'You're too good, Lara.

'Let me put you straight about the kind of man I am, in case you're harbouring the belief that I'm somehow better. I'm *not*. I don't consider others. I'm a taker—not a giver, like you. In the kind of world I inhabit the weak fall by the wayside and are quickly forgotten. I've had to learn to be tough. On the road to achieving what I want I've learned not to let anything or anyone stand in my way. If I come back into your life again I'm guaranteed to hurt you and make you rue the day you met me.'

'You're talking as if I'm nurturing some kind of hope that we might get together. Don't worry about that, Gabriel. I'm not.' She sniffed and wrenched her arm free.

'Is that right?'

In a flash Gabriel was on his feet and bringing her up towards him, moving his hands down to her slim waist to hold her fast and pulling her against the iron wall of his chest.

Then the world as she knew it disappeared as though it was nothing but a hazy dream and her eyelids shut tight as he crushed her lips beneath his. The frightening demand she sensed left Lara reeling. But it also stirred long-dormant feelings in her body, making them want to rise up and meet that furious hunger.

The day **Maggie Cox** saw the film version of
Wuthering Heights, with a beautiful Merle Oberon and
a very handsome Laurence Olivier, was the day she
became hooked on romance. From that day onwards
she spent a lot of time dreaming up her own romances,
secretly hoping that one day she might become
published and get paid for doing what she loved most!
Now that her dream is being realised she wakes up
every morning and counts her blessings. She is married
to a gorgeous man and is the mother of two wonderful
sons. Her two other great passions in life—besides her
family and reading/writing—are music and films.

Recent titles by the same author:

THE TYCOON'S DELICIOUS DISTRACTION
WHAT HIS MONEY CAN'T HIDE
DISTRACTED BY HER VIRTUE
A DEVILISHLY DARK DEAL

Did you know these are also available as eBooks?
Visit www.millsandboon.co.uk

THE MAN
SHE CAN'T FORGET

BY
MAGGIE COX

MILLS &
BOON

Published in Great Britain 2014
by Mills & Boon, an imprint of Harlequin (UK) Limited,
Eton House, 18-24 Paradise Road, Richmond, Surrey, TW9 1SR

© 2014 Maggie Cox

ISBN: 978 0 263 24649 0

Harlequin (UK) Limited's policy is to use papers that are natural,
renewable and recyclable products and made from wood grown in
sustainable forests. The logging and manufacturing processes conform
to the legal environmental regulations of the country of origin.

Printed and bound in Spain
by Blackprint CPI, Barcelona

THE MAN
SHE CAN'T FORGET

CHAPTER ONE

IT HAD SEEMED like a good idea at the time. If only Lara had remembered her brother Sean's sage advice to 'expect the unexpected', then she might have thought twice about agreeing to stay at their parents' home while they took a much needed restorative break in the south of France.

But then Sean wasn't there any more to remind her of that particular little pearl....

And, in truth, she would never have dreamt of refusing her mum and dad's request to house-sit for them when they were still reeling from the tragedy that had hit them all six months ago. *Their son, Sean, Lara's brother, was dead.* He had contracted malaria whilst undertaking the charity work that he loved in Africa and had not recovered from it. It hardly seemed real that such a thing was possible in the twenty-first century, but sadly it was.

Having already been back in the family home for a week now, Lara still expected him to walk through the door with a cheery, 'Put the kettle on, sis, I could murder a cup of tea!' just like he had done when they were teenagers.

Time seemed intent on playing tricks on her these

days. One minute it passed like a slow and choking mudslide, threatening to cut off her ability to breathe, and the next... The next it seemed to vanish completely, leaving her feeling that she was stuck in a desolate and unhappy dream that she couldn't wake up from.

Whilst she loved her work, she was glad that the college term had come to an end. Her duties and responsibilities in the library had been particularly arduous this past month, what with so many students wanting help with research to take home with them. But now that that frenetic time was over she had no choice but to fully embrace her grief and process the soul-deep pain that she felt at losing Sean.

But, truthfully, she didn't relish the prospect of the endless summer days stretching ahead of her as she normally would have done. With nothing to lighten her mood but the daily walks she would go on with Barney, her parents' devoted Border Terrier, Lara had been dreading the time to be spent alone at her parents' house.

She could have arranged to go on holiday herself when they returned from France, but she hadn't had the heart for it. A couple of friends had asked her to join them on a trip to Italy but she'd declined. How could she possibly be good company when she was still grieving so badly for Sean?

Now, in the middle of her second week's stay at the family home, Lara was sitting at the sturdy oak kitchen table, making a half-hearted attempt at eating a bowl of unappetising breakfast cereal, when the doorbell rang. Such a lyrical bell-like sound shouldn't pierce her to the very core, but it did. In fact it made her flinch. She seemed to be afraid of everything these days. But Sean being taken from them so suddenly like that had made her fear that nothing good would ever happen to her or her family again.

Rousing himself from the relaxed position he'd assumed, lying across her feet, Barney shot up and started barking and wagging his tail—just as though he was anticipating a welcome friend or visitor. Lara's nerves were jangled even more. It was eight-thirty in the morning.... Who on earth would be calling at this time?

'For goodness' sake,' she muttered beneath her breath, 'it's probably just the postman.'

Forcing herself to relax, she moved down the hardwood hallway in her bare feet, Barney eagerly following her. The day was already promising to be particularly warm, and the sun that shone through the door's decorated Victorian glass panes lit up the interior with the glare of a powerful spotlight.

Lifting her hand to shield her gaze, she squinted at the tall shadow behind the glass. Even though she didn't have a clue who it was she knew it wasn't the postman. Whoever it was, his straight, ominous stance suggested someone official. Lara's stomach executed a nervous cartwheel. *Please, God, not more bad news.*

She opened the door warily. 'Good morning.'

On the other side of the door stood a man with eyes so heartbreakingly blue that the sight of them made her catch her breath. Waves of disconcerting shock flooded her. Staring at the carved, high-cheekboned visage, with its cut-glass jaw and arresting dimple, Lara thought she was dreaming. To be confronted by the man that she'd thought never to see again, and so early in the morning, she found she was both lost for words and stunned right down to her marrow.

He was dressed in an exquisitely tailored dark suit with a dulled gold pinstripe, and the clearly custom-made clothing showed off her visitor's athletic, broad-shouldered physique to perfection. He had always looked classy, even when he was a student. Some people were just born with that exclusive air about them and this man was one of them.

As the sexy, expensive cologne he wore wafted tantalisingly beneath her nose she wanted to pinch herself, just to make sure she wasn't dreaming.

Her visitor proffered a tentative smile and she immediately sensed his uneasiness, as though for a disconcerting moment he wasn't sure what the appropriate greeting was.

'I was wondering if I might have a word with Mr or Mrs Bradley?' he asked. 'I'm a— I *was* a friend of theirs. I'm sorry I'm calling so early in the morning, but I've just got back from New York and I wanted to pay my respects to the family for their loss.'

Lara stared hard, her legs threatening to buckle beneath her. She was suddenly aware that Gabriel Devenish, her brother's best friend at university, hadn't recognised her.

Her initial reaction was to feel blessedly relieved, but that was quickly followed by a churning in her guts that made her fear she might faint.

The memory of Gabriel had haunted her for years.

He and Sean had studied for the same degree together. But while the big-hearted Sean had elected to go into charity work after graduating, Gabriel had followed in his rich uncle's footsteps and gone into the more lucrative and some might say cut-throat world of high finance.

Her brother had once told her that he'd heard on the grapevine that his friend had made an absolute fortune since moving to New York, but he'd said it in a way that had implied he almost felt sorry for him.

In any case, from the very first moment that Lara had set eyes on Gabriel, on a blistering-hot summer's day thirteen years ago, when she'd been just sixteen, she had developed the most massive crush on him. She might have been four years younger, and still at school, but that hadn't tempered her feelings. And a foolish impulse that she had lived to regret had once driven her to confess them to him.

Her memory was transported back to that night when Sean had thrown an impromptu party for some friends at the house when their parents were away.

Seeking to bolster her courage, because Gabriel had been there, Lara had drunk a little too much wine and had consequently embarrassed herself. Dancing with him a few hours later when the party was in full swing, delighted by his flirtatious comments and what she'd imagined was an invitational smile, she'd reciprocated by shyly telling him how much she liked him…that she liked him a *lot*, in fact. Then, shutting her eyes, she had moved her face up to his for a kiss.

She still remembered the look of shock on his face and the sensation of hurt that had flooded her when he'd firmly but carefully moved her away, telling her that she was his friend's little sister and that she'd read him wrong…he'd only been teasing her.

Lara practically remembered what he'd said to her word for word. He'd added, *'I'm sure there are plenty of boys your own age who would love to go out with you, Lara, but I'm a little too old for you, I fear. Anyway,*

I have my sights set on that tall, slim blonde standing over there. She's one of my tutors and has made no secret of the fact that she likes me.'

Even the false sense of courage that the alcohol had given her hadn't been able to protect Lara from being devastated by Gabriel's rejection…. Yes, devastated, and *humiliated*, too. Over and over again she'd speculated on the reasons why he'd spurned her. Had it really been just because she was younger than him and because she was Sean's 'little sister'? If you cared for a person—*really* cared—then what did it signify that there was a bit of an age difference?

Lara had been left with the conclusion that, apart from the bond of friendship that was between them because she was his best friend's sister, Gabriel didn't care for her at all. Even back then he'd set his sights on much more potentially lucrative opportunities—a prime example being the slim blonde tutor from his university.

Ever since that painful incident at the party Lara's relationships with men had never seemed to progress much beyond friendship, even when she'd wished that they would. The trouble was she no longer trusted herself to read the correct signals as far as the opposite sex were concerned. Also, in spite of Gabriel's rejection, she realised that she still harboured impossibly romantic feelings towards her brother's friend. Had she turned him into a bit of a fantasy figure over the years? A fantasy that no other man could possibly hope to live up to?

He had definitely been a hard man to forget….

Lara's throat was uncomfortably dry, but looking back at him now, she somehow managed to speak.

'It's Gabriel, isn't it? Gabriel Devenish? You were my brother's best friend when he was at university. I'm sorry but my parents aren't here at the moment. They've gone away to the south of France for a break.'

Behind Lara, hating to be ignored, Barney started barking again. Glad of the momentary distraction in order to gather herself mentally, she instantly dropped down to her haunches to stroke his rough wheaten-coloured coat affectionately.

'Hush, Barney, you don't have to make such a fuss.'

'You're Lara? Sean's little sister?'

Lifting her gaze, she fell into Gabriel's mesmerising crystal-blue stare like a diver plunging straight into the sunlit Mediterranean.

With her heart slamming against her ribs, she nodded slowly. 'That's right. Though not so little any more, I'm afraid.'

Rising to her full height again—five feet seven of slim limbs and womanly curves in light blue denims and a fitted white shirt—she was nothing like the plump, awkward teenager she'd been when she was sixteen. It was no surprise that Gabriel hadn't recognised her.

'Well, I'll be...'

He seemed to be genuinely shocked. Lara even detected a faint flush of heat in his chiselled countenance.

'You *have* grown up. Look...'

Tunnelling his long fingers through his thick chestnut hair, he inadvertently drew her attention to his strong, indomitable brow—a brow that was etched with two deeply hewn furrows. It didn't suggest he utilised that devastating smile of his very often these days. Whatever road life had taken him down it hadn't all been plain sailing, she thought. He might be rich, but no matter how much money a person had it didn't protect them from the slings and arrows that life aimed at everyone along the way... No one got off scot-free.

'I only learned of Sean's death yesterday,' Gabriel confessed. 'I saw an article in the newspaper about charity workers that had died of malaria and his name was mentioned. The piece said that he'd recently won a prestigious award for his work. I was stunned to hear that he'd died. I feel bad that I never kept in touch with him after we left university.'

'You took different paths.' Lara shrugged, her smile unsure.

She'd hate Gabriel to think she was criticising him, even though she'd never understood why he'd chosen to go into a profession that, in her view, was about taking rather than giving—a profession that was the polar opposite of Sean's.

'But it's good of you to call round to pay your respects. Mum and Dad will be touched when I tell them. I'm sure you must know they were very fond of you. Anyway, you're probably busy, so I won't keep you.'

Lara fervently willed him to take the cue she'd offered and leave. There was no way she wanted him to think that she was especially pleased to see him again. She was no longer the foolish sixteen-year-old whose crush on him had probably painfully embarrassed him.

But Gabriel sighed and stayed where he was. 'Look...I don't mean to be presumptuous, but is there any chance of a cup of tea? I promise not to take up too much of your time.'

As much as she wished she could come up with a convincing excuse that she was indeed busy, Lara had glimpsed an unexpected look of vulnerability in his eyes and she didn't have the heart to refuse him.

'Why don't you come in?' she invited. 'I was just about to have one myself.'

Feeling relieved, Gabriel followed Lara down the hallway towards what he remembered was a spacious and homely kitchen. As he walked slowly behind the brunette his astonishment that the sometimes shy and bookish teenager had blossomed into such a beauty made him stare at her shapely hourglass figure in wonder.

What her curvaceous body did for a simple pair of jeans and plain white shirt should be committed to art or poetry, he mused. Even though he wasn't remotely artistic or poetic himself, it certainly didn't mean he didn't appreciate the more aesthetically pleasing things in life—which was why he'd selected a New York apartment that had a stunning view of the Metropolitan Museum of Art.

Every now and then, when he found the time, he'd visit to remind himself that money wasn't the only thing in life worth appreciating. Yes, it gave a person a lot more options if he had it, but it didn't buy happiness. God knew he'd learned that to his cost over the years.... The contemplation of beauty and art 'soothed the troubled soul', as one wise guide at the museum had put it to him once, and although he would never dream of sharing such a view with any of his colleagues, Gabriel had agreed. That was why he admired the artists who created it.

But his admiration of Lara's beauty was set aside as he entered the kitchen. It was indeed as homely as he remembered. And the old-fashioned stand-alone fixtures and fittings, including the 1930s pillarbox-red

AGA, straight away transported him right back to when he and Sean had been young.

He recalled with fondness the countless delicious meals Peggy Bradley had made for them—in particular during that seemingly 'endless' summer when he and Sean, in between revising for their exams, had laughed and joked together, listened to the music of their favourite bands, mercilessly teased Lara and generally enjoyed being young and free of care, not burdened with responsibility as so many of the adults that they'd known had seemed to be. It had been easy to fantasise then that that those halcyon days would last for ever....

Gabriel's senses were suddenly awash in a sea of poignant and heartfelt memory. As if to compound his feelings, he saw that the cream dresser was full of engaging family pictures, and taking pride of place was an eye-catching photograph of Sean as he must have looked before he died. His mischievous brown eyes were full of laughter and his wide smile highlighted the chipped front tooth that Gabriel had accidentally broken when he'd too zealously bowled a cricket ball in the garden for him to bat. He had been the closest friend that Gabriel had ever had, and even though he hadn't kept in touch with him it cut him to the quick to think that he was no longer here....

'Everything looks just the same,' he remarked huskily, reaching his hand up to loosen the shirt collar that suddenly felt constricting.

'Mum and Dad aren't great lovers of change. They're old-fashioned like that.' Lara smiled fondly. 'Not to mention sentimental. They've become even more so since losing Sean.' Her smile vanished and, clearly needing a moment, she turned towards the sink to fill the kettle.

'It must have been a terrible shock to you all to receive the news that he'd died,' Gabriel murmured sympathetically.

'It was. One minute we were talking to him on Skype, hearing all about the events of his day, and the next…' Sadly shaking her head, Lara turned off the tap that had been gushing water into the kettle then moved across to the generous granite worktop to plug it into a socket to boil. 'How do you like your tea?' she asked, tucking some of her glossy dark hair behind her ear as she turned back.

'Don't you remember?' Gabriel teased, recalling with pleasure the numerous cups of tea an eager-to-please young Lara had made him whenever he'd stayed over or visited Sean. 'I used to tell you that, next to your mum, you made the best cup of tea in the world.'

'You did, didn't you?' Her generous mouth curved with pleasure. 'Okay, then, I'll see if I can remember how you like it. Don't tell me—just let me have a go. Pull up a chair and make yourself comfortable.'

He didn't need to be asked twice. This house was the only place he'd ever known that really felt like home, with everything that that word represented.

Jaded and tired from the demands and rigours of inhabiting the soulless world of high finance for what had probably been too many years to stay wholly sane, Gabriel had a secret yearning for some simplicity and comfort in his life. He was frankly weary of the kind of comfort epitomised by the opulent living of a lot of bankers in New York, although he himself had embraced it, thinking it was his 'due' for working so hard and making others as rich as he was.

He hadn't fully explored the realisation, but he was longing for the kind of comfort that might be attained by being amongst people who were authentic, with no hidden agendas and the ability simply to be themselves. In short, people who were naturally *good* rather than unscrupulously self-seeking.

And even as he had the thought his mind went straight away to Lara's parents. They had welcomed him into their home without any judgement or expectation when their son had befriended him, and had even expressed their sadness that he'd been raised by a wealthy but often absent uncle who more often than not had left him in the care of a hired nanny. They were appalled that Gabriel had never known the joys of growing up in a 'real' family as Sean had.

'Would you like some toast and marmalade with your cuppa?'

'Sorry...what did you say?' Blinking up into the melting chocolate-brown eyes of the lovely brunette who was suddenly standing in front of him, for a surreal moment Gabriel honestly forgot who or where he was because she was so enchanting.

Her brow puckering, Lara seemed taken aback that he hadn't heard her the first time. *Perhaps she didn't know how mesmerising she was?* He shrugged. He doubted it. He hadn't met a beautiful woman yet who wasn't intimately aware of her own appeal. Beauty was a very desirable cachet in the avaricious world that he inhabited—not to mention an *asset*. In his opinion every attractive woman who aimed for the top in his profession had no compunction in using such an advantage to the max.

'I just asked if you'd like some toast and marmalade with your tea….'

'Just tea will do thanks. Then, if you've got the time, I'd like you to sit down and talk to me. We've got quite a bit of catching up to do. It's been years since we've seen each other, Lara, and as well as talking about Sean I'd like to hear what you've been doing with yourself.'

'Okay.' She chewed down on her lip, as if taken aback by the invitation. 'But didn't you say you'd just flown back from New York? Don't you need to at least relax and unwind for a little while after your flight?'

Gabriel couldn't help but smile. It seemed that the once self-conscious and unsure teenager had inherited some of her mother's endearing natural ability to think of others' needs first. It wasn't something he often came across in his world—if *ever*—and he had to admit it was appealing. But he could just imagine the response of his more cynical male colleagues should they meet Lara and be exposed to her kind disposition for very long. They'd wonder if she was 'for real'.

'I assure you that right now I don't need to do anything else other than be here with you, Lara.'

If ever a man's statement had sounded more seductive and appealing then Lara hadn't heard one. And the huskily low-pitched velvet cadence of Gabriel's deeply arresting voice couldn't help but render the words even more provocative. Her insides felt as though they'd suddenly been heated by a fiercely burning erotic flame. Could it be that her teenage fascination for this man hadn't died with his rejection of her at that party, but instead had been quietly simmering inside all these years?

The realisation was akin to standing on a crumbling cliff edge and frantically trying to maintain her balance. It had been thirteen long years since she'd seen this man. She knew nothing about his life now, or what had transpired in the years since they'd last met, and she was pretty certain that if he had any interest in her at all at this moment it was only because of his past association with her family.

For all Lara knew, the man could be happily married to a stunningly perfect model wife in New York—the kind epitomised by the glossy magazines—with a brood of pretty blue-eyed offspring to boot. Her stomach helplessly churned at the thought.

'All right, then. I'll make us some tea and then we'll catch up. Just don't expect any tales of adventure or excitement. I live a very quiet and ordinary life that's probably miles away from how you live yours.'

Giving him a faintly wry smile, she moved back across the kitchen to the granite worktop and hurriedly arranged the teapot and matching china cups and saucers on a tray. But her hands were visibly trembling as she poured hot water onto the tea leaves, and her heart was pounding as though it would never be at ease or calm again....

They moved into the living room to drink their tea, and Lara opened the generous-sized patio doors that led out onto the garden so that they might enjoy the sunshine. She also didn't want to miss the opportunity of hearing the birds sing. That was one of the reasons why early morning had always been her favourite time of the day.

'You've made it just how I like it,' her handsome visitor announced, taking a sip of his tea as he lowered his long-limbed frame down into one of the comfortable Chesterfield armchairs. 'You've got a good memory.'

'Thanks.'

Suddenly self-conscious, Lara sat down in the chair opposite him and stirred her own tea. She'd never been able to drink the beverage without at least one sugar. *She'd bet that Gabriel never touched the stuff.* Even though he'd acquired a couple of lines on his forehead over the years, his lean, toned physique radiated the vim and vigour of a seasoned athlete rather than someone who spent his days immersed in making eye-popping deals on Wall Street.

The thought prompted a question. 'You said you'd just come back from New York? Is this a flying visit or are you going to stay for a while?'

A definitely guarded expression stole into his mesmerising blue eyes and his lean jaw clenched a little. Leaning forward, he placed his cup and saucer down onto the walnut coffee table arranged between them.

'I'm not sure. Right now I've no idea how long I'll stay. I've come back to deal with some legalities regarding my uncle's estate, to tell you the truth. He died a few weeks ago and I'm his sole beneficiary.'

'Oh, Gabriel, I'm so sorry...about your uncle dying, I mean. Did you come back for the funeral?'

'I did. Anyway, I have a meeting with his solicitor tomorrow.'

He shook his head, as though the matter pained rather than gratified him. But then why should he be pleased by the fact that his only family member had died? Lara reasoned. Even if he had bequeathed him everything he owned? If the scant details that she knew about Gabriel's upbringing by his uncle were right, then surely he would have preferred to have the man's love and affection, not to mention caring support, when he was a boy, rather than be left all his worldly goods when he died? Did he even *need* them when he was purported to be so wealthy in his own right?

'Did you see your uncle much over the years after you left to go to New York?'

'No, I didn't. We weren't close. He adopted me when my mother—his sister—decided she wasn't cut out to be a mother after all...that she wanted her freedom above all else. At least he was decent enough to do that, I suppose.'

'What about your father?' Lara frowned. 'What happened to him?'

In answer Gabriel's brow creased in a formidable scowl. 'Your guess is as good as mine. My mother put him down as "unknown" on my birth certificate.'

'How sad.' The comment was out before she could check it.

'Why? I grew up in an impressive home in a very desirable area and I wanted for nothing. What's sad about that?'

'It's sad that you never knew your real father, or had a relationship with him, and it's sad that you weren't close to the uncle who adopted you—that's all I meant.'

'Well, don't give it another thought. In the circles I move in I'm considered to be a great success, and everything I've achieved I've accomplished on my own. I wasn't held back by the fact that I wasn't close to my family or they to me. End of story.'

But Lara guessed that was *far* from the end. She was pretty certain that anyone who'd been abandoned by their mother as a child must have a river of pain and anger flowing through them that couldn't help but affect their sense of self-esteem and self-worth. But she sensed, too, that now wasn't the time to try and press Gabriel into telling her more. He'd come to pay his respects to the family for Sean, not to be grilled by his friend's sister about his less than idyllic upbringing.

'Anyway, I'd like to hear about what you've been up to since we last met.' Deftly, he changed the subject. 'What do you do for a living? If I remember rightly, you were either going to be a vet or a politician. We had some passionate discussions, you, me and Sean, about setting the world to rights, didn't we?'

His comment made Lara burn with embarrassment as she remembered their often heated and animated discussions. Especially when she recalled that her views had always been the most passionate and vehement. But when you were sixteen you thought you knew everything. You could even fool yourself into believing that a more experienced older man could seriously fall for you, when, in truth, he was only flirting with you because he could....

'Well, I didn't become a vet *or* a politician,' she said. 'Being responsible for setting the world to rights was too tall an order, so I became a librarian instead.'

'Well, well, well…a librarian?' Gabriel's expression was wry. 'I know you loved books, but I always thought you were far too passionate to squirrel yourself away in some dusty hall, lending them out to the great unwashed public!'

'In case you hadn't noticed, we're not living in the Dickensian era.'

Lara couldn't help but bristle at his mocking tone, but at the same time she couldn't help registering the disturbing fact that he'd called her 'passionate'. Had he always thought that about her? The thought made her heart race even as she reminded herself that he'd once painfully rejected her.

'Amongst other things, I issue books in a state-of-the-art college library with every bit of modern technology you can imagine at my disposal. If you think I chose a "safe" option in becoming a librarian, instead of a vet or a politician, then I can assure you that dealing every day with the demands of diverse and sometimes tricky students is no walk in the park.'

'But you love it?' Lifting a dark eyebrow, Gabriel smiled. 'I'm glad that you found a career you enjoy, Lara. And, just for the record, I still think you're passionate. I'm sure you would be whatever you decided to do in life. You can't help your nature.'

CHAPTER TWO

'AND WHAT ABOUT YOU, GABRIEL?' Lara asked, feeling suddenly hot again, because she seemed to be the focus of attention and she would much prefer to learn more about him. 'What line of work are you in these days? Are you still involved in finance?'

The smile Gabriel returned was faintly rueful. 'Yes, I am.'

'What exactly do you do? I mean, do you have a job title?'

In answer he rose to his feet, and it was clear to Lara that her questions were unsettling him.

'I'm a CRO on Wall Street—and, before you ask, that stands for Chief Risk Officer. I deal with analysing risk-and-reward formulas in financial businesses and banks.'

'Oh.' She raised her shoulders in a shrug, feeling none the wiser with the explanation. 'It sounds complicated.'

'Does it?' A visible muscle flinched at the side of his carved cheekbone. 'At any rate, I'd advise you not to lose any sleep trying to figure it out.'

'Meaning you don't think I'm intelligent enough to understand?'

'You always did take umbrage when you thought I

was being mocking, didn't you? Perhaps you should try not to take things so personally.'

As Lara mulled over the comment, to try and ascertain exactly what he meant, Gabriel moved across to where she sat, leaned down and gathered her hands in his. Then he silently pulled her to her feet.

There wasn't an adequate description for the huge wave of both panic and pleasure that suddenly engulfed her...except maybe abject disbelief that it was happening. Over the years, she had fantasised many times about what it might be like if Gabriel ever touched her or held her close as if he meant it, and while her heart sang to have him near she couldn't help but remember the time when he'd so purposefully moved her away from him and told her he could never be for her. But even that agonising memory couldn't stop her from thinking that being close to him like this felt so—so *right*.

Then she realised that his brilliant blue gaze was examining her with a searching intensity that couldn't help but make her apprehensive.

'Tell me about Sean,' he commanded quietly, his tone almost reverent, as though even uttering his friend's name out loud distressed him.

Relieved that it wasn't anything she'd inadvertently done or said that had made him study her so intently, Lara took a nervous swallow. It still upset her terribly to talk about Sean and remember afresh that he had died. The thought was akin to sharpened cold steel being plunged into her heart.

'What do you want to know?'

Gabriel didn't release her and she found she was in no hurry to be free. His hands were large and warm and they made her feel strangely secure, made her ache for the kind of loving, sensual protection that only a man like him could provide. She was suddenly aware of a small vein throbbing in his forehead.

'Why—*how* did he contract malaria?' he enquired huskily. 'Don't volunteers have to have some kind of protection before going out into these godforsaken places?'

'Of course they do.' Lara was taken aback by the underlying rage she heard in his voice...touched that he still felt so strongly about Sean after all these years.

She was angry, too, that the brother she'd loved so dearly had been ripped from her so suddenly and without warning, and the wounds of that loss were so great she feared they might never heal. Yet she wouldn't run away from grief, no matter how hard it hurt. She'd made a vow to face it head-on and not wound her heart further by denying how she felt. Something told her that it would be disrespectful to Sean if she did. But still, she utterly sympathised with Gabriel's confusion and pain.

'He had all the necessary jabs and medical examinations before he went over there,' she said softly, 'but malaria is caused by a mosquito bite from an infected mosquito, as I'm sure you probably know. Shortly after his death, a tear in the netting over his bed was discovered. Unfortunately the charity was always short of the money to be able to replace the old ones when they were no longer any good.'

'So he was given a faulty mosquito net?' His tone disparaging, Gabriel abruptly dropped Lara's hands and stepped away.

Feeling both bereft of his touch and chilled by the

memory of how Sean had died, she crossed her arms over her cotton shirt and nodded sadly. 'It seems so.'

As if he didn't know what to do with his rage to contain it, he strode over to the other side of the room to stare blindly out at the sunlit garden. Suddenly he spun round again to face her. 'How could Sean have been such an idiot?' he asked angrily.

'What?' The brutal question had the same effect on Lara as if Gabriel had slapped her hard across the face.

'I mean, why didn't he think of the consequences of being so careless about his own welfare? Probably because he'd never dream of putting himself first—and that was the problem. Why else would he accept a faulty net and risk being bitten? Even if he hadn't realised it wasn't intact. He should have checked. But he was always too busy thinking about others, wasn't he? No wonder he went into charity work. What a waste *that* turned out to be.'

His blue eyes glittered with fury and then, seconds later, looked utterly *desolate*.

'He was a genius at maths and science. He could have gone into any investment bank or financial concern and gone straight to the top. If it was so important to him to support worthy causes he could have done so from the safety of his office, using as much of his money as he wanted, without putting himself in the eye of the damn storm! It's a dog-eat-dog world out there—a world where it's every man for himself—and if you don't make yourself number one then you're dead in the water.'

As Gabriel angrily scraped his fingers through his hair it was clear that it was near impossible for him to contain his growing frustration.

'God knows I told him that enough times. You'd think he would have had the common sense to take it on board.'

Taking a deep breath in, Lara slowly breathed out again. Her anxious heartbeat started to ease and return to a calmer rhythm. Gabriel hadn't been being cruel when he'd asked how Sean could have been such an idiot—he was merely angry and frustrated at the senseless waste of his friend's life. As they *all* were.

'My brother was a good man—as I'm sure you know, Gabriel. And he was happy doing the work he'd chosen, helping others less fortunate than he was. It simply wasn't in his nature to put himself first. I don't know about you, but that's the way I want to remember him. Happy and fulfilled and enjoying his life. I know that if he were still here he'd want you to be happy and fulfilled and enjoying your life, too. *Are* you?'

Her question hung suspended in the air like the sword of Damocles. Gabriel was staring at her as though transfixed, but then he rubbed his hand round his jaw in a bid to stir himself from the seeming trance he'd fallen into and shrugged.

'In my view, being happy is given too much credence in this world. A far better goal is to aim to be successful. If you're successful then that's fulfilling. That at least gives you choices in life. Anyway...'

Moving back to his chair, he lifted his cup of tea to his lips and took a long draught. Then he put the cup and saucer back down and gave Lara a haunting smile that was part regret, part anguish.

'I'm sorry if I upset you with my rant about Sean. But he was a good friend to me—probably the best friend I've ever had. I only wish I'd realised it sooner. I should have stayed in touch with him—but it's too late now, isn't it? It's an absolute crime and a travesty that he was taken from us so soon. Please convey my heartfelt condolences to your parents, won't you? I'm sorry they aren't here for me to speak to personally. At any rate, I think it's probably about time I went.'

The thought that he was leaving and that she might never see him again hit Lara like a thunderbolt.

Before she was sufficiently recovered from the shock to think it through properly, she blurted out, 'Must you go? If you stay for a while we can have lunch together. You can even come for a walk with me and Barney first, if you like? A walk is the perfect remedy to blow the cobwebs away and clear your head. We've got woods at the back of the house, remember? I wish you'd seen them when the primroses were out in the spring—they were a picture.'

It was at that very moment that Gabriel knew he couldn't walk away from this woman as easily as he wanted to—as easily as he *should* walk away. Because he knew if he stayed he would only hurt her. The savage hunger and need that he had buried inside for so long—and from time to time had sought to assuage with pretty bodies who only saw him as a 'golden ticket' to the lavish and expensive lifestyle they craved—would only end up consuming the innocent Lara and filling her with the most bitter regret for issuing that invitation to stay a while.

But Gabriel knew already that he couldn't resist accepting it. And who could blame him for seeking sanctuary in her fresh and innocent company for a little while longer?

'All right, then. I'll stay…at least for lunch and a walk with Barney.'

'That's great. But you *do* realise I have an ulterior motive for asking?'

She smiled, and for the first time Gabriel noticed the two engaging and rather sexy dimples in her cheeks. But her words suddenly made him stiffen. He wasn't ready for his illusions about her—if illusions were what they were—to be shattered so soon.

'What motive would that be?' he asked warily.

She lifted her slender shoulders, then dropped them again. 'It's just that I've been a bit lonely here on my own, surrounded by memories of my brother. It would be nice to have some company for a change to help take my mind off things.… That's all I meant.'

Feeling ridiculously pleased at the admission, Gabriel relaxed. 'Then far be it from me to deny you the one thing I can give you today. Shall we go for that walk now? The sun is shining and it's a beautiful day. It would be a shame to waste it staying indoors.'

'I agree.' Lifting her long dark hair off her shoulders and dropping it down again behind her back, Lara moved gracefully across to the door. 'I'll just go and get my walking boots on—the terrain in the woods is quite rough and uneven in places. Will you be okay walking in those?' Her glance was doubtful as she surveyed the ebony Italian loafers that he wore. 'They look pretty chic and expensive.'

'I would have brought something more suitable to change into if I'd known you were going to entice me into the woods with you,' he remarked drolly, and his lips split into a grin when she blushed vividly.

'Don't kid yourself I'd even dream of such a thing. For one thing, I wouldn't know how.'

Beneath his immaculate white shirt Gabriel's heart started to pound disturbingly. More than that, a profoundly arousing heat invaded his blood.

'Now, there's a challenge if ever I heard one...' he commented huskily.

'I didn't mean it as a challenge. I was only— Oh, never mind. I'll go and get my boots on.'

Clearly flustered, Lara hurriedly left the room, and straight away Gabriel missed her presence and longed for her to return.

He was being introduced to a completely different world from the one he was used to inhabiting—a world that he realised he'd been missing for far too long.

Walking through the woods with the beauty he had once known as 'Sean's little sister' by his side was delightful. She laughed often and unselfconsciously—a huskily engaging sound that made all the hairs stand up on the back of his neck. And every now and then a waft of the delightful perfume she wore, which smelled like a bouquet of wild flowers, deluged Gabriel's senses and hit him in the gut. Coupled with the earthy, resinous scents that abounded in the woods, it made for a sensual experience bar none—a million miles away from the tense, charged atmosphere of Wall Street that was his usual daily experience.

'I'm going to take Barney's lead off now. This is his favourite neck of the woods. We know it well and I like to let him have a run.'

Gifting Gabriel with another sunny smile, Lara stooped to free the excited terrier from his leash and he bounded away through the thicket of dense under-growth and trees like a whippet, joyously barking.

'He's not the brightest chicken in the coop,' she commented affectionately. 'He's a natural hunter, but the trouble is he announces his arrival so that his prey can get away before he reaches it!'

Shaking her head in amusement, she laughed again, and Gabriel couldn't help but smile with pleasure. Driven by sheer instinct—for once letting his heart rule his head—he found himself drawing closer and reaching for her hand. The hotly fierce tingle that shot through his body when he touched her was like being glanced by lightning and almost made him stumble. The startled look Lara gave him in return indicated that she'd felt the electrifying sensation, too.

'I'd forgotten how funny you are,' he confessed. 'And that you have the most beautiful eyes. They glisten like jewels when you laugh.' It didn't come naturally to him to compliment a woman and mean it, but he meant this particular one with every fibre of his being.

'Thank you.'

Carefully she disengaged her hand from his, and the becoming flush on Lara's cheeks told Gabriel that he'd been right about her being disturbed by the shock of electricity that had arced between them.

'You're blushing,' he teased.

'If I am it's because I'm not used to receiving such effusive compliments.'

'Not even from the man in your life?'

He experienced no remorse whatsoever for shamelessly fishing. But Lara's expression looked troubled now, and the light in her eyes dimmed a little.

'There isn't a man in my life—at least not at the moment.'

Gabriel couldn't deny he was relieved to hear it, although he wasn't ready to explore *why* right then.

'You mean to say that there potentially *might* be someone? Someone you perhaps have your eye on?'

'No. I don't mean that at all.' She didn't bother to try and disguise her annoyance that he should quiz her on the subject.

'What about you?' she asked, turning the tables. 'Is there anyone significant in *your* life? For all I know you might even be married by now.'

'I'm not—married, I mean. And neither am I in a serious relationship. I'm married to my work, Lara. I know that sounds extremely dull and boring but it's true. However, that's not to say I lack the company of a pretty woman when I want it.'

'You mean you like to play the field? I suppose that's why there's no one serious in your life, then.'

She sighed. But whether that sigh signified disapproval or disappointment Gabriel couldn't guess.

Staring at the dense shroud of trees and bushes that her lively pet terrier had disappeared into, she suddenly called out, 'Barney! Here, boy! Come on back, now.'

When the dog didn't immediately appear, Lara turned her gaze back to Gabriel.

'I worry when he suddenly goes quiet,' she admitted, 'I'd better go and see where he's got to. He might have got stuck down a rabbit hole or something. It's happened before. Why don't you wait here for me? You've already got your posh shoes all muddy, and the ground on the other side of those trees and bushes is invariably quite boggy. Hopefully I won't be too long.'

'I don't give a damn about my shoes, and I haven't left my jacket back at the house and rolled up my shirt-sleeves for nothing. I'm not concerned about getting dirty. I'll come and help you find the dog.'

'His name's Barney!'

Again Lara looked affronted, and again Gabriel couldn't resist goading her.

'Who's he named after? One of your ex-boyfriends?'

'He's my parents' dog, not mine, you ninny.'

'You always used to call me that. You might be sur-prised to know I found it quite endearing.'

'Now, that I *don't* believe. My perception was that it irritated you. I was the pesky sixteen-year-old sister of your friend, remember? You didn't take me at all seri-ously. You put up with me out of politeness to Sean and my parents, I'm sure.'

'That's not true.' Gabriel frowned, perturbed that Lara had believed that.

'Come on, then.' As if intuiting his disturbance, she gave him a cheery smile. 'Let's go and find Barney.'

As he squelched through the dense and muddied undergrowth in his thousand-dollar Italian loafers, with the damp leaves of bushes and thickets brushing against his immaculate white shirt, occasionally stum-bling when he lost his balance, Gabriel had to smile at the ludicrous image he must present. His colleagues on Wall Street would have a field day if they could see him.

Strangely enough, that made him smile even more. In truth, he wasn't predisposed to be glum or morose. He honestly thought that he had the best of it. How could he *not* when he was following behind the long-legged beauty in tight jeans in front of him?

Lara was negotiating the uneven muddy trail through

the woods like a latter-day female Indiana Jones, hardly pausing for breath and calling out 'Barney!' every now and then with renewed gusto. Gabriel knew himself to be a fit man who welcomed a challenge—be it mental or physical—but his companion's agility and stamina had to be seen to be believed.

Suddenly coming to a halt, and with frustration and apprehension in her voice, Lara shouted, '*Barney!* This isn't funny. What do you think you're playing at, you naughty boy?'

'Sounds like you're expecting him to reply.'

'Ha-ha, very funny...*not.*'

This time Gabriel was treated to an irritated glare which, thankfully, he didn't take seriously—not when he guessed that Lara would be utterly distraught if they couldn't find the dog. It made him want to make more of a concerted effort to help her.

'Barney!' he yelled, striding towards an even denser section of the woods that they hadn't yet explored, at that point not giving a fig that his shoes were now more or less ruined by the rough, muddy terrain.

Was that a glimpse of a dark sandy-coloured coat he'd just spied through the trees? He squinted searchingly. Gabriel would bet his bottom dollar that it was.

'Barney! Here, boy!' he called again, moving more deeply into the shrouded area in front of him.

He hadn't gone very far when he saw the terrier's wriggling rear-end pointed upwards towards the sheltering canopy of leaves. The dog was furiously digging in the earth as though intent on finding treasure.

'I've found him!' he called out to Lara, spinning round only to find her hurrying towards him. Her white shirt was splattered with mud, as his was, her long dark hair was engagingly dishevelled, and her pretty face was visibly flushed pink with the heat of her exertions.

'Thank God!' she exclaimed as she flew past Gabriel to reach her adored family pet, dropping down onto her knees on the rough woodland floor.

She didn't seem to care that she might potentially hurt herself or ruin her clothes.

'Barney, you're a very naughty boy,' she scolded fondly, lifting the animal away from his enthusiastic digging and hugging him to her chest, uncaring that the terrier had made her white shirt even muddier.

Crazy as it was, Gabriel couldn't help but *envy* the small hound. He wouldn't mind his once spotless tailored shirt getting even dirtier if Lara held him to her fulsome breasts like that.

'He was probably digging for rabbits.' She grinned up at him, her dark eyes shining. 'He can't help himself.' Turning back to the dog, she crooned, 'You're a natural-born hunter, aren't you, baby?'

Then, before Gabriel could take command of his besieged senses and help her, she gracefully rose to her feet and slipped the leash back on the terrier's collar.

'I don't know about you, but I'm suddenly starving. Let's get back and I'll fix us some lunch.'

Starving didn't come close to describing Gabriel's appetite right then—and it wasn't food that he hungered for. His best friend's little sister was seriously challenging his libido and winning. Of all the things he might have envisaged happening on this trip to the UK, it wasn't that.

Just what the hell he was going to do about it he didn't rightly know. But to seriously consider bedding the shapely brunette and risk sullying his once good relationship with her and her family almost didn't bear thinking about.

'I want you to take off that shirt when we get home,' Lara instructed as she airily swept past him with Barney.

'What?'

Coming to a sudden halt, she turned to flourish at him a cheeky grin that would've shamed a mischievous schoolgirl.

'Don't worry—it's not because I have designs on your body or anything. You're quite safe. I was just going to put it in the washing machine. You can borrow one of my dad's shirts in the meantime. He's about the same build and height as you, although of course not quite as—not quite as…'

As her big brown eyes swept over him, and she clearly struggled to finish the sentence, Gabriel once again couldn't resist being provocative.

'Fit?' he suggested, smiling.

'You know that saying? It should be "Vanity, thy name is *Man*—not Woman".'

Crossing his arms over his shirtfront, Gabriel mockingly raised an eyebrow. 'That quote is from Hamlet, and it's, "*Frailty*, thy name is woman"—*not* vanity. Just thought you'd like to know that for future reference.'

His pretty companion tossed her head and spun away, striding through the undergrowth again with Barney yapping happily beside her—but not before Gabriel saw her look daggers at him, as if she'd like to abandon him in the middle of those dank, dark woods and leave him there.

Lara honestly didn't know where she was finding the courage to deal with the disturbingly charismatic presence that was Gabriel. And neither had she fully dealt with the shock of him turning up out of the blue like that at her parents' door.

As time had gone on, her day had grown more challenging. When they'd been chatting in the living room earlier and Gabriel had drawn her up from her chair to ask about Sean she'd really believed she might faint from the sheer dizzying pleasure of the contact—not to mention the mesmerisingly intense glance he'd given her. His brilliant blue eyes had stared back into hers as though wanting to see into her very soul…as though even that wouldn't be enough for him to find what he was searching for.

She'd seen so many things in that seemingly endless glance to take her breath away, but rage and hunger— for what, she didn't know—had been predominant.

The second time he'd touched her, catching hold of her hand in the woods and smiling down at her, as though her company genuinely gave him pleasure, the sizzling jolt of electricity Lara had experienced when he put his hand round hers had left her feeling dizzy and confused. Such an extreme reaction to a simple friendly touch didn't bode well for her peace of mind when the time came for her to say goodbye to Gabriel again. And this time she didn't doubt his departure would be for good.

He would go back to his high-octane life on Wall Street and she would return to her much more simple and ordinary routine as a college librarian. Except that would be no consolation for watching her brother's onetime charismatic best friend walk out of her life for a second time.…

On their return from the woods they stood in the

porch at the back of the house as Lara schooled Barney to wait while she and Gabriel removed their muddy footwear. Seeing that her companion's black loafers were liberally weighed down and caked in once-oozing but now dried sludge, she let out a groan.

'Oh, why, oh, why did they have to be *suede*?' she asked, sincerely regretful that because of her Gabriel had ruined what was an undoubtedly expensive pair of shoes.

She could just imagine Sean shaking his head and saying, *Not one of your best ideas, sis—taking Gabe on a woodland walk when he was wearing classy Italian loafers. What on earth were you thinking?*

It took her aback to remember that he'd always referred to his friend as Gabe, not Gabriel. Lara had never been bold enough to do the same. Aside from that, Sean would have been right to wonder what she was thinking about. The trouble was her wonderful brother hadn't realised that Lara never *had* been able to think clearly round Gabriel.

'I should have lent you my dad's walking boots,' she reflected ruefully.

'What size is he?'

'He's a nine.'

Grimacing as he stood up in the generous-sized utility room that his impressive physique had made appear suddenly small, Gabriel emitted a playful sigh. 'Wouldn't have been any good, I'm afraid. I'm a size twelve.'

Having removed her own boots, Lara rose to join him. 'In any case, I think your lovely shoes are completely ruined. Were they very expensive?' She flushed as she privately wondered how she could possibly find the money to replace them if they'd been even half as expensive as she guessed they had. God knew a college librarian didn't earn a fortune....

'If I told you, you'd probably read me the riot act for being so vain and wasteful. Forget about it. The damn shoes don't matter. Anyway, I've got a spare pair in the car.'

'You've got a spare pair in the car? Why didn't you tell me?'

His arresting gaze made him look to be carefully considering the question. 'I didn't think about it. Besides, it's no big deal. Now, if you'll go and get me that shirt you promised, I'll get out of this one and give it to you to put in the washing machine.'

He was already starting to unbutton the stained shirt as he spoke, and Lara suddenly panicked at the thought of seeing him standing there bare-chested.

'Okay...won't be a tick,' she murmured, hurriedly turning towards the door that led out into the hall.

Her senses were already bombarded by Gabriel's presence alone—how was she supposed to handle being presented with the arresting beauty of his naked male chest and act as though she were unaffected?

CHAPTER THREE

FOR A MAN WHO LIKED to be in command of situations, Gabriel found himself to be uncharacteristically all at sea in his old friend's home with Lara. Being in that house again, and recalling some of the happiest memories he had ever known, made him yearn to replicate the feelings they evoked—the predominant one being a sense of belonging.

He hadn't experienced that reassuring sense of being welcomed, being regarded without judgement or conditions being attached, since he'd left the UK all those years ago. God knew, the pressurised career he'd chosen wasn't likely to engender anything *close* to that feeling amongst the single-minded and driven individuals he worked with. The phrase about them probably selling their own grandmothers if it made a profit often sprang to Gabriel's mind.

From time to time it alarmed him to realise he was becoming equally mercenary, and he wasn't proud of the fact. But in truth, like all addictions, it was hellishly hard to give up—and making money was definitely his drug of choice. Yet it was strange that he wasn't exactly overjoyed at being bequeathed his uncle's substantial residence, plus all his possessions and a generous monetary legacy.

All attending the man's funeral had done for Gabriel was to remind him of the sense of abandonment and excoriating pain he'd lived with since he was a child and his mother had left, leaving him with a man who—although related to him by blood—had been as distant as the Milky Way and even *less* accessible.

And now, as well as the unwanted complication of having to deal with his uncle's legacy, there was the totally unexpected dilemma of *Lara*. Just knowing that she was in the homely kitchen right now, preparing their lunch, shouldn't give him the inordinate amount of pleasure that it did, but along with an undeniable sense of contentment that *was* how it made him feel. That in itself was unusual, because he hadn't met a woman yet he trusted enough to relax with—except perhaps Peggy Bradley, Lara's mother.

Occupying Lara's father's comfortable wing-backed chair in the living room, Gabriel knew his eyelids were drifting closed, but made no attempt to check their descent. Outside, the beneficent sun was shining and its soporific rays beamed in on him through the opened patio doors and inevitably made him feel sleepy.

On the scented summer air a distant melody floated by, teasing at the memory of a small gathering Sean had once spontaneously thrown at the house.... Lara in a long magenta-and-green dress, dancing for all she was worth, throwing her arms wide as if to embrace all that the world had to offer and drawing his eye more than once because she looked so pretty and so free....

'Gabriel? Sorry to wake you, but lunch is ready. I thought we'd sit out in the garden and eat?'

Hearing the velvet-toned voice of the woman he'd been thinking about, and unsure whether he was still in the throes of his dream or not, Gabriel opened his eyes. His startled gaze was straight away captured by the heart-shaped face that had once been so familiar to him.

Now the innocent young girl that he remembered from his youth had turned into a woman who made him catch his breath and made his blood turn molten simply by looking at her. Devoid of any artifice or make-up, her skin was as fresh and clear as the petals of the creamiest rose, and her lips… Her lush lips were the shape and kind that would draw any man's attention and make him long to know what they would feel like beneath his own if he were lucky enough to kiss them.

Straightening in the chair, he murmured, 'I was dreaming about you….' Playing for time in order to marshal his thoughts, he let a helpless smile tug at the edges of his mouth. 'Yes, I was dreaming about you at a party Sean had once. You were just sixteen and you were dancing like some ethereal wild child to a Jimi Hendrix track. You looked so free and pretty. I remember thinking you would have fitted right into the era of peace and love in the sixties.'

Lara's dark brows furrowed as though the reference displeased her. Clearly that particular recollection from the past didn't fill her with the same wistful pleasure as it did Gabriel.

'Sixteen was a horrible age for me. I was always so self-conscious and shy, and I sometimes said stupid things I didn't mean and came to regret. I said something *very* stupid that night at the party.'

'Did you? Well, you should put it behind you and forget about it. For goodness' sake that was *years* ago, sweetheart, and if my recollections are right I seem to remember that there was plenty of alcohol doing the rounds that night—no doubt that was partly to blame. Besides, we can all say stupid things sometimes. If you can't be stupid when you're sixteen, then when *can* you? Anyway, I was actually quite envious of you that night.'

'Were you? Why?'

'Because you looked so carefree. To me you represented a freedom that I longed for—the kind of freedom that no amount of money could buy me.'

Now it was *his* turn to feel self-conscious and awkward. Gabriel had never revealed anything quite so personal about how he felt to anyone before. Like many young men, the programming that he'd absorbed from an early age had taught him that expressing emotion was akin to revealing a weakness, and right then he kicked it strongly into touch.

Pushing out of his chair, he moved across the room to glance out at the sunlit garden again. Immediately he noticed that the wrought iron picnic table with its matching green umbrella was laid for lunch. It was just the diversion he needed. Too much introspection was liable to make him irritable. He was already regretting being quite so frank with Lara.

'Were you saying something about us eating outside?'

'Yes. Lunch is ready. Why don't you go and make yourself comfortable and I'll bring it out?'

Lara couldn't get Gabriel's remarks about how she had looked at Sean's party out of her mind. At no point had he given any indication that he remembered spurning her—first when she had lifted her face up to his for a kiss and then by tactlessly suggesting there must be boys her own age who were interested in her and telling her he had his sights set on the slim blonde who was his tutor.

He hadn't even taken the bait when Lara had mentioned that she'd said something stupid that night that she regretted. Had her flirtation with him been so insignificant to him that he didn't even remember it? The fact that he'd said he'd been dreaming about her with what sounded like genuine admiration seemed too unreal for words. But, however seductive it sounded, Lara would remain on her guard. She wouldn't let the immature behaviour of her past rule her present by repeating it.

But she also couldn't forget Gabriel's stark and heartfelt admission that her dancing that day had represented a freedom that he longed for—a freedom that 'no amount of money' had been able to buy for him. Had he been feeling trapped in some way?

She couldn't suppress the longing that infused her that one day he might reveal more of his innermost feelings to her—at least as a friend. It was easy to glean the fact that he was troubled. In the short time they'd spent together since his turning up at the door she'd begun to intuit that Sean's death wasn't the only grief that haunted him.

He didn't talk much during lunch, except to remark on how good the chicken salad she'd prepared was. Lara didn't mind. It was a glorious day and the warmth from the sun had helped ease any tension she might have felt because she was sitting opposite the man who had mesmerised her when she was just sixteen. The truth was he *still* mesmerised her. She'd fantasised about Gabriel so many times over the years—had even entertained the foolish hope that one day he might come back into her life, see the woman she'd become, and be enthralled by her.

But, seeing him again now, she knew that was just a pipedream. He was even more out of Lara's league than he had been all those years ago.

However, as they sat in the garden together she realised that the past association Gabriel had enjoyed with her and her family had definitely engendered an unspoken agreement between them that they could at least let their guards down enough around each other for a while and relax. They didn't need to present some awkward or uneasy façade that would prevent honest communication.

Reaching for the bottle of wine that she'd opened and stood in an ice bucket on the table, she poured some crisp white Chardonnay into their glasses and, raising hers in a toast, smiled. 'To old friends.'

A fleeting shadow passed across Gabriel's brilliant blue irises. His broad shoulders visibly tensed. Then he, too, raised his glass.

'To Sean, who once told me that the best bottle of wine was the one you shared with a trusted friend, whether it was vintage or a common or garden bottle of plonk.'

The expression on his sculpted, handsome face was indisputably wry, but it was tinged with a sadness and regret he couldn't hide.

'Your brother was far too generous. I wish I'd exhibited more of that quality towards him when I had the chance. But I was too set on carving my own path to properly consider him. I certainly wasn't around during the times he might have needed an ally or someone to confide in. Some "trusted friend" I turned out to be.'

'You're too hard on yourself, Gabriel.'

Not for a second could Lara deny the impulse that suddenly arose in her to touch him. God knew it was a big risk for her to give in to it, but she ached to give him some comfort. It was hard seeing him so down on himself like this…. Sean would have hated it, too.

Gently, she laid her hand over his. He stared down at it as though hypnotised. Then he shook his head.

'The fact is I'm not hard enough. I'm constantly creating strategies and contingency plans so that I don't have to face myself and confront the truth about who I've become…a man I'm hardly proud of.'

'But you've already told me what a success people think you are, Gabriel. You should be proud of what you've achieved.'

'So you think I've made a success of my life, do you?'

The pain Lara saw reflected in his gaze made her draw in a helplessly tight breath.

'What I think isn't as important as how you feel, Gabriel. You must have worked hard to get where you are, and you did it without help from either family or friends. That shows the kind of strength and determination that most people would love to have.'

'Does it?'

Shockingly, Gabriel seized her hand, as though he meant to make her his prisoner, and the intense, hungry glare he swept over her face made her heart thump hard.

'You're too damn generous for your own good, Lara. Let me put you straight about the kind of man I am, in case you're harbouring the belief that I'm somehow better. I'm *not*. I don't consider others. I'm a taker—not a giver, like you and your family. In the kind of world I inhabit the weak fall by the wayside and are quickly forgotten. I've had to learn to be tough. On the road to achieving what I want I've learned not to let anything or anyone stand in my way. If I come back into your life again I'm guaranteed to hurt you and make you rue the day you met me.'

Her mouth drying, Lara couldn't hold back the hot press of tears that surged into her eyes. His words had been like knives and her need to self-protect immediately kicked in.

'You're talking as if I'm nurturing some kind of hope that we might get together. Don't worry about that, Gabriel. I'm not.'

She sniffed and wrenched her arm free.

'New York has changed you, Gabriel—and not for the better. You used to be quite friendly and amusing. But it sounds like the path that you've chosen has corrupted you instead of made you happy. That worries me. And, just so that you know, I'm *not* looking for a man to be in my life. And I assure you that if I was I'm afraid it wouldn't be *you*.'

'Is that right?'

In a flash Gabriel was on his feet and yanking her up towards him, moving his hands down to her slim waist to hold her fast and pulling her against the iron wall of his chest. There was no time for Lara to think or even to feel alarmed. But her heartbeat went wild when his hand cupped the back of her head and forcefully directed her face up towards his.

Then the world as she knew it disappeared as though it was nothing but a hazy dream. Her eyelids shut tight as he crushed her lips beneath his, his hot silken tongue mercilessly invading and plundering the satin interior of her mouth in a kiss that seemed to be driven by passionate hunger and fury combined.

The frightening demand she sensed left Lara reeling. But it also stirred long-dormant feelings in her body, making them want to rise up and meet that furious hunger. Along with that shocking realisation there were other disturbing feelings and sensations that hit her. The foremost was how seductively delicious Gabriel tasted and how he exuded the most provocative scent— almost a primeval scent—that wasn't just down to the expensive cologne he wore. And the sheer strength of the man's hard, honed body against hers made her blood pound in her veins just as if he were some hungry lone wolf, intent on carrying her off to his lair to savour at his leisure.

But hers wasn't the only heart that was hammering. And when Gabriel suddenly and without warning let her go, cursing vehemently beneath his breath, Lara stumbled. Her legs felt as weak as strands of damp linguine.

Retrieving her balance as quickly as she could, she stood on her father's immaculately mown lawn and tentatively touched her fingertips to her lips. They were already slightly swollen and still throbbed from Gabriel's savagely hungry kiss. The man himself had already distanced himself and stood shaking his dark head in what looked to be disgust. When his gaze lifted to meet hers she had never seen an expression more nakedly stark.

'I'm sorry if I hurt you. Despite what I said, it was never my intention to do that,' he intoned huskily. 'But it's better you know now what I'm really like than find out later. At least now you have the chance to shut the door on me and vow never to see me again.'

Wiping the back of her hand over her tear-moistened eyes, Lara unflinchingly met his tortured gaze. It was then that she made a silent vow not to abandon him as his mother and uncle had done. Her friends might not have understood her decision if they'd been privy to his little speech about being 'a taker not a giver', but then none of them had known the Gabriel of old, and nor did they know how it felt to set your eyes on a man and believe that he might—*just might*—be your destiny.

Despite her private feelings about that, Lara was still determined not to let Gabriel have the upper hand. Even if she couldn't deny the powerful chemistry between them, she certainly wasn't about to let him use her and then discard her as if he wouldn't give her so much as a second thought. She didn't want to be one of the 'weak' that fell by the wayside.

'You probably didn't mean to hurt me, Gabriel, but the truth is you did. Perhaps you need to leave and reflect on that for a while?'

His glance was more than a little bemused. 'Do I take it that you'd be willing to see me again despite what just happened?'

'I would. But you won't behave like you have every right to kiss me like that again, Gabriel. Because I won't let you.'

Folding her arms across the fresh pink linen shirt that she'd donned after their walk as if she meant business, Lara sighed.

'I sense that you only did what you did out of sheer frustration at not knowing what to do with your feelings. Feelings that must have been building up inside

you since you heard about your uncle and then about
Sean. I can totally understand that. Grief can make even
the most stable of people go a little crazy sometimes.
It can make them act in ways they normally wouldn't.'

'So you think I kissed you purely because I didn't
know what to do with my grief and went a little crazy?'

Sensing her face flooding with heat, she twined a
long strand of rich brown hair round her fingers and
unwaveringly met his gaze. 'Yes…yes, I do.'

'Then clearly you've learned nothing about men and
their base desires, have you?' He raised a sardonic dark
eyebrow.

Shocked more by his remark than by his rapacious
kiss, Lara wanted the ground to open up and swallow
her. Clearly Gabriel still thought of her as Sean's innocent little sister after all—a woman who had probably
been sheltered from the world by kind but undoubtedly
misguided parents and was consequently too naïve for
words.

Gathering every ounce of determination and resolve
she could muster, she refused to let his mockery get to
her. Naïve or not, she still didn't believe Gabriel was
displaying his true nature. Her intuition told her that
presenting himself as cruel and uncaring was just a
ruse. It wasn't the truth. She'd put money on it.

'I may not have a lot of experience with men, Gabriel, and I know it's been a long time since we last
met, but I'm not as naïve as you seem to think I am. I'm
quite aware of what goes on in the world, and of the—
of the *desires* that people have. And, in spite of what
you said, I don't believe that it's in your nature to take
what you want just because you can. You've probably
built a wall around your feelings for a long time, and

it's only natural that those feelings should spill over since coming back home and being forced to face the losses in your life.'

She paused to take in a deep, steadying breath.

'I may not be as worldly-wise as you, but neither am I insensitive to the fact that you must be hurting.'

Even as she said the words Lara wondered how she'd dared express them when she saw Gabriel's lip curl disparagingly. He was rubbing his hand over the borrowed cobalt-coloured shirt that belonged to her father—a colour that brought out the intense glittering blue of his stunning eyes—and for a few heart-pounding moments she honestly thought he was about to walk away. To walk out of her life for ever.

'I hate to shatter another illusion, sweetheart, but I didn't kiss you because I was hurting.' Again Gabriel raised a rueful dark eyebrow. 'At least not in the way that you believe. I kissed you out of pure *lust*. If you find that shocking, then look in the mirror. The little girl that I once knew has grown up into a very beautiful and desirable woman. A very *sexy* woman. There's not a man in the world who would blame me for wanting you in my bed.'

'If you expect me to be flattered by that comment then I—'

He strode towards her again but Lara didn't flinch. Gabriel could taunt her all he liked, but she would stand her ground and refuse to believe him to be doing anything other than play-acting—seeking to divert her from the truth of what he was really feeling by making her think that he was a cold, heartless playboy with no remaining vestige of the friendly, teasing youth she'd known as a young girl.

'I don't expect you to be flattered, angel.'

Lifting his hand, he stroked his palm down over her cheek. The gesture both warmed and froze her at the same time. One thing she couldn't deny was the realisation that there had always been something unpredictable about his nature. Something *dangerous*, even.

Sean had once commented that women swarmed round Gabriel like bees round a honeypot because as well as having good looks he exuded a 'bad-boy' image they all seemed to find irresistible. Lara didn't doubt that was true, but she had never been frightened of him. She might be naïve, but she didn't think he would ever deliberately hurt her or cause her pain. Strangely, even his savage kiss hadn't changed her mind about that.

He sucked in a deep breath and the warmth of his ensuing sigh feathered over her cheek. It had the same startling effect as if she'd imbibed a shot of the most intoxicating brandy. The dizziness and weakness that flooded her made her wonder if her legs would ever hold her safely upright again.

'Rather than be flattered…for *both* our sakes…I'd prefer you to just tell me to go to hell and warn me never to darken your doorstep again.'

The exquisite carved male lips in front of her twisted, almost as if he wished she would put an end to his inner agony by readily acceding to his wish to tell him to go to hell. But Lara couldn't and *wouldn't* do it.

'No, Gabriel. I won't ever tell you that—not unless you deliberately cause me harm. Call me weak, or even stupid, but my brother would turn in his grave if I turned you away. My parents wouldn't be too pleased with me, either. I think our emotions have been heightened today because of what we've both been through….

losing people that we love. So let's put this upset aside for a while and finish our lunch, shall we? I've got some fresh fruit salad and cream for dessert.'

Feigning that she was unperturbed by what had just transpired between them, she lightly lifted Gabriel's hand off of her cheek and walked back to the table. But her heart was thudding like crazy as she pulled out her chair and turned back towards him. He was standing stock-still, staring at her as if he couldn't begin to fathom where she was coming from.

'No, Lara. I won't stay. Thanks for the lunch, but I think I'll pass on dessert.' He shrugged. 'In spite of what just happened I want you to know that I wish you a happy future—I really do. The *best*. I've no doubt you'll break a few male hearts along the way…that is, if you haven't done so already.'

Just as Gabriel finished speaking, Barney shot out through the patio doors like a bullet from a pistol. Fresh from the nap he'd been having after their woodland walk, he made a direct beeline for Gabriel, jumping up at him and yapping wildly with excitement as if he was his new best friend.

Lara could have kissed the terrier because, taken by surprise and with his defences down, Gabriel immediately dropped down to his haunches and appeared to gladly make a fuss of the animal. The action was just what was needed to defuse the tension between them.

'I think he likes you.' She smiled. 'I don't think he's going to easily let you go, Gabriel.'

'And how about *you*, Lara? Are you going to easily let me go?'

Even across the expanse of lawn that was between them the diamond glitter of his eyes seemed to burn a

hole right through the centre of her soul, and it shook
Lara. Licking lips that were suddenly achingly dry, she
smoothed a tremulous hand down the front of her jeans
and made herself hold his gaze unwaveringly.

'Probably not. I'm a bit like a terrier, too, when it
comes to my friends. It takes a lot to shake me loose.
By the time you go back to New York you'll probably
be heartily sick of the sight of me.'

'You think?'

Lifting a joyful Barney into his arms, Gabriel rose
to his full height again. The maddeningly enigmatic
smile on his face made her limbs feel as insubstantial
as cotton wool.

'Let's have that dessert now, shall we?' she suggested, aiming for a matter-of-fact tone and fearing
she'd completely missed the mark. 'It seems a shame
to let it go to waste.'

'Temptation personified—that's what you are, Lara
Bradley,' Gabriel drawled huskily.

'I'd probably make a good saleswoman, then, wouldn't
I?'

Hugging a now much calmer Barney to his impres-
sively broad chest, he smiled. 'Sweetheart, you could
sell me any damn thing you wanted and I wouldn't be
able to resist. See how much power you have over me?'

If only he knew it wasn't *power* over him that she
craved, Lara mused achingly, but something much
deeper and more lasting.

CHAPTER FOUR

When the time had come for him to bid Lara good-bye that day, his policy to keep them keen by not always being readily available—as was his habit with women—had made Gabriel strive to keep his tone and manner as non-committal and cool as possible. But all it had taken was one more lingering glance into Lara's big brown eyes to make him realise this was the *one* woman he wouldn't be able to employ his usual 'laissez-faire' technique with.

That incendiary kiss he had stolen from her might have left her thinking what a merciless bastard he was, but it hadn't been planned. He'd never known a hunger and a need for a woman like it, and in the midst of his surprising need to confess how driven he'd become in his bid for success his desire for her had reached fever pitch.

Add to that the fact that he had been mad at himself, mad at the world, and mad at the cards that fate had dealt him and it had been a recipe for fireworks. Now Gabriel couldn't get the taste of her or the memory of her soft and shapely contours out of his mind.

Realising he didn't want to leave before spending some proper time with Lara, he'd decided he would just let things unfold naturally between them instead of sabotaging his chances by being overly demanding and dictatorial. With that in mind, he had suggested that after his meeting with his uncle's solicitor the next day he pick her up and take her with him to see the house he'd been bequeathed, show her around. Somehow the thought of visiting his old home with her by his side was altogether more appealing than if he confronted the bittersweet memories it would undoubtedly evoke on his own. After the visit he would take her back to her parents' house so that she could walk Barney, and then in the evening he would take her out to dinner.

After hearing her gladly acquiesce to both those suggestions, Gabriel had left Lara to drive back to his hotel in Park Lane with his spirits raised even when by rights they shouldn't be—because not only had he lost Sean but he still had to face the ghosts of his past back at the manor house he'd grown up in.

That aside, he'd begun to sense that he and Lara had some 'unfinished business' between them. Why else would they have this chemistry after not even setting eyes on each other for years? Gabriel knew that he wouldn't be returning to New York any time soon without discovering the reasons for it.

'Do you mind if I ask you how your meeting with the solicitor went?'

In the sleek black luxury saloon car that Gabriel had hired for the duration of his stay Lara's tone was cautiously measured, as if she was unsure of what kind of response she would get from him. Gabriel couldn't blame her for being wary after what had happened yesterday. But right then, despite being secretly thrilled that she was sitting beside him, smelling as fragrant as a rose and looking breathtakingly lovely in her strapless pink summer dress, a more disturbing topic was dominating his thoughts.

That morning he had discovered that there was a surprising codicil to his uncle's will. How it would impact on his life should he go along with it had presented him with a dilemma he'd never anticipated. It seemed there was yet another complication for him to confront and deal with. Dear God! Was he *never* to be free of the demoralising legacy of his past?

Swallowing hard, he deftly steered the car off the main road and onto a thoroughfare that he knew led out into the countryside. It was an all too familiar route—one that he had travelled many times as a boy and rarely with any pleasure.

After travelling for a while in silence, Gabriel finally turned briefly towards Lara and answered her question.

'The meeting went as well as expected, I suppose, if not entirely to my satisfaction. Anyway, you'll see the house in a few minutes and we can go in and have a look round. I'd like to check a few things over and you can come with me. Then we'll have a cup of coffee. I'm expecting my uncle's housekeeper to meet us. She still maintains the place for me and sees to its upkeep.'

'It must be very reassuring for you to have somebody you know taking care of it.'

Seeing they were approaching the long fir-tree-lined drive that led up to the house, Gabriel grimaced.

'I don't exactly *know* her. Her name is Janet Mullan and I only met her when I came over for my uncle's funeral. She's nice enough, I suppose. A cheerful sort. God knows she would have to be to have put up with my taciturn uncle for so long. He wasn't the greatest conversationalist, that's for sure.'

Beside him, Lara emitted a soft-voiced sigh. 'You've never told me what his name was...your uncle, I mean.'

The question made his stomach clench. He'd always made a point of not calling his uncle by his name, because dignifying the man with a personal address might have suggested that he'd mattered to him—which he expressly *hadn't*.

'He was called Richard Devenish—or, to give him his full title, *Sir* Richard Devenish.' He wasn't able to prevent the acerbic inflection that crept into his tone. Being the man's only kin—apart from his errant mother, of course—Gabriel might have inherited the title but it meant little or nothing to him. He would probably never even use it. If he did, it would always be a bittersweet reminder of where he had come from.

His pretty companion shifted in her seat, and he sensed her big brown eyes staring at him in what was likely disbelief.

'You mean to say that you come from landed gentry, Gabriel? I didn't know that.'

'Why should you? I've never advertised it.'

'Did Sean know?'

'I must have mentioned it to him once, because every now and again when we got drunk he'd give me a mock bow just to rile me. Neither of us took it seriously, though.'

'You sound as though it embarrasses you. To have a title, I mean. I don't understand.'

'No.' Staring out through the windscreen at the gracious and mellow redbrick manor that had materialised at the end of the drive, Gabriel felt his insides lurch painfully. 'And I don't suppose you ever will…not unless I tell you. Anyway, we're here.'

Parking the car on the gravel and turning off the ignition, he turned towards Lara to survey her. Once again a rush of pleasure and a need so acute pulsed through him. It was hard to think about doing anything else but making love to her. The sleek bared shoulders in the fetching summer dress she wore didn't exactly help divert the idea. The way the bodice hugged her curvaceous breasts made it hard to look anywhere else.

'By the way…' He smiled, consciously changing his previously gruff tone to a gentler one. 'Have I told you how pretty you look today? That dress is sensational on you.'

Lara's small pink tongue slipped out to moisten her lips and the colour in her cheeks went from a beguiling tinted rose to a deep cerise. The desire that was already gripping Gabriel with a vengeance veered towards the painful.

'No, you haven't,' she answered. Clearly perturbed by the compliment, she quickly moved her gaze to make an interested examination of the imposing building in front of them. 'What an amazing house. It makes my parents' place look doll-size in comparison.'

'Yes, but I know which one I prefer.'

Before she could comment Gabriel put his hand on the door handle and stepped out onto the gravel, then he stooped down to glance in at her. 'We should go in.'

Last night Lara had found it nigh on impossible to sleep. She'd lain awake long into the night, thinking about Gabriel and the fact that he was returning the next day. The shirt that he'd worn during their walk through the woods was draped over a hanger that she'd hooked on the back of the slipper chair by her bed. She'd washed and ironed it, but it still smelled indelibly of its owner, and every now and then Lara had reached out her hand to pull the material to her and sniff it, to remind herself of how compelling and sexy Gabriel's scent was.

She had also touched her fingertips to her lips as she'd recalled the devastatingly passionate kiss that he'd stolen. And every time she had done so it had been as though she lay close to a furnace. There wasn't a single inch of flesh on her body that didn't feel scorched by the man. Just the memory of his heated passion had the ability to arouse her more than she'd ever been aroused before.

Although the beautifully tailored white shirt that belonged to Gabriel was no guarantee that he would keep his promise and return, Lara had chosen to believe it was. Even a man as rich as Gabriel surely wouldn't want to lose an expensive shirt...would he?

She needn't have worried. Gabriel had indeed returned, as he had said he would. And if yesterday when he'd shown up unannounced at her parents' door had felt like a dream, then the surreal sense had definitely intensified today. Lara knew her brother's friend came from wealthy stock, but she'd had no idea that the house he'd grown up in was as grand and palatial as *this*. Certainly Sean had never mentioned it. Had her brother sought to protect the other man's privacy by keeping the information a secret? Lara wouldn't be surprised if he had. Sean had always been fiercely loyal to his friends. Especially Gabriel.

Janet Mullan, the housekeeper, was a diminutive and pretty woman of around sixty, with a wing of silver hair amid surprisingly dominant chestnut curls, and she did indeed turn out to be just as cheerful as Gabriel had said she was. Her twinkling blue eyes lit with pleasure when she greeted them at the impressive Georgian double doors, and she seemed genuinely pleased to see the manor house's handsome new owner.

Straight away she demonstrated her thoughtful nature. If there was anything she could do to help Gabriel or his guest feel more at home, she told him eagerly, anything at all, then he shouldn't hesitate to ask. Would they like some iced tea or a cold drink before they looked around? The news this morning had forecast a 'scorcher' of a day.

Glancing briefly at Lara, Gabriel saw that she was happy to agree with his decision and declined. However, he did request some coffee and biscuits for after they'd finished touring the house.

After he had requested the key to his late uncle's study, because he needed to look at some correspondence that had been left for him, it was clear to Lara that her companion was restless, and she had the sense that Gabriel didn't want to spend any more time at the house than he absolutely had to.

It was hard to understand when he was now master of this incredible property.

When Janet Mullan returned with the key he politely thanked her and, touching his hand to Lara's back, partly exposed by the fitted pink dress she'd impulsively decided to wear that morning, Gabriel led her towards the palatial winding staircase that led to the upper floors.

After looking round several elegant and beautiful rooms they arrived at the light and perfectly proportioned library. Lara had been wondering if Gabriel would show her the bedroom he'd occupied as a child, in the hope that it would give her a little more insight into the man he had become, but she guessed he would probably prefer to visit it on his own. However, as soon as they entered the library, Lara fell silent in wonder. She couldn't help it.

Before her were floor-to-ceiling shelves perfectly arranged with books of every size and volume. More avaricious and ambitious girls might dream of diamonds and sports cars, but she would feel blessed beyond measure should she ever have a room totally dedicated to her books, a room that she could read and relax in—even if it was only small. Gabriel's library was beyond her wildest dreams, but she honestly felt privileged to see it and to experience its gracious ambience, however briefly.

Catching what looked to be a rare pleased smile on his handsome face as he noted her pleasure, Lara found herself walking across the gleaming parquet floor to the generous Georgian windows. Glancing out, she saw that the beautifully furnished book-lined room looked out onto a stunning river frontage, with acres of lush meadow stretching further than the eye could see beyond it.

But she quickly set aside her pleasure at the view when she realised that Gabriel had grown increasingly quiet. Was he unhappy or upset about something? Lara wished she knew specifically what was troubling him. However, what she *did* know was that she could hardly take her eyes off of him. Even dressed in jeans and a navy blue T-shirt, with a casually open chambray shirt, the man didn't look remotely out of place against the impressive grandeur of his childhood home. Yes, Gabriel Devenish exuded class, whether he was conscious of it or not.

Yet the serious, almost solemn expression crossing his strongly delineated features didn't suggest he was remotely pleased at the fact that, as well as being a rich financier, he was now a seriously wealthy landowner, as well. In fact his preoccupied expression suggested he wished he were anywhere else in the world but here.

Just what was going through his mind? Was he remembering his uncle, perhaps? Yesterday he'd confessed that their relationship hadn't been a close one. For a boy whose mother had already abandoned him that must have been cruelly hard. Seeing his home again, was Gabriel perhaps regretting the now lost opportunity to make amends with his uncle and work towards repairing their estranged relationship? If only he would share some of his feelings with her.

'Gabriel?'

'What is it?'

Turning towards her, he pierced her with a troubled yet forceful stare, as though challenging her to say anything that displeased him. Lara didn't need to be a trained psychologist to sense that his composure was balanced on a precarious knife-edge. Now definitely wasn't the time to quiz him about his past.

'From what I've seen so far, this is probably my favourite room in the whole house,' she declared, endeavouring to convey an upbeat cheerful tone. 'How lucky were *you* to have had a personal library at your disposal growing up? If I had lived here I know this is where I would have spent most of my time.'

'Of course you would. That's why you became a librarian, isn't it? Because you love books?'

'I don't deny it.'

'Well, sweetheart...'

To her surprise Gabriel joined her at the window embrasure—but he was still looking troubled, and his compelling blue eyes had darkened like the precursor to a storm.

'Although you might think I was lucky to have a library and such a beautiful house at my disposal, it was anything *but* a pleasurable or happy experience. In fact most of the time the house felt more like a prison than a home to me. It wasn't until I went to university and met Sean, and then you and your parents, Lara, that I got a taste of how different my life could have been if I'd had a similarly happy family.'

Resisting the urge to touch him, even though she badly wanted to, Lara proffered a sympathetic smile instead. 'I'm sorry that you didn't experience a happy family life when you grew up—I really am. But I hope you know that my parents and Sean practically thought of you as family. Mum and Dad were equally as pleased for you when you graduated as they were for Sean.'

'And what about you, Lara?'

Gabriel startled her by reaching out to coil some burnished strands of her silken dark hair round his fingers.

'Did *you* regard me as practically family, too?'

Even though her heart slammed hard against her ribs, and her mouth dried uncomfortably, she bravely met his searing intense gaze without glancing away. It was clear that her answer was important to him and it behoved her to tell him the truth, come what may.

'No, Gabriel. I can honestly say that I never thought of you as family.'

There was a definite hitch of surprise at one corner

of his sublimely carved mouth but he maintained his steady, searching glance.

'Well, well…' His voice lowered meaningfully, and then he freed the strands of hair he'd captured and slid his warm hand beneath her jaw instead. Tipping up her chin to trap her gaze, he said, 'I have to commend you on your honesty, Lara. So, if not family then what *did* you think of me as?'

A sudden attack of nerves seized her. Running her hand down over her dress, Lara sensed it tremble. Gabriel's nearness and the seductive warmth that emanated from his body made it hard to think straight, never mind string a sentence together.

'I don't mean that I didn't regard you highly. Of course I did. You were my brother's best friend and I—and I thought a lot of you.'

'And how do you think of me now?'

She supposed the question was inevitable, but it didn't make it any easier to answer. 'I'm—I'm still fond of you.'

'Fond?' His fingers gripped her chin a little tighter. His blue eyes had never looked stormier. 'That's got to be the most insipid expression of feeling I've ever heard and I can't say that I like it.'

Lara shivered. Inside her strapless dress her nipples had tightened almost unbearably against her bra. They were like molten steel buds and they stung as though burned by a flame as she helplessly watched Gabriel's mouth descend towards hers.

An instinctive need for self-preservation, along with the need to maintain a modicum of equilibrium before she found herself irretrievably lost, swept over her and she found herself halting his lips' descent by laying her hand flat against his chest to stop him. It felt like an impenetrable iron wall, and even as Lara halted him her body clamoured feverishly for his touch.

'We shouldn't— We shouldn't be doing this, Gabriel,' she breathed.

'Says who?' One corner of his devilishly teasing mouth twisted wryly and he caught the hand that was attempting to stop him and lightly threw it away. Then he crushed her against him without the slightest remorse. 'If it's what we both want, then who's to say we should stop?'

Again Lara made a last-ditch attempt to utilise common sense. But Gabriel's desire had lit hers like a flame to touch paper and being sensible was the last—the *very* last—thing her inflamed body wanted to do.

His hard, honed physique felt incredible, pressed up close to hers, and it was clear he was aroused. But somehow she managed to tell him shakily, 'What I want is to be your friend, Gabriel…a *good* friend—not one of the "pretty ladies" with whom you spend the night when you want some company. Our friendship means a lot to me. I wouldn't want sex to cheapen it.'

He immediately dropped his hands down by his sides, looking stricken. Then he looked furious. 'So you would feel cheap if you slept with me, would you? I can't say that does a hell of a lot for my ego. But perhaps in the fairy-tale world that you inhabit, Lara, you were hoping for some kind of knight in shining armour to bed you?'

Gabriel swallowed hard, and his fierce expression was disparaging.

'Well, that's *never* going to be a role I can play, sweetheart, and if all you want is a friend then I suggest you look elsewhere. It's not as if you don't know my history and what a lousy friend I was to your brother. Why would you think I'd behave any differently towards you?'

It was inexplicable why she was so prone to make him angry, but rather than try to understand it right then Lara preferred to try and get to the root of why he was so furious. In spite of his rejection all those years ago, she honestly didn't think it was because he disliked her.

'My statement about sex cheapening our relationship came out all wrong, Gabriel….' She chewed her lip in frustration. 'I didn't mean that the act would make me *feel* cheap—it's just that it would be a shame to reduce the quality of the long-held regard we have for each other just because we succumb to a desire that might be quickly forgotten and…' Her face flamed red as she said the next words. 'And regretted.'

His answering frown was formidable. 'So you think I'd be such a lousy lover you'd immediately regret it?'

Lara could hardly believe how adept she was at saying the wrong thing sometimes. Briefly glancing out of the window and wishing for some kind of mystical inspiration, she couldn't help sighing. 'I don't think that at all. You—you seem determined to misunderstand me.'

Folding his arms across his chest, Gabriel gave her another long, examining look. The sun streaming in through the window behind him made his chestnut hair glisten like copper and she found herself transfixed by the sight.

'Then tell me this,' he said soberly. 'Do you believe there's something wrong with succumbing to desire? Do you think you'll be somehow punished for giving in to it?'

'I'm not some kind of nun who's taken holy orders, Gabriel.' Feeling uncomfortably foolish, Lara flushed.

'Excuse the pun, but thank God for that,' he commented drolly, making her immediately feel weak again when his mouth curved into one of his devastating smiles.

'Is there anywhere else in the house you'd like to show me?' she said quickly, moving across to the door and impulsively taking the opportunity to put some distance between them in a bid to try and calm her wildly beating heart.

With a wry shake of his head he replied, 'That could easily be misconstrued as a leading question, sweetheart, and to save your very charming pretty blushes I'll keep the answer for later. Right now I need to go to my uncle's study and look over some papers. Think you can make your way back downstairs, find Mrs Mullan and ask her to make that coffee for us? Hopefully I won't be too long.'

'Of course.' Feeling glad of the temporary reprieve, in order to get her thoughts together, Lara was happy to agree. But then a thought occurred. *What if the correspondence his uncle had left for him upset or distressed him?* What kind of mood would he be in when he returned downstairs? And would she be able to handle it adequately and give him the support that he might need?

CHAPTER FIVE

APPROACHING THE REGENCY-STYLE oak desk in a room that was imbued with the familiar scent of Havana cigars, Gabriel stared down at the cream vellum envelope with his name on it that sat atop the green baize blotter and unconsciously clenched his fists. Recognising the imposing inked script with the letter 'G' curled with an exaggerated flourish as his uncle's hand immediately made him shudder.

He'd been instructed by his uncle's solicitor that a letter would be waiting for him back at the house and had been asked to read and digest its contents as soon as possible in order to help make up his mind about the unexpected demand in the codicil.

Having already had that document meticulously outlined to him by the solicitor, Gabriel was in no mood to read what would in all likelihood be another disagreeable demand. He'd quickly learned that inheriting the manor was not going to be the straightforward formality that he wanted it to be. But at the end of the day he was an astute businessman as well as a banker, and it just wasn't in him to relinquish the desire to add to his already considerable fortune if the opportunity presented itself, no matter how testing the task would be.

Having seen the house and its extensive grounds again, he was already certain that he would put it on the market and sell it as quickly as he could before returning to New York. He certainly didn't want to take up residence here for six months in order to decide what he was going to do with the place, as the codicil stipulated he would have to if he wanted to inherit.

Had his uncle seriously thought that he would? He was sick and tired of being tied to the unhappy childhood memories that dogged his adult life. The sooner he was rid of the house the better. At any rate, Gabriel knew he could hire the best damn lawyer in the business to help him get round that particular complication. And he personally knew of at least two property developers who would all but rip off his arm to get their hands on the place as soon as they got wind that he was selling it.

He didn't feel an ounce of loyalty either to his uncle or to his forebears when it came to making a profit from the sale. After all, what had his esteemed so-called family done for him?

Feeling impatient, because he'd much rather be spending time with Lara, Gabriel tore open the envelope, unfolded the enclosed letter and hurriedly scanned it.

His heart was thumping hard in shocked disbelief before he even got to the end of the first paragraph.

Dear Gabriel
If you are reading this letter then it must be because I am no longer here. Knowing that must be the case, it behoves me to finally tell you the truth about your mother, Angela. She did not wilfully abandon you, as I once told you. That is the

first important thing for you to know. The second is the tragic fact that my beloved sister took her own life.

She had a serious depressive illness that there was no known cure for, and shortly after you were born it became apparent that she was unable to take care of you by herself. She herself needed round-the-clock care and supervision because her illness drove her sometimes to harm herself and her pregnancy exacerbated the tendency.

I lived in fear that she would harm you, too, Gabriel, although with hindsight I should have known that she adored you and would have protected you from harm with her life.

It was a wretched disease that she endured, and I told you that she abandoned you because she begged me to do so should anything happen to her. She was convinced it would be better if you believed that rather than knew that she was sick. She feared that you would get it into your mind that you might have inherited the affliction and that it would stop you from having the successful and happy future that she envisaged for you.

As for your father—I honestly don't know who he was, Gabriel, because Angela would never say. She did tell me once that she loved him, and that he was good to her, but also that he was married. When she knew that she was carrying you she broke off all contact with the man, and I stopped asking her about him because I could see that it distressed her.

I have not been as good an adoptive father to you as I should have been, Gabriel. I know that

*now and I deeply regret it. But my own father was
an austere and uncommunicative man who never
displayed much emotion and I suppose I must
have picked up the traits. Consequently I fooled
myself into thinking that if I provided every material asset you would need to help you get on in
life that would be enough. But the truth is because
of my own emotional inadequacy I denied you the
one thing that you perhaps needed the most—love
and friendship.*

*I will never know if you can find it in your
heart to forgive me for the tragic lie that I told
you about your mother, Gabriel, but I hope that
given time, if you do, then my beloved sister and
I will rest in peace.*

*Look after the manor house for us, my boy,
and fill it with your own dear children. One day
the sadness and pain that has hurt us all beyond
imagining will, I hope, be banished for good and
be replaced with sunshine and laughter instead
of heartache.*

*I did you another grave disservice, Gabriel. I
once told you that money would buy you anything
you wanted—even love. I was wrong. I hope you
know that now and can find the woman of your
dreams to make a life with. Home and family—
that's where true happiness lies.*
Sincerely
Your uncle, Richard Devenish

As he finished reading, Gabriel felt numb to his very
core. The sensation was quickly replaced by a sense of

rage and despair the magnitude of which he had never experienced before.

With his hands shaking he watched the neatly folded letter slip out of his loosened grip and drop back onto the green baize blotter. Leaning forward to rest his arms on the desk, he dropped his head into his hands and squeezed his eyes shut tight. So many feelings, thoughts and sensations rose up inside him at the same time that he felt he would drown beneath the crushing weight of them.

Opening his eyes, he murmured, 'Dear God—why hit me with this now, after all these years? It just doesn't make sense. It makes no sense whatsoever!'

Unable to stay still for a moment longer, Gabriel shot to his feet, heedlessly scraping the chair against the immaculate parquet floor. Vacating it, he furiously kicked at one of the legs and it crashed to the ground and lay on its back like a floundering whale. He had no inclination to set it right again.

It was hard to breathe suddenly, and the desire to escape both the house and the shocking truth of his tragic past was strong in him—too strong to be overcome or ignored. Snatching up his uncle's letter, he slammed out of the room and hurried downstairs.

'Gabriel, please don't drive so fast!' Genuinely frightened at the speed at which her companion was taking the narrow country roads, Lara felt her spine rigid with tension. But she was even more perturbed by the furious tight-lipped expression that hadn't left his face since he'd sought her out in the kitchen, where she'd been talking to the housekeeper, and unceremoniously declared that they were leaving right away.

'But what about your coffee and biscuits, Mr Devenish?' Janet Mullan had asked mournfully, clearly concerned that her new boss wouldn't be staying for refreshments after all.

Gabriel had looked even more irritated, and his tone had been surly. 'Don't stress about it. I'll be in touch again soon, to let you know what I'm doing. Just do your job and take care of the place in my absence. That's all you need be concerned about, Mrs Mullan.'

And with that he'd grabbed Lara's hand and urged her towards the door without pausing even once to explain why.

Lara had already guessed that he'd discovered something in his uncle's study that had disturbed him. He *must* have, she thought anxiously, because although he'd been a little quiet he'd seemed more or less okay before he'd gone in there.

'I'll get you home safely—you don't have to worry,' he said now.

His classic chiselled profile was as coolly perfect as one of Rodin's marble sculptures and he didn't even steal a momentary glance round at her.

Twisting her hands together in her lap, Lara sucked in a breath and answered, 'I'm not worrying so much about your driving, Gabriel, as about your state of mind.'

'What the hell do you mean by that?'

This time he did deign to glance at her, and his crystalline blue eyes were fierce.

'I mean I can see that you're upset, that's all. Why don't we stop somewhere and talk? It's not a good idea to drive when you're feeling distressed.'

'Why don't you let *me* be the judge of that? And do me a favour, Lara—please don't treat me like I'm one of your family's infamous waifs and strays that you can pet and nurse back to health. In case you hadn't noticed, I'm all grown up now and I can perfectly well take care of myself!'

Gabriel was indeed 'all grown up now', she thought privately, but that didn't mean he had the tools to try and heal whatever had distressed him on his own. He at least needed to talk things out with someone.

Turning her head to glance out of the window at the verdant country scenes that flashed by, she hoped that perhaps later, when he'd calmed down a bit, there might be a chance of reaching him and getting him to confide what had so disturbed him when he'd gone into his uncle's study. She could only pray that an opportunity would present itself.

Back at her parents' house, as soon as Lara opened the door Barney leapt up at her, barking an enthusiastic greeting, his short tail furiously wagging as if she'd been gone for *years* instead of a mere couple of hours. As was her habit, she dropped down to make a fuss of him, tickling him behind the ears, stroking his back and talking to him as though he understood every word she said—which she didn't doubt that he *did*.

'Hello, you little scamp. Have you missed me? I know you don't like being on your own for long, do you?'

The terrier emitted a short, sharp yap as if to agree.

Staring down at Lara's slim back and silkily smooth bared shoulders in that far too alluring summer dress she was wearing, Gabriel couldn't help fantasising about how easy it would be for him to unzip the garment and, using every seductive technique he had—and there were *many*—coax her into bed with him, rather than let her waste any more time and attention on the family's dog.

He realised he was becoming more and more reluctant to leave the brunette's side for even a minute. And after reading the hauntingly disturbing contents of his uncle's letter he was in no mood to be on his own. The only thing that could possibly help ease his soul-deep distress was Lara, preferably naked and lying beneath him.

As if suddenly remembering he was there, she rose to her feet, her lips curving in a tentative smile. 'What are your plans for the rest of the day? Are you in a hurry to leave? Only I was wondering if I could get you a cup of coffee, since we didn't have one back at the manor house.'

Her comment couldn't help but raise Gabriel's hopes. 'Are you angry with me because I didn't stay at the manor longer with you?'

Her expression softened. 'Of course I'm not angry. I was just concerned because I could see that you were upset.'

'Nearly everything to do with that damn house upsets me. But that's not your problem, Lara. I'll make it up to you when I take you out to dinner tonight. I'll book us a table at the Dorchester.'

'You have nothing to make up to me, Gabriel.'

'Yes, I do.'

'In any case, shall we have that coffee now?'

Rubbing his hand round the back of his neck, Gabriel grimaced. 'I need something a lot stronger than coffee. Have you got any brandy?'

Absently smoothing back the curtain of dark hair that framed her face, Lara frowned. 'But you're driving back to your hotel at some point, aren't you? I won't give you alcohol if you're intending to drive, Gabriel.'

'You really *are* a little Miss Goody Two-shoes, aren't you? I bet you never once sat on the naughty chair at primary school, did you?' he jibed, hating himself for sounding so disparaging when she was only displaying her natural concern for him.

But his ill-mannered retort didn't seem to faze her. As she lifted her chin he saw her glossy brown eyes were defiant.

'Call me what you will,' she said, 'but I won't collude with any plan that might potentially harm you or get you into trouble, Gabriel—however much you insist on having your way.'

Not releasing her perturbed gaze, he deliberately stepped towards her. 'What if I want or need some help?'

He'd knowingly pitched his voice low to engage her intimately, and Lara's sharp inhalation of breath immediately drew Gabriel's avid glance to her cleavage. He witnessed the provocative rise and fall of her luscious breasts in the fitted bodice of that sexy pink dress and, God help him, what was a healthy male supposed to do in such testing circumstances?

'What kind of help?'

A corner of his lips quirked in a teasing smile. 'I'm sure you must know the answer to that by now, Lara.'

'You have a worryingly one-track mind—you know that? Do you *really* think us being intimate is going to help resolve whatever upset you earlier? Something disturbed you when you went into your uncle's study—don't you think it might be more help if we discussed that?'

'No, I don't. I'm far more interested in what's going to help me right now, sweetheart. Not in what happened in the past. And, yes, I really *do* think it would help if we were intimate. The last thing I want you to do is worry about what happened earlier. That's *my* problem. Can't you stop trying to be Lady Bountiful for a minute and just be a woman for a change?'

Her pretty face was immediately stricken. It was obvious he'd touched a nerve, but although he regretted that he might have hurt her it didn't stop him wanting to seduce her. It might not ease any of the devastation he'd felt on finally learning the truth about his mother, and the lie about her abandoning him that his uncle had colluded with, but fulfilling the intimate connection he craved with Lara would go a long way to help satisfy the burning desire that had mercilessly seized him since seeing her again.

It was a carnal hunger that made it almost impossible for him to think about anything else but being with her in the most intimate way. Had the woman put some kind of spell on him?

'That was uncalled for, Gabriel. I'm just as much a woman as you are a man and you damn well know it.'

Hands planted firmly on her shapely hips, her dark eyes glinting with fury, Lara had no compunction in displaying her temper—and in truth right then those fulsome breasts of hers, along with her rosily flushed satin cheeks, ensured she was a sight for sore eyes.

Gabriel couldn't help concluding that Sean's 'little sister' had turned into a woman who would stir lustful longings in a stone, let alone a healthy red-blooded male. It was an honest-to-God mystery why she was still single.

'And if your criteria for judging femininity means that a woman is only feminine if she agrees to have sex with a man when he tells her that he's "in need" then you're seriously deluded.'

'Of course I don't think that!' Now it was his turn to feel aggrieved. 'You make it sound like I'm some stranger off of the street, instead of someone who's known and regarded you since you were young. Is it so hard for you to believe that I'm attracted to you, Lara?'

Gabriel was finding it increasingly hard to tamp down his growing frustration at her reticence to be closer. Perhaps he should open up to her a little bit more? Let her know that he had just as much feeling and sensitivity as she had, even though he rarely displayed it? Could he risk revealing such a thing to her?

The thought instantly made him want to retreat in order to protect himself. What if Lara laughed at his confession and concluded it to be a cynical ruse he was using in order to persuade her into bed? What if opening up more personally to her turned out to be a colossal mistake he'd come to regret? He had never yet given a woman that kind of power over him and he didn't want to start now. If he couldn't seduce her with his usual prowess and the skill that was innate to him, then he shouldn't even waste his time trying.

Reaching out to push the door shut behind him, and unknowingly tantalising him with her alluring sun-kissed scent that reminded him of a garden full of honeysuckle, Lara sighed heavily.

'I don't want to argue with you, Gabriel, but I *am* going to make us some coffee. Then I really think we should sit down and talk.'

Frustratingly having to own to losing this particular

little battle, but reluctant to walk away, Gabriel ruefully shook his head. 'Okay, have it your way—at least just for now. Perhaps some coffee will help clear my head. God knows right at this moment it feels like a herd of buffalo are stampeding through it.'

'That's probably the jet lag. Unless you have some kind of cold or fever brewing? Let me see.'

Reaching up, Lara laid her hand against his forehead, as if to ascertain his temperature, and her silkily cool touch made Gabriel suck in a surprised and pleased breath. It renewed his hope that she would continue to play nurse should he stick around a bit longer.

'You feel a little warm, but I don't think it's anything to worry about. If you start to feel any worse I'll give you something to help take your temperature down.'

'It won't work.'

'Why?'

'Let's go and have that coffee and maybe I'll tell you.'

Finding a perfectly legitimate excuse to touch her, when it was becoming more and more difficult for him *not* to, Gabriel slid his hand beneath her elbow to lead her down the hallway and out into the kitchen.

CHAPTER SIX

It was one of the hardest things Lara had ever had to do—to sit down opposite Gabriel at the kitchen table and try to pretend she was impervious to the naked longing in his eyes. It would be so easy to give him what he wanted, what *she* wanted, too. But then what would that achieve other than fulfilling their mutual need for sexual gratification?

She didn't doubt he could get that anywhere. After all, what woman in her right mind could look at the man and *not* imagine what it would be like to make love with him? Never mind get the chance to actually find out! He was pure erotic female fantasy come to life. But although the thought of her body entwined with Gabriel's was a dream she'd often fantasised over—one that she'd longed to make a reality—she wasn't about to diminish her fantasy with just one or two stolen experiences in bed with him and then have him walk away. Not when she yearned for so much more.

'Can I ask you why you wore that particular dress today?'

'What?' Startled by the question, Lara stared back into Gabriel's darkly captivating blue gaze and frantically wondered what to tell him.

The outfit wasn't her usual style—that was for certain. When it came to more 'dressy' items of clothing she usually erred on the side of caution—not too revealing and not too showy. But her friend Nicky had persuaded her that this dress looked 'hot' and would be perfect for when she found herself going on a special date with someone.

She supposed that when she'd known she was seeing Gabriel the following day, and that he would be taking her to visit his ancestral family home, she'd decided it *could* constitute as a sort of date. Now, in the cold light of day, having his heated gaze examine her as if he'd like to peel off everything she was wearing, preferably slowly and stitch by stitch, Lara wished she'd been more sensible.

'I knew it was going to be a hot day, that's why.' She shrugged her shoulders as though it was scarcely worth even commenting on.

'Well,' he drawled, leaning across the table to pin her with a tantalising gaze it was impossible to wriggle out of meeting. 'I'd like to commend you on your choice. It shows off your figure to perfection.'

'Gabriel?'

'Yes, Lara?'

'I think we need to change the subject and talk about what's been troubling you. Can we do that?'

The answering scowl on that handsome hard-jawed face was not dissimilar to that of a small boy denied a treat. Under different circumstances Lara might have found it amusing. But she was becoming very familiar with Gabriel's avoidance tactics, and right at that moment she would have been hard-pushed to raise even the smallest of smiles. Not when anxiety about him was gnawing away at her.

'I know you probably think I'm being a bit too pushy, but I'm concerned. If you don't at least share with me what's troubling you then who *will* you share it with?'

Lifting his mug of coffee to his lips, he took a sip, then returned it to the table. 'So you want to hear the whole sorry tale of my hopeless and hapless family, do you?'

Straight away Lara registered the pain in his voice that he'd obviously hoped to conceal with self-deprecating mockery. Her heart twisted as apprehension and fear about what he might be going to reveal invaded her. She nodded slowly.

'All right, then.' Even though he'd agreed, Gabriel looked far from easy and stared down at the floor. 'My uncle left me a letter revealing things about my mother that I never knew.'

The words were followed by a near deafening silence that told her his feelings must be in utter turmoil. Somewhere outside a bird sang. The lyrical sound pierced the air, adding a heartrending poignancy to the moment.

Wanting to encourage him to resume his story, and fearing he wouldn't because the prospect of revealing his family secrets and potentially making himself vulnerable was something he no doubt despised, she remarked quietly, 'You said she left when you were very young. You don't remember her?'

He lifted his head. 'No, I don't. In any case, it turns out that that was a lie.'

'I don't understand.'

Gabriel's carved mouth twisted bitterly. 'Oh, she left, all right.'

He stared at her, lost in some unhappy reverie that he was still trying to make sense of, she guessed.

'She killed herself.'

Lara could scarcely think straight above the sonorous thump of her heart. 'Oh, Gabriel, I'm so sorry.'

As his confession sank in she felt even more stunned and sorry. She couldn't begin to imagine what it must be like to hear that your mother had committed suicide. How did a child—a child who was now an adult—pick up the pieces of his life and live anywhere *near* normally again after learning such devastating news?

Gabriel shook his head as though bemused. 'My uncle told me that she left because she didn't think she was cut out to be a mother. That was the story she begged him to tell me so that I wouldn't try and find out the truth about her.'

'But why—why would she do such a thing?'

Shrugging his big shoulders, the gesture momentarily straining the soft blue chambray of his shirt, he grimaced. 'He said it was because she was suffering from a depressive condition that was incurable. She was afraid that if I knew the truth I might think I'd inherited it and it would ruin my life.' A harsh semblance of a laugh left him. 'She must have really been disturbed if she thought it was better that I believed she'd deserted me!'

Leaning forward, Lara studied Gabriel as if seeing him for the very first time. There was no hiding his distress. She had a heartrending glimpse of the small boy who'd grown up believing that his mother hadn't wanted him and had consequently abandoned him. With every fibre of her being she longed to go to him and draw him into her arms. But she sensed there was a lot more yet to this terribly sad story.

'It sounds as though she was just trying to protect you, Gabriel,' she remarked softly.

'Protect me? From what, exactly? Her love and devotion?' His tone was bitterly disparaging. 'I may not be parent material, but I'm damn sure mothers are supposed to love and care for their children—not just abandon them on some whim!'

Several thoughts jostled for position in Lara's mind just then, but the strongest was her musing that if his mother had been mentally ill, then it was surely no 'whim' that had driven her to insist that her son didn't know the truth about her condition. The poor woman must have really believed it would hurt him.

But she didn't share the thought with Gabriel right then. The clenched fists he'd laid on the table and the tortured look in his eyes told her it was best to stay silent and simply allow him to express how he felt without interrupting the flow of pain and anger that must be coursing through him. Better that he let it out than keep it all in. Afterwards, bit by bit, Lara would do her utmost to try and help him.

'My uncle said in his letter that she'd been a danger to herself but he honestly believed she never would have harmed me. Did he think that would be a consolation when I learned that she'd killed herself? Did he never consider the effect it might have had on me, growing up believing that she'd left because she didn't want me?'

'Oh, Gabriel…'

It was no good. It was impossible for Lara to remain sitting in her chair when his feelings were clearly tearing him apart and she ached to console him. But when she got up and dropped her arm gently round his shoulders she sensed them instantly stiffen.

'Didn't I tell you not to treat me like some waif or stray that needs your help?' he growled, catching hold of her hand and gripping it.

Staring back into the starkly haunted blue eyes, she felt an answering quiver that was part fear and part desire run down her spine.

'I don't regard you as some kind of waif or stray, can't you see that? You're not a stranger to me, Gabriel. I'm treating you like I would any dear friend who needed my comfort and support.'

'So it's back to us just being friends again, is it?'

Her action purely instinctive, Lara retrieved her hand to lay her palm against his smoothly shaven cheek. His skin felt like sensually roughened velvet. 'Everyone can use a friend, can't they?' she breathed.

She didn't plan for her voice to catch on the final two words but it did. Even as she saw the pupils in Gabriel's blue eyes darken and flare she suddenly knew that it wasn't just comfort she wanted to dispense. Right then she needed him as much as he needed her and it was impossible to deny it.

'No, Gabriel, not just friends.'

In less than a heartbeat his big firm hands pulled her down onto his lap and without preamble he drove them deep into her hair. Although his warm breath fanned her face like a spine-tingling summer breeze, it still made Lara shiver.

'I want you so much I think I'll die if I can't have you,' he declared.

His voice was low and deep, the unfettered emotion it expressed so raw that it almost took her breath away.

Lara would have crumpled at the declaration if he hadn't been cupping her face and anchoring her. But his lips were against hers, his hot tongue invading her mouth and devouring her, and a low, hungry groan emanated from his throat that she couldn't help but echo as she surrendered to the irresistible fire that he'd ignited.

If it were possible she would kiss him for ever, she thought wildly, yet even for ever couldn't possibly be *enough*. Her hands weren't idle as Gabriel's lips worked their honeyed and stirring magic. They splayed out over the hard chest encased in sensuous cotton and chambray, her fingers helplessly curling against him in a voracious need to know and feel every part of him, to have the insatiable memory imbued in her mind and heart for ever.

Leaving her hair, Gabriel's hands slid down over her shoulders onto her back. Lara sensed his fingers fumble impatiently with her zip. As if shaken awake from a dream, she suddenly became aware that things were fast getting out of control.

Not wanting their first intimate exploration of each other to take place mindlessly and perhaps awkwardly on a chair, she twisted her mouth away from his and said, 'No, Gabriel, not here.'

Straight away she registered the confusion and protestation in his eyes.

Administering a reassuring smile, she gently extricated herself, then stood up and reached down for his hand. 'We'll go upstairs to my room,' she added softly.

'You're sure?' he murmured.

She hadn't expected to hear doubt in his voice, but doubt was what she heard—and it made her want him all the more because he wanted to make sure.

'Yes, I am. It's what I want, too,' she answered firmly.

Lara needed to show Gabriel that she was equally as aroused and needy as he was. She wasn't going to bed with him purely because she wanted to console him. The man turned her on like no other man ever *could*.

Rising to his feet, he impelled her into his arms as if he couldn't bear to let her go for even an instant. For Lara, too, it was difficult to contemplate leaving that safe haven when the familiar scent of his cologne and the arresting heat from his body made her feel as if she was, albeit briefly, abandoning a vitally integral part of her.

Staring down into her eyes as if he would see into her very soul, Gabriel loosely circled her waist with his arm. 'Then let's go.' He smiled.

The gesture was indisputably possessive and it thrilled Lara right down to her innermost core. Knowing that Gabriel really wanted her made her feel beautiful. How could it not when she'd loved her brother's charismatic friend from the moment she'd laid eyes on him all those years ago? There was an undeniable sense of inevitability about them meeting up again like this— as if they were meant to find each other again. Did Gabriel feel that way, too?

The seductive scent of her perfume lingered in the air as Lara took Gabriel by the hand and led him into her bedroom. The room was awash with afternoon sunlight but she made no move to draw the blinds. The most seductive shiver ran down Gabriel's spine as, instead, she led him across to a queen-size bed that was draped with a purple silk coverlet.

Truth to tell, it would have been difficult for him to note much else in that room other than Lara herself.

His blood was infused with a longing to hold her close so profound that it was as though he were caught in the grip of a dangerous fever that was steadily growing hotter. All he could think of to help ease his pain was getting her naked and joining his body with hers. And if he was seeking shelter from the storms of life that had battered him, seeking it in the only way he sensed might provide some brief respite, then he made no apology for it.

At the foot of the bed Lara turned to face him. Her silken dark hair framed her lovely face like a picture. Lifting her hands, she positioned them either side of his waist. As her melting brown eyes examined him it was as though she were touching him in the most intimate way. Gabriel burned to take her. But through the fog of his desire he vowed to take things slowly, so that the experience would be pleasurable for her. It would surely be worth the sacrifice.

Trailing his fingertips softly and deliberately over her mouth, he said, 'Will you undress or do you want me to do it for you?'

With a soft catch in her voice, she returned, 'You decide.'

He couldn't have wished for a better answer. Bending his head, he gently touched his lips to hers. As he did so he tugged at the zip at the back of the sexy pink dress and slid it down with ease. Momentarily breaking off the kiss, he stepped back so that he could tug down the bodice. The satiny material shimmered silkily down over Lara's bewitching form to the floor. As she stepped out of the dress she put her hand in Gabriel's to steady herself and then kicked off the cork sandals that she wore.

She lifted her head to study him. The undisguised need he saw reflected in her eyes all but undid him. He responded by deftly encircling her chest to undo the catch on her bra. When her beautiful breasts were freed, he was gratified that she didn't immediately try to cover herself.

For long seconds Gabriel just stared at her, drinking in the arresting sight before him as though not quite believing his good fortune. Then he put his mouth to one tip-tilted breast and suckled hard. Just as an electrifying bolt of heat ricocheted through his body and went straight to his groin, hardening him, Lara released a soft-voiced moan of pleasure.

Glancing up at her, Gabriel smiled. Flattening his hand, he laid it against her breastbone and gently pushed. As she gracefully fell back onto the purple counterpane the full extent of her curvaceous figure was at last revealed to him in all its irresistible glory. The luscious breasts with their peaked nipples, her slim concave belly and shapely hips, the silky smooth legs that were even longer than he'd imagined, the toenails that were painted with a sassy fire-engine-red.

After his initial heated examination Gabriel's thoughts were suspended as the urgent need to make love to her instinctively drove him instead. Tearing off his shirt and T-shirt, he jettisoned the clothing onto the floor. Ridding himself of his shoes and socks, he undid his belt buckle and left the belt to fall loosely against his jeans. Then he joined Lara on the bed.

He couldn't have said who welcomed whom first. The only thing he registered was their mutually ravenous need to hold each other close and be intimate. The rest of their clothes were quickly dispensed with as they embraced, and the vow he'd made to take things slowly fell mockingly by the wayside as soon as touched her. Ravishing her mouth more deeply and hungrily than he'd ravished any other woman's before, Gabriel ran his hands down over her shapely body and explored her. She was hot silk and sensuous satin, and the devastating revelation about his mother that had torn him apart that day freed some of its imprisoning hold on him.

When Lara disengaged her lips from his to whisper his name, Gabriel heard the unspoken invitation he was longing to hear and sucked in a shaky breath. Moving to sit astride her, his smile drowsy with pleasure and acknowledgment, he bent his head to continue the drugging kiss that he'd quickly become addicted to. Even as his mouth took hers captive he felt her silken thighs come round his waist to enfold him.

A second invitation was hardly necessary. He helplessly took her there and then, pressing himself deep inside her with a hungry primal groan. Her heat was like a honeyed river and Gabriel knew he would willingly drown in it—not just once but over and over until he was spent—until every hurt and bitter sorrow that had ever plagued him was laid to rest for good.

Lara had feared the relinquishing of her virginity to Gabriel. Not because she didn't want to lose it, but because she'd been afraid that the initial discomfort would prevent her from giving herself as wholeheartedly as she wanted to. But his heated sensual possession had quickly banished her fears. The most intimate core of her womanhood had softened so naturally to accommodate him that any discomfort she experienced quickly disappeared as she surrendered to the tidal wave of passion that consumed her.

But Lara did briefly wonder if, when Gabriel entered her, he had noticed that her muscles were a little tight—perhaps tighter than women with a lot more experience than her? She should perhaps tell him that this was her first time, but she was still wary of trusting him too much in case he either didn't understand or couldn't believe that she would wait so long to be with a man. If she were to confess that she only felt she could be intimate with someone she loved, would it scare him away?

The thought was swiftly quashed by the sensation of wondrous bliss and excitement that gripped her as Gabriel moved rhythmically inside her and her hands clutched the iron-hard biceps in his bulging arms to hold on. During that incredible, passionate ride Lara soon learned that imagination was no substitute for the breathtaking reality that was making love with a man she had been crazy about for years. Not for one second did he fail to live up to her hopes and dreams about the experience—in fact, he *exceeded* them.

As the heat between them gathered force Gabriel glanced down at her, his blue eyes blazing with hunger and desire as if there was no other woman on earth for him but her. It was then that Lara had to bite back her heartfelt need to tell him how much she loved him—how much she had *always* loved him.

She determinedly quelled the impulse as he moved deeper inside her and she wound her arms round his neck to pull his head down to hers. Even as they hungrily kissed, the need in her that had been helplessly building towards fulfilment suddenly reached its peak. She found herself on a trip to the stars that took her breath away, that made her feel mindless and boneless, that made her shake and quiver and cry out all at once.

Her heart thumped so loudly that she would swear Gabriel must hear it.

As she slowly came back to herself he gave her a lazy, satisfied smile, lowered his head and whispered in her ear. 'You're so beautiful you take my breath away.'

The edges of her lips curved in an answering smile and he lifted himself and drove into her even more deeply. Once again Lara had to hold on tight to the iron-muscled biceps as they contracted and grew hard beneath her fingertips. Then he stilled and convulsed with a harsh-sounding groan that seemed to emanate from deep inside his soul.

The sound made Lara shiver. It was as though every hurt and betrayal he'd ever endured had culminated in that groan and was now released. Feeling the hot press of tears against her lids, she wove her fingers gently through his hair and held his head, secretly thrilling that he stayed inside her instead of immediately moving away. Knowing he was a man who didn't trust easily, she was pleased and gratified that he must trust her enough to do that.

As he laid his head between her breasts, his warm breath skimming gently over her skin, she registered his racing heartbeat and murmured, 'It's all right, Gabriel, just let it all out. I'm here for you.'

He didn't look up, just stayed where he was, his body still as a statue. But Lara knew she didn't imagine the brief shudder that went through him or the near silent sob that was quickly suppressed in case she should hear it.

CHAPTER SEVEN

GABRIEL HAD NO IDEA how long he'd been sleeping. All he knew was that it was like the most delicious dream he could ever imagine finding himself waking up next to a softly slumbering and naked Lara.

Raising himself up onto his elbow, he gently moved the silken strands of dark hair that caressed the side of her face. She was lying on her belly, her lovely face turned to the side. At some point during the afternoon she must have pulled the purple counterpane over them, but it had slid back down to her waist to leave her back and shoulders exposed. It was then that Gabriel saw the perfect facsimile of an ebony and sky blue butterfly, whose delicate wings spread out over the base of her spine. The woman constantly surprised him. Who would have thought that the once shy young girl he'd known all those years ago would have opted for a tattoo, albeit one that only a lover would see?

Shaking his head, Gabriel breathed out a bemused sigh. But it was quickly followed by a stinging flash of jealousy. The thought of Lara being naked with another man, even if it *was* in the past, made him feel almost physically ill.

Making love with her had been one of the most ecstatic and meaningful experiences of his life since he had shared some of the hurtful secrets about his past with her. That had made the experience truly intimate. Never before had he shared such personal information with a woman. Shuddering, he remembered how he hadn't been able to hold back his grief when he'd climaxed—recalled too that Lara had gently advised him to 'just let it all out' and told him that she was there for him.

Then he remembered that he hadn't used protection. It hadn't even crossed his mind. That was another first and a not so acceptable one. Was Lara on the pill? Damn it all, he should at least have thought to ask her. But he had been so consumed by the fever of longing that she aroused in him that rational thinking just hadn't been on the agenda.

If she were to become pregnant after this, what would he do? What would Lara *want* to do? Would she agree to an abortion if he asked her? It was such a shockingly disagreeable notion that a knifing pain cramped his chest.

At that precise moment Lara stirred and opened her eyes. Gabriel couldn't believe he'd forgotten for even a moment how beautiful they were—dark-roast coffee fanned by long, luxurious ebony lashes.

She was staring blankly up at him, as though caught in a spell. Then her gaze fully registered his and she asked softly, 'Are you all right? I mean, how are you feeling?'

'I feel good,' Gabriel answered frankly. 'Better than I've a right to, probably. I can't help feeling that I'm very fortunate to have found you again, Lara. I guess I must have done something right to please the gods.'

She dimpled. 'Maybe you're not all bad boy, then?'

'Is that how you see me? As a bad boy?'

'I think you have a little bit of that in you, but rather than detract from it, it just adds to your charisma.'

'Tell me more.' He grinned. 'I'm not averse to hearing about all the qualities that make me attractive to a woman.'

'What? And pander to your already inflated ego?'

Gabriel chuckled and realised how much he was enjoying just lazing in bed like this with Lara, in the middle of the afternoon, without feeling remotely guilty or having the need to get up and think about work.

'You don't have to do that to make me stay here with you, baby. Whatever you've got, I'm already addicted to it. That's why I'm still here.' Stroking his knuckles gently down her cheek, he smiled. 'You don't get rid of me that easily, either. I guess you're not the only one with a touch of the terrier in her.'

'Talking of which…' Lara sat bolt upright, grabbed the silk counterpane and pulled it up over her breasts. At the same time her cheeks flushed pink as though she was suddenly aware that she was naked. 'I've got to walk Barney. I can't believe I actually fell asleep in the middle of the day. I *never* do that—even if I'm exhausted.'

'This seems to be a day of firsts,' Gabriel observed smilingly.

'What do you mean?'

'It's not important.' Shrugging his shoulders, he levelled his gaze at her more seriously. 'However, what *is* important is the fact that I didn't use protection when we made love. That's a pretty major mistake, Lara, and whether you believe me or not it's one that I've never made before.'

Frowning, she told him, 'You don't have to worry, Gabriel. I'm on the pill. I should have mentioned it earlier, but we—I...' Her smile was a shade unsure. 'We got a bit carried away.'

Gabriel felt as if he'd been sucker-punched and didn't know why. Then he did. If Lara was taking the contraceptive pill then she must have the occasional lover. If she did, then it must have been quite a while since the last one, because she'd felt exquisitely tight when he'd entered her—as if having sex wasn't a regular occurrence for her. But the thought hardly reassured him. It made him feel disappointed, when in fact he should be grateful that at least one of them was taking the proper precautions.

Mentally gathering himself, he murmured, 'Thank God for that.'

Lara flushed and glanced away. Turning back to him, she asked, 'Do you know what the time is?'

He checked his watch. 'It's just gone four.'

'Four o'clock? You're joking?'

Amused, Gabriel drawled, 'Why the panic?'

'The panic is Barney must be desperate to answer the call of nature and I've got to go and have a shower.'

'That's an interesting dilemma. And there's one more thing you have to add to your list of things to do.'

'What's that?'

'You need to kiss me hello.'

Finally succumbing to the irresistible impulse that had been growing steadily stronger from the moment he'd opened his eyes and found Lara lying naked beside him, Gabriel put his hands onto her slim shoulders and pulled her against his chest. The silk cover slipped away from her breasts to expose them, and his senses were immediately aroused by the silken texture of her soft flesh and the peaked nipples pressing against him.

His blood thickened and slowed at the thought of seducing her again. Just as he was about to capture her lips in a drowsily sensual kiss that he hoped would be the precursor to so much more, right on cue the terrier downstairs made his presence known with a round of impatient barking.

'Oh, Lord. I'll have to go and see to him. I won't walk him—I'll just let him out the back. Sorry.'

With a sheepish glance, Lara wriggled out of his embrace and moved to the edge of the bed. Glancing down towards the floor, as though searching for something, she murmured an audible expletive beneath her breath and huffed out a sigh.

'What have you lost?' Gabriel enquired innocently, even as he reached behind her to pick up the bra and panties that had been partially hidden in the folds of the silk counterpane. He quickly slid them under her pillow.

'My underwear. But never mind.' Rising to her feet, she hurried across the room to grab a pair of jeans and a pink T-shirt from her wardrobe.

Transfixed by the wholly arresting sight of her bare bottom and long, slim legs, Gabriel found his gaze drawn to the exquisite butterfly tattooed at the base of her spine. Leaning back against the pillows, he drawled, 'I think this is the best wake-up call I've ever had. So what's the story behind the butterfly?'

Lara was in the midst of pulling up her jeans. She completed the task and turned round. The pink T-shirt she'd retrieved was held protectively over her breasts, as if it was still important to her to preserve her modesty even though she'd just presented an uncensored view of her delectable derrière to Gabriel.

'Sean sent me a picture of a butterfly just like it in his last letter home before he died. He told me it was extremely rare and that he felt privileged to have seen it.' With a nervous swallow she glanced briefly down at the floor. 'I suppose I had the tattoo done as a kind of homage to him. He often used to tease me that I "played safe" and didn't take enough risks in life. It makes me smile to imagine what he would have said if he'd seen it.'

'I think it's a work of art—and so are you, angel. You and the butterfly are an exquisite combination.'

'Thanks.'

The smile Lara gave him was so endearingly shy that it provoked Gabriel's carnal hunger even more. In fact he didn't know why he had even let her out of bed. Broodingly, he watched her hurriedly don the pink T-shirt she'd been holding against her. Braless, the garment was more revealing than she was probably aware. One thing was for sure: he wasn't about to complain about the fact.

'I'd better go and see to Barney. I won't be long.'

His mouth drying, Gabriel couldn't resist a final comment. 'So you're going commando, are you? What are you trying to do? Torment me? Do you know how close I am to hauling you back into bed?'

'If you do, then who's going to clean up the mess that Barney will undoubtedly leave on my parents' prized parquet floor? I can tell you now, Gabriel Devenish, it won't be me!'

In spite of his frustration Gabriel was still grinning at

the quick-fire remark, and devising lascivious ways he might repay her for it, long after Lara had left the room.

Gabriel's relief had been plain when she'd told him that she was on the pill and didn't have to worry. But as Lara stood at the back door that looked out onto the garden and watched Barney scamper across the lawn she knew he must assume she was a lot more experienced than she actually was.

What Gabriel didn't and couldn't know was that she took the contraceptive pill to help regulate her monthly periods and ease painful cramps. And, whilst Lara knew it wasn't a good idea to risk pregnancy when she wasn't even in a steady relationship, she couldn't help feeling regret that Gabriel probably would have hated it if he'd made her pregnant. After all, he didn't know how deep her feelings for him ran, or that she'd surrendered her virginity to him because he was the only man she'd ever loved and she loved him still. Trying to be realistic, she guessed that he probably wouldn't welcome anything that cramped his high-octane lifestyle—least of all a baby.

Determinedly brushing aside the moisture that surged into her eyes as she recalled how wonderful it had been to make love with him, she unconsciously held her hand over her heart. She still throbbed and tingled where he had touched her, where he had united his body with hers.

Although she'd naturally wanted to help give Gabriel the comfort that he'd needed after learning the devastating truth of how his mother had died, and how his uncle had lied to him to protect her, what Lara had said to him just prior to the event still held true. Their lovemaking had been something that she had wanted, too. Not just wanted but needed. Whatever happened now, or in the future, she would never regret it.

'Oh, what a tangled web we weave when first we practise to deceive….' The famous quote stole into her mind as she thought of the pain and distress the deception had visited on Gabriel—the pain and distress that would probably plague him for the rest of his life. Now he would quite likely sell the magnificent manor house he'd inherited because he would see it only as a lucrative investment he could cash in on and not as a family legacy he could be proud of. How could he when the wounds of his past were so great that no one would blame him for wanting to turn his back on the whole scenario? After he'd sold the place he would probably just return to New York and Lara would never see him again.

'No.'

It jolted her to realise she'd voiced the protest out loud. But already she was making a vow not to let such a bleak scenario occur if she could prevent it. Somehow there must be a way to get Gabriel to see the gift he would be turning his back on—the gift that might be the key to helping him heal the grievous wounds from his past and make him see that he didn't need to bear them for ever, that his future could be so much brighter if he would only give himself the chance to explore the possibility and not run away.

Lost in her heartfelt reverie, Lara sighed. Then Barney started to bark and she glanced down to see the terrier scampering past her, no doubt in search of his basket and a nap. It was then she remembered that Gabriel was waiting for her upstairs. She almost wanted to pinch herself to make sure she wasn't dreaming. It wasn't necessary. The stinging tips of her tender breasts where Gabriel had kissed and suckled them were an apt reminder that this was no dream but instead a heart-poundingly wonderful reality.

Hugging herself, she headed out into the hall and quickly returned upstairs.

To her surprise, Gabriel wasn't in bed where she'd left him. Just as Lara sensed her stomach plunge at the thought that he'd slipped away whilst she'd been keeping an eye on the dog, the en-suite bathroom door opened and he stepped out, fully dressed and combing his fingers through his lightly tousled chestnut hair. His charismatic smile was both rueful and rakish at the same time.

Before she could ask what was going on he strode over to her and possessively wound his arms round her waist. Even though his embrace instantly rendered her weak with pleasure and desire, Lara suspected her secret hopes about how they might spend the rest of the afternoon weren't going to come to fruition.

'What's wrong? Why—why are you dressed?'

'I had a phone call from New York while you were downstairs. Sweetheart, I'm afraid I've got to go back.'

'You mean back to New York?'

Grimacing, Gabriel nodded. 'They've got a real crisis on their hands on the trading floor. They want me to go back and help sort it out.'

'But what about the legalities you said you needed to deal with here? I mean the ones concerning the house?'

'They're just going to have to wait. Right now my priority is getting back to New York. The sooner I leave, the sooner I'll be back.'

Lara stared into his captivating blue eyes and couldn't help offering up a silent relieved prayer that he intended to return. But she still didn't want him to go. 'So you *are* intending on coming back, then?'

Lowering his head, he captured her lips in a slow, seductive kiss that melted her and made her long for more. The touch of his mouth against hers was oh so drugging and sensual that she thought there couldn't be a woman alive who wouldn't surrender to the magic of it without the heartfelt hope that there would be more— much more—to follow.

'Of course I'm coming back. Do you honestly think I'd turn my back on the treasure that I've found?'

'You mean your family's manor?'

Gabriel tipped up her chin with his knuckle. 'No. That's not the treasure I mean at all, angel.'

As Lara stared back at him her heart skipped a beat.

'You make it very hard for me to leave when you look at me with those big brown eyes of yours like that, but nonetheless—' He abruptly dropped his hand and said briskly, 'I'd better be off. I've got to get back to my hotel and pack a bag. Can you give me your phone number?'

Retrieving his mobile from his jeans pocket, he looked at her expectantly.

'What do you want it for?'

'Do you really need to ask me that? So that I can let you know when I'm coming back, of course.'

'Oh.'

The number duly given, Lara gasped when once again Gabriel drew her into his arms.

'I know you've only been back a short time but it's going to feel strange not having you around,' she admitted.

'I feel the same, sweetheart.' Smiling ruefully, he cupped his hand to her cheek. 'Now I really do have to go.'

He moved across the room to the door and opened it. Then he pivoted, and the expression on his carved face was indisputably serious as he glanced back at her.

'I don't want you to be lonely but I hope you won't think of being with anyone else while I'm gone?'

Feeling her cheeks flame red, Lara couldn't help but be offended. Her telling him she was on the pill had made him naturally assume she was sexually active. The thought made her shiver with distaste, especially when she had always believed that the most precious thing you could give to the man you loved was your virginity. Yes, the idea was outdated and old-fashioned but Lara made no apology for it.

'Do you honestly think I would want to be with someone else after what we've just shared, Gabriel? I know we haven't committed to making our relationship serious or anything, but I'm not the kind of woman who operates like that. I'm loyal. How would you feel if I asked *you* the same question?'

His expression thoughtful, he answered soberly. 'You need have no worries on that score. Apart from the fact that I'll be too busy working, the only woman I'll be thinking about while I'm in New York is *you*, Lara.'

She released a soft breath of relief and followed it with a smile. 'That's all right, then. Have a safe journey and let me know that you've arrived safely, even if it's just a text.'

The corners of Gabriel's eyes crinkled with pleasure. 'Of course. It'll be nice to know that someone I care about is thinking of me while I'm away. That's another first.'

Feeling elated by his assertion that she was someone he cared about, Lara felt the rest of his poignant
comment squeeze her heart. How had he felt when he
was little and knew there was no one there to look out
for him and give him a cuddle when he got home from
school? A hired nanny could never have replaced a loving parent.

Right then he looked so endearing that Lara wondered how she didn't run to him and beg him not to go.
But she knew that she shouldn't reveal that she cared as
much as she did in case it made him want to back off a
little. That was the very *last* thing she wanted to happen.

'Well, here might be another first for you, Gabriel.
I'm really going to miss you when you're gone.'

He gifted her with another devastating smile that she
wouldn't easily forget.

'I'm going to miss you, too, baby.' Raising a rueful
dark eyebrow he opened the door and went out.

The days following Gabriel's departure dragged by in-
terminably. Lara's initial excited optimism and belief
that he would return, and that when he did he might
consider making their rekindled association more serious, started to evaporate distressingly.

Since he'd texted her that he'd arrived safely in New
York her mobile had been worryingly silent. To add to
her worry and concern, memories of that long-ago party
from her youth, when Gabriel had rejected her in pref-
erence for the tall slim blonde who had been his tutor,
returned to haunt her painfully and made her fear that
he wouldn't keep his promise if someone more attractive came on the scene when he was back in New York.

When her parents returned from France Lara stayed

on for a further couple of days to satisfy herself that they were coping and to give them whatever support she could. But she also stayed on because her family home now seemed indelibly imbued with Gabriel's presence. She almost feared to leave it in case it signified shutting the door on the magical and heartfelt time they had spent together there—a repeat of which might never happen.

CHAPTER EIGHT

IT HAD NOT BEEN the best of days. How could it have been when they were still experiencing the aftermath of a serious crisis on the trading floor and heads were starting to roll as some key players were called into account?

Gabriel had nothing to fear on that score—his record was exemplary and so were his dealings—but he still felt a huge responsibility towards the shareholders he had guided and advised. Especially when some of the companies he'd recommended for investment had gone to the wall during the past few days due, amongst other things, to bad management. God knew he'd warned the CEOs of said companies enough times that good management was key and they shouldn't be in a hurry to let go those with a proven track record in order to replace them with the current 'flavour of the month'.

But most of all it was a bad day because he couldn't be with Lara. He'd been back in New York for over a week now and already the separation felt interminable. As he had expected, work had consumed him.

Back in his high-rise apartment later that evening, he threw himself down on his opulent silk-sheeted bed fully clothed and mused on whether he should ring her just to hear her voice and assure himself that he hadn't dreamt the blisteringly hot connection that they'd shared.

The situation had undoubtedly rocked his world. When he'd read about Sean's death, Gabriel never would have believed that going back to see his friend's parents to offer his condolences would result in him meeting Lara again and finding himself insanely attracted to her. She had been a pretty teenager, but nothing could have prepared him for the stunning woman she'd become.

He'd since asked himself if he should actually be feeling guilty because he'd taken a long-ago friendship to a whole other level just because the opportunity had presented itself. But he hadn't been able to resist. After reading the gut-wrenching letter his uncle had left him which had revealed the tragic truth about his mother, Gabriel had found himself craving the kind of comfort that only a woman could supply. A lovely woman like Lara, whose caring and selfless nature was like a price-less gem that was rare to find.

Checking his watch, he noted that it must be about four in the morning over in the UK. Would he risk waking her from sleep simply just to hear her voice? Of course he would. Hadn't she told him when he was leaving that she would miss him? Well, now was a good opportunity to find out how much.

Sitting up, he undid his tie, then shrugged off the suit jacket he wore and carelessly threw it onto a nearby chair. Then he kicked off his shoes, plumped up the satin pillows behind him and rang her mobile.

Even the realisation that she would be asleep couldn't stop him from feeling impatient when she didn't pick up straight away. Holding the phone close against his ear, with his other hand he dragged his fingers wearily through his hair, thinking that if he had even half a mind to be sensible he should probably get some sleep himself. He'd been working flat out in a charged and nervous atmosphere since the early hours of the morning and felt like death.

But he instantly jettisoned the thought when he heard Lara's sleepily husky voice at the other end of the line.

'Hello? Who is this? Have you any idea what time it is?'

Gabriel couldn't resist chuckling. 'Who else would be ringing you at this ungodly hour if it wasn't me, baby?'

'Gabriel?'

He told himself he heard pleasure in her voice, as well as surprise, but he couldn't know that for sure. What if Lara hadn't missed him even half as much as he had missed her? What if, despite her asking him if he really thought she would want to be with someone else after being with him, she had sought out the company of an ex-boyfriend to help alleviate her loneliness?

Biting back a savage curse at the mere thought, he schooled himself to breathe more slowly. A potential coronary wasn't something he wanted to add to his already considerable cache of woes.

'Yes, it's me.' Despite his anxieties, Gabriel thought of her shining dark eyes and pretty face and his lips shaped a smile. 'I should say I'm sorry for ringing you so early in the morning, but if I were to tell you that then it would be a lie. Were you asleep?'

'Not really. I was only dozing. I don't fall asleep very easily these days. I just can't seem to settle.'

'Are you still at your parents' house?'

'No, I'm not. I've returned to my flat. Mum and Dad

came back from holiday a couple of days after you left. By the way, they asked me to tell you that they'd like to see you sometime. They've got a couple of photos of you and Sean they'd like you to have as a keepsake.'

Gabriel's insides churned at the prospect of meeting Lara's parents again when he had so recently seduced their daughter. Would he be able to handle the guilt that was bound to surface when he was in their presence? Their good regard had once upon a time been very important to him. It still was.

'It would be good to see them again,' he said warily. 'And I wouldn't mind having the photos.'

'Good. I'll tell them. Anyway, it's good to hear your voice. The last time I had word from you was when you texted me to say that you'd arrived in New York. How are you?'

'Never mind how *I* am. What do you mean, you can't seem to settle? Is there something on your mind? Tell me, Lara, I'd like to know.'

Registering her quietly indrawn breath, not for the first time Gabriel wished he hadn't left her so abruptly when he'd got the call from his office in New York. But when he'd learned his presence was urgently required because of a crisis that could potentially escalate if he didn't return and help resolve it, it had been unthinkable that he would refuse—especially when his professional reputation had been built on finding solutions that would fox many of his peers.

'I've—I've just been missing Sean, that's all. It's at times like these—times when I'm a bit low and down in the dumps—that I'd ring and talk to him. No matter what the situation he'd always help put things into perspective and make me laugh.'

'It's perfectly understandable that you're missing him, sweetheart. His death isn't something you're going to get over or come to terms with overnight. All you can do is to give it time. Isn't that what they say?'

'Yes, and isn't it ironic how plausible and sensible that sounds when it isn't someone that's personally close to you who dies?'

Dry-mouthed, Gabriel honestly didn't know how to answer her. He'd lost the one person who was universally meant to be the closest to a child, yet he hadn't known his mother at all. Not even for a little while. How were you supposed to grieve for a relative stranger? Because that was what she had been. Yet since he had found out that she'd taken her own life a sense of bitter sorrow at the futility of it all had slowly and undeniably crept into his heart and taken up residence there. Not usually given to fantasising, he had found himself wishing for the power to turn back time so that he might remake the past and ensure a different and better future for both of them. Perhaps he was experiencing grief after all?

He heaved a sigh.

'Gabriel? I wasn't being dismissive of your advice. I know you're dealing with your own grief.'

'Is that what you call it?' Even though he'd briefly flirted with the fantasy of remaking the past, he couldn't prevent the scathing inflection in his tone. 'What the hell would I know about it? Aren't you supposed to have a relationship with someone before you can grieve for them?'

'Just because you didn't have a relationship with your mother doesn't mean that you don't wish that you had. Look, let's talk about something else, shall we? Late at night, or even in the early hours of the morning, isn't the best time to be dwelling on things that make us sad.'

For a moment, Lara's gentle voice somehow subdued the influx of pain that had threatened to submerge Gabriel.

'And I hate to think of you being sad when you're so far away and I can't be with you to help make you feel better.'

'I'm not sad, for goodness' sake. I'm *angry*. Furious that the people who were meant to take care of me were such liars that they would deceive their own flesh and blood and not even consider the horrendous legacy that would leave me with. You can't possibly know how that feels.'

Shaking his head, Gabriel fought hard to recover his equilibrium beneath another crushing wave of emotion. What the hell did he think he was doing? He'd been longing to make contact with Lara for days—the mere thought of talking to her had been the light at the end of the tunnel when he'd been so consumed by work that there wasn't even a spare moment to ring her—and here he was, wasting precious time talking about his hopeless family.

He swallowed hard.

'Forget I said that, will you? I think it's just fatigue talking. Up until now it's been a hell of a day. But I already feel better knowing that you're thinking about me.'

'I'm glad. I know it doesn't solve anything, but it helps to know that you have a friend you can reach out to, doesn't it? I know it does for me.'

Trying hard to ignore the fact that she'd referred to him yet again as a friend and not as her lover—

had his lovemaking been *that* forgettable?——Gabriel sighed again.

'Look, don't you have some holiday left? Why don't you come over to New York for a few days?' Even as the idea made his heart race and his blood pump hard he knew it was a brainwave he couldn't ignore. Why hadn't he thought about it earlier? It was, after all, the perfect solution. If he had to spend many more nights without seeing Lara and having her in his bed he'd honestly go crazy.

'I do have some holiday left, but don't you have to work, Gabriel? Isn't there some big financial crisis or other you have to deal with?'

'There is indeed.'

The charmingly innocent question made him smile. The world Lara inhabited was a million miles away from the feverish atmosphere on Wall Street, where dealings often had serious global financial implications that could make or break economies overnight. He was fiercely glad that she wasn't part of that world.

He was also relieved that she wasn't remotely like some of the clever but brittle women he regularly came into contact with in that arena——women who had seemingly forgotten what it meant to be soft and feminine, who preferred to concentrate their energies on rising to the top of the career ladder, making their fortune, and didn't care what they had to do in order to achieve it. Some men might find such barefaced single-mindedness admirable, but oddly enough Gabriel *didn't*.

'It won't be sorted overnight,' he explained. 'But we're making some good inroads. Anyway, let's not talk about that. I really need to see you, Lara. You have no idea *how* much.'

The other end of the line went ominously quiet and Gabriel tensed. Her rejection wasn't something he wanted to contemplate even briefly.

'Say the word and I'll arrange the flight,' he said quickly. 'I'm not saying I'll be able to spend as much time with you as I'd like when you get here—especially not during the day when I'm working—but you'll have my driver at your disposal to take you wherever you want to go, and you won't want for anything. If you want to buy clothes, perfume—*anything*, in fact—I'll foot the bill. It will be my pleasure. And as often as I can manage it we'll have the evenings together. The nights, too.'

Again, Gabriel's blood heated at the thought. He blessed the photographic recall that, even throughout his pressured working days, helped him easily access the memory of Lara's seductive scent and the satin texture of her flawless skin.

'Are you sure, Gabriel? I mean, my coming to see you won't interfere with your routine?'

'My God, do you know how painfully dull that makes me sound? I don't deny that my work is important, but even *I* refuse to make it the be-all and end-all. Especially not now, when I know that I'll be seeing you.'

'All right, then. You can go ahead and arrange a flight for me. When you have the details you can ring or send me a text to let me know. My mum said just yesterday that I ought to have a holiday before I go back to work.'

'She was right—and if my memory serves me correctly your mum usually *is*, sweetheart.'

Rubbing his hand round his stubbled jaw, Gabriel was elated that his powers of persuasion hadn't failed him. If all went to plan Lara would be joining him in just a couple of days' time and his photographic memory would no longer be necessary to remind him of her charms—not when the delicious reality of her presence would be so much more satisfying.

Even though she'd accepted it—because what else could she have done?—Lara had been heartbroken when Gabriel had abruptly left her to return to New York. At that point she really hadn't known whether she would ever see him again. All she'd seemed to see in that carved, handsome face of his when he had announced he had to return to work to help alleviate a crisis was a man who put his career way above personal relationships and matters of the heart. *No question.* What if he had even felt *relieved* when he'd had the call telling him he was needed urgently?

Yet even knowing that Gabriel was a supremely driven individual, whose priorities were vastly different from her own, Lara didn't give up hope that one day soon he would come to see that there were far more important things in life than money and the admiration of his peers.

The devastation of his mother taking her own life and his uncle betraying him might have caused him to believe that love and family could never be for him—not when his trust had been so cruelly tested—but Lara refused to relinquish the hope that if only she could reach him—*really* reach him—then she might help him see that it didn't mean that love and family should be denied him.

It had lifted her beyond belief when he'd rung her in the middle of the night and invited her over to New York and she hadn't hesitated to accept the invitation.

Could it be that he'd been reflecting on the possibility of enjoying a serious relationship with her? She prayed that was the case. She certainly wasn't going to pass up the chance of finding out.

When he'd asked her what had been unsettling her she hadn't been completely truthful. Of course she was still grieving for Sean, but she'd also been missing Gabriel—missing him so much, in fact, that she could scarcely think about anything else.

Sometimes the memory of their lovemaking seemed like the most delicious dream she had conjured up to help compensate for the loneliness she had endured all these years. And other times, because it meant so much to her, it fuelled her fears about what she would do if she never got the chance to be intimate with him again. Lara had already lost the brother she'd adored. To lose Gabriel would be an equally grievous blow.

Now, travelling in the back of the beautiful limousine Gabriel had sent to the airport to collect her and heading over to Fifth Avenue, where his apartment was situated, Lara stared up at the high-rise buildings piercing the faultless blue sky and couldn't help shivering. It was as though she'd been dropped into an alien habitat in some distant universe, such was the contrast to the much more unhurried environment she was used to.

'This is it, Miss Bradley. If you tell the concierge at the door that you've come to see Mr Devenish, then he'll take you up to his apartment.'

'Thank you.'

'It's my pleasure, Miss Bradley. If you just wait there for a moment I'll get your luggage.'

When he came round to open the car door for her, Lara accepted the immaculately presented chauffeur's hand and stepped out onto the sidewalk outside the building. Already the concierge was approaching, and as she thanked the driver again she was rewarded with a genuinely warm smile.

'I'm Barry, by the way, and Mr Devenish will give you the number to contact me on when you want to go anywhere. He's already given me instructions to take you wherever you want to go during your stay,' he told her. 'So I'll look forward to seeing you again sometime soon, Miss Bradley. Have a good day, now.'

'You, too.'

It hit Lara then just how diametrically opposite Gabriel's lifestyle was to her own. She had just about got over travelling business class on the plane out here, but was he *really* expecting her to tour the city in a limousine every time she went out?

As the ultra-polite concierge took charge of her conservatively small suitcase and led her to the elevator she was suddenly seized by an acute attack of nerves. What would it be like, seeing Gabriel again? Would he still want her as much as he'd wanted her back home? Compared to the beautiful and fashionable women he must see every day at work, would he start to see her as painfully ordinary and homely? She glanced down at the royal blue, fluted-sleeved tunic dress she was wearing that she'd thought so pretty in the store and winced.

'This is Mr Devenish's floor, Miss Bradley.'

The ascent up to the top floor had been so swift that she'd hardly realised they'd been moving. She'd been too lost in anguished reverie about Gabriel.

The concierge pressed the doorbell and with a brief, officious smile asked, 'Would you like me to wait with you until Mr Devenish comes to the door?'

'No, thank you. I'm sure he'll be here in a minute.'

With a brief nod of his head, he left her. They had arranged that Gabriel would take a couple of hours off from work to welcome her and acquaint her with her new surroundings, but time seemed to deaden and slow as Lara waited outside the door for him, and she couldn't help worrying that because he was so busy at work he'd forgotten about her.

But suddenly he was standing there, immaculately dressed as ever, and even more devastating than she remembered. His eyes locked on to hers immediately. They drank her in, ate her up and all but consumed her, body and soul.

Lara opened her mouth to speak but no words came out.

Looking slightly dazed, he said, 'My phone rang just before you knocked and I stupidly took the call. My God, I've been waiting so long for you. Too long.'

And then further dialogue was abandoned as he hungrily drew her into his arms, drove his hands through her hair and pressed her against him as if she was as vital to him as taking his next breath.

If that first kiss he had stolen from her back in England had been akin to being scorched by flame, this one was an inferno that burnt her down to her very core. In response, her lips couldn't help but cling ravenously to his, and her heart leapt with sheer delight at the seductive velvety texture of his lips and the sensation of his hard body enfolding her. Then she greedily welcomed his hot searching tongue, taking breathless little gasps of air as she struggled to assimilate the tide of longing and desire that rendered her almost too weak to stand.

Gabriel groaned as if he couldn't bear being bereft of

her kisses for even a moment. Defenceless and desperate for his deepening touch, Lara was scarcely aware that he had dragged in her case and pushed the door shut behind her, then manoeuvred her up against it. But when his hand hotly covered her breast through the thin cotton of her dress, and when he replaced it with his lips to nip at the already tender flesh of her aroused nipple, she whimpered as an arrow of molten heat shot directly into her womb.

Even as she moaned her pleasure Gabriel moved his hands urgently down her back and onto her behind. In answer, Lara eagerly drove her fingers through his hair to hold him more tightly against her. A second later, he freed himself to examine her. As she met the intense azure gaze that had instigated her love and devotion all those years ago when she was not much more than a girl, she silently reaffirmed the vow she'd made that she would love him for ever.

'This wasn't the way I wanted to welcome you, baby,' he said wryly. 'But what can I do when I confess I'm an addict for you?' He bent and kissed her, capturing her plump lower lip with his teeth then slowly releasing it as he drew away. 'And I might just die if I don't get my fix.'

In one fluidly effortless movement he suddenly lifted her up high against his chest. Still avidly kissing her, he strode across the honey-coloured wooden floor and headed towards a closed door at the end of it. When they reached the door he kicked it open and carried her across to the palatial black-silk-covered bed that dominated the room. He toed off his shoes and Lara followed suit. And when he drew back the covers and lowered her down onto the sensual silk sheets niceties were forgotten as they tore at each other's clothes and breathlessly dispensed with them.

Their hungry eyes met in mutual wonder just once before Gabriel covered Lara's trembling body with his. And as soon as their skin made contact conversation was rendered redundant. There was simply no need for preamble to the seduction they both longed for.

Gabriel nudged Lara's slim thighs apart with his knee and she immediately sensed her hips soften and then naturally relax. But as she held on tight to the bunched iron biceps in his arms she found herself momentarily tensing as he urgently pushed his hard silken shaft deep inside her. He stilled for a moment. She was more than ready for him, but strangely she felt the eagerly anticipated invasion even more acutely this second time round.

She saw a briefly questioning look in Gabriel's eyes. But the suggestion of uncertainty—if that was what it was—was quickly banished as he started to move deeply inside her, bending his dark head to devour her lips, then her breasts, his searching hands exploring her even as he seduced her.

Yearning to tell him that she loved him, Lara didn't know how she suppressed the impulse. *I'll tell him afterwards*, she vowed, gasping aloud in shock and then pleasure as he bit down on the delicate skin at the juncture of her neck and shoulder with the edges of his teeth.

She couldn't help revelling in the thought that he would be leaving his mark on her in more ways than one. But then she was gasping for a second time when the hot, pulsating need inside her peaked and flooded her with dizzying warmth and she found herself riding an exhilarating wave of pleasure that stole every thought from her head to replace it with unmitigated joy.

The profoundly exquisite experience was heightened when Gabriel suddenly tensed and cried out, spilling his liquid heat deep inside her. His sculpted, handsome face looked to be deeply stunned by the intense release. Lara couldn't help but feel gratified that she had been the one to give him such a gift.

Just before Lara's hot satin heat had enfolded him and he'd driven himself deep inside her Gabriel had shivered hard at the terrifying realisation of how much this woman had come to mean to him. He had been like a cat on a hot tin roof waiting for her to arrive. Not even the demands of the trading floor had been able to distract him from the thought of her for long, and never in his history had he let his guard down so completely around a woman so that she might easily breach it.

He didn't doubt there would be a serious price to pay. But after the stunning satisfaction of their urgent love-making he almost didn't care what that price would be.

'That was amazing,' he breathed, lying down beside her and gathering her against him.

Glancing up, Lara smiled warmly into his eyes. 'I'm glad I wasn't the only one who thought so.' Dropping down again, she pressed her face close to his. 'Gabriel...?'

She whispered his name close against his ear, her soft lips brushing the tender lobe and sending a flurry of goosebumps scudding across his flesh.

'What is it, baby?' He lifted his head to examine her. When he saw that her sultry dark eyes glimmered with tears he immediately tensed. 'What's wrong?'

'Nothing.' Her lips parted in the most engaging and

bewitching smile, and again he was caught off-guard by her incandescent beauty—so much so that his heart *hurt* just looking at her.

'I just want you to know that I'm so glad I waited,' she said gently.

'Waited? For what, sweetheart?'

'To make love with the only man I've ever loved and to give him my virginity.'

If she had struck him hard Gabriel couldn't have been more shocked. He ached for her, body and soul, but somehow right then he found himself immobilised by the confession.

Lara had been a *virgin* when they'd first made love? It didn't make sense. She'd been so willing and ready. Even as doubt settled in the pit of his stomach and seriously unnerved him he remembered that when he'd first taken her she had indeed been exquisitely tight— not at all like an experienced woman…a woman used to having lovers.

In the throes of his passion he had stupidly dismissed the fact. However, he'd thought about it again just now, when they'd made love again.

But what had him reeling even more was Lara's declaration that she loved him—that he was the *only* man she had ever loved. Gabriel honestly didn't know how he felt about that. Love was not something he had ever figured as coming into the equation.

Clearly there was a red-hot attraction between them, but not *love*…surely? Besides, what could a relationship with him bring her other than more grief and pain? She deserved a man who was utterly devoted to her happiness, a man who was whole in every respect of the word, not some embittered automaton that just went through the motions of life but didn't truly enjoy any-thing very much.

As the waves of shock and surprise and, yes, *fear* continued to eddy through him, Gabriel expelled a long breath in a bid to try and regain his equilibrium. Then he lifted himself away from the lovely woman at his side to lie back against the bank of satin pillows behind them. Glimpsing the confusion in her eyes as he moved away, he felt his heart drum hard as he tried to think what to say to reassure her.

Sitting up, Lara lightly shook her head and folded her arms over her breasts. As she turned to face him he saw the silken skein of long, dark hair that nestled against her collarbone and he longed to give in to the impulse to wind it round his fingers as he had done once before, when things between them had been far less compli-cated than they suddenly seemed to be.

'Did I—did I say something wrong, Gabriel? Some-thing you didn't like?' she enquired hesitantly.

'You told me that you were on the pill,' he replied, endeavouring to keep his voice steady. No easy feat when his whole world had just been tilted on its head once more.

'It's true. I am. But why should that disturb you? Was it because you thought I must have had other lov-ers before you?'

'Frankly, yes. I *did* think that.'

'But—but couldn't you tell when you— When we…' Her cheeks reddening, Lara stared at him as if his an-swer was hard to comprehend.

Emitting a heavy sigh, Gabriel sat up. 'I seem to recall I was driven by lust and desire at the time and wasn't exactly thinking straight. But tell me this, Lara.

If it's true that you were a virgin then why in God's name are you on the pill?'

She drew up her legs beneath the covers and folded her arms round them. 'I take the pill to help regulate my periods. A lot of women do.'

'And you've never slept with another man before me?'

'No.' Her dark eyes flashed. 'I haven't. I don't tell lies, Gabriel.'

'No. Of course you don't. How *could* you, coming from the family that you do?'

It was a back-handed compliment and he wasn't proud of it. Lara had flinched when he'd delivered it. But things between them seemed suddenly to have gained a momentum he hadn't envisaged, and his instinct was to perhaps put the brakes on a little in order to have some time to reflect.

She'd given her virginity to him and told him that she loved him. Whilst both acts were significant in their own way, and had definitely pleased him, did it mean that she was hoping they could make their relationship more permanent? Right at that moment Gabriel didn't see how such a thing could possibly be achieved. How could it when both their lives and their lifestyles were poles apart? As much as he wanted to be with Lara, he couldn't see her taking to life in New York. As beautiful and intelligent as she was, she was more hometown girl than ambitious career woman, and he didn't deny he liked it that she was that way.

Moving across to the edge of the bed as he wrestled with what to do, he reached down for the black silk boxers that, in his haste to make love to Lara, he'd thrown onto the floor. Hastily pulling them on, he turned back to survey her and saw her shiver.

Despising himself for not being able to summon up the words that might help ease her distress, he remarked, 'You should probably get dressed.' Jerking his head towards another door, he continued, 'You can get a shower, then come and join me in the living room. You should find everything you need. I'll use the bathroom down the hall. We don't have much time before I have to get back to work and I need to tell you a few things.'

CHAPTER NINE

WHAT THINGS DID HE need to tell her? Lara wondered. She was sure that whatever it was it couldn't possibly bring more distress than she felt already.

Her heart bled because Gabriel hadn't exhibited the slightest pleasure or even *concern* that she'd been a virgin when they'd first made love. In fact he had sounded quite angry about it. Neither had he looked remotely pleased when she'd confessed that she loved him.

Was he really as cold-hearted and uncaring as all that? What if she had made the most horrendous mistake in confessing her feelings to him? She surely hadn't forgotten that he'd rejected her advances once before, albeit a long time ago. But it chilled Lara's blood as she contemplated that perhaps Gabriel really *couldn't* commit to her, or allow himself to love her.

She knew there was a genuinely good man behind those ice-blue eyes, even if the evidence was far too rare, but he was like a wounded bear that snapped at anyone who exhibited concern or ventured too near and she knew the reason why. His fractured—and some might say, dysfunctional—past haunted him. That was why he found kindness and concern so difficult to deal with. Maybe that was also the reason he couldn't immediately accept that she loved him or that she'd given her virginity to *him* rather than another man?

With that unhappy conclusion dominating her thoughts she hastily showered and dressed in the luxurious Art Deco bathroom, reapplied the lipstick that she kept in the pocket of her dress and went in search of the living room to find him.

Promising herself that she would play it cool and not let him see that he had hurt her, nonetheless she felt her heart skip an anxious beat when she saw him again. Gabriel was relaxing on one of the sleek black couches in the light and airy living room with its arresting clear-glassed views of the New York skyline. He had changed into another stylish Italian suit.

The far from welcoming expression on his hard-jawed visage made her insides plunge.

Standing in the doorway, she anxiously smoothed her hand down over the blue tunic dress she'd admired and bought especially for her trip to see him and made a silent vow never to wear it again. In her mind it was jinxed. Moistening her lips, she gave him a greeting that was understandably cautious. From now on she wasn't going to presume anything.

'You said you had some things that you needed to tell me?'

'Why don't you come over here and sit down?' he invited.

Lara thought she spied the merest glimmer of a smile on his lips, but because she wasn't sure she didn't allow herself to believe it. As yet she had no idea what he was going to tell her and couldn't help but fear the worst.

'Did you find everything you needed?' he asked.

'In the bathroom, you mean?'

Gabriel nodded.

'Yes, I did.'

She walked towards him, twisting her hands nervously together in front of her, then stopped, feeling her body helplessly warming when she remembered what they'd been doing just a short while ago. Who could have believed that such heated passion could turn cold so quickly? Gabriel had poured ice water on her feelings when he'd so hastily left her alone in his bed. What if he'd come to the conclusion that she should leave? That he'd made a mistake in inviting her to New York?

Sick with apprehension, she asked, 'Is my suitcase still out in the hall?'

'I've put it in the guest bedroom for now. Later on, when I return from work, I'll take it into my room.'

Even as relief washed through her Lara couldn't help feeling it wasn't right he should have everything his way. 'There's no need.' Lifting her chin, she defied him to disagree with her.

Making her knees knock together, Gabriel rose to his impressive height and covered the space between them. Just bare inches away from her, the scent of his arresting, sexy cologne sent Lara's pulse nervously skittering. Her tender nipples still stung from his attentions in bed, and as she came face to face with him again they burned and tingled fiercely.

'I know I might not be able to give you what you want, Lara,' he said, gravel-voiced. 'But I haven't brought you to New York for us to sleep in separate rooms. I should have been more thoughtful, more caring when we were together just now, but what you told me robbed me of all ability to think straight. I've been reflecting on things and I want to make amends.'

'And how do you plan on doing that? By buying me things? By showing me a good time as is probably your style with the women in your life before you kiss them goodbye and move on to the next one?' Despite her vow not to let him see that he'd upset her, Lara couldn't suppress the scalding angry tears that burned at the backs of her lids. She impatiently wiped them away. 'To be honest, I'd rather go home.'

'No. I don't want that.' A perturbed muscle flinched in the side of his hollowed cheek. 'I want you to stay. Whatever you think of me.'

'Why should it always be about what *you* want, Gabriel? Don't you think that I have needs, too?'

About to turn away, Lara choked back a gasp when she suddenly found herself slammed against his chest and her lips taken prisoner by a hard, hot, almost punishing kiss. Her resolve to leave melted like ice cream beneath the burning rays of a Sahara sun.

As the kiss eased in intensity to become surprisingly tender, Gabriel lifted his head to study her.

'I want you to have what you want, Lara, I really do. But while you're with me I'm afraid I'm driven to be greedy. Perhaps I can't quite believe that you'd surrender your virginity to a man who's notoriously selfish, who puts himself above everyone else when it comes to getting the thing he wants and consequently doesn't consider feelings. But I'm too enamoured of you not to see it as the most unbelievable blessing that you're here, and I can't help but want to make the most of it.'

Reaching out, he cupped the side of her face and looked to be aiming for a smile, but he didn't quite manage it.

'Don't go. Please don't go.'

Lara caught her breath. It wasn't just the simmering desire she saw reflected in his eyes that took her aback, but the almost childlike need that told her he would be nothing less than devastated should she insist on leaving. It was then that she was poignantly reminded that he'd grown up bereft of his mother's love and care, and likely believed he didn't deserve similar consideration from any woman who came into his life.

Moistening lips that still throbbed from his ravenous kisses she carefully examined his carved features. 'I'm not going to leave, Gabriel.' She breathed out a gentle sigh. 'I wouldn't walk out on you when I've given you my word that I'll stay—at least until my holiday comes to an end.'

Seeing the relief that spread across his handsome features, Lara was pleased that he seemed to be reassured.

Recovering her good humour, she teased, 'Besides, do you really think I've come all the way out to New York not to see some of the sights while I'm here?'

'I'll make sure you get to see everything you want to, I swear. Just say the word and I'll arrange it.' His hands dropped to her shoulders. 'And, by the way, one of the things I needed to tell you was that we're going out tonight to a function. It's a corporate dinner at a restaurant not far from the Stock Exchange. I can't duck out of it, I'm afraid. I have to go and I want to take you as my escort.'

It was on the tip of Lara's tongue to say no. She would be so far out of her comfort zone in such elite company and in surroundings that were about as alien to her as the grand Regency house where Gabriel had grown up that it would be no joke. But then she saw the hint of steel in his eyes that told her it would be a waste of time even attempting to refuse, because one way or another he would persuade her differently.

He had never felt more possessive of a woman than when he walked into that stylish New York bar and restaurant with Lara. From the moment they'd arrived heads had turned—not just to greet him, because Gabriel knew everybody who was *anybody,* but to cast curious, admiring glances at his companion. And how could he blame them when Lara added a whole other level to the term 'drop-dead gorgeous'?

The little black dress that she'd insisted was the only suitable garment she'd brought with her to wear to a 'posh' dinner made Gabriel feel like the mythical Ares worshipping at the feet of Aphrodite. It didn't cling to her sublime curves but it couldn't help but pay homage to them whenever she moved. And the way that she wore her hair, in a very feminine loose topknot, with curling tendrils brushing the sides of her cheeks, and with her shoulders bare courtesy of the halterneck style of the dress, she looked utterly exquisite.

Gabriel's hand gripped Lara's a little tighter as they moved through the crowd milling around the bar. There were more greetings and back-slapping as people recognised him, and frankly for once he could have done without it.

When he sensed that his companion was drawing back, and guessed she was feeling overwhelmed, he deliberately pulled her near and his smile was reassuring. She wasn't used to this. The stylishly attired Wall Street patrons and the competitive atmosphere they created whenever they were together was a million light years away from the world Lara inhabited.

Although the air was drenched with the smell of alluring perfume and expensive cologne, the predominant scent was that of money. It was strange how the realisation didn't give Gabriel his usual sense of pleasure or the satisfaction that he'd grown to depend on.

Looking for an out, he caught the eye of the maître d' and asked him to show them into the private dining room where they were scheduled to eat.

The gathering had been set up in one of the most intimately sophisticated rooms of the restaurant which was frequently the chosen venue for the private meetings he had with his executive clientele. But tonight Gabriel's fellow guests would be some of the key players who had worked with him to help avert yet another serious financial crisis. After the tough few weeks they had endured, and the intense few days when it had been touch and go and Gabriel had been called in to join them, they would be in the mood to celebrate. Although by no means could anyone rest on their laurels yet.

The effusive greetings of his fellow diners over, Gabriel was relieved to be able to sit down next to Lara and look at the menu. It didn't escape his notice that her slender fingers shook slightly as she perused what was on offer, and neither did he miss her soft-voiced sigh. His broad-suited shoulder brushed against hers as he leant towards her and he caught the faint but arousing scent of her honeyed perfume. His stomach clenched hard with desire.

Lowering his voice he asked, 'How are you bearing up? I promise this won't go on for too long.'

His reward was a too brief glimpse of a smile.

'I'm all right. I think.'

Gabriel's own smile was more generous. 'I can't

say that *I* am. I'd much rather we were alone together than here at this dinner,' he confessed. 'And, trust me, I wouldn't be here at all if I had the choice.'

It was impossible to suppress the need and desire that crept into his tone. In truth, it was hard even to think straight when Lara was around.

'I'm bowled over by the fact that you're actually here,' he went on, 'and that you came all this way just to see me. By the way, this is a very good menu. "Bankers' fare", they call it. If you want a recommendation, can I suggest the filet mignon?'

Unable to resist, he let his avid gaze into her sultry brown eyes deliberately linger, quite aware that there was running speculation round the table about their relationship. After all, Lara was an unknown entity to them. A very beautiful and desirable unknown entity.

Before she could comment on his suggestion of cuisine, one of the top city bankers across the table—a man called Lars Jensen—leaned towards them and asked confidently, 'So, Lara—can I call you that?— I'm intrigued, as all my colleagues are. How did you meet Gabriel? He has a reputation of being a bit of a wizard here on Wall Street—a regular Croesus. Whatever he touches turns to gold. Did you perhaps have some business dealings with him in London? If you did, lucky you.'

The suited young man seated opposite her, with his fashionable, close-cut fair hair and too-inquisitive green eyes, had honed in on Lara like a missile poised to attack. Having no idea how much or how little Gabriel wanted her to reveal, she made her quietly voiced response carefully measured.

'I know nothing about the financial world and, no,

we didn't meet in London. Gabriel went to university with my brother. That's how we met.'

'I'm even more intrigued. You mean that you've known him all these years and he hasn't mentioned you? At least not in my hearing.'

'Why should he mention me? We're just friends.'

Catching an expression that was almost a glower on Gabriel's handsome face, Lara sensed herself flush. Had she said the wrong thing? What else could she have said? That she was an ex-girlfriend of his? That patently wasn't true.

'So you're "just friends", are you?' Lars's tone was mockingly doubtful as his laserlike glance pinioned them both. 'Is that a new euphemism for lovers in the UK?'

'No, it isn't,' Gabriel interjected firmly, his hard jaw clenching. Out of sight, his hand folded possessively over Lara's. 'And if I tell you that Lara was only sixteen when we first met, I doubt you'd think we would have been lovers, would you?'

This time the other man's searching gaze lingered over-long on Lara, making a mental inventory of her assets almost as if she was some kind of lucrative deal he was convinced would add to his fortune.

Lowering his voice, he briefly turned his attention back to Gabriel, commenting, 'Don't tell me you weren't tempted?'

Beside her, Lara intimately sensed the silent fury and tension in her companion's body as if it were her own.

'I think we should drop the subject. don't you? Lara is my guest here and your inappropriate insinuations are making her uncomfortable. That's not acceptable.'

His ice-blue gaze swept the table. 'And that goes for all of you.'

There was a sudden marked silence and Lara wanted the floor to open up and swallow her. If anything Gabriel's warning had only increased the curiosity in the other guests' eyes. Squeezing his hand to get his attention, she felt her heart thump hard when she immediately got it. His eyes shot little sparks of tangible electricity at her.

'What is it?' he demanded.

'You don't have to defend me. I'm sure your friend didn't mean anything by what he said.'

'You know that for sure, do you?' Tugging her towards him, so that what he said would be for her ears and her ears only, he whispered, 'Number one, he's not a friend—he's a colleague, and a very ambitious and ruthless colleague. You should be aware that we're sitting at a table full of hungry sharks, my angel, and right now *you're* the bait.'

Lara shivered. As her eyes strayed across the table to the rest of the glittering company, clad in their perfect Italian suits and breathtaking haute couture, she was stunned to realise that everyone was examining her and trying to figure out exactly who she was, as if it wasn't a usual occurrence for Gabriel to bring an unknown woman to these functions with him.

Feeling her face flame self-consciously at being the centre of so much attention, she turned back to her companion. 'I need to go to the ladies' room,' she murmured.

Gabriel immediately signalled to a nearby waitress and asked her to direct her. But as he stood back and helped her to her feet Lara sensed his reluctance and frustration at having to release her even for a second.

* * *

Lara felt as if she deserved a prize for enduring one of the most discomfiting and tense evenings of her life. But at the end of it one thing was absolutely clear. What she'd witnessed of the superficial and pressured life of the New York financial 'elite' wasn't for her.

Even though it was a dream come true to be with Gabriel, she was already longing to return home to the simple yet satisfying day-to-day routine she was familiar with—a way of life where she didn't have to be overly concerned about what people thought of her or whether she was wearing the right outfit to go to dinner or to work. Even at the college library she could get away with wearing jeans and a T-shirt.

That said, Gabriel looked nothing less than *edible* in his flawless Italian tailoring. One of the female guests at their table had obviously deliberately followed her out to the loo, and had blatantly quizzed her about her relationship with him. When Lara had frostily declined to tell her, the other woman had immediately shared a 'no-holds barred' graphic illustration of what she'd personally like to do with him in bed.

Lara's jaw had dropped at the woman's sheer temerity. It was obvious that Gabriel's warning to his assembled peers not to make her feel unduly uncomfortable was only to be adhered to as they sat round the dinner table. Out of his sight it was open season for the sharks to feed. Lara had quickly discovered that going to the dinner as Gabriel's guest didn't automatically grant her immunity from the other women who desired him and wouldn't hesitate to tell her so.

It was a relief to return to the apartment, even though Gabriel had been broodingly quiet on the journey home.

Inevitably her anxiety had been building because of his lack of communication, and as soon as they were alone again Lara immediately turned to him for some answers as to the reason why.

'What's wrong?' she asked as he shrugged off his suit jacket and hung it on the steel coat stand inside the door. 'I get the feeling that you're unhappy. Didn't you enjoy the dinner? Your colleagues were certainly glad to see you.'

He curled his lip. 'It may come as a surprise to you, Lara, but on Wall Street it pays to stay on good terms with the boss. With the money, as they say here. If you think that people were glad to see me simply because they love my company then you're more naïve than I thought.'

Toeing off her shoes, as was her habit when she was at home, Lara heaved an annoyed sigh.

'Do you get off on cutting me down to size, Gabriel? Does it stroke your ego to do that? Obviously it must. And anyway why *shouldn't* people be glad of your company? You can be quite pleasant when you try, though I confess that's not very—'

The final word of her little speech was unceremoniously cut off as Gabriel hauled her against his chest and devoured her lips with a hard, open-mouthed kiss. As soon as his silken tongue drove into her mouth and his hands moved down her body to lift up her skirt and touch her intimately Lara felt immediately and frighteningly powerless to deny him anything. It appalled her that she couldn't even put up a fight. But then why would she want to, she reasoned, when she loved him so much that it hurt?

'Right now I can't take it slowly,' he breathed hotly

against her mouth. 'I confess you've become irresistible to me, and I can't take it slowly because I want you too much, but afterwards…'

Lara momentarily held her breath as she sensed his hand slide into her panties. When his searching fingers invaded her and pushed up she gasped, her head falling against his hard-muscled shoulder. Her senses were instantly drowned by the heat from his body and the seductive, sultry scent of his masculine cologne. If he hadn't been holding her she might easily have sunk down to the floor, because her limbs were rendered weak as a kitten's.

'Afterwards,' he continued, his free hand caressing the back of her neck, 'we'll take it nice and slow and really get to know each other, find out what gives us the most pleasure.'

Unable to reply because she was suddenly swept away on a sea of delectation so profoundly erotic that she couldn't speak, Lara pressed her cheek against Gabriel's pristine white shirt, registering the wild beating of his heart against her ear and wondering what she could do to make him feel similarly swept away.

She hardly seemed to know herself when she was with this man. All she could think about in his company was fulfilling her most carnal desires and hopefully fulfilling his, too. Had her self-enforced celibacy all these years turned her into some kind of insatiable siren?

When she lifted her head it was to find Gabriel staring down at her with an intensity that almost stopped her heart. 'What you do to me…' she murmured softly, tenderly touching her hand to his cheek.

His piercing blue eyes crinkling in acknowledgement, he lifted her up into his arms as though her weight didn't even signify. Then, still holding her gaze he affirmed huskily, 'We need to go to bed. *Now.*'

CHAPTER TEN

THE FOLLOWING WEEK passed like the most fantastical dream. Whilst her days were spent sightseeing and touring the city—courtesy of Barry, Gabriel's attentive chauffeur—Lara's nights were all given over to Gabriel. On occasion he wined and dined her at wonderful restaurants, took her to the cinema or to see a show on Broadway, but whatever the entertainment or pleasure they participated in, the high point of every evening was always when they returned to Gabriel's apartment and to each other's arms.

Knowing that her short holiday was quickly coming to an end, and that soon she would be going home to England to resume her post as college librarian, Lara started to feel painfully anxious about the future of her relationship with Gabriel. Did they even *have* a future together? They had a powerful connection, certainly, and there was no disputing the fact that she loved him, but as he had noticeably avoided discussing commitment and making their association more meaningful, Lara couldn't help but be apprehensive.

She had seen first-hand how devoted he was to what he did, and how seductive it must be to be so highly regarded in the financial arena he worked in. His colleagues all seemed to view Gabriel as practically irreplaceable. But did that mean he would never consider returning to the UK and once more making it his home?

During the time Lara had spent with him in New York he had never even mentioned the family home that he'd inherited. She was wary of trying to get him to discuss it in case it stirred up the fury and despair he'd expressed when he'd read his uncle's letter, yet she knew that Gabriel would never come to terms with what had happened and start to heal his past if he never even addressed the issue.

What did he intend to do about the Regency manor house that he'd grown up in? Did he plan to sell it and not even consider going back to reside there?

If that were the case, and he stayed in New York, Lara was pretty certain she wouldn't be joining him. The elite, sophisticated lifestyle and relentlessly driven aims of the bankers and financiers to make and acquire even more money and kudos epitomised everything she and her family disliked about the pursuit of material success in the world. As her brother, Sean, used to say, 'What good is being rich if you don't do something good with your wealth to help those less privileged on the planet?'

But Lara's dilemma was more than just the fact that that particular way of living didn't chime with her personal values. It had much more to do with her despair that Gabriel had never even once told her that he loved her. She had begun to suspect that he never would. Already she feared their heated, passionate union would be very quickly put aside to be replaced by even more work demands and perhaps occasionally the company of one of those 'pretty ladies' he'd mentioned that he called upon whenever he got lonely.

Was she really so hard to love? And would he honestly prefer that lonely and ultimately empty existence over enjoying Lara's love and devotion for the rest of his life? Not to mention the possibility of creating a family of their own....

Sipping at a glass of orange juice in the living room as she waited for him to reappear that evening—he'd got back late from work and was still getting ready so that they could go out to dinner—Lara stared out at the stunning New York skyline of silver and shadows and felt unbearably sad.

Her sojourn here was rapidly coming to an end, and as yet nothing had been resolved between them about their relationship. This was to be her last night in the city because tomorrow she was flying home, and so far, aside from giving her the details of her flight, Gabriel had hardly even mentioned it.

'Hey.'

The smoky cadence of his voice had her turning quickly, and just in time she managed to avoid spilling juice all over the pretty midnight blue silk dress Gabriel had bought her.

She had never sought for him to buy her gifts, and had frequently told him so whenever he suggested it, but when he'd told her he'd stepped out of his office one afternoon to visit a high-end store so that he might get her 'something pretty to wear to dinner', Lara had been helplessly touched by his thoughtfulness. Pleased, too. The garment was sleek and fitted, and when she'd taken it out of the stylish carrier bag and unwrapped it from its carefully folded tissue paper she'd been taken aback at just how perfect it was.

She shouldn't have been surprised that it fitted as though made for her, because her lover had an astute eye for the details that many men might miss—not to mention intimately knowing the lines and curves of her body. The thought that he'd committed them to memory made her blood throb and heat in anticipation of the next time they would make love.

Setting the tall glass of juice aside, she curved her lips in an affectionate smile of awe and admiration. Gabriel stood before her dressed in another flawless suit, combined with a navy silk shirt and sky blue tie. His chestnut hair was swept back off his face to reveal the carved, clean lines that she was sure Michelangelo himself would have hungered to paint or sculpt.

'Hey, yourself.'

'I see you're wearing the dress.... Stand up—let me see how it fits.'

Getting to her feet, Lara obligingly made a slow turn to show off the dress from every angle.

An array of tumultuous feelings hit Gabriel all at once. But first and foremost was the dizzying sensation of warmth that flooded his heart—flooded it like a cascading waterfall where, if you were to stand underneath it, you would scarcely be able to draw breath with the force of it.

As he stood and surveyed the bewitching combination of beauty and sensuality that was Lara, and sensed his blood start to pound with the inevitable hunger and need that always arose when she was near, he wondered if that alien feeling was love. That sense of complete and utter helplessness in the face of something that he'd always told himself he didn't want? That hitching of his heart and the weakness in his limbs whenever he caught sight of the woman he intuitively knew he would be willing to *die* for in order to keep safe? And—more than that—the feeling of devastating loss he imagined he would suffer if he were never to see her again? Surely they were all signs that pointed to him being head over heels in love with Lara?

But what followed that wondrous revelation was the dark demon of fear. Fear that he might ruin her life because he had no experience of caring for such a priceless jewel.

For so long Gabriel had held himself apart from any sensitivity or feeling around women in case he got hurt. Look what his own mother had done to him. With such a precarious introduction into the world, trust—particularly when it came to women—was surely going to be an ongoing issue for him.

His thinking ran along the lines of what if he allowed himself to get involved with someone and then got hurt so badly he would never be able to recover enough to do the one thing that he did well? That was acquiring money and status in his chosen field. At least that gave him options with regard to how he lived. And in any case, surely it was better to be rich and miserable rather than the reverse?

Mentally giving himself a shake, Gabriel turned his attention back to the dress Lara was modelling. It could indeed have been tailor-made for her exquisite form— and, being personally acquainted with just *how* exquisite that form was, he knew, with a glimmer of pride, that he had chosen so well.

'You look utterly beautiful—in fact, you're ravishing,' he told her.

'It's the dress.'

'Can't you accept a compliment for once without putting yourself down, for goodness' sake?'

As soon as the words left his lips Gabriel wanted to take them back. His thoughtless remark had made Lara's cheeks flush with embarrassed heat and he was once again reminded of his fears around loving her. In truth, he couldn't bear the idea of hurting her even *once*, let alone the many times he might thoughtlessly hurt her should they spend the rest of their lives together.

Tucking her hair behind an ear, she lifted her shoulders in a shrug. 'Perhaps I'm not very good at receiving compliments—which is why I try and deflect them with humour. It doesn't mean that I don't appreciate you saying nice things to me, Gabriel. What woman *wouldn't* want a man to tell her she looks beautiful?'

'I'm sorry I snapped at you. I guess I'm just feeling a little on edge, knowing that you're leaving tomorrow,' he admitted, his chest tightening at the thought. He went to her then and folded her into his arms. Resting his chin on the top of her head, he stroked his hand down her back and immediately sensed her quiver. 'I should kidnap you and stop you from going,' he murmured.

Moving back a little, so that she might examine him, Lara knew her luminous brown eyes couldn't hide her disquiet.

'You don't have to resort to kidnapping me to get me to stay with you, Gabriel. I'd gladly stay with you if you just simply asked.' She sighed and shook her head. 'But you *won't*, will you? Just simply ask, I mean?'

She was beginning to know him too well. 'Aren't

you looking forward to going back to England—to your family and your job…your life there?' he replied, hoping to divert her.

'Of course I am. Can I ask you something?'

Her voice had lowered softly and he guessed she was wary of upsetting him. He hated the idea that Lara felt she had to walk on eggshells around him.

Releasing her, he restlessly drove his fingers through his hair. 'What is it you want to ask?'

'Have you… Have you ever thought of coming back to England to settle? I mean, what about the house that you inherited from your family? Have you made up your mind about what you're going to do with it?'

'Yes, I have. I'll be travelling back in a few days to sign some papers. I'm sorry I didn't tell you before, but it just never seemed to be the appropriate time.'

'You're selling it, aren't you? That means you won't be coming back to settle, doesn't it?'

Gabriel swallowed hard. It was time to tell Lara the truth—the *whole* truth.

'In my uncle's letter, he stipulated that I could only inherit if I came back to live in the manor for at least six months. After that I could do what I liked with the house.'

Her eyes lit up and he saw the hope that flared in their silken depths.

'Then you *could* come back to live there? We could see each other whenever we wanted?'

'Sweetheart, as difficult as it might be for you to understand, I don't want to live in that house again. It holds too many unhappy memories for me. I'd be much better off selling it and staying here.'

The colour drained from Lara's face. 'But didn't you

just say that your uncle stipulated in his letter that you could only inherit if you lived there for six months? If you're not planning on doing that, how will you sell it? It won't be yours to sell, will it?'

'I have a very good lawyer. There are ways and means to get round the legalities.'

'I don't understand....'

Her voice faltered a little and she looked as if she might cry. Gabriel felt like the worst criminal.

'I mean, it's not as though you need the money, is it? Why not just keep the house? Keep it for your family?'

He stared at her. 'You know I don't have any family.' He ground out the words as if they might choke him. What was Lara playing at, coming out with such a thing?

'I mean that you might one day have a family of your own. That would help dispel the unhappy memories of living in the house, wouldn't it?'

'I'm happy to take risks in my working life, Lara, but not in my personal one. Don't you know that by now?'

He saw her take a nervous swallow, then slide her palms down over the pretty blue dress he'd bought her. She lifted her shimmering gaze to his.

'I suppose I do. I just hoped that, given time, you'd come to see things differently. The eternal optimist— that's me.' Her lips quirked in a self-deprecating smile. 'Shouldn't we go to dinner now? It's getting late, and I ought to try and get a good night's sleep before travelling tomorrow. I'll just go and get my jacket.'

As Lara left the room, Gabriel stared blankly ahead of him out of the window at the winking lights of the city that had helped him to make his fortune. And right then he despised himself and *it* for contributing to breaking the heart of one of the sweetest and loveliest women in the world....

They sat down on their last night together to what should have been a wonderful meal at a local Thai restaurant, but for Lara the delicious food might as well have been gruel for all the enjoyment it gave her.

She was numb from her head down to her toes. The realisation that Gabriel wasn't any nearer to changing his mind about returning to England to face the demons from his past or to consider the possibility of committing to a proper relationship with her had finally sunk in. He'd asserted that he was happy to take risks in his working life but not in his personal one. The declaration had shattered her heart because she knew it was the death knell to all her hopes and dreams where he was concerned. What else could she do now but accept his decision to continue living his life in New York without her?

'Don't you like the food I ordered for you?' As he laid his fork down by the side of his plate, Gabriel's lean, hollow-cheeked face was grim. He reached up to loosen his tie as if he suddenly couldn't bear the constriction.

Biting back the tears that precariously threatened, Lara dabbed at her lips with her napkin. 'I know you meant well, bringing me here to eat, but I'm afraid I don't have much of an appetite.'

'You should have said.'

'I didn't because you've been working all day and I didn't have anything at the apartment to cook for you. I knew you needed to eat. That's why I agreed to go out to dinner with you.'

'As usual, putting others before yourself.' Although he'd lowered his voice, the muted volume didn't disguise the disparagement in his tone.

Lara flinched. 'You make it sound like it's something you despise—to think of others, I mean. I can't help my nature, Gabriel.'

His blue eyes were as clear and cold as flawless diamonds. 'No, you can't, can you? That's why I knew it was probably a mistake to start this affair. But I'm only human and I simply couldn't resist.'

If she hadn't been trembling so hard at his words, and feared losing her balance should she attempt to stand, Lara knew she couldn't have remained sitting in her seat. For the first time ever she honestly felt she disliked the man who gazed back at her across the table.

'Is that really all you thought us being together was? An affair? Something you could take or leave? I knew you had the potential to be cruel, Gabriel, but I never guessed just *how* cruel.'

'Why? It isn't as though I haven't given you enough evidence.'

'You're right. You started giving me evidence all those years ago, when I was just sixteen.'

Lara's comment drew a disturbed frown between Gabriel's brows. 'When you were sixteen? I doubt it. You surely didn't take it seriously when I used to rib you about not having a boyfriend because you were so choosy?'

'It wasn't that. Don't you remember Sean's party? The one he threw at our house? I know you do because you talked about it that first day, when you showed up to offer your condolences for Sean. Well, that night you were flirting with me, and in my innocence I took it to

mean that you liked me. I mean *really* liked me. I foolishly told you how I felt about you....'

Lara paused. The memory was suddenly more acute
than it had ever been. The power of it made her ribs
hurt.

'I don't think it pleased you. If anything, you were
probably highly embarrassed. You told me I should look
to be with someone my own age. Then you saw that
blonde tutor from your university across the room and
you all but pushed me aside to get to her. So yes, Gabriel. I *do* know that you can be cruel.'

He shook his head. 'That was a long time ago. You
were just a kid. I wouldn't have wanted to encourage
your interest because you were my best friend's little
sister and your family's regard was important to me.'

'But feelings are feelings, no matter what age you
are, and even then mine ran deep, Gabriel. Anyway,
we're talking about what's happening *now*. What I
want to know is are you reducing what we have to the
description of a mere affair because you're trying to
protect yourself from being hurt should you commit
seriously to me? I don't understand. How can I hurt
you if you don't really let me into your life, Gabriel?'

'As hard as it might be for you to hear, Lara, I don't
need anyone in my life. My life is just fine the way it is.'

'Is that true?' Sadly shaking her head, Lara barely
knew how to proceed. Gabriel was implacable when he
erected his defences. As hard as iron. She knew that.

'It's pointless continuing this conversation.' Throwing down his napkin, he signalled for the waiter. 'I'll
only hurt you even more if we continue, and you're
going home tomorrow.'

Lara stayed in her seat and said softly, 'You're probably right. Okay. Why don't you just pay the bill and we'll go?'

'Wise decision,' he murmured, just at the same moment as the smiling waiter arrived at their table.

It truly amazed Lara how quickly she had got back into the routine of working after the long summer break. In the endless days and long, sleepless nights following her departure from Gabriel in New York she'd wondered if she'd ever find pleasure or satisfaction in the job she loved again. But as soon as she had returned to the college, and the requests and demands of the students for help with their research, she'd taken both refuge and pleasure in the familiar routine of the life she was used to.

It helped her not to dwell on Gabriel too much. She would have been utterly useless doing her job if she had.

Yet the memory of their agonising goodbye at the airport and his comment that he'd known it was a mistake to start their affair still had the power to make her cry.

The distance he'd put between them at the restaurant with his remark the night before she was due to leave had grown even wider when he'd told her he thought it best they slept in separate rooms, so that Lara could get a good night's rest before catching her flight the next day. Even though he'd been hateful at the restaurant she hadn't slept a wink. Without Gabriel in the bed next to her—the Gabriel who had been so loving and passionate—she'd felt as if an essential part of her was missing.

Although she'd told herself she didn't understand his sudden cold impulse to distance himself from her not just physically but emotionally, in truth she did understand. He'd been running away again. Not just from

Lara, but from his fear of love and all that that might mean. He simply didn't trust it in case it was taken away, just as his mother had been taken away from him when she took her own life. That was why he'd taunted Lara with his remark that their 'affair' had been a mistake. He'd been trying to push her away. He wouldn't run the risk of caring for her too much in case she ended up hurting him.

The next morning, although they'd sat at the dining table together for breakfast, Gabriel had busied himself making several calls on his cell phone that had ensured his attention was on his work and not on her.

Lara might as well have been invisible. She'd tried hard to make conversation, hoping to engage him with her heartfelt declaration that she was still going to miss him despite what he had said at the restaurant, and that it would be hard to go home knowing they might not ever see each other again.

Gabriel's handsome face had remained worryingly impassive, as though he was deliberately locking her out—locking her out of his mind and his heart—and finally, when his chauffeur had called to tell him the car was ready to take them to the airport, out of his life, too.

When he'd left her at the airport he'd hesitatingly laid his hands on her shoulders and bent his head to kiss her. Lara had tensed helplessly, hoping and praying that he was going to have a change of heart and declare he couldn't just let her disappear out of his life without making some plans for the future. But to add to her distress his parting kiss hadn't been the least bit passionate or heartfelt. They might have just been mere acquaintances. The touch of his lips had been briefly warm and perfunctory, nothing more. Then, after telling her to take care of herself, that he'd probably be in touch just as soon as he 'got his head straight', he'd turned on his heel and hadn't looked back even once as he'd exited the airport.

Back at work, despite her vow not to dwell too much on her longing for Gabriel, memories of his warm, hard body against hers, of the smiles that had tugged at her heart because they were so rare and therefore even more precious, of the sound of his voice especially before he made love to her, when he'd seductively enticed and teased her, would sneak up on her when Lara least expected it. She would wonder what he was doing and if he even gave her a second thought. Had Gabriel already replaced her in his bed with some pretty, ambitious girl who viewed him as a sure-fire ticket to success and fortune? A girl who might please him sexually but would never love him—not like *she* loved him.

'Hello, Miss Bradley. Did you have a good holiday?'

She blinked, then glanced up from the paperwork she'd been desperately trying to apply herself to before thoughts of Gabriel had intruded once again.

A tall, slim young man dressed in skinny jeans and an unironed T-shirt stood on the other side of the counter. He had a shock of sandy-coloured hair in dire need of a wash and a comb. Lara immediately relaxed. Danny Fairfax was one of the most pleasant students you could wish to meet—charming and affable, in spite of his sometimes unkempt appearance. She always made sure to make time for him when he needed help with some aspect of the research he was struggling with.

'It was fine, thanks.' She followed up this answer with an unguarded, warm smile. Danny immediately flushed beetroot-red, which endeared him to her even more. 'And I told you before to call me Lara. "Miss Bradley" makes me sound like some elderly spinster.'

His lips broke into a grin. But he quickly looked serious again. 'I'm sorry I asked if your holiday was good. I forgot that you told me your brother had recently died. Obviously you must still be grieving for him.'

The comment took Lara aback. Not just because Danny had remembered the fact but also because she realised she'd probably been thinking more about Gabriel than about Sean. Of course she still missed her brother's presence, and not a day went by when she didn't mourn him, but Gabriel was a living, breathing reality, and when she'd been with him he had reached deep down inside her and stolen both her heart and her soul. She knew Sean would understand, even give her his blessing. He had loved Gabriel, too.

Staring back into Danny's strangely still grey eyes, Lara wondered if he would ever experience the depth of love and passion that she had experienced with Gabriel. She could only pray that he wouldn't have his heart splintered and broken as hers had been.

'Yes, I'm still grieving. But losing someone like that… It still feels like they're around. You know what I mean? His presence is everywhere.' It didn't pass Lara by that she might have been talking about Gabriel.

'Yes, I do know what you mean,' Danny answered gravely. 'I lost my dad two years ago at Christmas and sometimes I hear his voice as though he's in the room with me, especially when I'm trying to work out a problem. He was from Yorkshire, and when things got tough he always used to say, "Don't let the man grind you down!" Funny how that used to help me.'

'He sounds as though he was a very wise man, your dad.'

'He was. He was the best.'

'So, Danny…' Lara purposefully switched back into work mode. It wouldn't help her to dwell on her personal sorrows too much and nor would it help Danny— although she was touched that he would share the story of his personal loss with her. It was good to know that she wasn't the only one walking around with the feeling that life had pulled the rug from under her and she might never walk on firm ground again. 'What can I do for you today?'

Gabriel had been revisiting his old bedroom. Although his initial reaction on entering it had been wary, his stomach clenched hard in readiness for the deluge of hurtful memory that would inevitably swamp him, he had been mildly surprised to see that the room was newly decorated, freshened up.

Had Richard Devenish undertaken to get a decorator in before he'd fallen ill? Why on earth had he done that? It wasn't as though he'd needed an extra room. Had he perhaps believed that his nephew would return and make the manor his home again?

Bemused, Gabriel allowed his gaze to sweep his surroundings in a preliminary search. His glance falling on the neatly arranged books in the two maplewood bookcases that he remembered from his childhood, he leant down to retrieve a first edition copy of *Brave New World* by Aldous Huxley. It had been a Christmas present from his uncle when he was just nine. He had all but devoured the book. He'd loved it so much he had even written an essay about it at school.

That year his teacher had commented in his report, *'Gabriel is a precocious reader with a highly inventive imagination that I am sure will take him far!'*

His lips nudging a bittersweet smile, he replaced the book and turned round. Janet Mullan, the housekeeper, had left the large picture windows open to let in the sunshine. The scent of stocks and roses from the garden below also drifted in delicately, filling the air with the heady summer perfume that Gabriel had always loved even as a boy.

Releasing a slow, contemplative breath, he walked to the windows to stare out at the stunning vista. He recalled thinking at that time that it wouldn't be so bad living here if he could have a few of the boys from school to come and stay with him in the holidays. But his nanny—a middle-aged lady called Margaret—had shaken her head and reminded him that his uncle had forbidden it, in case any of the valuable antiques in the house got broken.

To make up for his disappointment she'd given him a hug, ruffled his hair and said she'd take him to the local fair on the village green…perhaps he'd see some of his friends there? Well, Gabriel had gone to the fair, munched at a toffee apple and a sticky bun, palled up with a local boy and had a whale of a time, sliding down the helter-skelter and riding the carousel. That had been one of the best days of that summer, he recalled.

But sadly, events like that had been too few and far between. His taciturn uncle had grown more and more distant, seemingly preferring to stay away rather than share the house with Gabriel when he was home, and concepts like heritage and family had quickly grown to mean less and less to his nephew. The next summer holiday that Gabriel had properly enjoyed had been after his first year at university, when he had met Sean.

Inevitably, the thought of his best friend brought with it a new deluge of heartfelt memories—of Lara and the stricken look on her pretty face when he'd bade her goodbye less than warmly at the airport. It had been the hardest thing he'd ever done, and every night and day that had passed since had given him plenty of cause to regret it. It had been a cruel way to end their too-brief relationship—pretending that he didn't care how she felt. It had been the act of his life.

The truth was he cared too much. He just hadn't been able to deal with the outpouring of love and affection that he'd received from Lara. It had been a totally unfamiliar experience to have someone love him and want to be with him—not because of what he could materially provide for them but because they wanted to be with the man behind the facade Gabriel had affected all these years. The *real* Gabriel Devenish.

But why should he let Lara waste her love on him? Sooner or later she'd find out that he just wasn't worth it. In years to come, when she was married to a really decent man, she'd thank him for it.

Feeling an overwhelming sense of weariness and despair descend, he lowered himself onto the bed, put his hands behind his head, and lay down. His uncle's solicitor was waiting for him downstairs in the drawing room—waiting for Gabriel to give him his decision about what he intended to do with the house. Remembering that he'd also promised his property developer friend that he would ring him to discuss some figures regarding the potential sale of the manor, Gabriel loosed a heavy sigh and shut his eyes.

CHAPTER ELEVEN

LARA COULDN'T FATHOM what on earth was wrong with her. Yes, she'd been through the mill, losing first Sean and then Gabriel. But were those heartrending events enough to make her feel queasy and persistently light-headed, which was how she'd been feeling for several days now? She should perhaps go the doctor, but she was sure she would eventually shrug it off so steered clear of pursuing that option. Instead she determinedly focused on work, even putting in some overtime in a bid to shake herself out of whatever was ailing her.

Besides, she wasn't the only one who had lost a loved one or had her heart broken. What she should aim to do was to be more stoical. She should just endeavour to take one day at a time and somehow, some way, garner some optimism about life again.

Then one morning, as she got ready for work, Lara reached into her purse to dig out the foil packet of contraceptive pills. She immediately realised she'd picked up the previous month's packet instead of the current one. About to jettison the empty container into a nearby wicker basket, she did a double take. At the beginning of the empty rows there was one tablet remaining. How had that happened? More to the point, why hadn't she noticed it before?

Her heart started to pound as she calculated back to the week of the remaining pill. Without a doubt it was the week that she'd spent in New York with Gabriel. Six weeks had passed since then. Six weeks with no sign of a period. Lara had put the absence down to the emotional rollercoaster she'd been on, telling herself that everything would sort itself out just as soon as her emotions calmed down.

Hadn't she started to take the pill in the first place to help regulate her periods because they tended to be erratic? She shouldn't be alarmed that she'd missed one. Yet some instinct told her that she *did* perhaps need to be concerned.

Dragging her hand feverishly through her tousled dark hair, and still in her pyjamas, she sat down on the bed and let the realisation that had shockingly dawned wash over her. Wasn't it true that you had to be consistent when taking an oral contraceptive? If you missed one then you risked the inevitable. Suddenly, the reason for her queasiness, her feelings of being light-headed and her missed period became disturbingly clear. She was pregnant. Pregnant with Gabriel Devenish's baby!

It was the strangest thing, but suddenly Lara's sense of confusion and worry about her health dissipated like ice crystals beneath the sun. She would need to take a test to be absolutely sure, of course.... Touching her palm to her cheek, she sensed her skin flush warmly. A sense of joyous excitement filled her. It went racing through her blood like life-giving oxygen.

How or why she had omitted to take one of her pills no longer seemed to matter. She certainly hadn't forgotten to take one deliberately. In any case, Gabriel hadn't got in touch when he'd 'got his head straight', as he'd promised he would. He hadn't even let her know when and if he'd returned to the UK to deal with the sale of his family's manor house.

As much as it grieved her, Lara could no longer make that her driving concern. In her mind and in her heart she had left the door open for him to come back to her— of course she had. But if he didn't—and right now it didn't look as if he would—well, she would have their son or daughter to take care of, and that would in time help to ease the hurt of his desertion.

At least she hoped that it would. But whatever happened one thing was certain: she intended to be the most loving and adoring mother she could be. She might not be wealthy, but her child would be the recipient of far more important riches—her love and devotion. He or she might not have a father in their life, but that would have to be enough.

Gabriel had spent the morning with his architect, perusing and discussing the renovation plans for the manor which were already well under way. The genteel old orangery was being redesigned, along with the bedrooms, and he'd also had discussions with one of Britain's top garden designers about what could be done to make the most of the gardens.

The day the solicitor had visited the house to find out what Gabriel intended to do about it, Gabriel had made the surprising decision to fulfil the terms of the codicil to the will and live there for the six months stipulated so that he could inherit. Shortly after that he had rung his office in New York and told them he was taking a year's sabbatical in order to decide what he wanted to do about his future.

His decision to take a year off had dumbfounded his employers, and they had immediately offered him a myriad of financial temptations and seductive inducements like a prestigious house in the Hamptons to get him to rethink. Gabriel had firmly declined.

The most surprising thing of all was that when he had come off the phone he'd felt as if a huge weight had been lifted off his shoulders. Until that cathartic moment he hadn't fully realised how much his work and his drive for more success, more money and more power had dominated his life. It certainly hadn't left much time or space for anything else. In particular, for the loving and committed relationship he secretly craved but had always feared he would never be able to sustain even if he found it.

During the past few weeks since he had returned to the house and reread his uncle's letter—particularly the part where he had told him of his hopes that he would return to live at the manor and raise his children there—Gabriel had been filled with new hope and optimism about his future. A future quite unlike the usual picture he had envisaged for himself.

What had helped tremendously was the fact that he had actually started to fall in love with the house. Bit by bit the sorrow of his childhood and his damaged past had loosened its grip and he had started to heal.

One afternoon, whilst exploring one of the larger bedrooms which the housekeeper was convinced must have been his mother's, he discovered a framed photograph tucked away in a bureau. It was a picture of his mother, Angela, holding him as a baby, and it bore out the housekeeper's theory that the room must have been hers. There was no doubt that Angela had been a beautiful woman, with glossy dark hair and vivid blue eyes, but it wasn't just her beauty that drew the viewer in. Her smiling face exuded warmth and love in equal measures as she held her son firmly against her heart.

How she must have hated being ill and unable to look after him, Gabriel thought.

The idea jolted him.

Up until now, Angela Devenish had been an almost ghost-like figure in his mind—hardly real. As if she'd never existed at all. Now her life and the woman she had been started to fascinate him. He studied the photograph for a long time. He even took it with him into his bedroom and stood it on the dressing table so that he would see it every morning when he woke up.

But even though he had begun to make genuine inroads into seeing his mother in a different light and healing the wounds from his past, there was one face that he longed to see again more than any other. And that face was Lara's.

The only thing that had held Gabriel back from going to see her when he'd returned to the UK was the sickening memory of how he had behaved towards her when they'd parted in New York. He also couldn't forget the story of how he'd rebuffed her when she'd been just sixteen at Sean's party. She hadn't had to elucidate how hurt she must have been. It had been written all over her face.

He honestly wouldn't blame her if when she saw him again she told him to go to hell. But he hoped to God she wouldn't. Until he had made the decision to live in his family's manor so that he could inherit—not so that he might sell the property but so that he could make it his home—he hadn't known how he could legitimately approach her. All he had known was that he wanted to show Lara that he could be a better man, a truly good man—a man she could depend on.

And to do that he would have to show her evidence that he intended to stay in the country and make his life there.

If Lara agreed—and it was a big *if*—she would be an absolutely vital and crucial element in helping Gabriel create the new life he wanted. A much happier and more fulfilling life than he had ever experienced before.

Three months later...

Lara pressed her palm to the base of her spine and rubbed it. Having been on her feet since the early hours of the morning, she was so tired she could drop. Why did her tiredness and stress always seem to go straight to her back these days? she wondered.

With a jolt, she remembered that she was pregnant. The realisation still came as a shock every time she thought about it, but it had all been confirmed by her doctor so there was no more doubting. It still seemed like the most unbelievable dream.

With a wistful sigh, Lara started to go through her usual routine of shutting up shop for the day. All she could think about now was the prospect of a long and leisurely soak in the tub with some scented bubbles. That should help ease the ache in her back.

'Any plans for the evening, Lara?' her young colleague Marisa asked as she shut down her computer beside her.

'Only to have the longest, most relaxing soak in history, in a bath full of deliciously warm and sudsy water.'

'Sounds heavenly.' Marisa smiled.

'What about you? Have you any plans?'

'I'm going out for a pizza with Mark, my boyfriend.'

'You're still seeing him? I thought you two had had a big row and you had decided not to see him any more.'

Marisa's plump cheeks suffused with heat. 'Every now and again we fall out. But we quickly patch things up.' She smiled. 'He's a nice boy. I'd miss him if we weren't together. Sometimes he feels like a missing part of me I didn't know I'd lost. Do you know what I mean?'

Lara *did* know what she meant, and helplessly she felt the other girl's comment catching her off guard. Her eyes filled with tears. The thought of Gabriel and the memory of his passionate caresses and kisses was never far away. Those memories were even more poignant now that she knew she was carrying his baby. Did he ever think about her and wonder how she was doing? Did he ever miss her?

It had been neither simple nor easy to slip back into the predictable routine of the life she'd had before he'd walked in and ignited all her hopes and dreams with a fierce burning light that would never go out. So far it had been the biggest challenge of her life. Lara wondered how Gabriel would react if he knew that. It all but killed her to think he might just brush it off and put it down to experience.

'Lara?' Stepping towards her, Marisa looked alarmed to see that she was weeping. 'What's wrong, love? Do you feel sick? Do you want me to get you a glass of water?'

She suddenly sounded much older than her years,

and the younger woman's concern made Lara want to weep even more.

Touching her fingertips to the moisture that had tracked down her face and dampened her cheeks, she shook her head and forced a smile. 'No, I'll be fine, thanks. I think I just need to get out of here and go home and have that bath.'

'That's bound to help. A long hot bath is a bit of a cure-all for me, too. It's the same as having a cup of tea, isn't it? It somehow makes you feel better.'

Marisa's sage remark had the effect of making Lara want to hug her—so she did. The other girl flushed with pleasure.

'You're wise beyond your years—you know that?' Lara told her. Then, moving away, she glanced over at all the empty chairs and tables that would be full of diligent and not so diligent students again tomorrow. One thing was for certain: life went on, despite what was happening in your personal life.

Reaching for the red wool cardigan she'd hung over the back of her chair, she hurriedly pulled it on. Lifting up the heavy swathe of hair that had fallen down her back she let it fall again and shook it free. Absently glancing towards the twin glass doors of the exit, she frowned. A man dressed in a classic raincoat thrown over a dark sweatshirt and jeans was pushing them open.

Stepping inside, he took a brief inventory of his surroundings before tunnelling his fingers through his hair and moving towards them. Even if she hadn't seen his face Lara would have known that smooth athletic gait anywhere. Staring in disbelief, she found it hard to think, never mind *speak*. In fact, she suddenly felt quite faint.

'Who could that be?' Marisa whispered next to her. 'Doesn't he know that we're closed?'

'His name is Gabriel Devenish.'

Still in shock, Lara knew her voice wasn't much above a whisper. But it was almost as if she'd had to say his name out loud in order to believe that he was there and not just a figment of her imagination, or some seductive ghostly visitation from one of her nightly dreams of him.

When he stepped up to the counter and turned the vivid azure beam of his too-arresting gaze on her, a well of hurt and long-suppressed fury at his cavalier treatment rose up inside her and made her stiffen her shoulders defensively.

Lifting her chin, she looked him straight in the eye and announced, 'We're closed. If you need any help I'm afraid you'll have to come back tomorrow.'

The beautiful carved lips in front of her edged into an amused smile—a smile that unscrupulously stormed Lara's heart and turned her insides to mush.

'I'm afraid what I need can't wait until tomorrow,' he remarked, and the smoky voice and piercing eyes mercilessly imprisoned her, locked her up and threw away the key.

For a long moment she fell into a kind of trance. Then the sound of Marisa pointedly clearing her throat behind her and touching her hand to Lara's sleeve had her turning round to see what was wrong.

There was nothing amiss. The younger girl's eyes were alive with curiosity and what might have even been delight as she commented, 'I'm sorry, Lara, but I have to dash. Mark is meeting me in the car park. Take care of yourself, won't you? I'll see you tomorrow.'

'Enjoy your pizza,' Lara murmured automatically.

As the twin glass doors swung shut behind the slender blonde, her heart hammered at the realisation that she and Gabriel were alone. The impulse to do something, *anything*, to help still her nerves took hold, but Gabriel's handsome face was suddenly looking ominously serious and she couldn't help but stare. Just what did he want to say to her? Whatever it was, she was determined that she would have her say first.

'What on earth are you doing here—and how did you know where to find me? I don't recall giving you the college's address.'

'I went to see your parents,' he replied. 'Your mother told me where to find you.'

'When was this?'

'This morning.'

Lara's hand automatically shot to her abdomen. She gently rubbed it through the soft grey tunic she wore beneath her cardigan, then realised she was drawing attention to the one place she didn't want Gabriel's eyes to be drawn to.

Had her mum told him about the pregnancy? Even though she had been over the moon on hearing Lara's news about the baby, declaring it was the blessing she had been praying for, Lara was confident that she wouldn't have told him anything without checking with her first. But her insides still churned at the thought of how Gabriel would take the news.

'Why did you go to see them? Was it to collect Sean's photographs? And when did you get back to the UK? Is this another flying visit, Gabriel?'

Seeing that Lara's slender hands were gripping the edge of the fibreglass counter as if her life depended on it, and hearing the distress in her voice, Gabriel frowned. He hated the idea that his appearance had upset her, even though he knew she had plenty of reason to be distressed. The need to alleviate her unhappiness became imperative.

'I'll explain everything in a moment. Trust me, there's nothing to worry about. Right now all I want to do is look at you.'

He ached with an unholy ache to take her in his arms and kiss away every hurt, every moment of unease or despair he had ever visited on her, but he forced himself to wait. This wasn't the moment to blunder back into her life and just take what he wanted as if it was his God-given right. That was the *old* Gabriel. The man who had been too selfish and self-obsessed to know what a gift had been bestowed on him when Lara had surrendered her virginity and confessed that she loved him—had *always* loved him.

'You look tired. The shadows under your eyes look like bruises and you're far too pale. What have you been doing to yourself? Burning the candle at both ends?'

Gabriel hadn't meant his observation to sound critical, but he saw straight away that Lara was immediately defensive—*angry*, too. Her animated reaction confirmed it.

'What do *you* care what I've been doing? You didn't even bother to ring me after I left New York, and nor did you have the decency to let me know you were back in the UK! I'm done with worrying about you, Gabriel. I really am. I think it's time I focused my attention on myself and my own needs.'

Her dark eyes crestfallen, she leant towards the desk

and switched off the lamp that was there. Then she opened a drawer and collected her shoulder bag.

'I'm going home now. It's been a long day.'

'We need to talk, Lara. I know you probably think I'm not worth giving the time of day to, but I want the opportunity to help change your mind about that. Did you drive here?'

'Yes, I did.'

'Then I'll follow you in my car.'

She didn't answer. With her head held high, and clutching her bag in front of her, she came round the counter and started to walk towards the exit.

Although she hadn't argued with his intention, Gabriel felt oddly hurt that she wouldn't even look at him. Instead she arranged the strap of her bag more firmly onto her shoulder and drew the sides of her long wool cardigan together as if she was cold. Almost as if needing to protect herself. Then she proceeded out of the building to the car park.

The journey back to Lara's flat was thankfully a short one. Afraid that too long a delay before they were able to talk would give her added time to mull over past events and decide she would be better off without him, Gabriel couldn't help but be anxious. She'd seemed so adamant just now that they were over. But then he remembered the times when she'd openly demonstrated how much she cared and once again hope flared inside him.

Standing beside her as she inserted the key in the lock and opened the door of the Victorian semi where she lived, he stayed silent as a reluctant Lara invited him in.

'We'll talk in the living room,' she declared, her

brown eyes issuing him with a mere cursory glance before sliding quickly away again. 'The sooner we get this over and done with, the better.'

In spite of its lofty ceiling, the room Gabriel followed Lara inside to was surprisingly cosy and welcoming. The space couldn't help but reflect the personal touches and preferences of the woman who lived there. From the small collection of family photographs that sat atop the pine bookcase and the mantelpiece to the several wooden shelves that were literally crammed with books, it was eminently clear what the occupant's priorities were.

A seriously comfortable-looking dark gold couch with an embroidered throw on the back was strewn with brightly coloured cushions, and an old Chesterfield armchair sat before an uncurtained window overlooking the garden.

'You may as well sit down.' Her tone less than inviting, Lara threw her shoulder bag down onto the couch and, with her arms folded, moved her head to indicate he take the armchair.

Murmuring 'Ladies first', Gabriel waited until his reluctant hostess had settled herself on the couch and then, shrugging off his raincoat, he folded it over the back of the venerable old armchair and sat down.

'You said you were going to explain everything?'

Her pretty face was inevitably troubled as she leant forward in her seat to study him. Sighing, Gabriel scraped his fingers through his thick dark hair and smiled. 'I will. What I want to tell you is that I decided what I wanted wasn't in New York after all, but here.'

'You mean your family's home? Have you decided to sell it?'

'I'm not just talking about the manor, Lara. Although in answer to your question I have to tell you I'm *not* intending on selling it. My plan is to live there. In fact I've been living there for the past three months now, attempting to make my peace with the past and turning the place back into a home—a *real* home.'

'You have? Oh, Gabriel, that's wonderful.'

The surprise and pleasure that shone from her beautiful dark eyes couldn't help but melt Gabriel's heart. But he hadn't finished telling her the full extent of his plans yet, and a lot depended on her answer to his next question as to whether he carried them out or not.

'The truth is, Lara…' he continued. 'The truth is it won't be a real home until you agree to marry me and come and live with me there. Will you?'

CHAPTER TWELVE

IT WASN'T THE MOST romantic thing in the world to have happen, but when the full impact of Gabriel's question hit her, Lara sensed a sudden, urgent need to be sick. Hurriedly rising to her feet, she threw him an apologetic look and ran out through the door to her bedroom's en-suite bathroom. Once there, she crouched down in front of the toilet and was violently ill even as she heard Gabriel come in behind her.

'Sweetheart, what's wrong?'

As his deeply concerned voice asked the question, he stooped down behind her and gently gathered her hair behind her head so that it wouldn't fall over her face. When she'd finished, it was to find him running some cold water into the sink and dampening a washcloth. Almost as if she was a little girl he proceeded to wipe her mouth, dabbing gently at her lips, and then he carefully helped her to her feet.

'Wait here,' he instructed, and as the familiar, warm, musky scent of his cologne besieged her senses and rendered her even weaker he briefly disappeared, to return with a glass of cold water. 'Take a good long drink,' he ordered her.

Although he patiently waited for her to finish, Lara easily sensed the concern that gripped him.

When she glanced up again Gabriel removed the glass from her trembling hands and stood it on the shelf above the sink. Then he stared at her. Many times before she had been the recipient of that intensely direct examination, but it had never been as intense as this. Disturbingly, what she saw in the depths of that glittering gaze were varying shades of anger—like the precursor to a storm—and deep, deep anguish and pain.

'What the hell is going on, Lara? You'd better tell me.'

'Haven't you guessed? Don't you know the signs?'

Suddenly overwhelmed with the situation, she shouldered past him into the bedroom. Once there, she dropped down onto the bed and brought her hands up to her face. Incredibly, Gabriel had just asked her to marry him. But was he now going to reject her because she was pregnant? She almost couldn't bear the thought. Before she knew it scalding tears were trickling down behind her palms.

Suddenly the door opened and Gabriel was there. He was staring down at her, a muscle flinching in the side of his carved cheekbone, his expression mirroring hurt disbelief.

'You're pregnant.'

It was a statement of fact, not a question. Raising her head, Lara met his accusing gaze with her heart thudding and her mouth as dry as sand. 'Yes. Yes, I am.'

'So no sooner had we parted than you found yourself another man? I thought I was getting to know you, Lara, but now I realise I didn't know you at all.'

Sounding despairing, Gabriel started to move back

towards the door, as if he had already made up his mind what he was going to do about her admission.

But then he turned and said furiously, 'You certainly didn't waste your time missing me, did you? And to think I believed you when you said you were a virgin the first time we made love. What a prize idiot I was to fall for such an unlikely story!'

With his hand on the doorknob he glared at Lara, then stalked from the room. Ice-cold fear poured through her like white-water rapids as she realised he was going to leave.

Lara jumped up and ran after him.

'Gabriel!'

She got to the living room just as he was collecting his coat from the back of the chair and she rushed forward to grab his wrist and stop him from going. Suddenly it was *her* turn to be furious.

'You *are* an idiot. Such a stupid, *stupid* idiot!' Even as the accusation left her lips a fresh bout of scalding tears rolled down her cheeks and Gabriel stared at her, clearly uncomprehending either her meaning or the reason for her distress. 'Do you honestly think I would sleep with another man when it's *you* that I love—have always loved and always will?'

His lip curled with disdain. 'But you've just admitted that you're pregnant.' He shook off her grip on his arm. 'Or are you going to try and convince me it was some kind of immaculate conception?'

Lara sucked in her breath in a bid to try and steady herself. 'Before you go any further I need to tell you—I need to tell you it's true that when we first slept together I was a virgin. I waited all these years to give up my virginity to a man I really loved because it was im-

portant to me. That man has always been you, Gabriel.'
She paused to take in another steadying breath and saw
the interplay of hope and uncertainty that crossed his
face. 'The baby is *yours*, Gabriel,' she finished.

'What?'

'Just hear me out, will you? I fell pregnant when I
forgot to take one of my contraceptive pills that week
we were together in New York. I didn't do it deliberately. I would never try and trap you like that. But
my head was in the clouds the whole time I spent
with you—it was like a dream. I only discovered I'd
missed one of my pills a few weeks after I got home.
I'd been feeling nauseous and light-headed, but I put
that down to being upset because I was missing you
and you hadn't been in touch. I didn't even know if I
would ever see you again.'

'The baby is mine?' The raincoat Gabriel was holding slid out of his hand onto the floor.

Raising her hand in an attempt to dry her tears, Lara
nodded. 'I swear it. I'll show you the foil packet with
the pill I didn't take still in it. You can trace it back to
our week together in New York. But if you still don't
believe me then I don't know how else to convince
you. I foolishly thought my word and the devotion I've
shown you would be enough. I don't tell lies, Gabriel.
Remember I told you that once before?'

The man standing in front of her looked seriously
stunned. 'Why didn't you tell me you were pregnant
as soon as you found out? I would have come back
straight away.'

Shrugging, Lara gave him a wobbly smile. 'I didn't
want to put any pressure on you or make you feel ob-
ligated, that's why. I especially didn't want that be-

cause of the way you were when we said goodbye at the airport. You seemed so angry, Gabriel. Angry and distant. It was as though you resented me. I knew you were already in turmoil because of your uncle's letter and what he'd told you about your mother. I didn't want to add to your worries.'

Gabriel was shaking his head as if he couldn't quite believe what he was hearing. 'You really are unbelievable—you know that? You had every damn right in the world to demand I come back and take up my responsibility to you and the baby. When will you learn that *you're* the important one, Lara—not me?'

'Don't say that. You're very important to me, too, Gabriel.' She followed this declaration with a puzzled frown. 'But why didn't you tell me you'd decided to come back and live at the manor? Were you thinking that I would automatically expect us to take up where we left off when you clearly had doubts about our relationship?'

'You crazy woman,' he breathed.

Fastening his hands around her slim upper arms, he pulled her against his chest. Lara's heart went wild. As he pushed back a stray curl where it brushed against the side of her cheek she saw his intimate smile was candid and unguarded as he gazed back at her, and it rendered him even more beautiful in her eyes. That heartrending smile suggested he'd made the decision to reveal at last the *real* Gabriel Devenish. To reveal the honourable and decent man behind the steely corporate facade and the much admired financial acuity that he was known for. The man Lara had always known he was.

'I didn't want to tell you I was coming back to live

at the manor until I'd taken some proper time to examine some of the hurts from my past and tried to make some headway into healing them. You didn't deserve to be with a broken man, Lara—a man who didn't know how to love anyone but himself.'

He grimaced painfully.

'And I didn't even make a very convincing job of that. I poured all my energies into my work, and my relentless desire to be the best at what I did was only because I wanted to have the admiration and praise of my peers. I was looking for validation that I was worthwhile. It wasn't even about the money. But that ambition became the most important thing in my life. A very empty and meaningless life, when all was said and done.

'Apart from being good at my job, I didn't regard myself as being good at very much at all. And I didn't have meaningful relationships because I couldn't allow myself to be close to a woman in case I was betrayed in some way—that's another reason why I directed all my attention into my work.

'And as far as doubts are concerned, I can tell you that the only doubts I had were whether I was good enough to be with an angel like you,' he continued huskily. 'I always intended on coming back for you, Lara. Was I hoping for too much when I hoped that you would want to share the rest of your life with a man like me? As I want to share my life with you?'

Lara lifted her hand to lay her palm gently against his roughened cheek. 'No,' she said earnestly. 'You weren't hoping for too much. I can't think of anything I'd like more than to share the rest of my life with you. Besides…no one else would want me if I couldn't be with you Gabriel. I'd be like an empty shell. Don't you know that you've ruined me for any other man because my body and soul belongs to you?'

A profoundly dazed look stole into the eyes that gazed back at her.

Gabriel's hands tightened as they dropped down to her hips and pulled her harder against him. 'And now you're going to have my baby. I'm going to be a father. *We* are going to be parents, with a family of our own. I can't help asking myself if I deserve to be this happy.'

'So you don't mind that we'll have a baby to take care of so early in our relationship? We can't pretend it won't be challenging.'

'We'll weather any storms that come, sweetheart,' Gabriel reassured her warmly. 'We'll weather them because together we're strong and our love won't let the challenges of life overwhelm us. Look at what we've already overcome. This baby will bring us ever closer— just you wait and see.'

His face came towards hers, but with a quick shake of her head Lara gently but firmly pushed him away. 'You have to let me go and freshen my mouth before you kiss me,' she declared. 'Then I'll let you kiss me senseless if you want!'

His carved lips quirked in an amused grin. 'That's like asking me if I need to take my next breath. If you take longer than ten seconds then I'm coming to find you—and I warn you…if you're not ready there'll be a hell of a penalty to pay.' As she smiled and walked towards the door, he added, 'And you still haven't answered my question.'

Feigning ignorance, Lara stopped and turned to examine him. 'What question might that be?'

'Will you marry me? Put me out of my misery, woman, and give me your answer. A man can only take so much before he cracks.'

Her expression softening, Lara laid her hand over her heart and then, with a graceful flourish, indicated that it was his. 'Of course I'll marry you, Gabriel. That's always been my intention—ever since Sean brought you home with him that very first time. He'll be so pleased that two of the people he loved best are going to be together, don't you think?'

It was as she turned and left the room that Gabriel finally realised fully the immense capacity to love that Lara had. Sean had possessed that capacity, too. Shaking his head, he didn't even try and stem the tears that welled in his eyes.

His head was spinning. The woman he loved had agreed to be his wife and she was pregnant with their baby. All the things Gabriel had thought would be denied him were coming true.

He already knew that his future goals didn't have anything to do with continuing to be a 'mover and shaker' on Wall Street, but were to do with being a loving husband and father, with his children growing up happy and content with two parents who adored them and who would do everything in their power to help them have a wonderful life. And they would all live together in the beautiful manor house that Gabriel had inherited from his family. Uncle Richard's heartfelt hope was going to be realised.

The architects and designers Gabriel had hired were already helping him bring his home into the twenty-first century without encroaching on the Regency building's historic innate beauty and grace, and he was already pleased with some of the results they had achieved. Lara had agreed that she was, too, and the room that had given them both the most pleasure was the beautiful nursery—although Lara was already insisting that the baby would share their room until she was confident that he or she was ready to sleep in a room by themselves.

Suddenly aware that the small gathering behind him in the glass-ceilinged conservatory had fallen into a reverent silence, and knowing that Lara's parents were closest to them at the front of the seated rows, he brought his mind right back to the present and the radiant and beautiful woman at his side.

Lara looked absolutely stunning in her simple but elegant wedding gown. It was fashioned in lavender-coloured floor-length satin and her mother, Peggy, had helped her decide on it. It was the perfect choice for her daughter's timeless beauty. The strapless design had a sweetheart neckline and a beaded appliqué underneath the bust, and the material flowed down over the waist that five months of pregnancy had clearly but not yet too obviously swelled.

His clasp on her slender hand tightened a little possessively as Lara lifted her shimmering dark eyes to his. For a man who had prided himself on addressing many corporate banquets and dinners with aplomb, Gabriel suddenly found himself bereft of words.

Clearing his throat, he leant towards his bewitching wife-to-be and asked in hushed tones, 'Are you ready for this? You don't want to change your mind?'

Momentarily taken aback, Lara blinked. Then her soft pink-painted lips curved in a loving, amused smile.

'Are you serious? To use an often used cliché, for which I won't apologise, I've been waiting for this moment all my life.'

Gabriel chuckled and claimed her lips in a briefly hungry kiss that he had no intention of apologising for, either. When he looked up again the professional celebrant who stood in front of them—a slender woman with copper-coloured hair and merry brown eyes—bestowed an indulgent smile upon them and reprimanded him teasingly.

'You're meant to kiss the bride when I pronounce that you're man and wife, Mr Devenish, *not* before!'

Unable to resist, Gabriel remarked, 'No offence, but nobody tells me when I can and can't kiss the woman I love—the woman I adore more than life itself.'

Briefly stunned into silence, the celebrant bestowed another smile on him. Then, her gaze encompassing both him and Lara, she said, 'Shall we proceed with the ceremony now?'

Unable to stop himself from having the last word, Gabriel twined his fingers with Lara's and answered, 'Trust me, I'm as anxious to get the ceremony under way and make this amazing woman my wife as you are!'

There was a delighted ripple of laughter from behind them at that declaration, and a gently respectful round of applause. As for Lara—she glanced up at the handsome blue-eyed man at her side, dressed in a flawless midnight blue tuxedo, and offered up a silent prayer of thanks for her great good fortune.

Then the voice of her brother stole into her mind, saying, *I always told you to go for what you wanted in life, and that if you wanted it enough you would get it...remember?'*

Swallowing back her tears, Lara murmured under her breath, 'Yes, Sean, I remember—and you were right. Thank you.'

* * * * *

"We said no touching."

Rafiq inched his palm higher. "You said no kissing."

"Rule two: no touching."

Despite Maysa's assertions he did not bother to lift his hand, and she did not bother to shove it away.

"Yet you have been touching me."

"As a physician."

"And I have reacted as any man reacts to a woman's touch."

"For that reason I should go now."

Rafiq had predicted that she would stand and leave, but she remained positioned next to him, both hands still resting lightly on his shoulders. He straightened, bringing their faces close. Their gazes connected immediately. He saw indecision in her eyes, as well as a spark of need.

And then Maysa did something Rafiq did not expect—she broke her first rule.

Kristi Gold has a fondness for beaches, baseball and bridal reality shows. She firmly believes that love has remarkable healing powers and feels very fortunate to be able to weave stories of love and commitment. As a bestselling author, a National Readers' Choice Award winner and a Romance Writers of America three-time RITA® Award finalist, Kristi has learned that, although accolades are wonderful, the most cherished rewards come from networking with readers. She can be reached through her website at www.kristigold.com or through Facebook.

Recent titles by the same author:

FROM SINGLE MOM TO SECRET HEIRESS
THE RETURN OF THE SHEIKH
THE CLOSER YOU GET

Did you know these are also available as eBooks?
Visit www.millsandboon.co.uk

ONE NIGHT
WITH THE SHEIKH

BY
KRISTI GOLD

Published in Great Britain 2014
by Mills & Boon, an imprint of Harlequin (UK) Limited,
Eton House, 18-24 Paradise Road, Richmond, Surrey, TW9 1SR

© 2013 Kristi Goldberg
ISBN: 978 0 263 24649 0

Printed and bound in Spain
by Blackprint CPI, Barcelona

ONE NIGHT
WITH THE SHEIKH

To my beautiful daughter, Kendall.
One of the best athletic trainers in the business,
one of my biggest fans,
and one of my major sources for chocolate.

One

King Rafiq ibn Fayiz Mehdi possessed keen intelligence, vast power and infinite riches. Yet none had aided him in preventing a devastating tragedy—a tragedy for which he had been partially responsible.

As the sun began to set, he stood on the palace's rooftop veranda and peered at the panorama stretched out before him. The diverse terrain he once revered now seemed ominous, inviting disturbing recollections that cut into his composure like a well-honed blade.

A dark, winding road at midnight. Silence and dread. Flashing lights illuminating the bottom of a cliff. The twisted metal wreckage…

"If you believe you'll move mountains by staring at them, I assure you it will not work."

At the sound of the familiar voice, Rafiq glanced back to see his brother standing only a few steps behind him. "Why are you here?"

Zain claimed the space beside Rafiq and leaned back against the stone wall. "Is that how you greet the man who so generously handed you the keys to the kingdom over a year ago?"

The same man who had abdicated the throne for the sake of love, an emotion Rafiq had never quite embraced. "My apologies, brother. I was not expecting you for another month."

"Since I completed my initial preparation for the water conservation project, I felt the timing was right for my return."

Under normal circumstances, he would appreciate Zain's company. Lately he preferred solitude. "Did you travel alone?"

"Of course not," Zain said in an irritable tone. "I do not travel without my family unless absolutely necessary."

Rafiq had never believed he would hear his womanizing brother utter those words. "Then Madison is with you?"

"Yes, and my children. I've been anxious for you to finally meet your niece and nephew."

Rafiq did not share in Zain's enthusiasm. Being in the presence of two infants would only serve to remind him of what he had lost. "Where are they now?"

"Madison and Elena are tending to them."

At least he could temporarily avoid the painful introduction. "I am glad you have finally returned Elena to her rightful place. The household does not run well without her."

"So I have heard," Zain said. "I have also heard you are in danger of causing an uprising among the palace staff if you continue to terrorize them."

Rafiq admittedly had trouble maintaining calm in recent days, but he did not care for the exaggerated accusation. "I have not terrorized the staff. I have only corrected them when necessary."

"It's my understanding you have found it necessary to *correct* them on a daily basis, brother. I've also learned you have not been cooperative with the council."

Rafiq began to question the real reason behind Zain's surprise appearance. "Have you been speaking with our younger brother?"

Zain's gaze faltered. "I have been in touch with Adan on occasion."

His anger began to build. "And you have clearly been discussing me."

"He only mentioned you've been having a difficult time since Rima's death."

Rafiq's suspicions had been confirmed—Zain had arrived early to play nursemaid. "Despite what you and Adan might believe, I do not need a keeper."

Zain leaned forward, his expression suddenly somber. "We both understand how devastating it must be to lose your wife and your unborn child—"

"How could you understand?" No one would ever understand the constant guilt and regret unless they had experienced it. "You have a wife and two healthy children."

"As I was saying," Zain continued, "it's understandable that you are still harboring a good measure of anger, particularly with so many unanswered questions about the accident. However, your attitude is proving disruptive. Perhaps you should consider taking a sabbatical."

Impossible and unnecessary. "And who would run the country in my stead?"

"I would," Zain said. "After all, I prepared many years to assume that responsibility before I gave up the position. Adan is willing to assist me."

Rafiq released a cynical laugh. "First, Adan has no interest in governing Bajul. He's only interested in flying planes and seducing women. As far as you are concerned, our people have not forgotten you abandoned them for a second time."

Barely contained fury called out from Zain's narrowed eyes. "I still have an abiding love for this country, and I am quite capable of seeing that it runs smoothly, as I promised before I returned with Madison to the States. Do not forget, I alone developed the water conservation plan that will secure Bajul's future. And I have earned the council's support."

Rafiq recognized he had been wrong to criticize Zain. "My apologies. I do appreciate your support, but I assure you I do not need a sabbatical."

"A sabbatical would allow you to assess your feelings about the situation."

Rafiq was growing weary of the interference. "My *feelings* are not significant. My duties to Bajul are of the utmost importance."

"Yet your emotional upheaval has understandably begun to affect your leadership. Grieving requires time, Rafiq. You have not allowed yourself enough for that."

He had grieved more than anyone would know. "It has been six months. Life must continue as planned."

Zain whisked a hand through his dark hair. "Plans go awry, brother, and life sometimes comes to a standstill. You have suffered a great loss and if you choose not to acknowledge that, you will only suffer more."

He could no longer suffer through this conversation. "I prefer not to discuss it further, so if you will excuse me—"

The sound of footfalls silenced Rafiq and drew his attention to Zain's blonde American bride walking toward them, a round-faced, dark-haired infant propped on one hip. He immediately noticed the happiness reflected in his sister-in-law's face and the obvious adoration in her blue eyes when she met Zain's gaze. "I have a baby girl who insists on being with her daddy."

Zain presented a warm smile. "And her father is more than happy to accommodate her."

After Madison handed the infant to Zain, she drew Rafiq into an embrace. "It's good to see you, my dear brother-in-law."

"And you, Madison," he said. "You are looking well, as usual. I would never have known you had given birth." Ironically, only a few days after he had buried his wife.

She pushed her somewhat disheveled hair back and blushed. "Thank you. Elena told me to tell you that she'll see you as soon as she has Joseph in bed. She seems to be able to calm our son better than anyone, but then after raising the Mehdi boys, she's had quite a bit of experience."

Zain moved closer to Rafiq and regarded his child. "Cala, this is your uncle Rafiq. And yes, we do favor each other, except for that goatee, but I am much more handsome."

Rafiq experienced sheer sadness at the sound of his mother's name that his brother had given his daughter.

The mother he had barely known yet still revered. "She is a beautiful child, Zain. Congratulations."

"Do you wish to hold your niece?" Zain asked.

If he dared, he risked destroying the emotional fortress he had built for protection. "Perhaps later. At the moment I have some documents to review." He leaned and kissed Madison's cheek. "You have honored my brother by giving him the greatest of gifts. For that, I am grateful."

Needing to escape, Rafiq strode across the veranda, only to be halted by Zain, who handed the child back to Madison and followed him to the door. "Wait, Rafiq."

He reluctantly faced his brother again. "What is it now?"

Zain rested a hand on Rafiq's shoulder. "I understand why it would be difficult to discuss anything involving emotional issues with your siblings. For that reason, I believe you should seek out a friend who understands you better than most."

He could only recall one soul who would currently meet that requirement, and they had not interacted as friends in quite some time. "If you are referring to Shamil Barad, he is away while the resort is being renovated."

"I am referring to his sister, Maysa."

The name sent a spear of regret through Rafiq's heart, and a rush of memories into his mind. He recalled the way her long, dark hair cascaded down her back and fell below her waist. The deep creases in her cheeks that framed her beautiful smile. He remembered the way she had looked that long-ago night when they had made love—their greatest mistake. He also remembered the pain in her brown eyes the day he had told her they could never be together. "I have not spoken with Maysa at length in many years. She severed all ties when—"

"You chose Rima Acar over her?"

He did not care to defend the decision, but he would. "I was not consulted when the agreement between our fathers was made."

Zain rubbed his shaded jaw. "Ah, yes. I believe Sheikh Acar trumped Maysa's father's offer during the bridal bartering. I also recall that you did nothing to plead your case. You never attempted to convince either party that you belonged with Maysa."

And he had regretted that decision more than once. "In accordance with tradition, it was not within my power to do so."

Zain's expression turned to stone. "A tradition that forced me to choose between my royal duty and my wife. An antiquated custom that has done nothing but lead to your misery, and Maysa's, as well. The choice the sultan made for Maysa resulted in divorce and nearly ruined her, and you were anything but happy with your queen."

Anger as hot as a firebrand shot through Rafiq. "You know nothing about my relationship with Rima."

"I know what I witnessed when I saw the two of you together." Zain studied him for a long moment. "Were you happy, Rafiq? Was Rima happy?"

He could not answer truthfully without confirming Zain's conjecture. "I cared a great deal for Rima. We were friends long before we wed. Her death has been difficult for me, whether you choose to believe that or not."

"My apologies for sounding insensitive," Zain said.

"As I told you earlier, it's very apparent you are in great turmoil, which brings me back to my suggestion you talk with Maysa. She will understand."

Perhaps so, but other issues still existed. "Even if she agreed to see me, which I suspect she will not, any liaison with Maysa would not be considered acceptable. She is divorced and I have been widowed for only a brief time."

Zain's frustration came out in a scowl. "First of all, I am only suggesting you speak with her, not wed her. Second, if you are concerned that someone will assume an affair, then steal away in the night to prevent detection. It has always worked to my advantage. Should you need assistance, I will be glad to make the arrangements."

He had no doubt Zain could. His brother had made covert disappearance an art form. "I do not need your assistance, nor do I plan to see Maysa."

"Do not dismiss it completely, Rafiq. She could be the one person to see you through this difficult phase."

At one time, that would have held true. Maysa had known him better than any living soul, understood him better, and she had been a welcome source of support during their formative years. She had also been his greatest weakness, and he had been her greatest disappointment.

For that reason, he should stay away from her. Yet as he left his brother's company and returned to his quarters, alone with his continuing guilt, he began to wonder if perhaps Zain might be right. Reconnecting with Maysa again, if only for a brief time, could very well be worth the risks.

* * *

As the village's primary physician, Maysa Barad answered the midnight summons expecting a messenger requesting she tend to an ailing child or a mother in labor. She did not expect to find Rafiq Mehdi, the recently crowned—and newly widowed—King of Bajul. Her childhood friend. Her first love. Her first lover.

The changes in Rafiq were somewhat apparent, but subtle. He was still tall and lean. Still as incredibly handsome as he'd always been, despite that he now chose to wear a neatly trimmed goatee framing his sensual mouth. His eyes and hair were still as dark, much the same as hers, yet maturity had lent him an even greater aura of power. A power that had crushed her resolve on more than one occasion many years before.

She could not remember the last time he had called on her. She couldn't imagine why he was here now, but she intended to find out. "Good evening, Your Majesty. To what do I owe this pleasure?"

"I need to speak with you."

His serious tone and intense gaze prompted Maysa to press the panic button. "Are you ill?"

"No. I will explain why I am here as soon as we are in a private setting."

Maysa glanced around him to see a black car parked in the portico, and surprisingly not one of the requisite sentries. "Where are your guards?"

"At the palace. Only select members of my staff know I am here."

Being completely alone with him somewhat concerned Maysa. She considered asking him to return in the morning, when she was appropriately dressed, well rested and better prepared. However, he was still the king and his wish would have to be her command, an all too familiar concept. During their youth, she would have done anything he asked of her. One fateful night, she had.

Despite all the concerns racing through her mind, and the threat to her composure, she opened the door wide to allow him entry. "I suppose you may come in for a while."

After Rafiq stepped into the foyer, Maysa closed and locked the door, then faced him to find his dark, pensive gaze leveled on hers. "I sincerely appreciate your willingness to see me at this hour," he said without a hint of familiarity.

She sincerely questioned the wisdom in allowing him in her home. "You are welcome. Follow me."

Maysa led him down the corridor and paused when one of the staff appeared from around the corner. She waved the befuddled woman away and continued past the myriad rooms comprising the expansive house belonging to her father, and on loan to her. The same house where she'd gone from teenager to woman in her childhood bed, courtesy of the man walking behind her.

Once they reached her private living area, she shut the door and gestured toward the settee. "Feel free to be seated."

"I prefer to stand," he said as he began to pace the room like a caged tiger, his hands firmly planted in the pockets of his black slacks.

Maysa dropped down onto the sofa, curled her legs beneath her and adjusted the aqua caftan to where it covered her bare feet. She chose to continue to speak in English, should one of the staff decide to eavesdrop. "What can I do for you, Rafiq?"

He stopped to stare out the window overlooking the mountains. "I could not sleep. I've had difficulty sleeping since…"

"The accident," she said when his words trailed away. The mysterious, single-car accident that had claimed the queen's life six months ago. "Insomnia and restlessness are understandable. Rima's death was tragic and unexpected. If you would like me to prescribe a sleep aid, I would certainly be willing to do that."

He turned toward her, some unnamed emotion in his near-black eyes. "I do not wish a pill, Maysa. I wish to go back to that night and find a way to prevent my wife's death. I want to find some peace."

His feelings for his queen apparently were much deeper than Maysa had realized. "It takes time to recover from losing someone you cared about, Rafiq."

"It has been six months," he said. "And I did not care enough, which directly contributed to her demise."

Evidently she had made an erroneous assumption. It seemed Rafiq's marriage to Rima Acar had been little more than a long-standing agreement between their patriarchs. Yet she didn't understand why he blamed himself for her death. "You weren't driving the car, Rafiq."

He crossed the room and joined her on the opposite end of the small settee. "But I did drive her away that night."

She wasn't certain she wanted to hear the details, but since he'd decided to take her into his confidence for the first time in years, she chose to listen. "Did you argue before she left?"

He lowered his head and streaked his palms over his face, as if to erase the bitter memories. "Yes, immediately after she informed me she was with child."

Rima's pregnancy had been kept from the press, but the revelation came as no surprise to Maysa. Unbeknownst to the king, the queen had come to her for confirmation instead of consulting the palace physician, though she never quite understood why. Rima had always been aware of Maysa's close relationship with Rafiq, at times pitting them as rivals. "Were you not happy to hear the news?"

"I was pleased to know I would have an heir. She was not at all pleased to be having my child."

Maysa had witnessed Rima's distress when she'd delivered the results, but she had attributed that to slight shock. "She told you that?"

He released a rough sigh. "Not in so many words, but I sensed her unhappiness. When I questioned her at length, she did not deny it. She disappeared some time later without my knowledge."

Maysa experienced a measure of satisfaction that he'd chosen to release his burden and a good deal of guilt over what she'd chosen to withhold from him. She suspected she knew where the queen had been before the accident, though she had no solid proof. "Do you know where she might have been going when she left?"

His expression remained somber. "No, and I most likely will never know. I do know if I had been kinder to her, then perhaps she would not have felt the need to leave."

She offered him the only advice she could give him at the moment. Advice she had been forced to follow since the day he'd told her he would be marrying another, shattering her dreams of a future with him. "Rafiq, you can spend a lifetime wondering what might have been, or you can move on with your life."

"I told Zain only hours ago that I intended to proceed with my life," he said. "I did not admit the difficulty in that. To him, or until recently, myself."

"It would be nice if your brother were here during this trying time."

Rafiq kept his gaze trained on the floor. "He arrived in Bajul today with Madison and their children."

She realized having the children around could be the basis for his lack of enthusiasm and distress. "That must be very difficult for you."

He finally looked at her. "Why would you believe I would not welcome my brother's family?"

She laid a hand on his arm. "Of course you would, but being in the presence of two infants might remind you of your recent loss."

"I can handle that, but I cannot abide Zain's advice. He is convinced I need a sabbatical."

"Perhaps he is right. Time away would aid in the healing process."

He frowned. "He is wrong. I only need time to adjust. I can accomplish that and still tend to my duties."

As far as she was concerned, he was overestimating his strength. "Does Zain know you're here?"

"Yes. He insisted I talk with you."

Maysa's hopes had been dashed once more. "I thought perhaps you came on your own."

"I would never have thought to bother you," he said.

"It's no bother, Rafiq. I considered visiting you after the funeral, but I wasn't at all certain I would be welcome."

He looked at her somberly, sincerely. "You will always be welcome in my world, Maysa."

The memory hit her full force then. The memory of a time when he'd spoken those same words to her.

No matter what the future holds, you will always be welcome in my world, habibti....

Yet she had not been welcome at all. After his marriage contract had been finalized, they had been expressly forbidden to see each other, yet they had continued to meet in secret. Those clandestine trysts had only fueled the fire between them until one night, they had made love the first—and the last—time.

Maysa wondered if Rafiq remembered. She wondered if he recalled those remarkable moments, or if he had pushed them out of his thoughts. She wondered why she had been such a fool to believe he would have changed his mind about marrying Rima.

She rose to her feet and crossed the room to pour a glass of water from a pitcher set out on a side table. She kept her back to Rafiq as she took a few sips, and swallowed hard when she heard approaching footsteps.

"Have I said something to upset you, Maysa?"

His presence upset her. Her feelings for him upset her. She set the glass on the table and turned to him. "Why are you really here, Rafiq? Why have you come to me after all these years?"

His expression reflected confusion. "You are the one person I have always turned to for solace."

"Not always," she said. "We've been virtual strangers for well over a decade."

His expression implied building anger. "You were the one who left Bajul for the States, Maysa. I have always been here."

"I had no choice after I divorced Boutros."

"A man you should have never wed."

A heartless, angry sultan who had almost stolen her sense of self-worth and security. Almost. "As it was with you and Rima, my marriage was no more than an edict from my father."

Rafiq inclined his head and studied her. "Why did you risk your name and reputation to divorce him?"

She did not dare tell him the entire truth. "He refused to allow me to pursue my profession. I refused to allow him to tell me how to live my life."

He looked as if he could see right through her. "That is the only reason?"

"Isn't that enough? And what other reason would there be?"

Now he appeared cynical. "Everyone is quite aware of Boutros Kassab's reputation for suspect business arrangements and questionable connections."

She would simply allow him to believe that rather than reveal the harsh reality—Boutros was a sadistic, uncaring lecher. "I was eighteen when we married, Rafiq. I had no involvement in his business dealings. I was only required to play the dutiful wife."

He raised a brow. "In his bed?"

She hesitated slightly. "Do you wish me to lie and say no?"

"He is thirty years your senior. I hoped you would say he had little interest in anything of a carnal nature due to an inability to perform."

Many nights she had wished that had only been the case, but it had not. "Boutros is a man, and men rarely lose interest in sex, no matter what their age."

"Did he satisfy you, Maysa?"

She was momentarily stunned. "That is none of your concern."

He streamed a fingertip down her cheek. "I am only curious if he knew how to please you. If he learned, as I did, how to make you tremble with need."

She circled her arms around her middle as if that might afford her protection from his magnetic pull. From the memories. "Did Rima satisfy you, Rafiq? Or did you simply go to her for the sake of producing an heir?" The moment the words left her mouth, she silently cursed her thoughtlessness.

Rafiq reacted by turning away, crossing the room and moving to the window to stare at the mountains once more. She approached him slowly and rested a palm on his shoulder. "I am so sorry, Rafiq. I did not mean to be so unkind. I know how much you are hurting over the loss of your child. I also know that you did care very much for your wife, and you were a good husband to her. You would never ignore her needs."

"And in doing so, I was forced to disregard what I needed most."

"And that was?"

"You."

Without warning, Rafiq spun around and crushed Maysa against him. He claimed her mouth with a vengeance, with a touch of desperation. And as she always had, she willingly accepted the kiss.

She hated that he could so easily mold her into a willing, wanton woman, but not quite enough to stop him. She despised herself for wanting to give in to the ever-present desire. To do so could lead to undeniable pleasure, and quite possibly disaster. He didn't necessarily want her. He only wanted comfort wherever available, as it had been all those years ago. And that made her furious enough to recapture her common sense.

With all the strength she could muster, Maysa moved back, putting some much-needed distance between them. "How many women were there after me and prior to your marriage to Rima?"

Confusion crossed over his expression. "Why does that matter?"

"Perhaps you could call on one of them to provide the escape you so obviously need."

His handsome features turned to stone. "You truly believe that is all you mean to me?"

She folded her arms beneath her breasts. "Yes, I do. You're only seeking a temporary diversion, and after you receive it, you will be gone again."

"I seek the company of someone I trust. Someone I have always cared about."

"If you truly cared about me, you would not have kissed me."

"Perhaps the kiss was a mistake," he said. "Perhaps I should not have come here."

She released a disparaging laugh. "You're right. It was a mistake. Someone could find out, and that would not go over well with the elders. I am a scorned woman, remember? A divorcée and to some, the equivalent of a harlot. And let us not forget you are the almighty king."

"You have never been a harlot in my eyes," he said adamantly. "And at times I wish to forget I am the king."

The sudden dejection in his tone tugged at Maysa's heartstrings. "It sounds as if you *could* use a sabbatical."

"I have nowhere to go where I would be left alone." He fixed his gaze firmly on hers as his lips curled into the familiar teasing smile. The one that had always crushed her determination. "Unless, of course, you would be willing to open your home to me. I would keep to myself. You would not know I am here."

She would know he was there every moment of the day, whether in his presence or not. "I question the wisdom in that plan."

He took her hands into his. "I only wish for time away from my responsibilities, and to become reacquainted with a friend."

How very easy it would be to agree to his request, but… "You have no wish to become reacquainted in bed?"

"I would never ask anything of you that you are not willing to give."

That alone presented a problem—she could find herself willing to give him everything, receiving nothing in return aside from nights of pleasure and more good memories to temporarily overcome the bad. He could also break her heart once more.

Maysa tugged out of his grasp and strolled around the room, all the while weighing the pros and cons. Then something suddenly occurred to her. She could use his presence to her advantage. She could finally show him that improvements to health care for the poor should be paramount during his reign. She could introduce him to exactly what his people endured in the face of illness. And she would do so while keeping her wits about her.

After all, the guest wing was far removed from her private suites, allowing them physical distance. Aside from that, she was a strong, independent woman. She had superb skills honed at the best medical facilities in the United States. She had survived and divorced a known tyrant. She could handle a king—or so she hoped.

On that thought, she faced Rafiq again, lifted her chin, and centered her gaze on his. "All right. You may stay." When he began to speak, she held up a finger to silence him. "As long as you abide by my rules."

He sent her a suspicious look. "What would these rules entail?"

"I prefer to reserve the details for later." When she actually knew what they were.

"All right," he said. "Is there anything else you require of me tonight?"

One response vaulted into her brain. An inappropriate response that she shoved aside. "Not at this time."

Rafiq regarded his watch before bringing his attention back to her. "I must return to the palace now. We shall continue this discussion when I arrive tomorrow to begin my respite."

Tomorrow? "I thought perhaps you would need more time to make arrangements." Or to change his mind.

"I have complete control over when I stay or when I leave the palace. After all, I am—"

"The king. I know." All too well. "I'll see you out."

They walked side by side to the door where Rafiq paused and regarded her earnestly. "I am forever in your debt, Maysa, and I assure you I will give you no cause to distrust my motives."

That remained to be seen. "I'm pleased to know that. And I reserve the right to add conditions should your motives come into question."

"I will strive to win back your trust. The way you once trusted me before our lives intruded on our relationship."

Maysa wanted to believe him. More important, she wanted not to be so drawn to him. Wanted not to feel so lost when he looked at her as he looked at her now—with a heated gaze that traveled from her forehead to her mouth.

They stood for a few long moments, face-to-face, the tension as thick as the mountain mist. Maysa recognized that it would only take a slight move toward him before they found themselves lips to lips. Body to body.

She finally cleared her throat and stepped back before her resolve shattered. "Have a good night, King Mehdi. I will see you tomorrow."

"I will be here before day's end, Dr. Barad."

The formality surprised Maysa and sounded false to her ears. Yet if that formality kept her grounded, she would avoid calling him by his given name. Avoid touching him altogether. Avoid any circumstance that could lead to risks neither could afford to take. But when he leaned and brushed a soft kiss across her cheek, and presented a soft, sensual smile, she worried danger could lurk around every corner when he returned to her home.

After Rafiq opened the door and strode out of the house toward the awaiting car, Maysa considered the first rule. An important rule that could save her from herself. "Rafiq," she called before he could settle into the seat. "I have one more thing to say before you go."

He turned with a wary look on his face. "You have reconsidered?"

She hadn't, though she probably should. "No. I have thought of one rule that we both must follow."

"And that is?"

"There will be no more kisses."

He sent her a knowing smile before he slid into the car. And as Maysa watched the taillights disappear, she worried that King Rafiq Mehdi could convince her to break all the rules.

Two

No more kisses...

As Rafiq sat alone in his office, attempting to tie up loose ends, kissing Maysa remained foremost on his mind. Making love to her again did, as well. He could no more resist the fantasies than he could pick up the palace with his bare hands and move it down the mountainside.

"Have you mentally vacated the premises, brother?"

Rafiq glanced up from his desk to discover his youngest sibling standing before him, wearing his usual standard beige flight suit and mocking smile. "I am preoccupied by my duty."

"Too preoccupied to speak with me, your most loyal supporter?"

Adan rarely supported anyone aside from himself. "Unless you have something important to say, you may return later."

"I do have something of great importance to tell you," Adan said as he claimed the opposing chair.

Frustrated over the intrusion, Rafiq tossed his pen aside and leaned back in his seat. "You have found yet another aircraft you are determined to add to our fleet."

"No. I came to deliver a message."

"From whom?"

"Maysa Barad." Adan's grin widened, as if privy to a secret. "She requests that you arrive before 6:00 p.m., and that you limit your guards if at all possible."

He could only imagine where his brother's thoughts had turned. "Duly noted. You may leave now."

"Not until you explain why you are visiting Maysa, and why she would ask that you not bring along too many guards. Either she feels she does not pose a threat, or she wishes to make certain she has your undivided attention."

"What business I have with Maysa is not your concern."

"Perhaps, but I am curious."

Rafiq resisted telling his brother what he could do with his curiosity, and his British accent. "If you must know, Maysa has agreed to allow me to take a brief respite in her home."

Adan rubbed his chin. "I see. Will you be spending this respite in her bed?"

He was not at all surprised over the assumption, but he *was* angered by it. "Rest assured, I will not be attempting to bed her." Though preventing that possibility would prove to be a great challenge.

Adan released a cynical laugh. "Ah, that is where we differ. I for one would give up flying before I would not take advantage of being alone with a beautiful woman in close confines. And you should consider doing the same."

He felt the need to explain his resistance, whether Adan deserved an explanation or not. "First, I have only been widowed a short while—"

"To a woman you did not love."

"A woman I had known for quite some time before she became my wife. No matter what you believe, I did care for Rima."

"Yet not as much as you've always cared for Maysa."

His patience was beginning to grow thin, frayed in part by the truth. "Maysa is only a friend who has agreed to accommodate my needs."

"Which needs would those be, brother?" Adan asked.

"My intentions are honorable." Though his thoughts and actions the previous evening had not been at all honorable.

"How honorable will you be while spending time with a friend who at one time fancied herself in love with you?"

He could not argue that point. "What Maysa and I shared in the past had more to do with camaraderie than with love."

"Teenage lust, you mean. And that lust could quite possibly carry over into adulthood."

He had spent most of the night considering it. "I am older and wiser. I have learned to maintain self-control."

Adan presented a skeptic's smile. "You are a Mehdi male, Rafiq, and self-control can and will escape you in the presence of a woman you have always desired. You are not made of steel."

Rafiq folded his hands atop the desk and glared at his brother. "Do not project your lack of restraint on me. I have not made bedding women my favorite pastime."

"I have not had as many women as you might believe," Adan said. "And although you have practiced more discretion, I suspect you were not celibate during the time between your agreement to marry Rima and when you finally did wed her."

That fact was not up for debate. "If you are finished delving into my private life, you may take your leave immediately."

"Actually, I'm not quite finished. Did it disturb you that Rima was not a virgin when you wed her?"

Adan's audacity made Rafiq's blood boil. "Why would you assume this?"

"Are you denying it?"

Unfortunately, he could not. Yet he did question how Adan would know something so personal about Rima. He was tempted to ask, but he in turn feared the answer. "This topic is not up for discussion."

"I only wanted to point out that Rima was not destined for sainthood," Adan said. "Neither are you. In fact, you're human, and a man with needs."

The reason behind his brother's insinuation finally dawned on Rafiq. "If you are worried I will bring scandal upon the Mehdi name by sleeping with Maysa, I assure you that will not happen. And if you are also hoping that I will abandon my duty and pass the crown to you, as Zain did with me, you may set those wishes aside immediately."

Adan's expression turned suddenly serious. "I have never possessed any desire to be king, Rafiq. And as far as your relationship with Maysa is concerned, I am an advocate for letting nature take its course. If you and Maysa find you cannot resist each other, then don't. You certainly have my blessing."

Adan had failed to weigh the most important fact. If Rafiq took Maysa as his lover again, the liaison could only be temporary since he would be expected to choose a suitable queen. The thought of being with another woman aside from Maysa was unthinkable. The thought of wounding her again, unimaginable. Yet he could very well head down that path if he acted on impulse.

For that reason, perhaps he should consider canceling their arrangement. Perhaps it would be best if he found another location for his sabbatical. "I will take your counsel under advisement. Now if you do not mind, I have work to complete."

"So much work, *il mio bel ragazzo,* that you cannot give your former governess a few moments?"

Rafiq turned his attention from Adan to Elena Battelli, who now stood at the doorway, a dark-haired infant balanced on her hip. Her silver hair contrasted with her topaz eyes that at times hinted at mischief, and other times reflected wisdom. She had been the Mehdi sons' surrogate matriarch since their mother's death, and always a welcome presence. She had also been free with her opinions, and he expected no less from her now.

Rafiq came to his feet, rounded the desk and accepted her embrace. "I am glad to see you have returned home, Elena. You are looking quite well."

"You are looking tired, *cara,*" she said as she handed the baby off to an overtly surprised Adan. "Take your niece to her father and allow me some time alone with your brother."

Rising from the chair, Adan gripped the child awkwardly and looked as if he had consumed something unpalatable. "What if she begins to cry on the way?"

Elena frowned. "She would not be the first female you've made cry, so I suggest you hurry."

As soon as Adan left with the squirming infant, Rafiq seated himself behind the desk while Elena claimed the chair opposite his. She studied him for a long moment before she spoke. "What is this I hear about you spending time with Dr. Barad?"

He should not be surprised Elena would join his brothers by presenting her thoughts on the matter. Yet her opinion had always mattered most. He also suspected she would side with Zain. "It is not what you might believe it to be."

"I believe, *cara mia,* it is a good idea."

He had not predicted that reaction. "I am beginning to question the wisdom in the plan."

"Because you fear what others might think?"

Because he feared his possible absence of strength in Maysa's presence. "I do not wish to add undue stress to her life."

Elena waved a hand in dismissal. "Maysa is well equipped to handle stress, Rafiq, and perhaps even better equipped to handle you."

He was taken aback by her assertions. "What are you saying?"

"I am saying she knows you very well." Elena laid a palm on his hand. "She has always been your touchstone, and I believe you need that right now, more than you need the throne. And if you are concerned that you might succumb to inadvisable urges, I trust you to be the honorable man you have always been."

If only he could trust himself. "Then you sincerely believe I should continue with my plans?"

"Yes, I do." She rose with the grace of a gazelle. "Do not forget what I've taught you. *Chi trova un amico trova un tesoro.*"

He who finds a friend, finds a treasure.

As Elena started toward the door, she sent Rafiq a smile over one shoulder. "Maysa is your treasure, *cara.* Do not squander that gift."

Maysa had begun to believe Rafiq had changed his mind. When the doorbell chimed, she hurried down the hall to answer the summons but then slowed her steps so as not to seem too anxious, though she was. Yet when she opened the door, the bearded man on the threshold happened to be her brother, not the king. "What are you doing here, Shamil?"

"I expected a more enthusiastic greeting, considering my recent absence," he said as he breezed past her and entered without an invitation.

"My apologies," she said as she faced him in the foyer. "I'm just surprised to see you."

"Were you expecting someone else?"

She chose to withhold the truth and settled for a change in subject. "Are the resort's renovations complete?"

"No, and that is why I am here now," he said. "I will be returning to Yemen tonight, and I would respectfully request you supervise the workers from time to time in my stead."

The request did not surprise her in the least. Shamil

always seemed to have an ulterior motive when he bothered to call on her. He had protested the loudest over her divorce, and had chastised her at every turn—until he wanted something. "I have a medical practice that requires my attention, Shamil. I do not have time to oversee a project that you took on."

"Need I remind you the resort is partially your responsibility?"

She could not believe his audacity. "Our father handed the keys to the resort to you, not me."

"And he handed this house to you," he said as he made a sweeping gesture over the area. "All because he is a generous and forgiving man. I would be remiss if I did not mention that he initially arranged for the hotel's restoration. I am certain it would please him if he knew you were assisting me. He would not be pleased if he learned you refused to provide that assistance."

Maysa was beyond trying to please her father, and immune to Shamil's veiled threats. "I can only promise that I will stop by once a week, provided I find the time."

"Twice a week, or perhaps three times, would be preferable."

She would agree to most anything if it encouraged her sibling's speedy departure. "I will try. Is that all you wish from me?"

"For the moment. I will notify the staff you will be periodically stopping by."

"All right."

When Maysa moved toward the door and yanked it open, she heard the sound of a car pulling into the portico.

"What is *he* doing here?" Shamil asked, both his tone and expression balanced on the brink of contempt.

She ventured a backward glance to see Rafiq emerging from the sedan with a heavily armed guard standing nearby. "First of all, he is the king, and he is allowed to go anywhere he pleases. Second, he is a friend, and at one time, your best friend."

"He no longer holds that distinction."

Maysa's attempt to question her brother further was thwarted when Rafiq joined them at the doorstep.

Rafiq smiled at Maysa and briefly nodded at Shamil. *"As-salam alaikum."*

"Wa alaikum as-salam," Shamil replied in a voice that heralded indifference along with a touch of disdain. "Have you forgotten the way to the palace, Sayyed?"

"Not at all," Rafiq replied. "I am here by invitation."

Shamil sent Maysa a lethal look before returning his attention to Rafiq. "If you are here to discuss health care issues with my sister, it would be appropriate to do so in a less private setting."

Concerned over her brother's caustic demeanor, Maysa stepped aside to allow Rafiq entry. "The staff will show you to your quarters, Your Highness."

"As you wish," he said without offering Shamil even a passing glance.

She sensed her brother's glare before she actually contacted it. She turned and gave him a glare of her own. "How dare you be so ill-mannered."

"How dare you invite him into our father's house."

"Our father has always had close ties to the Mehdi family," Maysa said. "He would not be opposed to having a member as a houseguest, particularly if that member happens to be the sovereign ruler of Bajul. A king who is in need of a respite, which is why he will be staying here for a time."

"Our father would be opposed to you becoming the king's mistress."

Her fury simmered just below the surface of her feigned calm. "You have no right to speak to me this way, nor do you have any reason to hate Rafiq. Or do you still envy his marriage to Rima?"

He looked as if he might strike the wall, or worse, his sister. "Rima meant nothing to Rafiq," he growled. "He did not deserve her."

Clearly Shamil had not moved beyond the past, or his desire for a woman he could never have. But hadn't she been guilty of the same with Rafiq? No. She had moved on, and would continue to do so. "How would you know what privately transpired between the king and queen, Shamil?"

"She deserved far more care and concern than Rafiq afforded her. She deserved the chance to live, and he stole that chance from her."

"Rafiq had no hand in Rima's death."

"You would not agree if you had seen her that night."

Maysa felt as if they might be hurling toward the truth of what had transpired that evening. What she herself had witnessed. "Perhaps I did see her after all."

That seemed to momentarily douse Shamil's wrath. "Where would you have seen her?"

"I drove to the resort earlier that evening and when I saw you embracing a woman on the veranda, I immediately left. Am I correct to assume that woman was Rima?" When he failed to respond, she added, "Shamil, was it Rima?"

His gaze faltered. "She was there for a brief time."

"And how many times before that?"

"That is not your concern."

Oh, but it was. "Were the two of you having an affair?"

"Enough!"

She'd obviously struck a nerve encased in the truth. "And Rafiq knew nothing about your liaison with his wife."

"Rafiq knew nothing about Rima's life because he chose not to know." He sent her a steely look. "And he will never know. Is that understood?"

One more threat among many. "He has a right to know what happened in the minutes leading up to her death."

"He gave up all rights to that knowledge when he discarded her feelings and deprived her of freedom. And if you utter one word of this conversation to the king, then I will see to it you are removed from this house and I will make certain your reputation is ruined beyond repair."

She clung tightly to the last thread of civility. "You do not have that much power, Shamil. You never have. I can find another place to live, and the villagers respect me not only as their doctor, but as a person. They care not about my past."

He narrowed his eyes and stared at her. "Will they be so accepting if they learn their doctor is also the king's *sharmuta?*"

She pointed a shaky finger at the SUV parked at the end of the drive. "Leave now and do not return unless you arrive with an apology."

He released a bitter laugh. "Oh, I will return, yet I

will not rescind what I have said. If you reveal any details to Rafiq, there will be consequences."

With that, he rushed to the waiting SUV and drove away, leaving Maysa standing on the threshold, worrying over how she would tell Rafiq about his wife's whereabouts that fateful evening. *If* she decided to tell him.

Should she confess, the outcome would still be the same. Rima would still be gone, her secrets following her to the grave. Shamil would be bent on ruining Maysa's life if she told Rafiq the details. She had very limited loyalty to Shamil, but she possessed enough common sense not to risk losing everything she had worked so hard to build. Yet the thought of keeping such a serious secret from Rafiq fueled her guilt.

Fortunately, she would not be forced to choose which course to take in the immediate future. Right now, her focus would be on making Rafiq feel welcome.

She seemed uncomfortable. Rafiq noticed that about Maysa during dinner, and now as they relaxed on rattan sofas in the private courtyard beneath the night sky. Regardless that she seemed on edge, she still looked beautiful as she sat with her legs curled to one side, revealing her bare feet and a delicate silver chain circling one ankle that matched the heavy bangles at her wrists. Her long, dark hair cascaded over her slim shoulders, strands of amber highlighted by the moon, and the sleeveless white gauze dress she wore contrasted with the golden cast of her skin. He remembered touching that skin during a time when they had both been completely captivated by one another. So hungry for each other that it seemed they might never be sated—until the one and only night they crossed the forbidden line and made love.

She captivated him still, fed a fire that he had wrongly assumed would be extinguished by time, mistakes and regrets. He wanted to leave the sofa he had claimed and take the space beside her. He wished to do more than only sit with her. Yet her moratorium on kissing left him with only one option—remain where he sat and simply admire her from afar.

Maysa sighed, her attention focused on the jasmine lining the edge of the stone terrace. "I love summer evenings."

He loved the sound of her voice—soft, lyrical. "You have lost most of your accent."

She smiled, deepening the dimples creasing her cheeks. "The time I spent in the States is responsible for that."

"Do you still know how to speak our native tongue?"

She frowned. "Of course I still know how. I have to communicate with my patients here."

He thought of one question he had wanted to ask. "Why did you return to Bajul to practice medicine knowing how you would be treated following your divorce?"

Her gaze wandered away as she began twisting the bracelets around her right wrist. "Bajul is my home, Rafiq, and since Boutros lives elsewhere, it seemed logical to return. I also missed the quiet pace and the peaceful existence."

"You do not seem at peace tonight," he said. "Is something bothering you?"

She shifted slightly and finally raised her gaze to

his. "Actually, yes. I'm concerned about the lack of care for the poorest in Bajul."

"It is my understanding you are an excellent doctor, therefore they are receiving the finest care."

"But I'm only one person, Rafiq. Other physicians could assist, yet they refuse. They only provide services to those who can pay. It's a travesty."

He understood her frustration, yet he had no solution. "I cannot force other physicians to work for no pay."

"But you could see to it that newer doctors are enticed to come here to fill in the gaps."

He leaned back and set his glass of mango juice on the adjacent table. "How do you propose I do this?"

"By offering government-sponsored grants."

"Our current funds are earmarked for the water conservation efforts. We have no surplus to devote to anything else at this time."

"Then perhaps sell one of the new military planes Adan has recently acquired. It would seem you have more than enough for a country the size of Bajul."

"At times it seems we do not have enough to bolster our defense. But I will take your suggestions into consideration."

He noted a spark of anger in her dark, almond-shaped eyes. "That is all you have to say?"

"Maysa, I am only one voice on the council."

"You are the supreme voice, King Mehdi. You have the last word."

He had less power than she realized. "I must do what the majority dictates to keep the peace."

"At the expense of your people?"

"Again, I will consider your concerns and present

them to the council when it is time to prepare the next budget."

She straightened her legs, planted her feet on the ground, and seared him with a glare. "That is over five months away. People could die before then, both elderly adults and children. Mothers with difficult births."

He did not have the means to accommodate her at this time, yet he could not disappoint her. "I will see what I can do, though I can make no promises."

"I suppose that is enough," she said, her expression somewhat more relaxed. "At least for the time being."

Fatigue began to set in, yet Rafiq could not force himself to leave her. He also could not rid himself of the slight pain resulting from an injury he'd suffered in his youth. He lifted the shoulder slightly, once, twice, before he settled back against the cushions.

"It still bothers you, doesn't it?" Maysa asked.

He was not surprised she had noticed. "What bothers me?"

"Your shoulder. The one you fractured in that ridiculous fight with Aakif Nejem."

"I believe we were fighting over you." He smiled. "And I came away with two black eyes and a lacerated lip. I would have been unscathed had it not been for my falling against the iron gate."

Maysa returned his smile, though she appeared to be attempting to keep it at bay. "The very gate you drove through earlier, designed by my father to ward off unwelcome suitors."

"Yet that gate was not strong enough to keep me from you that night."

A brief span of silence passed between them, as well as an exchanged glance that Rafiq remembered very clearly. The same knowing look they had given each other when he had laid her down in her bed, cloaked only by the cover of darkness, the threat of discovery heightening their desire.

Maysa broke the visual contact first and turned her focus back on the flowers. "That was a long time ago, Rafiq. We were both young and very foolish."

"We were consumed by each other."

She raised a thin brow. "Consumed by lust, you mean."

Had it only been lust, he would have long forgotten that evening. Forgotten her. "Have you never considered what would have happened had your father come upon us?"

"Would he have forced us to marry?" She shook her head. "He would have sent me away from you."

In many ways, that is exactly what had happened. The sultan had sent her into another man's bed. A man who had not deserved her.

When Maysa hid a yawn behind her hand, then stretched her arms above her head, Rafiq suspected she would soon be leaving him again, at least for the evening. "It is time for me to go to bed," she said, confirming his theory. "I have several early visits to make in the village tomorrow."

He struggled for some way to keep her there awhile longer, and returned to the issue that had begun their journey into the past. "Would you examine my shoulder before you retire?"

"What do you believe I'd accomplish by doing that?"

She would be closer to him, at least momentarily. He pressed his palm against the spot that always gave him the most pain. "I would like to see what you think about this ridge. Perhaps you can advise me if it is an issue I need to have evaluated further."

She sighed, rose from the sofa and took the space beside him. "Lean forward." After he complied, she rested her left hand on his left shoulder and examined the offending shoulder with her right hand.

"Well?" he asked.

She pushed against one spot, causing him to wince. "Does that hurt?" she asked.

"Slightly." More than he would allow her to see.

"That's your deltoid muscle," she said as she continued to knead the area. "You have quite a bit of tension there."

The tension behind his fly began to increase with every caress of her fingertips. "Perhaps it is only stress-induced?"

"Perhaps, but I cannot tell for certain without an X-ray. You could probably benefit from physical therapy."

The therapy she was offering him now was quite beneficial in terms of soothing the soreness. He could not say the same for his libido. And when she leaned over and applied more pressure, his palm automatically came to rest on her thigh, immediately above her knee, where he drew small circles with his thumb through the dress's thin material.

Her hand froze midmotion. "What are you doing, Rafiq?"

"Nothing." Not presently.

She released a shuddering breath. "We said no touching."

He inched his palm higher. "You said no kissing."

"Rule two, no touching."

Despite her assertions, he did not bother to lift his hand, and she did not bother to shove it away. "Yet you have been touching me."

"As a physician."

"And I have reacted as any man reacts to a woman's touch."

"For that reason, I should go now."

Rafiq predicted she would stand and leave, but she remained positioned next to him, both hands still resting lightly on his shoulders. He straightened, bringing their faces close, their gazes connecting immediately. He saw the indecision in her eyes, as well as a spark of need.

And then Maysa did something Rafiq did not expect—she broke her first rule.

Three

She had taken complete leave of her senses, but at the moment Maysa didn't care. She only concerned herself with the play of Rafiq's mouth against hers and the impressions he made with the gentle glide of his tongue.

At some point—and she had no idea how or when— he had shifted toward her and she had moved fully into his arms. A nagging voice demanded she stop before she could not, but she disregarded the caution. For once she wanted to be softly kissed, without undue force. Willingly kissed. She wanted to remember how it felt to be a desirable woman, not simply an object of brutal lust.

Yet all the reasons why she shouldn't be doing this kept crowding her mind. She could be only a means to an end for Rafiq. A source of comfort. A temporary diversion. She was also keeping a secret from him. A secret that could ultimately destroy him emotionally, and her reputation literally.

Still, when he cupped her breast, she focused on the sensations, not solid rationale. He traced her nipple with a fingertip, causing her to shift restlessly against the building heat. But when he left her mouth to feather kisses down the column of her throat, sliding the dress's strap down her shoulder, a barrage of bitter memories prompted her to automatically tense.

Rafiq reacted to her sudden change in mood by abruptly rising from the sofa, leaving Maysa alone steeped in self-consciousness. He walked away, his hands laced behind his neck, and stopped in the middle of the terrace, keeping his back to her.

"I'm sorry," Maysa muttered as she readjusted her clothing. "I have no idea what has come over me. We shouldn't be doing this." She'd begun to wonder if she could do it, even if she wanted to.

Rafiq dropped his arms to his sides and faced her again. "I am not sorry, yet I am convinced this will keep happening between us."

So was Maysa, unless she revealed the absolute truth behind her reluctance. She wasn't willing to do that. "We'll simply need to avoid situations such as this. Following dinner each evening, I will return to my quarters, and you will return to yours. We will keep our distance during the day, as well."

He shifted his weight slightly. "And I will lie awake all night, imagining how it would be to touch you with my hands and my mouth in ways I never did when we were younger. I will dream about how it would feel to be buried deep inside you. And each time I see you, I will want the reality."

The heat returned, prompting Maysa to cross her legs. "Then perhaps it would be best if you found another place for your respite."

"I care not to be anywhere else."

Truthfully, she didn't want him to leave, either. "Then I suppose you will be forced to rely solely on your imagination."

"Or we could both choose not to fight our desire. No one would know if we became lovers again."

How very easy it would be to agree. How very foolish if she did. "I would know, Rafiq. Nothing could ever exist between us beyond temporary physical pleasure. You are the king, and I am a woman who most believe is unfit to keep company with you, let alone be your lover."

He rubbed a palm over his nape. "Again, we could be discreet. We could enjoy each other during the time we have."

The fact he didn't say she wasn't unsuitable was as effective as a frigid shower. Maysa stood, hands fisted at her sides, nails digging into her palms. "I have already been one man's whore, Rafiq. I will not be another's."

"I am prisoner to tradition and acceptable mores, Maysa, as are you. Yet that does not mean I would view you as my *sharmuta*."

"Yet that is exactly what I would be to you, a woman not fit to be your queen, yet expected to do your bidding in bed. Answer your every need, yet receive nothing in return, as it was with Boutrous. That would make me your mistress."

Maysa expected to see anger in Rafiq's expression,

but he only seemed concerned. "What did Boutros do to you, Maysa?"

"This has nothing to do with him." Only a partial truth. "This has to do with us. I have developed a great deal of self-respect during our time apart. I am not that smitten schoolgirl who would have given everything to you, knowing I could never have a future with you."

He released a rough sigh. "What do you wish me to say, Maysa?"

That he would tell the elders to go to hell. That she was an acceptable partner by virtue of her intelligence and skills, not her past. That he would make an effort to change the archaic laws governing the role of women. "Nothing, Rafiq. I wish for you to say nothing. You have already said it all."

When she turned to retire to her room, Rafiq called her back. "I would rather die a thousand deaths than to wound you again, Maysa."

And she would experience a thousand more regrets if she gave in to the sincerity in his dark eyes. "Then don't, Rafiq. Be my friend."

He approached her slowly. "I am your friend. That has never changed, despite the distance between us."

Before she made another monumental mistake and walked back into his arms, Maysa left the terrace and returned to her quarters. And once she was safely in bed, she let herself imagine what it would be like to make love with him again, too. Yet the fantasies could never replace the reality. But the reality was she'd invited him here for a reason, and tomorrow she would begin to implement her plan. And with that plan came the opportunity to educate a king. The beautiful, sensual king of her heart.

* * *

Shirtless, Rafiq faced the double-paned window overlooking the veranda, allowing Maysa a premiere view from the partially open door. The strong planes of his broad shoulders, broken by a slight scar on his right, demonstrated he was still as physically fit as he'd always been. The indentation of his spine tracked into the waistband of his navy pajamas, surrounded by supple, golden skin. And below that, narrow hips and a toned buttocks looked quite touchable.

But she wouldn't touch him. Not today. She had more pressing matters at hand, provided he cooperated.

Maysa moved quietly into the room, several items of clothing clutched in her arms. "Did you sleep well?"

If he was at all startled by her appearance, he didn't show it. He simply turned and presented a half smile. "I slept as well as can be expected in a strange bed alone, knowing that a desirable woman is such a short distance away."

She disregarded the innuendo, but she could not seem to keep her eyes off the downward stream of masculine hair below his navel, or that he seemed quite pleased to see her from an anatomical standpoint. "Well," she said as she forced her gaze to his dark eyes, "I hope you are sufficiently rested since I have plans for us today."

"Plans?" He rounded the foot of the bed and stood a few feet from her. "What do these plans entail?"

"I am traveling to the Diya region and I want you to come with me."

He frowned. "That is over two hours away."

"Yes, and I make the journey every Wednesday to

treat the sheep farmers and their families. Today is Wednesday."

"Why would you wish me to accompany you?"

"Because I believe it's important you begin to understand the health care issues facing your country, including the lack of resources in remote areas."

He appeared to mull that over before he spoke again. "The people of Diya never supported my father. It has been reported several possible insurgency camps exist there."

"Perhaps they did not embrace being ignored by your father," she said. "You could change that."

He strolled around the room for a moment before turning to her again. "Would we be able to communicate by cell phone with the outside world?"

She rolled her eyes. "There are no cellular towers. The villagers only recently received regular phone service, and many do not have electricity. Some do not have adequate water supplies."

"If I accompany you, I would require a contingent of guards for both our protection should I be recognized."

"Not if you are unrecognizable." She tossed him the army-green shirt and cargo pants. "If you put these on and wear sunglasses, no one will know a king walks among them."

He unfolded the clothes and inspected them. "I doubt a change of attire would serve as an adequate disguise."

"If you wear sunglasses and shave, that should suffice."

He laughed. A deep, low, sensual laugh that sent chills down the length of Maysa's body. "I have no intention of shaving."

"Your goatee will grow back, Rafiq. Most likely in two days' time."

He leveled his gaze on her. "Is it that important I join you?"

"Yes, and it should be important to you. A good ruler knows his people. Especially the poor and less fortunate."

He sighed. "All right. I will do this for you, but I still believe it is necessary to bring along a guard."

"That isn't necessary. I've traveled the terrain many times and I have yet to encounter any trouble. I also travel with a firearm should I need it."

His grin arrived slowly. "Do you know how to use it?"

She returned his smile. "I'm certain I could shoot straight should the situation arise. So rest assured, as long as you are with me, your royal body will be safe."

"You are willing to take my royal body into your own hands?"

Ignoring the suggestive words, she pointed at the clothes. "Dress, Your Majesty. I'll meet you at the back entrance to the house."

His smile disappeared. "And I will drive."

"No, you will not."

With that, she flipped her hair over one shoulder and left the room to prepare for the journey. With a reluctant king in tow, it could prove to be quite an adventure.

Rafiq had always known Maysa to have an adventurous spirit. He had seen her take risks most women would not dare undertake. Yet he had never seen her dressed as she was now. She wore a long-sleeved white blouse covered by a white laboratory coat, as well as khaki pants and a pair of heavy boots. Her official apparel concealed her feminine attributes, yet her absence of makeup did not take away from her natural beauty. He knew exactly what existed beneath the clothing— full breasts, round bottom, soft skin.

While Rafiq's discomfort began to grow, Maysa looked entirely comfortable behind the wheel of the Hummer, navigating the rugged terrain with practiced ease. He, on the other hand, was sweltering due to the August sun and in part due to his inability to take his eyes off Maysa. Since last evening, he had not been able to escape the memory of her kiss. Could not erase the images of what he wanted to do with her. To her. But he also could not forget her reaction to his touch, as if she had been somewhat repulsed.

He streaked a hand over his forehead and took a drink of water from the canteen she had brought along. "How much farther?"

"We're almost there," she said, keeping her eyes trained on the dirt road. "Over the mountain."

As soon as they topped the rise, Maysa continued down the incline past a tribesman herding sheep and several young boys playing barefoot along the path. Once they arrived in the primitive town, she pulled in front of a large canvas tent where several people had gathered around the opening.

After Maysa shut off the ignition and climbed out, Rafiq remained seated to observe the interaction between doctor and villagers. Women, men and children converged upon her, shouting greetings and presenting smiles that she returned.

After a time, she managed to make her way to the passenger door to address him. "Keep your sunglasses on at all times," she said in a low voice. "I will tell everyone you're from the States and you do not speak Arabic. In fact, it's best if you do not speak at all."

That could take effort. "If that is what you wish."

She favored him with a smile. "And by the way, I like you better clean-shaven."

His hand immediately went to his bare chin. "Be that as it may, I will begin growing it back as soon as we are finished with this adventure. Otherwise, someone might mistake me for my brother."

She pulled a stethoscope from the pocket of the lab coat and draped it around her neck. "Do what you will, Rafiq, but take it from a woman. Kissing a man with a beard is not always comfortable." With that, she rounded the SUV while Rafiq remained to ponder her words. Did she intend to let him kiss her again? One could always hope.

Rafiq slid out of the Hummer and joined Maysa at the rear to haul the large supply trunk into the tent while she carried a smaller medical kit. She signaled him to be seated in a rattan chair in the corner of the tent and pressed a fingertip to her lips, reminding him to be silent, as if he were an errant schoolboy. She then went to work, tending to the villagers with both speed and skill. She periodically handed out treats to the children and advice to worried mothers. Several men stood nearby, eyeing Rafiq with suspicion and occasionally watching Maysa with lust. He could not blame them though he did not care for their leers. Yet defending the physician's honor would most likely incur the physician's wrath.

As Rafiq continued to witness Maysa deliver her expert ministrations, he experienced a sense of pride, though he had no right. He had never discouraged her from entering the medical field, but he had not encouraged her, either. He had always believed she would be destined to abandon her dreams for the life of a sultan's wife. But she had bravely defied convention and custom, and had suffered severe consequences for her choices.

Watching her care for these downtrodden people, receiving their adoration and appreciation, Rafiq realized that perhaps she had not suffered as much as one would believe. Perhaps she was living the life she was meant to live. A life without him.

A commotion coming from the tent's entrance drew his attention. A young man elbowed his way through the awaiting crowd, shouting, *"Tâbeeb!"*

When he rushed toward Maysa, Rafiq immediately shot to his feet to intervene. Maysa gave him a quelling look as she took the farmer aside and spoke to him quietly.

He could not hear most of the conversation, but he understood the gravity of the situation from the concerned look in Maysa's eyes. She turned and addressed the woman who'd been assisting her and instructed her to do what she could until she returned. Then she gestured Rafiq to follow her out of the tent. Once they were back in the SUV, Maysa followed a truck out of the village and toward the mountains.

"Where are we going?" Rafiq asked as Maysa made one hairpin turn without braking.

"There is a woman in labor," she said. "She's having difficulty delivering."

"Her first child?"

"Fourth, and that's what concerns me."

The man had not looked old enough to father four offspring. But he did not have time to voice his opinion as Maysa pulled into a drive leading to an earthen hut. She had stopped the vehicle, retrieved the smallest medical kit and had arrived at the front door before he had barely left the passenger seat.

Rafiq made haste and entered the house to see Maysa disappearing through a door to the right of the living area. He discovered three children sitting on the low blue sofas, their eyes wide with fear. The oldest could not have been more than six years old, the second perhaps four and the youngest about two years of age. He surveyed the room to find it absent of any adult and assumed the father had chosen to be at his wife's side.

When he claimed another smaller sofa to wait, the oldest little girl came to her feet and crossed the room to stand before him.

He remembered Maysa's insistence he not speak, yet he could not pretend he was not concerned over the child's well-being. *"Shu esmek?"*

She twirled a lock of dark hair around her tiny finger. "Aini."

The name suited her, he decided. With her dark curls and equally dark eyes, she was as pretty as a spring flower. He remembered Elena once saying that children only wanted to be fed, clothed and to feel safe. Aini was clothed, she did not appear undernourished, yet he imagined she did not feel secure at the moment.

For that reason, Rafiq began to recite a story about a lost sheep in search of its mother, a tale he had learned from his own mother. One by one, the other children gathered around and listened intently. When they looked at him with complete trust, he realized, though he had been born to royalty, he had never felt quite as important as he did now. He also experienced a fierce need to protect them. The protection he had not afforded his unborn child.

The sound of mournful moans began to filter from the adjacent room, thrusting away the regret. Rafiq waved the children onto the sofa beside him and set the youngest in his lap. He raised his voice in an attempt to muffle the scream that made his blood run cold. He could only imagine what these innocents were feeling at the moment—hearing their mother in such abject pain.

Maysa emerged from the chamber holding a bundle in her arms, a cap of dark hair showing from beneath the white blanket. To Rafiq, she looked completely natural holding a baby, and in one fleeting moment, he imagined her holding his child.

She approached the sofa and smiled. "Here is your baby brother," she said to the children in Arabic, followed by, "The baby was breech," in English, directed at Rafiq. "The mother has lost a lot of blood and needs a hospital."

While the two oldest children slid off the sofa to view their new sibling, Rafiq moved the youngest child from his lap and stood. "Is the mother in danger?"

"Yes."

Her somber tone demonstrated to Rafiq the gravity of the situation. "How much time does she have?"

"I fear not long enough to make the three-hour drive, but we have no choice."

Rafiq would give her another choice. "Is there a telephone?"

Maysa looked around the room and pointed at an

ancient handset hanging from the wall. "There, though I cannot guarantee it works."

He would soon find out. Fortunately, the telephone was operable, though it took several attempts to connect with the palace, and another two to convince the staff he was in fact the king. Finally, he managed to reach his brother. "Adan, I need your immediate assistance."

"You have bedded Maysa and you need to know how to proceed?"

He was in no mood to put up with Adan's questionable comments. "I need a medevac helicopter sent to Diya immediately. Make certain to have medics onboard, and that it arrives in less than fifteen minutes."

"What is this about, Rafiq?"

"A woman's life is at stake," he said. "We have only a small window of time to deliver her to the hospital."

"I will do the best that I can on such short notice."

"You will do exactly what I say, and you will be expedient!"

"Calm down, Rafiq. I will have the helicopter there in ten minutes, even if I must fly it myself."

"Good. I am counting on you, Adan."

As soon as he hung up, Rafiq recognized his heart had been racing at breakneck speed. He had done what he could and hoped that it would be enough. He had not been able to save his own wife, but perhaps he could save this one.

Even after she'd treated the last remaining patient in the tent, Maysa could not recall feeling so utterly helpless. A few hours ago, she'd watched the helicopter fly away while she stayed behind since there hadn't been room for her and the woman's husband. "I should have left for the hospital hours ago."

Rafiq came up behind her and rested his palms on her shoulders. "She is in competent hands," he said. "The hospital was prepared to receive them immediately. I am certain all will be well."

If only she could feel so confident. "I hope so," she said as she gathered supplies and put them in the kit. "I cannot imagine how her poor husband would feel if he lost his wife, not to mention having to raise four children on his own."

"It is not something you would wish to imagine," he said. "So do not."

Maysa understood all too well what Rafiq was probably feeling at that moment—his own loss. "I hope we receive some news soon."

"Adan said he would find a way to get word to us when there was news to report."

Maysa was grateful Rafiq had been there to offer support, and thankful that his position had opened doors she would not have been able to open herself. She turned with a smile and handed him the kit. "Please put this in the Hummer and we'll be on our way."

"We cannot leave now."

He couldn't be serious. She was so tired she could barely stand. "Why would we wish to stay any longer? I've finished with my work here for the week."

He smiled. "I have been told the villagers have arranged a feast in honor of the *Tâbeeb* and her *American* friend."

As much as Maysa would like to attend, she was simply too tired for a celebration. "As it stands now, we won't be home until midnight."

"You have not eaten all day."

"I had some goat cheese and *lahvash*."

He frowned. "Would you insult those who have prepared a fine meal in your honor?"

Before Maysa could respond, "I wouldn't if I were
you, Dr. Barad" came from behind her.

She glanced back to see a tall, lanky, sandy-haired
man with a full beard approaching. A familiar face she
hadn't seen in quite some time.

As soon as he came to her side, Maysa drew him
into an embrace. "It is so good to see you, Jerome."

He set her back and surveyed her face. "It's good to
see you, too, Maysa. It's been at least a month."

"Longer," she said with a smile. "I assumed you returned to Canada."

"I did for a time, but I didn't stay long. After making a few stops, I'm back in Diya to finish my work."

After Maysa heard Rafiq clear his throat, she faced
him again. "Jerome Forte, this is..." She struggled to
come up with a proper—and false—introduction.
"This is Rafe."

Jerome presented a cynical smile. "No. This is Rafiq
Mehdi, ruling king of Bajul."

She should have known she wouldn't be able to put
anything over on the photographer. "You're right, but
I prefer you keep his identity to yourself."

"You may count on my absolute discretion," he said
before he regarded Rafiq once more. "It is a pleasure
to meet you, Your Majesty."

Rafiq stared at Jerome's extended hand for a few
moments before accepting the gesture. "What brings
you to this part of the world, Mr. Forte?"

"Please, it's Jerome." He wrapped an arm around

Maysa's waist, much to her chagrin. "I've been photographing the area for an international magazine. Not only did Maysa suggest the region, she has been instrumental in convincing the villagers here to allow me to take their pictures."

Rafiq looked as though he might throw a punch. "Is that all she's been assisting you with?"

She moved away from Jerome and frowned. "Yes, that is all. Jerome and I have been friends for several years."

"Yes, we have," Jerome said as he smiled down on her. "And I've missed our talks."

"We must decide whether we are staying or going," Rafiq said, a definite edge in his tone. "If you choose to leave, then we must do so now."

He suddenly sounded as if he wanted to leave. "We should stay for a while," she said. "You're right. I wouldn't want to seem ungrateful."

Rafiq moved beside her and possessively took her arm. "If you will excuse us, Mr. Forte, we have a celebration to attend."

"As do I," Jerome said. "The party is being held a block away. We can all walk together."

Considering the disapproving look on Rafiq's face, Maysa was somewhat concerned that accompanying Jerome could lead to trouble. She would certainly hate to have to intervene, though she would. She did not appreciate male posturing in any form or fashion. "Then I suppose we should be going before the sun has completely set."

The trio walked the brick streets of the village, Maysa flanked by the men. While Rafiq remained stoic and silent, Jerome chatted nonstop about his recent travels to Tunisia. Fortunately they arrived at the expansive field without incident.

Several fires blazed throughout the area, providing the means to cook the fare for the feast, including spits with roasting lamb. She'd never cared for that delicacy due to her fondness for baby sheep. But tonight she would sample everything to avoid appearing unappreciative.

As they wove their way through the throngs of people, Maysa answered each greeting with one of her own as Rafiq and Jerome hung back. The village men wore summer-weight *bishts,* their heads covered by *mashadahs,* while the women wore the usual *hijab.* She, Rafiq and Jerome seemed out of place in their civilian clothes, yet no one seemed to notice—except for a group of young women who stood to the side of the banquet table, giggling behind their hands when the men walked up to fill their plates.

Maysa leaned toward Rafiq and whispered, "You are making quite an impression on the female population here. Perhaps you could find a suitable wife among them."

"Perhaps you have discovered a suitable lover in your Canadian friend."

She found the jealousy in his voice somewhat amusing. "As I have told you, Jerome is only a friend. Nothing more."

He kept filling a bowl full of *ogdat* until the stew almost overflowed from the vessel. "He would like more. He would like to have you all to himself."

"Don't be foolish, Rafiq. If you'll look to your left you'll notice he is preoccupied with a young woman as we speak."

Rafiq followed Maysa's gaze to where Jerome was standing near one of the fire pits, charming a pretty young woman who seemed to be hanging on his every word, as well as his arm. "She does not appear to be more than a teenager," he said.

"I predict she is well over the age of consent," she said. "And interested in Jerome. I've seen them together before."

Rafiq frowned. "Her parents approve of this liaison with a foreigner?"

She sighed. "I have no idea, and it is not any of my concern. Now let's eat so we can leave as soon as possible."

Maysa followed Rafiq to the nearest fire and sat beside him on the ground. They ate their meal in silence, then afterward watched several men perform the *dabke* in their honor. As badly as she wanted to leave, she felt it would be impolite to depart during the dance. A dance that seemed to go on and on for an eternity.

By the time the group had finished, and the applause had died down, Maysa worried she could fall asleep and land face-forward in the fire. "We should go now, otherwise I might be forced to let you drive."

Rafiq regarded his watch. "It is late. Perhaps we should find lodging here for the night."

Finding herself in a hotel room with Rafiq did not seem wise. "As far as I know, Diya has no inns."

"Is there a family who would take us in?"

"The two of you can use my tent, Your Excellency."

Once more, Jerome had interrupted the discourse by stealing into the area without Maysa's notice. "Then where would you sleep, Jerome?" she asked, though she knew the answer.

He grinned. "I have made other accommodations."

Of course he had—with the young woman who happened to be standing behind him. "I appreciate the offer, but from what I recall, your tent is not that large." At least not large enough to house two former lovers battling chemistry.

"I disagree," he said. "It's very large, and it has enough room for three people, provided you're willing to sleep side by side on the ground. Actually, there's a sleeping bag covering the ground, and a spare should you need it. It's really quite comfortable."

"I really don't think—"

"I believe it will be suitable for the evening," Rafiq chimed in. "We appreciate your generosity, and we accept."

Maysa momentarily gaped. "I don't accept. I am quite capable of driving."

"You are exhausted," Rafiq said. "As am I. We will rise early in the morning and return refreshed and fully awake."

She doubted she would sleep at all with Rafiq in such close proximity. "I truly don't believe it's necessary."

"His Majesty has a point, Maysa," Jerome added. "There's no need to hurry home when you have a perfectly good tent for the night. It's in the same location, so I'm sure you'll have no problem finding it."

With that, Jerome took his paramour's hand and disappeared into the darkness.

Maysa brought her attention back to Rafiq. "I'm not certain it's wise for us to spend the night together in a tent."

"And I do not think it is wise to drive hours in a state of exhaustion."

She decided to give up on that argument, in part because she was extremely tired. "All right, you may have the shelter and I will sleep in the Hummer."

"No one is sleeping in the Hummer, Maysa. We are both adults and I vow to maintain control, if that is your concern."

That was precisely her concern. "Do you promise to stay on your side of the tent?"

He raised a hand as if taking an oath. "I promise that I will be the gentleman Elena has taught me to be."

Could she trust that he was telling the truth? Could she trust herself around him? Of course she could. She would keep her distance, and demand he keep his. And in the morning, she would return home without any regrets.

"All right. We'll stay in the tent."

And she sincerely hoped it *was* big enough for both of them.

Four

The shelter was much larger than Rafiq had envisioned, and not a tent in the true sense of the word. The structure was comprised of a wooden frame covered by canvas, and tall enough to allow him to stand. Yet it seemed much too small for a man who greatly desired the woman with whom he would share the space.

As he sat on the blanket-covered ground to remove his boots, Maysa stood in the corner, washing her face in a basin set out on a small side table. She had removed her blouse, leaving her clad in a fitted, sleeveless undershirt. While he continued to watch her, she slipped the band securing the braid, unwound it and then shook out her hair that cascaded down her back, the ends touching the top of her waist. He recalled that fall of hair surrounding him, flowing over his bare skin. How many nights had he imagined it happening again? Too numerous to count. And when he had made love to Rima, Maysa had oftentimes been foremost in his mind, fueling his fantasies. A shameful secret he would carry to the grave.

Maysa turned and stretched her hands above her head, drawing the shirt tighter, revealing she wore no bra. She removed a brush from her bag and ran it through her hair. "Thank you for all you did today. And be sure to thank Adan for getting word to us that both mother and child received a clean bill of health."

"Do not forget your part in that good news," he said as he followed the movement of her hand sliding the brush through her long locks, back and forth.

"I was only doing my job."

She was clearly bent on torturing him at the moment.

He stripped away his own shirt for the sake of comfort, and as soon as she turned off the lantern, he intended to remove his pants, also for comfort. If that somehow offended her, then so be it. After all, she had made certain their makeshift beds were almost a meter apart. Still, the distance would not prevent his fantasies, or discourage him if she gave him the least bit of encouragement.

Wise or not, he wanted her still. He would continue to want her even after they parted ways. Yet her reaction the night before when he touched her indicated she did not want him as fiercely as he wanted her, if at all.

After replacing the brush in the duffel, Maysa returned to the pallets, lowered herself onto the blankets and crossed her legs before her. "Are you tired?"

Sleep was the last thing on his mind with Maysa so close. "Surprisingly I am not."

"Neither am I. I thought perhaps we could talk."

He stretched out on his side facing her, and bent his elbow to support his jaw with his hand. "What do you wish to talk about?"

"Your relationship with Rima."

He had not expected that, nor did he care to discuss it. "She was my wife for a brief time and that is all that needs to be said."

"Actually, that's what I wanted to talk about. Why did you wait so long to marry her?"

He had had many reasons, but he chose to omit one—he had hoped Rima would eventually tire of waiting. "I attended university, and when I returned, I had to assist my father since Zain had left for the States. We had no indication when he would return, or even if he would return at that point."

"That seems like a logical justification for a man, but I don't understand why Rima would agree to delay a wedding for the sake of duty when your responsibility would still exist after the wedding."

Rima had never pressured him to set a date. He had done so only because it had been expected. "She decided to travel and then after her father passed, she spent a good deal of time with her mother. We were both in no hurry." And they had both believed they had a lifetime to spend together. A life that would include polite conversation and little passion.

"I would say that's obvious," Maysa said. "You waited almost fifteen years to make it official."

In many ways, fifteen years had not been long enough. "I understand why you would be confused over the decision, considering you married Boutros almost immediately after the betrothal."

Her gaze faltered. "I wasn't given a choice. My father demanded I marry him immediately, per the terms of the agreement. Boutros wasn't getting any younger, and he wanted an heir."

"An heir you did not give him."

"Fortunately, no."

When Maysa began to rub her right wrist, only then did Rafiq notice the ropelike scar circling it. When he had called on her the first night, she had been wearing heavy bangles that concealed the mark. Tonight, the wound was uncovered and he needed to know its origination, though he suspected he already did.

He immediately sat upright and took her hand to study it further. "What is this?"

She wrenched out of his grasp. "It's nothing."

He needed more evidence to substantiate his theory. "Take off your watch."

"No."

"Then I shall do it for you."

He anticipated she would fight him when he unbuckled the strap, yet she sat motionless with a blank stare, as if shielding herself from the truth he sought. And he found that truth when he removed the watch— another circular scar.

Rafiq bit back his anger and tempered his tone. "Did he bind you, Maysa?"

"Rafiq, I—"

"Did that *kalet* tie you?"

"Yes!" she said, her voice heralding her fury. "Yes, the bastard bound me. He grew tired of me fighting him."

Rafiq gritted his teeth and spoke through them. "He forced himself on you against your will?"

"Yes, he did, and he also did this." She twisted around and raised the back of her shirt, revealing a series of slashes across her flesh. "He tried to beat me into submission, and when it did not work, he would go for the rope."

Unable to remain still, Rafiq stood and began pacing the area. He longed for a solid wall to hit, a means to expend his rage. "I will kill him with my own hands."

Maysa's laughter spun him around. "You are too late to ride to my rescue, I fear. It's my understanding his heart is failing, though I'm surprised to learn he has a heart at all. I have no doubt it is as black as midnight."

Rafiq returned to her and claimed the space beside her. "Did you not mention this to your father?"

"Yes, I did. He told me that to be a good wife, I would do what was required. Even Shamil sided with him."

His respect for the sultan and his former friend plummeted. "And your mother?"

"She always left the room, most likely to hide her tears. But I never cried. I was determined not to let any of them see my tears or my weakness, especially Boutros."

"Yet you suffered for your strength."

She raised her chin, defiance reflecting from her eyes. "I called on that well-honed strength the night I left him."

He needed to know all the details, both bad and good. "How did you manage to escape?"

"We were at his home in Oman. He was out with one of his many mistresses. I broke into his desk, stole several thousand riyals and caught a plane to Canada. That's where I first met Jerome, on the plane. He assisted me in finding temporary housing. He was also instrumental in finding me employment. I worked as a waitress in a busy café, and once I'd saved enough money, I traveled to the States and began my studies."

Her resilience amazed him. "Your father never offered financial assistance?"

"Of course not. He was furious. But my mother eventually sent me money whenever she could. She enabled me to hire an attorney for the divorce. And as they say, the rest is history."

He formed his palm to her face. "Though I admire what you have accomplished on your own, you should have come to me for help."

"Why would I do that, Rafiq? You all but bid me a final farewell after we spent that one night together, or have you forgotten?"

The bitterness in her tone caused him to drop his hand. "I have never forgotten that night." Nor had he forgotten the sorrow in her eyes when he had told her they could not be together again.

"You told me we would remain friends," she said. "Yet we never really spoke again."

"We were forbidden to have any contact."

"We were forbidden after you were officially betrothed to Rima, but that didn't stop you from taking my virginity, did it?"

"And I recall you came to me willingly that night. You begged me to make love to you."

She lowered her eyes. "Yes, I did, and I never regretted it. I only regretted…"

He raised her chin with his fingertips, forcing her to look at him. "You regretted what?"

"That we only had that one time. But it was enough

to get me through those horrendous times with Boutros. I would close my eyes and escape back to that night. I reminded myself that what we shared was pure and good, not ugly and brutal. Those memories helped ease the pain and tolerate the reminders I still carry with me."

He suspected her internal scars still ran deep. "I did the same with Rima," he said, surprised at how easily the admission flowed out of his mouth. "She came to me willingly, and I always treated her with care and respect. Yet I sensed her thoughts were somewhere else. Perhaps on someone else, as were mine. I always thought of you."

"And the women before Rima?"

"I always imagined you. And the men after Boutros?"

"There have been no other men."

Perhaps that should not surprise him. "No one?"

"No. When you kissed me the other night, that was the first time since I left him. I thought I was immune to desire, but you proved me wrong." She attempted a smile but it faded quickly. "Although when you touched me, I realized I still have lingering issues."

He had mistakenly believed she had no intention of returning his affection. "I understand why you would feel that way, but I would have hoped the passage of time would have aided in your healing."

Her hand went to her wrist again, as if she needed to remember. "My emergency room rotations served as a constant reminder of what I had endured. I treated women who had suffered the same, and I began to realize that marital violence spans all cultures. Some still turn a blind eye to the problem because they believe that a wife should persevere to save the marriage. Fortunately, I was wise enough to leave."

He took her hand again and kissed her palm. "You were brave, Maysa. You still are. Braver than most men."

He saw the first sign of tears in her eyes, but she quickly blinked them away. "I am also damaged, Rafiq. No man would want me."

I want you. "You are a beautiful, desirable woman, *habibti.* Any man would be fortunate to have you."

"Well, I do not intend to give anyone that option. But I do have a favor to ask of you."

"Whatever you wish."

"Would you hold me tonight?"

She asked so little of him, yet so much. "If that is what you desire."

"But can you only hold me without wanting more?"

He could offer her a lie, or be completely honest, which is what she deserved. "If I said I did not wish to make love with you again, that would be untrue. But I will honor your request and be satisfied having you in my arms as we sleep. Shall I turn off the lantern?"

"I'd prefer to leave it on."

To chase away the demons, Rafiq presumed. "Then we will leave it on."

She stretched out on her back and sent him a sincere smile. "Then, Your Majesty, you are cordially invited to join me for an evening of celibacy."

He returned her smile, despite his disappointment. "I accept your invitation, Dr. Barad, as long as you do not steal the blankets."

"I will try to refrain."

When Maysa shifted to her side, Rafiq covered them

both and slid his arm beneath her. He decided to remain clothed from the waist down, at least until he was assured she slept. Then he would strip off his slacks and hope she did not notice.

Yes, she was inadvertently bent on torturing him with her request. And with the floral scent of her hair teasing his senses, her warm body fitted to his, she had succeeded in her mission.

At some point during the night, Maysa roused from a fitful sleep to the sound of steady breathing. A few moments passed before she became fully awake and turned to find Rafiq lying on his back. The lantern had begun to dim, washing his bare chest in an amber glow, yet allowing her to covertly study him. Human anatomy had been a part of her daily existence for years, but she was not immune to prime physical specimens, and the king definitely fit into that category.

His right arm curled above his head on the pillow and the other rested at his side between them. His dark lashes fanned out beneath his closed eyes, and his lips were pressed together. His clean-shaven jaw had already begun to show the signs of a light spattering of whiskers.

She continued her visual journey down the column of his throat and on to the prominent pectorals that indicated he still worked out with weights. He'd developed that passion in his teen years, while his brothers had stayed in shape picking up women, literally and figuratively, according to Rafiq. He had been a serious student, so bent on earning his father's respect. Bent on being his father in many ways. Yet she had known a different prince, the one who had spoken sweet words in soft whispers. The young man who had touched and kissed her so gently.

Those memories prompted her to reach out and touch him now. She sifted through the triangular shading on his sternum and slid a fingertip lightly down his belly, pausing where the sheet was draped loose and low, covering his hips. Realization that she didn't see a waistband dawned on her. She rose up to view his pants piled in a heap at the end of the pallet. Only his pants?

Morbid female curiosity caused her to lift the sheet to take a peek.

Hello...

As she suspected, he was unequivocally—and beautifully—bare. And for some reason, she could not quit staring.

"Are you enjoying the sight?"

She dropped the sheet and glanced up to see Rafiq's half smile and his open eyes full of amusement. "You're naked."

He propped a bent arm behind his neck. "I am, and you seem quite fascinated by that fact."

His voice hinted at arrogance and pride and Maysa had to admit, he had much to be proud of. "The question is, why did you take off your pants?"

"I always remove them when I am in bed. Otherwise, I have difficulty sleeping. You do not remember this?"

Oh, yes, she did, though they had only slept together one time. "I remember."

"Do you wish me to put them back on?"

Did she? "I wouldn't want you to be uncomfortable on my account, Your Excellency."

"Good. Feel free to carry on, although should you

proceed, you are in danger of waking the sleeping dragon."

She sent a downward glance to the place she'd recently inspected. "I believe the dragon has already been roused."

His grin expanded. "And you are surprised by this?"

Not in the least, but she was surprised by her reaction. She felt winded and flushed and...needy. "I apologize for touching you without your permission."

"Never apologize for something so pleasurable. I am yours to do with what you will."

She so badly wanted to return to the time when she had been secure in her sensuality. When she hadn't been afraid to explore, or be explored. She had the perfect guide next to her, a man she could trust. A man she had desired for as long as she could recall. Perhaps he couldn't promise a future, but he could bring her back to that land known as the living. First, she had to ask.

"I have a request for you," she said.

"Your wish is my command."

Before she reconsidered, Maysa sat up, drew in a deep breath, pulled her undershirt over her head and tossed it aside. "I want you to touch me the way you did when we were young, Rafiq."

Obvious desire, as well as a cast of concern, called out from his coal-colored eyes. "Are you certain?"

She stretched out on her back, closed her eyes and fisted her hands at her sides. "As long as we go slowly. I need—"

"I understand what you need," he said. "And you may rest assured I will treat you with the greatest of care. You only need tell me to stop, and I will."

She knew he would, otherwise she would never allow this to happen.

After Maysa nodded, Rafiq took her arm, unclenched her hand, and kissed her palm. He then leaned over and kissed her forehead, then each cheek before brushing his lips over hers. "Open your eyes for me." When she complied, he added, "I want you to see me touching you. I want you to know it is me."

He did understand, she realized, and she loved him for it.

Loved him...

She would take that out and examine it later. At the moment, her attention was drawn to Rafiq as he brushed his knuckles down her throat. He circled a fingertip around one breast, then the other, all the while keeping his gaze trained on hers. He seemed to be gauging her reaction, and she reacted with an increase in her respiration. He placed a kiss between her breasts, then sought her eyes again before he dipped his head and closed his mouth over her nipple. The circular movement of his tongue, the gentle pull, caused her to shift restlessly from the sensations. She was so lost in the heat, the yearning, she hadn't realized he was caressing her abdomen. She wanted him to keep going, yet when he slipped the button on her fly, illogical fear enveloped her.

"Stop." Her command came out in a raspy whisper.

But she'd been forceful enough to cause Rafiq to raise his head, taking the welcome warmth of his mouth away from her breast. "Do you wish me to stop completely?"

"Yes... No..." She streaked both hands over her

face. "I'm not certain. A part of me is still fearful, and I despise feeling this way."

"I do not want you to be afraid. I want you to feel only pleasure."

She lowered her eyes. "I know. I'm sorry."

"Do not apologize, Maysa. I promised I would stop when you asked, and I am a man of my word."

She finally looked at him. "You're a good man, Rafiq, and always patient with me."

"I will continue to be patient," he said. "You will determine if you wish to continue. Now we should sleep. We have a long drive ahead of us in the morning."

She didn't want to think about morning. She wasn't certain she could sleep. "I suppose you're right."

"First, may I kiss you?"

How odd that he'd asked, yet she appreciated that he had. "Yes, you may."

"You are not concerned with the no-kissing rule?"

She couldn't help but smile. "I believe it's too late to enforce that now."

"I want to make certain you have not changed your mind."

"I will if you do not hurry up and kiss me."

He rolled her toward him, framed her face with his palms and pressed his lips against hers softly. Yet it didn't last long before Rafiq pulled back and smiled. "Now if you would please put your shirt back on, I might possibly be able to sleep."

Feeling strangely wicked, Maysa leaned over him to retrieve her top, intentionally rubbing her bare breasts against his chest. She rose up and replaced the shirt slower than necessary. "Is that better?"

He swallowed hard. "Somewhat. Should I put on my pants?"

"I'm a doctor, Rafiq. I've seen quite a few naked men in the course of my medical career." In afterthought she added, "But I would prefer you keep the dragon covered."

Rafiq laughed then. A grainy, sensual laugh that almost had her reconsidering sleep. But she wasn't ready to move forward in their intimacy. At least not yet.

When she settled back onto the blanket, Rafiq again folded her in his arms, providing the security she needed at the moment.

Concerned over the future, Maysa listened to the cadence of Rafiq's breathing and determined he wasn't sleeping. "Are you awake?"

"Yes."

"After all the years, I still feel a connection between us. Do you?"

"Of course," he said. "Time does have a way of standing still when it involves friendship."

Friendship... That said it all. "Where do we go from here?"

He brushed a kiss across her forehead. "Wherever we choose to go. And wherever that might be, I promise we will both find pleasure in the journey."

Did she dare continue with this dangerous emotional game? Did she risk losing herself to him again? Yes. She was no longer that starstruck young girl with unattainable dreams. She could never play a role in his future, but she could be a part of his present. They needed each other. He needed comfort, and she needed confidence.

Wise or not, she would make love with him again, provided she wasn't too broken.

Five

He was surprised she had allowed him to drive. He was more surprised by her current demeanor.

As Rafiq navigated the barren terrain, he afforded Maysa an occasional glance. At the moment, her face was turned toward the morning sky shining in through the moon roof, her unbound hair blowing back in the breeze from the open window. He could not see her eyes, now covered with sunglasses, but he could definitely see her smile and the twin dimples framing her mouth. She had also left her blouse unbuttoned, providing a view of the undershirt drawn tight over her breasts. That had almost proved enough distraction to cause him to veer onto the shoulder, coming dangerously close to the edge of the cliff.

Freedom…

That word immediately came to Rafiq's mind. Both yearned for it, yet Maysa captured the essence of it. He wished to see more of that absence of inhibition in the near future. He wanted more of what they had shared last night. Most important, he wanted revenge on the man who had stolen her security and left her scarred for life. Death was not good enough for Boutros Kassab.

"We should keep driving past the city," Maysa said, turning her vibrant smile on him. "We should escape and not tell anyone where we're going."

Her enthusiasm was contagious, and familiar. Many times in their shared pasts they had spoken about this very thing. "And where do you suggest we go?"

She lifted her shoulders in a shrug. "I don't know. South to the sea, maybe. Or perhaps we could travel north into Saudi. Dine at the finest restaurants and stay at the best resort."

He only wished they could be that carefree. "You have responsibilities, as do I."

She frowned. "What happened to your sense of adventure?"

"Replaced by the crown." Determined by duty.

"That, Rafiq, is a travesty." She pointed to his left. "Pull over up there."

She'd indicated a thirty-meter expanse of dirt breaking into the pavement and a sheer drop-off beyond. "Why?"

"Please, just do it. And back into the spot."

Far be it for him to question Maysa once she had her mind set on something. He slowed the Hummer, pulled off to the side of the road and then put the vehicle in Reverse. He made certain to leave sufficient room between the SUV and the drop-off, though he was tempted to inch close enough to earn a scolding.

Once they had stopped, Rafiq shut off the ignition

and draped one hand over the wheel. "Do you wish to watch the traffic the go by?"

She unbuckled her seat belt and opened the door. "No. We're going to sit for a while and look at the mountains."

When Maysa exited, Rafiq did the same and followed her to the back of the vehicle. She opened the tailgate, boosted herself up onto it, and patted the space beside her.

They sat quietly for a time, staring off into the distance. He had seen the panorama countless times, yet he had often taken the majestic mountains for granted. They served as a fortress surrounding the city, nature's protection against those who envied Bajul's peaceful existence and autonomy, as well as its resources.

"You can see the palace from here," Maysa said, breaking into silence. "And of course, who could miss *Mabriruk*. We should take a day to explore there before your respite is over."

He did not care to consider the ending of his time with her, though it was inevitable. "When Zain and Madison visited the mountain, they returned with not one but two souvenirs. Zain knew the possible consequences, and he chose to take that risk regardless."

"You don't truly believe that fertility mythology, do you?" she asked.

Perhaps not, but he did not wish to take any undue chances. "I only know the villagers still believe it."

"Well, I can't say that I do. It takes more than a mountain to make a baby."

He sent her a teasing smile. "I was not aware of that."

She playfully swiped at his arm. "I'm certain you don't need me to explain the procreation process."

He rubbed his chin and pretended to think. "I would not object to hearing it in terms I would understand."

She laid a hand above her breast. "Why, Your Majesty, are you asking me to talk dirty to you?"

Precisely. "It would not be the first time if you did."

A blush colored her cheeks. "I was incredibly young back then."

"And extremely bold." He still recalled that night when she had verbalized what she had wanted him to do to her, causing him to shift against the uncomfortable effects of that memory. "I appreciated your candor, and I would hope you still feel that you may say anything to me."

"I do, and I have." She leaned back and supported herself on straight arms. "Do you remember that night when we spent several hours not far from here, looking at the same view?"

He remembered it well. "The night you stole your father's car and whisked me away from the palace?"

"I borrowed his car," she corrected.

"Without his knowledge or permission."

She looked extremely proud of her subterfuge. "I returned it later, and he was never the wiser."

"True. Do you remember the code we used when you would summon me?"

Her smile gave the rising sun competition. "How's the weather. And you would always answer—"

"Hot." And that would start the scramble to find a way to be together.

The silence returned, this time rife with tension as

they centered their gazes on each other. She finally favored him with a smile. "How is the weather?"

"Hotter than a desert blaze."

She leaned to his ear and whispered, "So am I."

He answered the obvious invitation with a kiss. Maysa responded with the passion Rafiq had learned to appreciate years before, and had greatly missed. He had never received the same reaction from his wife, but then their kisses had been obligatory. Absent of passion or undeniable need.

He experienced all those emotions with Maysa, and the intense desire to have her again overwhelmed him. He slid his hand beneath the back of her blouse to feel her bare skin against his palms. She surprised him by guiding that hand around to her breast. The desperate sound she made when he feathered his thumb across her nipple was almost his undoing.

Momentarily releasing her, he shoved the medical kits aside to make a place for them. No words were spoken as they crawled inside the vehicle and immediately moved back into each other's arms. He kissed her again, harder, deeper, as he divided her legs with his knee until they were completely twined together as tightly as braided rope.

"I want to touch you," he said. "Everywhere."

"I want you to touch me." Her voice was winded, her eyes hazy. "I need you to touch me."

The reality sudden dawned. How easy it would be to grant her wish. And unwise. Should anyone come upon them on the verge of making love, the scandal would rock the country. A scandal neither could afford.

He placed a kiss on her forehead. "Not here. Not now. You deserve better than this." That all-important next step would be best taken in a feather bed, not in the bed of an SUV. "We are less than twenty minutes away from your home."

"I'm not sure I can wait another twenty minutes."

Neither was Rafiq. "Then perhaps we should leave immediately."

"Are you sure you wouldn't rather stay here?"

He kissed her again, this time with more restraint to prevent rousing the dragon again. "I am sure. We will have the entire evening to spend together and a bed at our disposal. Provided you are ready to take that next step."

Her smile expanded, showing her dimples to full advantage. "Then what are we waiting for?"

Fortunately, they had waited long enough not to have their burgeoning affair confirmed by another member of the royal family. Had they arrived ten minutes earlier, Zain and Madison Mehdi might have caught them in a thoroughly compromising position.

Maysa wasn't altogether unhappy to see the couple, though their timing wasn't exactly the best. But when they'd come upon Zain and Madison in the living area, both looking extremely serious, she worried this might not be only a casual visit.

Rafiq crossed the room and targeted his brother with a glare. "Why are you here?"

Zain rose from the sofa, his gaze honed in on Maysa. "We have simply stopped by to see how the two of you are getting along."

"That's not true," Madison said as she stood. "We're here because all hell is breaking loose back at the palace."

Maysa exchanged a wary look with Rafiq before she brought her attention back to Madison. "What exactly do you mean?"

"Although arranging for the helicopter was noble, Rafiq," Zain began, "you might have been a bit more discreet. It seems the media has learned you were in Diya with Maysa. You might have made us privy to your plans so that we would have been prepared for the fallout."

"Rafiq had nothing to do with it," Maysa said. "This was all my idea. Had I known it would create a scandal, I would never have considered it."

With his eyes flashing anger, and his hands fisted at his sides, Rafiq looked as if he might fly into a rage. "I was in Diya observing one of Bajul's finest doctors treating the sick and downtrodden. What scandal is there in that?"

Madison lowered herself onto the sofa and folded her hands together. "Because rumor has it you spent the night with the country's finest doctor."

Searing heat began to work its way from Maysa's throat to her forehead. "We slept together in a tent." Could that have sounded more questionable? "In a large tent, and all we did was sleep." Excluding some minor foreplay and major kissing. Hopefully they wouldn't ask about the ride back from Diya.

"Did anyone see you together on your return from Diya?" Zain asked.

Clearly that had been too much for Maysa to hope for. "No one saw us."

"There was nothing to see," Rafiq interjected, sounding a bit too defensive in Maysa's opinion.

"Everyone, please sit," Madison said. "We need to implement a plan."

Rafiq slid his hands into his pants' pockets and remained frozen on the spot. "I prefer to stand."

Maysa preferred to leave for the closest exit, but she claimed the chair adjacent to the sofa before she answered that urge. "What do you suggest we do about this misunderstanding?"

Zain draped an arm over his wife's shoulder. "Madison held a press conference this morning to—"

"Without my permission?" Rafiq interjected.

Maysa affected the calm Rafiq failed to show. "What did this press conference entail?"

"Attempting to answer the usual questions," Madison said. "What business did the king have in Diya? What is the true relationship between the king and doctor? In other words, are they having a sordid affair? Nothing I haven't faced before in my career."

"I really feel badly you're having to work on your holiday, Madison," Maysa said.

Zain kissed Madison's cheek. "Even after blessing me with two babies, my wife is still the best at what she does."

Madison smiled. "Sweetheart, I can lactate and change a thousand diapers a day and still handle my job. That's part of why you love me."

This time Zain kissed her on the mouth. "And you love me for my overt charm, as well as my royal staff."

While Maysa couldn't hold back her laughter, Rafiq grumbled an Arabic curse. "Could the two of you stop mooning over each other and bring your minds back to the issues at hand?" he said. "Specifically, I demand to know every detail of this press conference."

Maysa could only guess at that, but she was certain karma had arrived, telling her to steer clear of any intimacy with the king. Steer clear of him altogether. "I would assume Madison denied the conjecture, Rafiq."

Madison shrugged. "Of course. I said the king wanted to investigate medical care in the outlying villages, and that's why he accompanied Dr. Barad to Diya. He preferred to do so anonymously to allow him a better advantage. I ignored any questions about the sleeping arrangements."

"Madison successfully dodged those bullets," Zain added. "But there will be plenty more if someone discovers the two of you cohabiting here."

As usual, Rafiq began his restless pacing. "Are you saying I should return to the palace?"

"Not necessarily, Rafiq," Zain said. "Madison also informed the press that following your information-gathering, you would be taking a brief sabbatical."

Maysa could see several problems with that plan. "Are you certain that's a good idea with the media already making assumptions?"

Zain wrapped an arm around his wife's shoulder. "Madison and I both agree Rafiq still needs time away."

"But he can't stay here with you," Madison added. "He's going to have to find another place for his mini-vacation."

Rafiq stopped his pacing and stepped forward. "Would you please address me directly? And do not forget I have the ultimate decision whether I stay or go. If I decide to remain here, then that is what I will do."

Maysa looked directly at Rafiq for the first time since they'd received the news. "Madison's right, Rafiq.

You cannot remain here with me. The gossip will escalate, whether it's true or not."

"And that is the last thing you need right now," Zain said. "We are so close to having the council's full support for the water project. They need to know your complete focus is on your duty and not on a woman who…"

When Zain's words trailed off, Maysa's defenses went on high alert. "Whom they deem not worthy to wipe the king's feet?"

Madison reached over and patted Maysa's arm. "Believe me, I know exactly what you're going through, and I personally think the mores are ridiculous and archaic."

"This is not the time to try to change customs," Rafiq said. "It seems I have no other option than to lock myself in my suite and demand I not be disturbed."

"And that holds no guarantees you will not be disturbed," Zain added. "Should anyone learn you are there, the intrusions would continue. I suggest perhaps you leave the country. You could stay in our home in Los Angeles."

Rafiq released a caustic laugh. "If you recall, California is home to the press and paparazzi. I would be bothered there perhaps more than I would here. And I refuse to be so far away should an emergency arise."

"He's right," Madison said. "It would be best if we find a remote location near Bajul."

"He can stay at the resort." Maysa's abrupt, and somewhat loud, declaration had the effect of a gunshot. All eyes turned to her.

Madison appeared totally unimpressed by the suggestion. "I don't consider staying in a resort full of tourists as the best place to relax and avoid publicity."

"No one is presently staying there," Maysa said. "The main hotel is currently closed for renovations, but the stand-alone villas on the far side of the property are available. They're a perfect hideaway."

"What about the staff?" Zain asked.

"Shamil gave them all a vacation. In fact, he requested I stop by from time to time to oversee the workers."

Rafiq frowned. "With no staff available, then I would be charged with preparing my own meals and laundering my own clothing?"

Heaven help him if he had to lift a royal finger to do menial chores. "Every villa is equipped with a full kitchen and normally a private chef. Since that isn't the case at the moment, I would be willing to see you have the proper meals and I can have my own staff do your laundry."

"This could definitely work." Madison pointed a finger at Maysa. "But you'd have to find a way to remain undetected. Zain's guards ran off a few reporters who were hanging around at the gate when we arrived. I assure you, they'll return as soon as we leave."

"I'll travel at night," she said. "The building crews will be gone by then, so the risk of anyone seeing me would be minimal."

When Rafiq failed to respond, Zain turned his attention to him. "Does this appeal to you at all, brother?"

Rafiq finally dropped into a chair and stretched his long legs before him, as if he'd settled in for the unforeseeable future. "I am thinking."

"Don't think too long," Madison said. "We have to

decide now, otherwise you'll be forced to return to the palace whether you're ready or not."

Rafiq remained silent a few moments before sending a quick glance at Maysa. "I will agree to the plan, as long as Maysa is also in agreement."

She saw no reason not to agree. He would have his time away, and she would have time away from him. If he had stayed under her roof, the temptation would have been too great. As it stood now, they would be better off keeping their distance from each other. She would simply deliver his meals and laundry, then leave. If only she truly believed it would be that simple. "I agree it's the best option."

"Excellent." Zain shot to his feet, held out his hands to his wife and pulled her up from the sofa. "Now if the two of you will excuse us, as soon as we return the guards to the palace, we have plans of our own."

Madison checked her watch. "And we only have a couple of hours before your children demand to be fed."

"That is why they invented bottles," Zain muttered.

Madison patted his cheek. "Patience, sweetie. The lake isn't going anywhere, and neither is the mountain."

"Are you planning to have more children?" Rafiq said, sounding somewhat appalled.

Madison's cheeks flushed. "Well, no, we're not. But then we weren't planning the last two."

Maysa couldn't help but laugh again. "Then I suggest you make certain you are prepared to battle the powers of *Mabrúuk*. I have condoms available should you need them."

Zain winked at his wife. "Thank you for the offer, Maysa, but we have everything under control."

Madison sent him a smile. "We better. As much

as I love our babies, I'm not sure how well we could handle two more."

Maysa experienced a tiny bite of envy over the couple's obvious love for each other. A love that had encouraged a king to give up his throne for the unacceptable woman he adored. If only she could be so fortunate.

Shaking off the melancholy, she gestured toward the corridor. "Since I certainly do not wish to delay you further, I'll see you both to the door."

Rafiq didn't bother to stand. "Before the two of you leave, I would caution you both to take care. But if you wish to provide a diversion by swimming nude in the lake during the light of day, you have my blessing."

"We are married and I am no longer the king," Zain said. "The press is not interested in my life any longer. In fact, I can parade naked in the streets if I so desire without earning a second glance."

"I don't know about that," Madison added. "I've seen you naked and it's pretty impressive."

Zain grinned before continuing the lecture aimed at his brother. "On the other hand, you, Rafiq, *are* the king. You are expected to behave with a measure of decorum, so I suggest you avoid being naked anywhere other than the shower."

The warning was not lost on Maysa. "I will make certain he keeps his clothes on in public." Her tongue seemed determined to get her in trouble. "I'll see you to the door so you may get on with your day."

After a brief exchange of goodwill between the brothers, Maysa escorted Zain and Madison to the door while Rafiq stayed behind. "You can both rest assured that we will be on our best behavior."

"I trust you will," Zain said as he kissed her cheek. "Do not let him have the upper hand and order you around. Stand firm."

"I'll try my best, Zain, but you and I both know your brother. He's nothing if not stubborn and persistent." And persuasive.

Once Zain started toward the awaiting car, Madison took Maysa's hands into hers. "If that whole best intentions thing to avoid Rafiq's charms doesn't work out for you, just make sure you're discreet. And most important, don't go anywhere near that damn mountain."

With that, Madison hurried away to join her husband, leaving Maysa alone to ponder her options. She couldn't exactly avoid the mountain since it shadowed the resort, as it did most of the town. And she definitely couldn't avoid Rafiq's charms as she saw to his comfort. But she could—and she would—stand firm. At least she had work to occupy her time and her mind.

"Are you certain you have to work tomorrow?"

They'd barely made it into the villa's door before Rafiq posed the query that sounded like the prelude to a proposition. Maysa set one of the paper sacks containing supplies on the kitchen's black granite counter and began rifling through it. "I have to be at the clinic tomorrow. I have a full schedule."

Rafiq leaned around her and placed another sack next to hers. "Will you not consider staying with me tonight?"

Oh, she had considered it on the drive to the resort. She was considering it now when he rested his palm on her waist and she could feel the warmth of his hand through the dress's cotton fabric. But she still planned to give him an emphatic no. Eventually. Right then she chose to ignore the question and his touch. Or at least try.

"My chef prepared these pastries for your breakfast," she said as she pulled a metal tin from the bag. "She also provided a nice lunch that I'm sure you will enjoy."

She took said lunch, sidestepped Rafiq and placed it in the refrigerator. After she closed the door and turned around, she found Rafiq leaning back against the opposite counter, arms folded across his chest, his eyes looking as dark and intense as a midnight storm.

"I will make it worth your while if you stay with me tonight." His deep, sensual voice, as well as the promise in his words, went straight to Maysa's head like a glass of fine French champagne.

Stand firm...

Turning her back, she continued to unload the last of the supplies. "It's almost a half-hour drive to the clinic."

"I will have one of the guards drive you."

"I have my own vehicle, remember?"

"Yes, I remember. I also recall what we almost did in that vehicle, and our plans to finish what we had barely begun. Had my brother not arrived, we would still be in your bed, and I would be deep inside you."

Maysa fumbled the coffee canister on her way to placing it in the overhead cabinet. The container hit the countertop with a thump, landed on the bamboo floor and rolled behind her. She closed her eyes and cursed her clumsiness. She opened her eyes the minute she heard Rafiq come up behind her. He brushed against her back as he set the coffee in the cabinet with little effort.

Maysa's effort to avoid him began to wane. She ducked under his arm, strode to the adjacent dining room and began rearranging the artificial flowers in the vase set in the middle of the heavy wood table. "I have to admit Shamil did a good job modernizing the villas. With all the granite and stainless appliances, the place looks almost American. There is a nice private pool in the courtyard and…"

A persistent king pressed against her back, generating enough heat to fuel the six-burner stove. Rafiq rested his right hand on her waist and his left hand higher, where he grazed his thumb back and forth along the side of her breast. Then he swept her hair aside and whisked a series of soft, warm kisses along the side of her neck. She could ignore him. She could pretend to ignore her body's immediate reaction. Or she could simply enjoy the moment.

When she tipped her head back against his shoulder, he kissed the corner of her mouth, and without warning, he turned her around and set her atop the table.

A laugh of surprise slipped out of her gaping mouth. "Are you attempting to disarm me?"

He rested his hands on her thighs. "I am trying to persuade you allow me to resume what we began earlier today."

"We're in the kitchen."

He planted his palms on her knees. "We are in the dining room next to the kitchen."

She narrowed her eyes. "Are you having some sort of sexist fantasy about having your way with a woman in a domestic setting?"

"You are my fantasy, and I would like to have my way with you in any setting."

He punctuated his point by kissing her without mercy. So lost in his gentle yet complete exploration of her mouth, a few moments passed before Maysa realized Rafiq was working her dress up her thighs. When she tensed, he brought his lips to her ear.

"Trust me."

She did trust him, so much so she didn't launch into all the reasons why they shouldn't do this as he reached beneath the dress and clasped the band low at her hips. She didn't issue one protest when he began to lower her panties. In fact, she lifted her hips, allowing him to pull them down her legs to drop onto the floor. She didn't question why she was sitting on a table with her hem almost to her waist. She didn't care that she was exposed to Rafiq's eyes as he nudged her legs apart. She certainly didn't care when he formed his hand between her thighs.

She tipped her head against his and lowered her gaze to watch the patently erotic scene. Not once had she climaxed with her former husband, and she worried she might not be able to now. But this was Rafiq, the one and only man who had ever given her one—several—before the foreplay culminated into full-blown lovemaking. He knew exactly where to touch her, how much pressure to apply until she bordered on begging him to hurry. Yet he continued to take his time, measuring each stroke until her legs began to tremble. A sense of relief blended with the heady sensations when she experienced the impending release. She inadvertently dug her nails into Rafiq's shoulders as the orgasm began to build in intensity. She bit back the scream resulting from sheer pleasure, not pain. He captured her gasp with another kiss, moving his tongue in sync with the finger he had eased inside her.

As the final wave subsided, Maysa kept her head lowered and tried to hold the unexpected tears at bay, to no avail. She quickly swiped away the few that slipped free and hoped Rafiq didn't notice.

"Did I hurt you?"

The distress in his voice drew Maysa's gaze to his. "Not at all. I wasn't certain I could feel that way again."

He kissed her forehead so tenderly she almost sobbed. "I despise what that monster did to you, yet I knew he would never break you."

"No, he did not." But Rafiq could very well break her heart again.

He leaned over, swept her underwear from the floor and handed them to her. "Now get dressed, return home and try to have a good night's sleep."

She was stunned he hadn't made another attempt to convince her to stay. "What about you?"

"I will be fine until you are ready to take the final step."

Was she ready? A few moments ago she would have gladly followed him into the bedroom. But perhaps he was right. Perhaps she needed more time to weigh the consequences. "You heard what Zain and Madison said. We should not be entertaining thoughts of further intimacy under the circumstances."

He visually tracked her movements as she slipped her panties back into place. "No one would need to know, Maysa."

"But I would know, Rafiq. If we made love, and a reporter asked me about our relationship, the truth would be written on my face."

"All the more reason for you to take some time away from your practice."

If only it were that simple. "My entire day is booked tomorrow, morning until late afternoon."

"Say the word and I will have my personal physician treat patients in your stead."

"He doesn't know my patients. They rely on me. They know me."

Rafiq clasped her waist, lifted her up and set her on her feet. "Then see your patients and come to me tomorrow night."

The temptation to say yes lived strong in Maysa. Temptation had gotten her into trouble before. "I'll think about it."

"That is all I ask."

His agreement came much too swift. "Then you'll be fine should I decide to have one of your guards deliver your dinner while I remain home?"

"Of course."

He gave her a brief kiss with only a light graze of his tongue. Yet that was enough for her to reconsider.

Before she did, Maysa grabbed her bag and began backing to the door. "I will let you know if I decide to join you tomorrow night."

A slightly arrogant grin lifted the corners of his beautiful mouth. "And if you decide not to come to me, mark my words, I will eventually come to you."

Six

"You have one remaining patient, Dr. Barad."

Maysa leaned over the counter and frowned at Demetria Christos, the fiftysomething office manager, who normally ran the clinic's office like a ship's captain. Tonight the woman seemed as tightly wound as her salt-and-pepper curls. "You told me fifteen minutes ago the last patient had left, Demetria."

She began rapping the desk with a pen. "He's a walk-in. An American traveling through the region. He says he requires a complete physical, although he looked well to me. Very well indeed."

She could refuse treatment, but then again, he could actually afford to pay for the services. She could always use extra money for supplies and salaries. "Where is Jumanah?"

"She left a few minutes ago with her husband, before the man arrived."

And that meant Maysa would be without a nurse to assist. Not necessarily an issue, but it would delay the process if she had to handle the entire treatment herself. "Fine. But please lock the door and hang the closed sign."

"I have already done both."

"What room is he in?"

Demetria resumed her annoying pen tapping. "Room one."

Maysa pushed off the counter then turned when she came upon an idea. "I have a favor to ask. Would you mind having Paulos prepare his eggplant moussaka to go, please?" One of Rafiq's favorites during the time when they would eat together at the Greek restaurant. Now that she had the dinner situation solved, she had to tackle the other—whether she would personally deliver it or summon one of his guards.

She sent Maysa a suspicious look. "You do not like eggplant, Doctor."

A faux pas of the first order. "It's for a friend. Someone who's in Bajul for a visit."

"A man friend?"

A royally gorgeous man friend. "Yes, but he is nothing more than a casual acquaintance." And that was nothing less than a colossal lie.

Demetria looked crestfallen. "I am disappointed you have yet to find a suitable companion. Perhaps you would reconsider using my matchmaking talents?"

She would rather eat eggplant. "No, thank you, and feel free to go to the restaurant now."

"You want me to leave you alone with a stranger?"

The woman had a point. "Does he look threatening?"

"He is very tall and lean and quite handsome." She topped off the comment with a smitten smile.

Not the answer Maysa needed. "But does he appear to be the criminal sort?"

"My instincts say he is harmless, and my instincts are never wrong."

Except for the time Demetria had coerced her into a date with a local banker who was eight years' Maysa's junior and as interesting as a spreadsheet. "Then clearly there isn't any reason why you shouldn't leave."

"This is true. His chart is on the door."

"Thank you, and I'll be by to pick up my order as soon as I'm finished here." Maysa spun around and headed down the tiled hallway, exhaustion weighting her steps. She grabbed the chart from the holder and scanned the intake form only containing his last name as she entered the room. "What can I do for you, Mr. King?"

"I am open to all suggestions."

She glanced up from the page to see Rafiq casually perched on the edge of the exam table, one leg slightly bent, one foot planted on the floor. He wore a tailored white shirt, black dress slacks and an expression that said he was greatly enjoying his little surprise.

"What are you doing here?" she asked as soon as she found her voice.

"As I told your secretary, I am here for a complete physical."

That came as no real surprise. "You have your own physician."

"He is not presently available."

As if she believed that. "Did Demetria recognize you?"

"She did, but I asked her not to tell you."

That certainly explained the office manager's odd behavior, yet it did not explain Rafiq's lack of wisdom. "Do you realize the risk you took coming here? Anyone could have seen your armored car and—"

"I walked from the palace," he said. "I had the guards deliver me there and then set out on foot. That served as a sufficient decoy."

"Since it's at least a mile from the palace to the clinic, obviously you're not in dire straits as far as your physical health is concerned." She would have to question his mental health for walking the streets in broad daylight.

He leveled his dark gaze directly on hers. "I do have an ache that does not seem to want to go away."

She decided to play along, probably at her own detriment. "Where exactly is this ache?"

"I will show you."

When Rafiq slid off the table and began unbuckling his belt, Maysa pointed at him. "Do not remove one article of clothing, Your Majesty."

He had the gall to grin. "Then how will you treat this ache if you do not see its origin?"

Do not humor him, Maysa. She smiled in spite of herself. "Believe me, I don't have to see it to know how to diagnose it. It could possibly be priapism, although that usually occurs when the erection remains long after sexual intercourse."

"I see." He rubbed his shadowed jaw and studied the ceiling before returning his attention to her. "Then how do I find relief, Doctor?"

She tossed the chart onto the counter housing the sink. "I don't believe the answer to that requires my expertise. However, I do require an answer from you. Once again, why are you here?"

He took two slow steps toward her. "I am here to ask if you will be coming tonight."

If he had his way, she would be—in every respect. "It's been less than twenty-four hours since you asked, and I still have not decided."

He moved as close as he could, pinning Maysa against the counter, his hands braced on either side of her. "Is there something I could do to persuade you?"

The images from the dining table incident filtered into her muddled mind. The feelings of absolute desire were still fresh, and threatening to reappear. "Give me more time, and some space."

He straightened and slid his hands into his pockets. "I will not pressure you to make a decision, yet I will be disappointed if you leave me to while away the hours all alone, with no relief for my condition… What is it called?"

"Priapism, and you don't actually have it. You do have the means to relieve it by taking matters into your own hands."

That earned her another one of his deadly smiles. "And what would be the pleasure in that when you could take matters into your hands?"

Maysa was growing very hot, and very bothered. "I suggest you go back to the villa and await my decision like a good little king."

"How will I know what that decision will be?"

"When you see me at the doorstep. Or not."

"Then I will wait all night if I must." His expression turned suddenly serious. "Before I leave, I need you to know I understand your hesitancy, and the reason behind it. You fear the loss of control."

Rafiq had definitely hit the mark with that assumption. "You're right. Losing control is something I no longer take lightly."

"You might also believe I am being selfish." He released a rough sigh. "Perhaps I am. Yet I have learned that life holds no assurances, and the time we have is relatively short-lived. But at the moment, time together is all we have, no matter how brief."

And brief it would be. Once this affair was over, should it actually begin in earnest, they would go back to leading separate lives, as they had been for well over a decade.

He took her hands, turned them over and placed a tender kiss above the scar on one wrist, then the other. "If you decide to join me tonight, I will promise to give you my complete attention, and I will allow you all the control."

He then strode out the door, while Maysa remained in the room to mull over his vow. Rafiq Mehdi wasn't the kind of man to give up control under any circumstance. He was still the man she'd known long ago—an abiding tenderness existed beneath the steel exterior. He'd demonstrated that only moments ago. Would it be worth the risk to her emotional health if she made love with him again? Could she walk away as if nothing had ever existed between them?

She had traveled down that treacherous road before, and she had survived. She would definitely survive this time.

Maysa Barad would never allow any man—not even the man she had always loved—to break her again.

* * *

Rafiq had constantly been decisive when it came to duty. When it involved lovemaking, he was much the same. He had always taken the lead after making the first move. To relinquish that power would be completely foreign to him, yet he would for Maysa—provided she finally arrived.

She had phoned a half hour ago to inform him she was on her way. He had walked the floor as he'd waited, wondering if perhaps she had changed her mind. In accordance with his plan, he wore only a robe and nothing else. A distinct risk, but he had a point to prove. He also had a tenuous hold on his libido when he heard the lock trip.

Maysa entered the front door carrying a brown paper sack. She stopped short the moment her gaze fell on where he now stood, attempting to affect a calm he did not remotely feel.

She clutched the bag tighter and cleared her throat. "Obviously you've run out of clean clothes."

"I still have a surplus. I decided to wait to shower until after your arrival."

The discomfort in her expression indicated she understood what he was proposing. "I brought dinner from the Greek restaurant."

The low-cut yellow gauze dress she wore almost brought him to his knees. "Would you be dining with me?"

She shook her head. "No. I had a late lunch."

"As did I. You may put it away and I will reheat it later in the microwave."

"You know how to use the microwave?"

"I have two graduate degrees. I believe I can find

which button to press." He had one particular button in mind, but it would not be found in the kitchen.

"Far be it for me to force you to eat," she said. "I'll put this in the refrigerator."

"And I will retire to the shower." Without formality or fair warning, Rafiq removed the robe and set it aside on the sofa. "You are welcome to join me."

He expected Maysa to protest his boldness or perhaps leave out the door. Instead, she took a slow visual voyage down his body. He reacted as any man would, particularly a man in the presence of a woman he wanted with a fierceness unlike any he had known.

Her eyes widened slightly when she arrived at the destination that heralded the obvious results of her perusal. "I see your condition hasn't improved."

"It still requires treatment. After your hectic day, are you up for a further examination?"

"You are clearly up for it." She raised her gaze and smiled, presenting her dimples as one more weapon in her female arsenal. "I might be persuaded to lend a hand in a while. In the meantime, I suggest you retire to the shower."

"And you will join me?" He was quite surprised by the eagerness in his voice, and evidently so was Maysa.

"Perhaps, but first I must return a phone call from a patient."

Her profession seemed destined to intrude on their time. "Will this require you to make a home visit?"

"I won't know until I speak with him."

He inclined his head and narrowed his eyes. "Is this truly a patient, or a secret lover?"

She rolled her eyes. "It's a seventy-year-old farmer with a cold. I highly doubt his wife of fifty years would approve of me taking him as a lover. Besides, one lover at a time is all I can handle."

The promise in her words and her eyes lifted Rafiq's spirits. "Then I shall be in the shower, awaiting your care."

Gathering his strength, Rafiq turned away from Maysa, though he sincerely wanted to take her down on the sofa and dispense with further delay, as well as her clothing. He crossed the expansive master bedroom and entered the bath that was truly fit for a king. The stone shower was equally large, perhaps large enough for five people, and well appointed. He depressed the control on the wall that slid the ceiling open to reveal open air and a host of stars. He then set the temperature and started the water for two of the four showerheads.

After stepping beneath the spray, he braced both hands on the tiled walls and attempted to regain some control. If he failed, Maysa's examination would be over before it had begun. *If* she had not decided to take up with the farmer and leave him behind. He decided to bathe and hope for the best.

When several minutes had passed, and he was thoroughly clean and somewhat composed, he began to believe Maysa had changed her mind. Perhaps she had...

"The doctor has arrived."

The sound of her voice drew his attention to the shower's opening. The sight of her standing there, without any clothing and seemingly relaxed, shattered his calm into a million shards of human glass. He had never seen Maysa completely nude, even in their youth when their covert meetings had been conducted in darkness. The golden cast of the overhead light illuminated each detail, from the fullness of her breasts capped with light brown nipples, the indentation of her waist, the curve of her hips and the shading between her thighs.

When she stepped into the shower, he grew painfully hard and extremely aware that he would have to develop superhuman strength in the next few moments.

Maysa moved beneath the spray opposite him and closed her eyes as the water flowed over her. After Rafiq pushed aside the showerhead above him to gain a better view, his anticipation heightened while he watched her bathe. He followed the movement of her hands as she washed her breasts, then her abdomen and lower still. He wanted to go to her, touch her, kiss the moisture from her body one blessed inch at a time. Yet he had promised to relinquish his control. Therefore he had no choice but to wait until she came to him.

She rinsed the soap from her body, slicked back her long hair and finally approached him. But when he reached for her, she took a step back. "Before we continue, I need to outline some rules."

He could not conceal his frustration. "More rules?"

"For now," she said. "First, do not touch me until I give you permission."

"That is not acceptable—"

She held up a hand to silence him. "Don't forget that I am in control, as you ordained."

He had not forgotten, though he had begun to regret it. "Continue."

"Next, you cannot kiss me, at least for the time being."

He was quickly taking exception to her rules, yet he knew better than to argue. "All right. Is there anything else I might do to accommodate you?"

"Yes." She closed the space between them and reached up to move the spray over them. "Enjoy being stripped of your control."

Her eyes seemed alight with fire as she placed her hands on his chest, pausing to touch his nipples with deft fingertips. He sucked in a deep breath when she drew a path down his belly. He clenched his jaw tightly when she circled his navel, and tighter still when she raked her nails lightly down his thighs.

She seemed to be purposefully avoiding his erection, or perhaps bent on torturing him until he begged her. She undeniably had torture in mind, he realized, when she lowered herself onto her knees. The minute she took him into her mouth, he began the battle to remain in control of his body, the only control he still retained.

When she used her tongue like a feather, from tip to shaft, Rafiq focused on trivial details in an effort to prolong the experience—his least favorite foods, his agenda for the next council meeting, the extreme heat in August. He even attempted to recall the words to the Petrarca poem Elena had forced him to memorize. Nothing worked as a sufficient distraction, until he ventured a glance at Maysa kneeling before him. Seeing her there, appearing subservient, gave him pause, as well as a temporary respite from the need for gratification.

He broke a rule by lifting her to her feet, immediately earning him a look of displeasure. "Did I do something wrong?" she asked, sounding unsure.

"You were doing everything right, and it took great effort for me to stop you."

"Then why did you?"

"Because you should never be on your knees before any man." Least of all him—a man who could give her nothing more than temporary pleasure.

"But you didn't force me on my knees, Rafiq. There is a difference."

"Still, I wish to see your eyes when you touch me."

Her smile reappeared, soft and sensual. "Let's see how long you can keep them open when I continue."

And continue she did, using her hands as effectively as she had her mouth. She increased the cadence of her strokes, making it difficult for Rafiq to draw a breath, or to keep his eyes open. In a matter of moments, he would lose both the battle and the war. He would lose the opportunity to carry her to the bed and bury himself inside her.

"Stop." The demand echoed in the shower like a gunshot.

"No," she replied, then sent a pointed look at his hand circling her wrist.

He reluctantly released her and prepared to plead his case. "If you continue, I am in grave danger of—"

"I know. That is my intention."

She had turned the tables on him, implementing her own plan that would surely drive him to the brink of pleasurable insanity. Yet she was empowered, and he was powerless. Powerless to stop her determined, thorough touching. Powerless to hold out any longer when she brought her lips to his ear and whispered, "Be grateful you are surrendering your control to a physician."

And without warning, she pressed her free hand between his legs at the same time the climax crashed down on him with the force of an explosion. He tipped his head back against the wall as a harsh, guttural moan slipped out of his mouth. The orgasm continued longer than any he had experienced before, and the impact almost buckled his knees. By the time the sensations began to wane, he realized his heart was beating dangerously fast.

He finally opened his eyes to Maysa, who seemed very proud of her accomplishment. "What did you do to me?" he grated out.

She streamed a fingertip along his jaw. "Aside from giving you the most intense orgasm you've ever experienced?"

"*How* did you do it?"

"I happen to know a certain trigger point that reportedly increases a man's pleasure. I've never tried it before, but I assume it worked."

"Had it worked any better, I would be dead."

She laid her cheek on the left side of his chest before returning her gaze back to his. "Your heart is still beating strongly, so I do believe you will live."

"For a moment I was in doubt." And in less than a moment, he would kiss her, damn the rules.

"I'm certain you have no doubts about one particular aspect of the experience."

"What would that be?"

Her expression turned from amused to sultry. "Isn't handing your control to a woman a complete rush?"

And now the time had come to reclaim that control.

He spun her around against the wall, framed her face in his palms and kissed her without hesitation, using his tongue to simulate the act of lovemaking that he planned to undertake tonight. He would need time to recover, but he knew exactly what to do with that time.

He broke the kiss but kept hold of her face. "You do not have the market cornered on your so-called trigger points. I know where they exist on you, and I intend to explore each and every one, perhaps more than once."

"But—"

He pressed a finger to her lips. "This is my plan, and these are my rules. I expect you to touch me, and I will be kissing you often. Everywhere. Do you understand?"

She appeared as if she might respond but nodded instead.

"Good. Now before I carry you to bed, I have one last remark."

"Please do, but hurry." Her words came out in a raspy whisper.

"If you trust me enough to give up your control to me, I will give you an experience you will not soon forget."

Seven

Maysa wouldn't soon forget the expectation in Rafiq's dark eyes as he awaited her answer. If she agreed to his request, she would acknowledge that she was finally ready for that next all-important step—letting go and letting him make love to her in every possible way, and the possibilities were endless. She wanted to experience each and every one with him. She needed to forget the horror her life had been with Boutros. Rafiq alone could erase those memories from her mind with only a kiss.

She took both his hands into hers. "I trust you, Rafiq. Do with me what you will, as long as you do it very, very soon."

When he swept her up into his arms, Maysa laughed from surprise and a sheer sense of freedom. She continued to laugh as he strode into the bedroom and deposited her on the edge of the mattress. She stopped laughing when he stood before her, his golden skin and thick dark hair still damp from their water play, arms dangling at his sides, every astounding inch of him exposed to her eyes. One prime, naked, beautiful male. All hers to enjoy with touches and kisses. Definitely kisses, and she craved one now.

She turned her focus on his mouth and made a rather ridiculous observation in light of their current situation. "You shaved again."

He rubbed a hand over his jaw. "Yes, and with good reason. As you've said, women at times find facial hair irritating. I would not want that for you."

"I like you better without the goatee."

"I am pleased you are pleased."

Maysa would be more pleased if he would make some move to touch or kiss her. Anything to put her out of her misery. After the shower escapade, she was so sexually keyed up she could jump out of her skin, or jump all over him.

Yet he continued to survey her as if intentionally prolonging her agony. "Rafiq, are you simply going to stand there all night and assess me?"

"No." He leaned forward and planted his palms on either side of her hips. "I am trying to decide exactly what I wish to do with you."

"I don't care. Just do it."

He barked out a laugh. "Patience has never been one of your virtues, but since I am now in control, you will have to find some."

She sighed. "You're frustrating me so much I want to scream."

He gave her a wry grin. "I assure you, screaming

could very well be involved. Or at the very least, moaning."

His words blanketed her body with another round of heat. His sudden, deep kiss landed that heat right between her thighs. After he had kissed her quite thoroughly, he began a trek down her body with his lips, pausing at her breasts to pay each equal attention with the tip of his tongue and the steady pull of his mouth.

When she tried to take him back onto the bed, he rejected her efforts and straightened. "Patience," he reminded her. "I want you to remain where I have placed you."

He wanted her to continue to sit up? "What if I want to lie back?"

"I will inform you when that is permissible."

He was beginning to take the power play to the extreme, but who was she to question him? She had stripped him of all control in the shower, and seeing him that helpless had been a complete and utter turn-on. "Your wish is my command, Sayyed."

"And my command is that you take pleasure in the experience," he said, tossing her words back at her.

"I'm sure I will, as soon as you give it to me."

"I have every intention of giving it to you." When he raked his gaze down her body and back up again, she literally squirmed. "Do you know what you deserve?" he asked.

A medal for remaining upright. "No, what do I deserve?"

He leaned forward again and kissed her lightly. "A man who is willing—" he lowered himself to the floor "—to fall to his knees before you."

His tender words and actions shot straight to Maysa's heart. "I don't know what to say."

"Say nothing," he said. "Only feel."

When he parted her legs, Maysa trembled from anticipation. She became keenly aware that he was about to undertake what no man had ever dared. She had been with two men—and the one before her had never attempted this. The other had only been concerned with his own sadistic gratification, not hers.

Still, she wasn't a child. She knew all there was to know about human sexuality and female anatomy. But she had no personal barometer with which to measure how this ultimate intimacy would feel. She would soon find out, she realized, as Rafiq slid his hands beneath her bottom and kissed his way up her inner thighs.

The minute he reached the intended target, she acknowledged he had a wonderfully wicked mouth, and he used it on her with the skill of a man experienced in the art of lovemaking. As she witnessed the act, she had trouble catching her breath, but couldn't. With every pass of his tongue, she tried very hard to take in all the sensations, but she was beginning to enter the realm where thought was impossible. Her hips involuntarily tilted toward him, prompting Rafiq to be even more deliberate. And that in turn brought about a climax that jarred her like an unpredictable bolt of lightning.

The impact left her weak and winded and momentarily incoherent from the wonder of it all. But she wasn't so mentally jumbled that she didn't notice the typical male pride in Rafiq's expression as he rested his chin on her shaky knees.

"That was quick," she said when she'd recovered enough to speak. "And totally amazing."

"I agree it was over too quickly for you to enjoy the full effect. It will not be that way the second time."

Surely he didn't mean... Oh, yes, he did. "Rafiq, I can't..."

"Do not underestimate yourself," he said. "Or me."

Multiple orgasms had never been a part of her limited sexual repertoire. She knew they were possible, but could she truly hope they were possible for her? She sought confirmation as Rafiq went back to his ministrations, this time using his hand as well as his mouth. She remained more aware of what he was doing this time, but no less excited to have him do it. No less in need of a release. The climax began to gain momentum, more tempered this time, but still potent. And when Rafiq hit her "trigger spot," the orgasm caused her to curl over his head to anchor herself.

Maysa fell back on the bed, closed her eyes and waited for the endless tremors to subside, willing her pulse to steady. Only a few moments passed before she felt the mattress bend beside her.

"Are you all right?"

She opened her eyes and focused on that remarkable, endearing smile. "I have traveled to that state known as euphoria."

His deep laugh gave her the chills all over again. "I believe I visited there in the shower."

"I never knew," she said, struggling to express what she was feeling.

"Never knew what?"

She rolled toward him and touched his face. "I never knew I could feel so much. I truly did believe Boutros had destroyed all that was good about lovemaking. I have you to thank for helping me to see it can be good. Better than good."

He pushed her damp hair back and kissed her forehead. "You are not required to thank me, and the best is yet to come. If you are ready."

How could she not be? "I am more than ready, and weary of waiting."

"Good. Get dressed."

She had not expected that perplexing order. "Is this some new technique you've learned, making love fully clothed?"

"No. I want to take you somewhere special to make love to you."

He was certainly full of surprises tonight. "Where would that be?"

"Our past."

If only they could actually return to those carefree days. If only they could change the course of their history and the confines of their culture. If only they had found some way to be together permanently.

Maysa dealt daily in reality, not impossibilities. Time could not be rewound, and even if it could, she wasn't certain she would turn back the clock. Every heartbreak, every moment of torture, had driven her to succeed. Every disappointment had made her who she was today—a strong, independent woman. A physician. If she had been chosen to be Rafiq's wife, she would have eventually been relegated to entertain dignitaries and churn out royal heirs. She had always wanted to be a doctor, and she probably would not have been allowed the opportunity had she married Rafiq. Resentment might have destroyed their love.

Nevertheless, the past was dead and buried, and the present was all that mattered right now. She would concentrate on that as they set off on their mystery journey.

Yet the mystery ended the moment Rafiq steered the Hummer off the main highway and Maysa realized exactly where they were going—their secret sanctuary.

Ancient olive trees lined the narrow lane, welcoming them back to the large parcel of Mehdi-owned land that bordered the palace grounds. The private grove where she and Rafiq had come of age in each other's arms. Where they had first declared their love, all the while knowing that love would never be enough to sustain their relationship. Not when culture and customs had intruded.

As pavement turned to gravel, Maysa powered down the window, allowing the warm breeze to reintroduce her to the scents and sounds of nature in its purest form. Rafiq pulled between two acacia trees adjacent to the small clearing that had served as their special meeting place. He shut off the ignition and left on the parking lights that illuminated the tufts of grass and aloe plants in a golden glow.

After taking in the sight, she shifted slightly toward Rafiq. "It looks the same as it did before. I do hope the caretaker still keeps the wolves away."

He draped an arm over the steering wheel and stared out the windshield. "No one has spotted a wolf in a number of years."

That gave her only a small measure of comfort. "I suppose we could have brought along one of your guards, although having an audience would be rather awkward."

"They are positioned on the main road in front of the entrance to the property."

Wonderful. "They're not going to be patrolling the area, are they?"

"They will remain in the car, as I have instructed. We will not be disturbed."

"Good. I'd hate to be caught—"

"Naked?" He accentuated the comment with a sensual grin.

"Exactly."

"I will protect you from prying eyes if necessary."

She smiled at a sudden recollection. "If my memory serves me correctly, you insisted on coming to my bed that first time because you worried someone would catch us here without our clothes. Now you're suggesting we take off all our clothes here and the threat is still real."

He reached across the console and took her hand. "With age and experience comes the need for adventure."

"As long as that adventure does not include ants and other creatures of the night."

He brought her face around and kissed her. "I will protect you from all predators."

Maysa fished two condoms from the side pocket of her casual dress and prepared for Rafiq's reaction. "And I am in charge of protecting us from pregnancy."

As she'd predicted, he scowled. "Although I understand the necessity, I am not pleased with having a barrier between us."

"A thin barrier. You'll barely know it's there."

"I will know, and why only two?"

She slapped playfully at his arm with the back of

her hand. "I have a whole box at the resort if this is not enough."

"That is good to know." He reached behind the seat and brought out two of the hotel's blankets. "Now it is time to put these barriers to good use."

Maysa waited while Rafiq rounded the Hummer and opened her door. After he took her hand to help her out, they walked, arms around waists, toward the far side of the field that contained more sand than foliage.

Rafiq let Maysa go to spread out one of the blankets, then dropped the other on the ground beside the pallet. "In case we need to cover ourselves should we be visited by an intruder."

She truly hoped that wouldn't be necessary. "Well?" she asked when neither made a move to undress.

"Shoes first," he said as he lowered onto the blanket and began removing his boots.

Maysa slipped off her sandals while Rafiq stripped out of his shirt. Although the light was limited to a three-quarter moon, she could still make out his body's finer details—the webwork of masculine veins in his strong arms, the bulk of his biceps and the ridged plane of his belly. She had seen those details earlier, among others, yet she found she would gladly study them for hours. She also discovered a sense of daring that had been missing from her life for several years.

After she stepped onto the edge of the blanket, she pitched the condoms to Rafiq, who made a perfect one-handed catch. She reached behind her, slid the back zipper down and then lowered the straps. She let the dress fall in a pool of gauze at her feet, drawing Rafiq's attention to her bare breasts. When she shimmied out of her panties and kicked them aside, he released an audible groan.

"Have I told you how beautiful you are?" he asked, his voice noticeably strained as he lowered his fly.

She didn't need to hear the compliment—she could see the appreciation in his eyes, and elsewhere when he had dispensed with the rest of his clothes. And she had no qualms about taking a long look elsewhere. "Thank you, Your Highness. I feel the same about you." She felt so much for him that her emotions were heading into a tailspin.

Rafiq patted the space beside him. "If you are ready to proceed, join me."

Deciding to take that daring for another spin, Maysa went to her knees, crawled toward him and reached over to retrieve one discarded packet. After withdrawing the condom, she nudged Rafiq onto his back and took the liberty of rolling it into place, with a few added unnecessary adjustments for good measure.

She then stretched out atop the length of him. "I believe I've proven I am more than ready." She shimmied her hips against him. "So are you."

With one smooth move, he flipped her onto her back. She expected to see amusement in his eyes, but instead, she saw worry. "Again, if you wish me to stop, say so. If you experience any pain, tell me."

She loved him for his concern. She loved him for more reasons than she could count. "I'm positive that will not happen. After all, this is what we've been waiting for, and I trust you'll make it worth the wait."

He lifted her chin and kissed her briefly. "I will do everything in my power to make it right for you."

"And you are a very powerful man, Rafiq Mehdi, oh, king of the female climax."

Finally, his smile reappeared. "I will endeavor to continue to earn that title, beginning now."

And he did, without a moment's hesitation. After a few expert touches and one long, hot kiss, he quickly took her to the brink and she was on the verge of pleading and promising him anything if he would take her all the way. Then he removed his hand, raised slightly, moved over her.

Maysa braced for the inevitable, so certain she could handle the culmination of all their foreplay. Yet when he began to ease inside her, her body tensed even though her mind told her this was not an invasion. This was Rafiq, the man she trusted with her life.

Rafiq stilled and responded by uncurling her fisted hands and kissing her palms. He then began speaking to her in Arabic. Soft words. Sensuous words. Descriptive words that painted a picture of how she felt surrounding him. How he had waited a lifetime to be this close to her again. How his greatest desire was to give her the utmost pleasure.

Before Maysa realized it, they were completely joined; she was entirely free of any resistance and once more caught in the throes of an orgasm the moment he began to move. As the cadence of his thrusts increased, she smoothed her hands over his back, memorized every nuance, reveled in his power and remembered that one night when she had given herself to him the first time. When she had willingly handed over her heart, only to have it shattered by his duty. And it would invariably happen again if she allowed it.

She refused to consider that now. She only wanted

to concentrate on these precious moments when nothing mattered but making love with him. Loving him.

After Rafiq collapsed against her with a low moan, Maysa's unwanted tears again broke through despite her determination not to cry in front of him for the second time in as many days. The emotional fortress she had erected for self-protection had begun to crumble in his presence.

"Once more, I have brought you to tears, and I am sorry for that."

Maysa opened her eyes and tried to smile, a shaky one. "These special moments made me cry, Rafiq. Not you. They're good tears."

"I have never known tears to be good."

Spoken like a man who probably hadn't cried since childhood. "Sometimes they're necessary. An emotional release of sorts. You don't need to worry."

He brushed a damp strand of hair away from her cheek. "Yet I do worry. I worry about what will happen after we part ways again."

So was she. "Let's not ruin this by talking about that. We still have time. Tomorrow is Saturday, which means I have nowhere I need to be."

"I need to be with you," he said. "The entire weekend. I do not want to be away from you for even an hour."

"Then I am yours." For the weekend. Beyond that, who knew?

He brought her against his chest and rubbed her arm in a soothing rhythm. "Perhaps we should begin our time together in a real bed."

Maysa smiled in earnest. "I agree. I think I'm lying on a tree root, or perhaps a tortoise."

He shifted to where they faced each other. "Shall we drive back naked?"

"Oh, no, let's walk back naked. If we're lucky, we'll stumble upon some hapless reporter and provide a story that will span the ages. I can see it now—King Rafiq Mehdi Plays Doctor with Local Doctor."

Their shared laughter echoed over the olive grove, drowning out the night sounds and the inevitable goodbye hanging over them like a guillotine. Maysa wanted more laughter in the time they had left. She would reserve the tears for after he was gone.

Rafiq could not recall a time when he had been consumed by such fierce emotion. As Maysa slept in his arms, he held her as tightly as he dared for fear of rousing her. She needed rest as much as he needed her. He planned to wake her in the morning with kisses and make love to her most of the day. Lose himself in her for as long as possible, until he was forced to leave her behind again. Forced to find a more suitable woman in the eyes of the elders and the country at large. He knew no woman who would be as suitable for him as Maysa. But he would not subject her to the cruelty he inherently knew would exist if he took her as his future queen. He would not risk failing another woman.

Oddly, the guilt over his role in Rima's death had subsided over the past few days, yet it once more reared its ugly head. He had selfishly and willingly drawn Maysa into this doomed affair, and now he would suffer the consequences of his actions by losing her a second time.

Before that happened, he had much he needed to tell her, including all that had transpired the night of

Rima's death. Perhaps then Maysa would understand why he did not deserve her devotion. Perhaps then their parting would be easier. Swift and sure, as it should be. Once he confessed, she would not look upon him the same way. She would not be able to forgive him, as he had not been able to forgive himself.

In the interim, he would cherish this fleeting fantasy they had created, and he would show Maysa the depth of his feelings by giving her his undivided attention. He dared not put those feelings into words, for to declare them out loud would only wound her further.

Yet as he gazed upon her beautiful face and saw the girl she had been, as well as the remarkable woman she had become, he whispered those words without thought. With the reverence of a prayer.

"Ana bahebik."

I love you....

Eight

Maysa had always looked forward to Monday mornings, a day when she could leave the boring weekend behind to face the challenges of her profession. Today, with a remarkable man sleeping soundly at her side, she hated Monday.

In a little over an hour, she would reluctantly leave Rafiq to go work after spending a weekend with him that had been anything but uneventful. On the contrary, she'd experienced the best two days of her life to this point. She'd become someone unrecognizable to herself, a woman transformed into a high-voltage mass of sexual energy. She and Rafiq had made love in many different ways, and in many different places. She had done things with him that she'd never dreamed she would do, and the rewards had been phenomenal. He'd guided her into a paradise built on experimentation and a total loss of inhibition. They'd foregone clothing for easy access whenever the lovemaking mood struck them, and it had quite often.

But during the aftermath, when they'd been temporarily satisfied to only hold each other, they talked about times gone by and the road to her career. They'd discussed world politics and Rafiq's role in Bajul's future. They had covered everything but their impending goodbye.

Maysa had been grateful for that. She preferred to focus on the present and quiet, unforgettable moments such as this. She propped up on one elbow, supported her cheek with her palm and took the opportunity to study Rafiq, now stretched out on his back. He had a perfectly sculpted profile, as did all the Mehdi sons, only one of the reasons their photos had been in high demand and plastered all over the internet. Extraordinarily beautiful men with political power and untold wealth. The pinnacle of masculinity in a package of three.

But right now, with his eyes closed and his features slack, Rafiq looked more teenage boy than adult monarch to Maysa. More innocent than experienced. The motherless child who had strived to be worthy of his father's respect. The king of her damaged heart.

When he began to stir, she smoothed a wayward lock of hair back and kissed his forehead. His eyes opened slowly, followed by a patently sensual smile. The adult Rafiq had returned.

"I am surprised you are awake," he said in a sexy morning voice.

"I have to go into the clinic in a bit."

He turned toward her and outlined her lips with a

fingertip. "Can I persuade you to take another day off to spend with me?"

He could, if she let him, but she wouldn't. "This is my life, Rafiq, taking care of people. I have a responsibility to my patients to show up and..."

Her words trailed off the minute Rafiq's hand landed on her breast. She should move it immediately, before he moved that hand significantly lower. But as he began that predictable downward trek, his cell began to ring, momentarily keeping Maysa from throwing caution and obligation to the desert winds.

Rafiq fell back against the pillow, snatched the offending phone from the nightstand and answered with a gruff, "What do you want, Zain?"

Maysa settled her head on his shoulder, her palm resting on his sternum. She listened to the steady beat of his heart, as well as the one-sided conversation that seemed somewhat tense.

"I will be preoccupied for the next hour," he said. "But you may call after that if any issue arises."

Then out of the blue, Rafiq guided Maysa's hand beneath the sheet to show her exactly what had arisen. She attempted to ignore his personal "issue," not by taking her hand away, but by leaving it still.

Rafiq caught her gaze, smiled and winked at her before he continued. "I trust you can handle it." Maysa stifled a laugh when he added, "No, I was not speaking to you, Zain," followed by a long pause when Maysa could no longer resist the temptation to drive him crazy with a few practiced touches.

"What am I doing at the moment?" Rafiq drew in a broken breath and let it out slowly. "I am considering a long morning ride. I will see you this afternoon."

After he hung up, Rafiq immediately tossed the phone aside, while Maysa threw back the covers. After that, everything happened very quickly—fumbling for a condom, touching with abandon, making love as if tomorrow would not arrive. After the frantic session was over, they remained in each other's arms while their bodies calmed and their breathing returned to normal.

Yes, these were the moments she appreciated the most. She would take them to memory and bring them out when they were all she had left of him.

The shrill of the alarm forced Maysa out of the fantasy world and back into reality. She reluctantly left him and sat up. "I have to get ready for work." When Rafiq didn't respond, she glanced to her right to find him staring at the ceiling. "Is something wrong?"

"A complication with one of the council members," he said without looking at her. "I must return to the palace this afternoon."

"Permanently?" She despised the disappointment in her voice, but she wasn't prepared for their parting.

"I am not certain," he said. "It will depend on the outcome of the meeting."

She rose from the bed, grabbed the robe from the nearby chair and slipped it on. "I hope it goes well."

"As do I."

On the chance this could be the final time they would be together alone, she decided to make an offer he wouldn't refuse. "I'm going to shower now. Would you like to join me?"

He moved up against the wood headboard and raked both hands through his hair. "I will shower in the secondary bath. After you are dressed, meet me in the living area. We have a few things to discuss."

A strong sense of dread shot all the way to her soul. "All right. I will see you in a while."

As she bathed, Maysa tried to tell herself this could only have to do with Rafiq's duty, and not their relationship. She had little luck in convincing herself that was the truth. By the time she was finished dressing and out the bedroom door, she was resigned to hearing goodbye.

When she entered the living room, Maysa discovered Rafiq leaning forward on the edge of the small divan, his head lowered and his hands laced together between his knees. When he looked up, she immediately noticed the weariness in his eyes.

She swallowed around the knot in her throat and took the space beside him. "I am fairly certain I know what you are about to say."

He sighed and leaned back against the magenta cushion. "You have no way of knowing what I am about to say until after I say it. And once the words leave my mouth, you will never view me in the same light again."

She clasped his hand to reassure him that nothing he said would ever change her mind about him. "Rafiq, we've both known our time together would eventually come to an end sooner than later."

"You misunderstand," he said. "This is not about us."

Now she was sincerely confused. "Did something happen at the palace in your absence?"

"No. I need to tell you what transpired the night Rima died. I have been carrying the burden far too long."

Relief washed over her, though she was still concerned. "Go ahead. I'm listening."

He hesitated a few moments before he continued. "Shortly after dinner that evening, she came into my study and told me of the pregnancy. I was pleased with the news and hopeful that having a child together would restore our civility, if not our friendship. She did not agree."

"Then she wasn't even the least bit happy about the baby?" Maysa asked, though she had seen indications of that unhappiness when Rima had come to her for confirmation.

"No, she was not happy. I requested we make a formal announcement, yet she refused. She said she did not want anyone to know until she was more than two weeks along in the pregnancy."

Warning bells rang out in Maysa's head. "Are you certain she wasn't further along?"

"I am certain. Why would you believe otherwise?"

She had no one to blame but herself for walking into this snake pit. Still, she was trapped between upholding patient confidentiality and being up front with Rafiq. She chose the former for the time being. "I apologize. You were her husband and you would most likely know when she conceived."

"I knew the exact night she became pregnant," he said. "I had recently returned from a diplomatic mission encompassing several countries. It was the first time she had allowed me in her bed for several months, and that was only after I pursued the matter of producing an heir."

The tangled web of deceit had now grown, wrapping Maysa in its clutches. If he had been traveling during the time of Rima's actual conception, that left only one probability—Rafiq had not fathered the child she'd been carrying at the time of her demise. "You said something else happened that night. What was it?"

"We debated the announcement for a time," he continued, "and then she informed me she did not care to be pregnant with my child, but she did want out of the marriage. I told her that was impossible and I would not divorce her."

Having heard that from her own husband, Maysa experienced a fleeting moment of sympathy for Rima. "I'm sure that upset her further."

He released a rough sigh. "Yes, but not as much as when I told her if she left the country after the birth, I would seek her out and bring the baby back to the palace. I would see to it she would have no contact with our child. She said she would see me in hell before she allowed that to happen. That is when I ordered her out of the palace. I arranged for the car she was driving that night."

And Maysa knew exactly where she had gone— ironically the resort where they were now having this disturbing discussion. "No one knows about this?"

"Only my assistant, Mr. Deeb, who had the car delivered to the palace." He turned his weary gaze on her. "And now you know everything."

She did, but he did not. She could fill in the blanks, and possibly annihilate everything she had worked so hard to gain, because of one man who had played in integral part in this twisted triangle. Her own flesh and blood.

Rafiq streaked a hand over his jaw and sighed. "I

would not blame you if you choose to leave now and never look back."

She rested a hand on his arm. "If you are expecting harsh judgment from me, you won't find it. You're human and not infallible. Neither am I. We all make mistakes, and we can only move on and learn from those mistakes if they cannot be rectified."

He appeared stunned by the comment. "I deserve no less than your condemnation. What honorable man threatens to tear a mother away from her child, then arranges to send that distraught woman to her death?"

"An angry man," she said. "And you had no way of knowing Rima would have an accident. Her death wasn't your fault any more than your mother's death was your father's fault."

He sighed. "I cannot believe you would forgive me so easily."

"Yet I do, Rafiq. More important, it is past time for you to forgive yourself."

The time had also come to tell him the truth about Rima's relationship with Shamil, and the result of that relationship. But after she consulted the clock on the wall, she decided to wait until she wasn't facing a clinic full of patients in less than twenty minutes. As it stood now, she would probably arrive late.

She came to her feet, leaned over and kissed his cheek. "When I return here tonight, we'll continue this discussion, provided you decide not to end your sabbatical immediately." She held her breath while waiting for his answer.

"I will be here," he said. "I cannot stand the thought of leaving you today."

She couldn't stand the thought of him leaving her

ever. But he might not be so willing to stay once she revealed the truth, as well as how long she had kept it from him. "I have to go now, and I'll see you this evening."

Rafiq rose from the sofa, took her hand and walked her to the door where he kissed her soundly and said goodbye. She hoped it wasn't the final one.

After she was well on her way to the clinic, Maysa mulled over everything Rafiq had told her, particularly the part about Rima lying about the length of her pregnancy. She was without a doubt certain of one thing—Rafiq had not been the father of Rima's child. Her instincts told her she knew the responsible party. And as soon as she had a break at work, she planned to track him down and confront him by phone.

When her cell began to ring, Maysa fished it from her bag to find her brother's name on the screen, as if she had somehow willed him to contact her. "Hello, Shamil," she answered with feigned composure.

"Hello, my dear sister. Are you enjoying your status as the king's whore?"

Evidently the rumors had traveled all the way to Yemen. "It's not like you to listen to idle gossip, Shamil."

"True, but I do tend to believe what I have seen with my own eyes. That was quite a passionate kiss the two of you shared at the door of my finest villa only minutes ago."

Utter panic settled over Maysa. "Where are you now?"

"I am staring at two armored cars, but I am about to pay His Excellency a long overdue visit. I have done some soul-searching during my time away and I have decided the bastard should hear the truth."

Unable to concentrate on driving, Maysa pulled onto the shoulder. "The guards will never let you near him."

"That is where you are wrong. I have already notified the king I will be there soon, and he was more than happy to welcome an old friend."

She highly doubted that. "You call yourself a friend when you have betrayed his trust by sleeping with his wife?"

"You are not one to judge after you have spread your legs for him in *my* resort. I will derive great pleasure from demanding he leave at once."

A sense of dread prompted Maysa to tighten her grasp on the steering wheel. "Shamil, please, think about what you are about to do."

"I have thought about it, and nothing you can say will stop me from exacting the revenge the *king* so deserves."

When the line went dead, Maysa jumped into action. She executed a U-turn in the middle of the road and depressed the accelerator, spewing gravel in her wake. If Shamil made good on this threats, she refused to allow Rafiq to face the truth alone—provided she wasn't already too late.

At one time, Rafiq would have welcomed seeing his onetime closest friend. But after learning from Zain that Shamil was still attempting to thwart the conservation project, he was anything but pleased over his unexpected appearance. "I believe our meeting was scheduled at 4:00 p.m. at the palace."

"And I believe this meeting cannot wait."

When Shamil entered the villa without a proper invitation, both guards immediately moved forward to follow him. Rafiq raised a hand to halt their progress. "Remain here. I will notify you if you are needed."

He returned inside to discover Shamil had made himself at home in a chair across from the divan. "Please, sit down on *my* sofa, Rafiq."

Rafiq complied and assumed a relaxed position, though he was anything but relaxed at the moment. "Your insistence upon calling me by my given name is an act of subordination. I will forgive you this time in light of our shared past."

He stroked his graying beard as if it were a cherished pet. "I am sorry to say I cannot forgive you for seducing my sister. But then I suppose she was an easy target."

The true reason behind the visit had become all too clear. "I refuse to discuss Maysa with you."

Shamil crossed his legs and folded his hands together in his lap. "Perhaps then we should discuss the other woman formerly in your life, until you drove her to an untimely death."

Rafiq clung to the last thread of restraint. "I will not speak to you about Rima, either."

"Then I will speak to you about her. I know everything about your sham of a marriage, Rafiq. Every last detail. Who do you think she told about her misery over being wed to the likes of you?"

He momentarily rejected that notion, until he recalled Rima mentioning having lunch with Shamil a few weeks before her death. "I am aware you and Rima maintained your friendship and that you spoke to her on more than one occasion. We were all friends at one time."

"Friends?" Shamil barked out a caustic laugh. "You were never Rima's friend. You were her captor and she, your prisoner."

Rafiq had begun to suspect Shamil knew much more than he had initially believed. "We were bound by a contract made a long time ago. Rima accepted her role as queen and my wife."

Shamil leaned forward and sneered. "Let me ask you something. Did it disturb you to learn you were not Rima's first lover?"

A repeat of the conversation he had had with Adan a few days before. "What Rima did before our wedding was immaterial to me. I only asked that she remain faithful after we exchanged vows."

"Were you faithful?"

"I was." Though he had been tempted a time or two during the year following their marriage. Yet he had never acted on that temptation.

"Perhaps physically true to her," Shamil said. "But not mentally. You have always lusted after my sister."

"You know not of what you speak." A false denial, but Shamil did not deserve the truth.

"When you were forcing Rima to do your bidding in bed to produce another arrogant Mehdi, were you not imagining driving your *sambool* into Maysa?"

It took all Rafiq's strength not to wrap his hands around Shamil's throat. He settled for a curse. *"Ibn il sharmuta!"*

Shamil appeared only mildly insulted. "Please leave my mother out of this. She was a good woman. Unfortunately, Maysa does not appear to have inherited that goodness. She has brought nothing but shame to our family, first by divorcing her husband, and now by allowing you to bed her."

He refused to acknowledge any intimacy between him and Maysa. He would definitely address Maysa's ruthless ex-husband. "Do you know what Boutros Kassab did to her? Are you aware of the torture he inflicted upon her? Or do you have so little regard for Maysa that you do not care?"

Shamil did not seem the least bit disturbed, leading Rafiq to believe the latter held true. "Maysa has always been prone to exaggeration. I am certain the accusations she leveled against Boutros were overblown."

Having his conjecture confirmed, Rafiq's hatred burned bright for this man whom he once considered a confidant. "At one time I greatly respected you, Shamil. Now I see that you are nothing more than a power-hungry, misguided man without a conscience. It is no wonder you have not found a suitable wife. No woman would dare tie themselves to you."

His smile was cynical. "Your wife did not feel that way, Rafiq. Had she not been bound to your contract, she would have been with me. In fact, she was. Many times when you left her alone to travel. Did you not wonder why she always chose to stay behind?"

He had never questioned her reluctance to travel, nor had he objected to the decision. "She had duties to oversee at the palace."

"She had an aversion to spending time with you. And for your information, I was Rima's first lover, and I was her last."

"You are a liar."

"It is not a lie. She came to me that fateful night

when you ordered her out of the palace. She told me you arranged for her transportation and threatened to take your child away from her."

Rafiq now realized he spoke the truth. "That proves nothing other than she came to you seeking advice."

"She came to me seeking comfort, which I gladly gave to her in my bed. If you require further confirmation, ask my sister."

He had erroneously believed the shocking secrets were over. "What does Maysa have to do with this?"

"She saw Rima and I together in this very place that night."

If Shamil spoke the truth, Rafiq did not understand why Maysa had withheld the information. He intended to find out, but first he must deal with the turncoat before him. "I could have you hanged for this."

Shamil appeared unmoved by the threat. "Yet you will not do that. I hold the power to halt the conservation project, as well as destroy your standing with your people. Once they learn you demanded the queen leave her rightful home, subsequently leading to her death, they will not be quick to forgive you."

Rafiq inherently knew that to be true, but he would not give Shamil the satisfaction of an admission. He would present a defense for his actions. "The people are aware Rima's death was an accident, and I do not need your vote to see the project to fruition since I have the majority of council's support."

"Then consider this. Should word leak out that you have taken a scorned woman as your mistress, then you will take Maysa down with you. Since the day you appointed me health minister, I began to make many contacts in the medical field. I will make certain she is stripped of her hospital privileges and quite possibly her license to practice."

Rafiq glared at him. "You would have to show cause to do that. An unfounded rumor of an affair is not cause."

"Ah, yes, but it is amazing how a proof of physician's grave mistakes can suddenly surface, whether they are founded or not."

His patience now in tatters, Rafiq shot from the sofa and pointed at the door. "Get out."

Shamil's ensuing laugh sounded sinister. "You are ordering me out of my own establishment?"

"Yes, and if you do not leave, I will have you forcefully removed by my guards and have you escorted to the airport. They are very loyal to me, and I have no control over what they might do on the way. A man would have a difficult time surviving in the mountains without supplies, clothes and transportation."

He saw the first sign of fear in Shamil's eyes. "You would not dare give that order, as you would be the primary suspect."

No, he would not, yet he would allow Shamil to believe otherwise. "It is amazing how people mysteriously disappear. Since in all likelihood no one has been made privy to our meeting, and since it is well-known you are currently living in Yemen, you would not be missed for quite some time."

Shamil finally stood, strode to the door and opened it. But before he exited, he faced Rafiq again. "When you see Maysa, give my whore of a sister my fondest regards."

On the heels of his fury, and driven by absolute betrayal, King Rafiq Mehdi, who had always prided

himself on control, strode across the room, drew
back his fist—and centered it in the middle of Shamil
Barad's face.

Nine

Maysa arrived in time to see Rafiq deliver the blow that sent her brother back against one stone column bracing the portico. She watched in horror when the guards restrained Rafiq as he went after Shamil, who used that window of opportunity to throw a punch. The impact to his jaw snapped Rafiq's head back and split the corner of his mouth. Two more sentries appeared from across the road, grabbed Shamil and wrenched his arms behind his back.

Shock kept Maysa momentarily planted in place, until she came around and found the wherewithal to retrieve her medical bag from the backseat. She rushed toward Rafiq, only to be restrained by the bodyguard who had kept Rafiq from mostly doing serious damage to Shamil.

"Unhand her!" Rafiq shouted and then swiped his

shirtsleeve across the trickle of blood seeping from the laceration.

"Did he break my nose, Maysa?" Shamil asked, stopping her progress.

She took a quick glance at the wound. "Yes, it looks broken. They'll take care of it at the emergency room."

"You will not treat it?"

"No, I will not."

"Sharmuta!"

"Perhaps I am a bitch, but at least I fight fairly."

"Take him to the hospital," Rafiq ordered the guards.

For some reason Shamil looked terrified. "I will drive myself."

"You will remain in custody until I decide what I will do in regard to your assault on the king."

"And you will make certain I arrive at the hospital safely?"

Maysa could not believe he was being such a sniveling child. "I will call ahead and inform them you're coming." That would be the only favor she would grant him.

As the security detail began tugging him toward one of the cars, Shamil turned a hateful glare on Rafiq. "Remember what we have discussed, Your Majesty."

Rafiq muttered an Arabic oath as he turned and strode back into the villa before Maysa could get to him. She followed him even knowing she could very well be walking into a hornet's nest, with the king serving as the head hornet.

After she closed the door behind her, Maysa came upon Rafiq restlessly circling the living area, his hands balled into fists as if he would like to hit something else. "Look, Rafiq," she began, "I know you're most likely angry with me—"

"I am not angry with you," he said without looking at her. "I am angry at myself for not maintaining control. For being such a fool and a failure."

"Who have you failed?" she asked, though she already knew the answer.

He finally looked at her, the weight of the kingdom in his eyes. "My wife, and now you."

She set her bag aside on the coffee table, hoping to eventually put it to good use when she treated Rafiq's cut. If he let her treat it. "You and Rima failed each other, Rafiq. You two should never have married in the first place. But you did marry her, she turned to another man, and it all ended in tragedy. No matter what happened that night, it's done and it cannot be undone."

He paused his pacing in the middle of the room. "How long have you known about her affair with Shamil?"

The query came as no surprise. "Not until he told me the day you arrived at my house. I had my suspicions, but I never confirmed them."

"Yet you chose not to tell me."

"Shamil threatened to ruin my medical practice. At the time, that mattered most to me." Before Rafiq had come to matter more. "You and I were barely on speaking terms. I had no idea we would reconnect the way we have."

"Yet when we did become close, you still did not reveal what you knew. You should have said something, Maysa."

"Then you are angry with me."

"Disappointed that you did not feel you could tell

me after what I told you earlier." He both looked and sounded resigned.

"I did plan to tell you tonight, if that's any consolation." And now she was charged with delivering the final betrayal blow. "There is something else you need to know."

"Nothing you could say would surprise me at this point in time."

"Perhaps you should sit down, just in case."

He remained planted in the same spot. "I would rather stand."

Of course he would. "It's about the baby Rima was carrying. Shamil was the father." She waited a moment for the news to sink in before she continued. "I only discovered that this morning, after you mentioned the timing of the pregnancy. Rima was close to entering her second trimester."

"How do you know this?"

Maysa decided she needed to sit and selected the straight-back rattan chair in the corner. "Rima came to me to confirm the pregnancy, although I wasn't certain why. I now believe she wanted to avoid using one of the palace's physicians for fear they would be suspicious since you had been traveling at the time she conceived."

He sighed. "I find little comfort in the knowledge the child was not mine. An innocent life was still taken, regardless of its parentage, and I find that incredibly sad."

The declaration demonstrated the depth of his honor. Some men would be relieved, and not at all upset. "Did Shamil mention the baby to you?"

"He did not, yet I find it hard to believe that Rima would conceal it from him."

Maysa had no problem believing it. "I hate to speak ill of the dead, but Rima was always about appearances. I honestly believe she would not have divorced you for Shamil. She would never put herself in the midst of a scandal. I do think she let him believe she would for the attention."

"The attention I did not give her?"

"It wouldn't have mattered if you'd showered her with it every moment of every day. For Rima, it would never be enough."

"I did not realize you thought so little of her."

Clearly he had been blind to the ongoing competition for his affections between her and Rima. "She craved that attention when we were schoolmates at the palace, and she would find it through whatever means." Including shamelessly flirting with the other two Mehdi brothers behind Rafiq's back. But he had heard enough secrets for one day.

When Maysa noticed Rafiq's lip had begun to swell, she stood and gestured toward the sofa. "I need to take a closer look at your cut."

He trudged toward the divan as if on his way to the gallows. After he settled onto the cushions, Maysa went to work. He winced when she applied antiseptic, yet he remained still when she applied the strips to close the wound.

"That should hold the edges together if you're careful. But if it opens, you may need stitches."

As she began to put away the supplies, Rafiq clasped her wrist. "What are we going to do about us?"

"Is there an us, Rafiq?"

He released her and forked his hands through his hair. "Shamil continues to threaten to expose our affair. We would have to be cautious if we continue to see each other."

If they continued to see each other. "Then I suppose it's probably best we end it now, as originally planned."

"You are willing to walk away after what we have shared?"

She summoned all her courage before she answered. "Yes, because you are not willing to defy tradition and have an open relationship with me."

"To do that would only subject you to constant contempt and ridicule."

"Are you certain you are not referring to yourself?"

"I am the king and will remain so, whatever anyone might believe about me. But I would face resistance from the council when attempting to make decisions for the country. The majority still adhere to the old ways."

"Then in part this is also about your reputation and your unwillingness to discard the old ways."

"I am only trying to protect you, Maysa."

A spear of anger mixed with resentment hurled through her. "I divorced a husband who was basically a terrorist. I left my homeland for a strange country with only the clothes on my back. I worked my way through medical school and returned to Bajul to face the worst possible scorn, and I have survived it all. What makes you believe I need your protection?"

"I care about you and your well-being."

"If you truly cared about me, Rafiq, you would never propose I be your *sharmuta,* as Shamil so aptly put it. That being said, you may consider your sabbatical officially ended, and our affair permanently over. Feel free to return to the palace knowing your secrets are safe with me. Now I have to return to the clinic and salvage what is left of the day." And what was left of her heart.

Fearing she might reconsider or cry, Maysa snatched the bag and headed for the door. She didn't have time to open it before Rafiq came up behind her and slid his arms around her waist. "I do not know how to let you go a second time."

"Then don't, but only on my terms."

He turned her to face him. "I cannot risk failing you the way I failed Rima. I cannot abide you hating me. If avoiding that possibility means letting you go, then I have no choice."

Little by little, her heart began to splinter, one fissure at a time. One word at a time. "Everyone has choices, Rafiq. You have to decide whether you want to risk making them, or if you wish to settle for safety. I will not play second chair in your royal orchestra. I will not stand by while you choose another queen and enter another loveless marriage for the sake of building a fortune and making Mehdi babies. Either we are truly together, or we are not. I need all, or nothing."

She held her breath while she waited to hear his choice, and silently prayed it would be the right one.

Her hopes soared when he held her closely. They plummeted when he said, "I cannot risk hurting you again."

Oh, but he already had. Twice. She pulled away to gain some distance, at least physically. The emotional ties would be much harder to sever. "Then I wish you well, Rafiq, in your endeavors. And please do not try to contact me for I will not accept your calls."

"Will you honor one last request before you leave?"

The pain in his eyes called to her, and she tried not to listen. "That would depend on the request."

"Will you kiss me goodbye?"

Her mind rejected the appeal, while her shattering heart told her to answer. And she would for the sake of what they had meant to each other. A lasting memory to live on until she was ready to move forward.

Maysa wrapped her hand around his neck and brought his lips to hers. They remained that way for a long moment until the threat of tears forced her away from him. "God speed, Rafiq."

"Ana bahebik, habibti."

How long had she waited to hear those words? And now they had come too late. "I love you, too, Rafiq. I have since the first time I saw you. But I find it tragic that we still live in a place where love is simply not enough."

She walked away with her head held high and her soul in tatters. This time, the goodbye hadn't broken her. Not completely.

In the two weeks since Maysa had told Rafiq good-bye, she'd immersed herself in work, thankful for the diversion. Yet the nights had been the most difficult, and uninterrupted sleep had been at a premium.

Fortunately, today she finally felt more like her old self and prepared to meet any challenges. She was not prepared for the patient seated on the exam room table. "What are you doing here, Madison?"

"Guess."

Maysa didn't dare. "I hope you have a cold or some other minor ailment."

Madison tightened the band securing her blond

ponytail. "I'm not sure what I have exactly. I've been a little queasy in the morning and tired. But then being a mother to triplets can be exhausting."

Apparently the overtired mother was having a mental lapse. "You mean twins."

"I'm counting the father of my babies, so that basically makes three children. Did you know the man has no clue how to fold towels?"

She smiled. "Of course not. Someone has always done it for him."

"That someone is me because I refuse to have the staff do something I am quite capable of doing."

As much as she wanted to visit with Zain's wife, she still had six more patients to see before day's end. "Back to your symptoms. Is it possible you could be pregnant?"

"I have no idea. My periods are still irregular even after my one functioning ovary spit out double deuces."

"Let me rephrase the question then. Have you had unprotected sexual intercourse?"

Madison looked more than a bit sheepish. "Yes. The day we went to the lake."

The day they had stopped by to reveal the rumor mill was in full spin. "I knew I should have given you condoms."

"Zain hates using condoms."

"So does Raf…" She wanted to yank her wayward tongue out of her mouth. "Many men take exception to them, but they're necessary if you wish to prevent disease and pregnancy."

"It's okay," Madison said. "I know you and Rafiq were sleeping together. I could tell the minute I saw the two of you together at your house."

"Actually, we weren't sleeping together at that time."

"But you did sleep together later, right?"

Maysa grasped for an excuse to change the subject. "Let's get you a pregnancy test, just in case." She turned to the counter, retrieved the box, then offered it to Madison. "You know the drill. The restroom is right across the hall."

"Gotta love peeing on a stick," she said as she hopped off the table and headed out the door.

While Madison was gone, Maysa debated whether she should ask about Rafiq. Probably unwise. She would hate to learn he had already begun the queen candidate search.

After Madison returned, Maysa placed the test on the counter and set the portable timer to await the results. "In ten minutes, we should have the answer."

Madison scooted back onto the table and sent her dangling legs into motion. "I'm having a moment of déjà vu from the last time you gave me a pregnancy test. We have to stop meeting like this."

Maysa laughed. "I agree, but it's better than if you had something serious, such as malaria."

"Very true."

A few moments of awkward silence ticked off before Maysa spoke again. "How are the children?"

"Fine. Getting fat as little pigs."

"And Zain is doing well? Other than his domestic issues."

"Very well and frisky as ever. He has been busy with the water project, but he's never too tired for… you know."

Yes, she definitely knew, and she couldn't quell the envy onset. She studied the anatomy poster on the wall to her left in an effort to avoid Madison's scrutiny. "Elena and Adan are doing well?"

"Yes, and it's okay if you ask about him, Maysa."

Could she possibly be more obvious? "All right. How is he?"

Madison scowled. "He's horrible. He has turned into the meanest king in all the Middle East. He orders everyone around nonstop and refuses to come to dinner. And that blasted pacing. Makes me want to glue his butt to the office chair."

She smiled in part over Madison's comment, and in part because she liked to think Rafiq was experiencing some regret over his decision. "The pacing is a longtime habit. He's nervous."

"He's lovesick. He misses you, Maysa. I don't really know what happened between you, and you certainly are under no obligation to tell me."

She needed to tell someone, and she felt she could trust Zain's wife with the information. "Archaic tradition happened. He can't be openly involved with a divorcée, and I refuse to be his mistress."

"I don't blame you." Madison suddenly shifted her weight from one hip to the other, a possible sign of discomfort. "I do know about Rima and your brother's ongoing affair, and that the baby wasn't Rafiq's."

"Rafiq told you that?" she asked, attempting to temper the shock in her voice.

Madison shook her head. "No. He told Zain, and Zain told me. We don't have any secrets between us. He's also concerned that if Shamil decides to leak the information, I'll have to do damage control."

"It could definitely be damaging, depending on how

the information is perceived. The country seemed to take a liking to Rima immediately."

"I personally never cared for her," Madison said. "She seemed a bit self-absorbed at times, and cold. But then maybe I'm being too harsh. I never really had the chance to know her that well."

Maysa had known her all too well. "She's always been aloof since our teenage years."

"Then you knew her before she and Rafiq became engaged? Or maybe I should say before they went under contract."

"Actually, Rafiq and I were seeing each other up to that point in time." And after, a fact she decided not to divulge. "We were very close."

Madison sent her a sympathetic look. "It must have been difficult knowing she was taking your man right out from under you, and you could do nothing about it."

"It was very difficult, and at times it seemed she went out of her way to flirt with Rafiq in my presence. But then we were teenage girls, and you know how petty they can be sometimes."

"Speaking of teenagers, did you know Rima slept with Adan when he was only seventeen?"

She could tell Madison regretted the statement the moment it left her mouth. And Maysa had a difficult time believing Adan would betray his own brother.

"Are you certain that really happened?"

"Positive. Adan told me the night of the wedding. He claims Rima had argued with her one true love and she turned to him for comfort. Adan being Adan, he jumped at the opportunity. When I mistakenly thought he meant she'd argued with Rafiq, he hinted someone else was involved. I assume that someone else was your brother."

That made perfect sense to Maysa. "Does Rafiq know?"

"Not hardly, and I hope Adan doesn't have a sudden crisis of conscience and blurt it out. That would probably send Rafiq right over the edge. Losing you has been bad enough. That's why I wish you could work it out and save us all some grief."

She saw no end to the impasse. "In order to work it out, one of us will have to give in, and it will not be me. I highly doubt Rafiq will, either."

"You never know, Maysa. Just look at what Zain did to be with me. He gave up the crown and moved back to America."

Rafiq would never do something so drastic when it involved duty. That much she knew.

When the timer dinged, Maysa walked to the counter and picked up the test to read it. "This is either good news, or not so good news. You'll have to tell me which one it might be."

The woman looked as though she might vault off the exam table. "I'll let you know as soon as you tell me what it says."

"You're not pregnant."

Madison's shoulders slumped. "In a way, I'm a little disappointed. In a bigger way, I'm glad. I'm not sure either Zain or I could handle having another baby after dealing with twins. At least not for another year or two."

Maysa tossed the test into the trash and smiled. "If that happens, you must be sure to confirm the pregnancy with me. We'll make it our own tradition."

"And maybe before then, you'll be the one in need of a pregnancy test."

Not likely. "Single mothers are not always viewed favorably, and I don't intend to look for a husband in the near future."

"You could always go the artificial insemination route." Madison snapped her fingers and pointed. "You could even do it yourself."

That appealed to Maysa about as much as having a tooth filled. "No, thank you. I'm also fairly sure sperm donors are few and far between in Bajul."

"I know of one man who would gladly donate his sperm the natural way. Of course, he'll first have to realize he's in danger of giving up the best thing that has ever happened to him, meaning you."

"Forgive me if I don't hold my breath until that happens. I'd require a ventilator."

Madison slid off the table, gave her a hug and paused before she left the room. "Don't give up on him yet, Maysa. He just might come around, marry you and tell all of Bajul to go to hell if they don't like it."

As far as Maysa was concerned, that would take a full-fledged miracle. And though she had witnessed a few miracles in her career—the birth of a child, a patient's unexpected recovery from a devastating illness—she wouldn't let allow herself to hope for one this time.

Ten

"Miracle of all miracles. You are actually sitting down."

At the sound of the grating British accent, Rafiq looked up from his notes to see Adan filing into the office, Zain and Madison trailing behind him. "I do not recall summoning any of you."

Zain claimed the chair across from the desk without seeking Rafiq's permission. "Since you did not summon us in response to our request for a family meeting, we have taken the initiative to seek you out."

Rafiq gripped the gold pen in both hands with enough force to break it in half. "The council meeting will be held tomorrow afternoon, and I need to prepare. Therefore, this meeting is officially over."

Adan assumed his usual perch on the edge of the desk, as if he had been raised by baboons. "We are not leaving until we have our say, Rafiq."

If he chose to argue the point, he would only prolong their departure. "Then have your say and be done with it. But make it quick or I will leave the whole lot of you here, retire to my bedroom and lock the door."

While Madison remained a few feet away, Zain and Adan exchanged a glance before Zain began to speak. "We are here on Maysa's behalf."

The sound of her name instantly filled Rafiq with further regret. The same regret that had haunted him every moment of every day since they had parted. "She has contacted you?"

"She has no idea we're discussing her," Adan said. "However, since you apparently have left her high and dry, we feel it is necessary to advocate for her. In other words, remove your head from that part of your anatomy in which no self-respecting head belongs, and beg her to come back to you."

If only that option existed. "Impossible. Any public connection she has with me will only serve to destroy her good standing in the community. She has already endured entirely too much hardship as it is." Some of which he had recently imposed on her life.

"If you're referring to her status as a divorcée," Zain began, "it's a common occurrence in America. People change spouses as often as they change underwear."

His brother had clearly forgotten he was in Bajul, not Los Angeles. "Need I remind you we are not governed by the same laws and customs here?"

"No, you need not," Zain said. "I personally experienced the results of those antiquated customs. Perhaps I should remind you that I chose to marry Madison, and we have suffered no serious ill effects from that decision."

"You are no longer king, Zain. You handed that honor to me. My private life is put under a microscope daily, and I will not subject Maysa to constant scrutiny."

"Instead, you are willing to subject all of us to your bad temper because you are so consumed with her, you can barely function," Zain said.

His ever-present anger began to escalate. "My duty has not been affected by my decision to cut all ties with her." The decision that she truthfully had made for him.

Adan scowled. "Duty be damned, Rafiq. Your duty cannot replace a woman's affections, or save you from your determination to punish the world for your own failures."

He did not need to be reminded how he had failed, or whom he had failed. "If you know what is good for you, Adan, you will go fly a plane and leave me be."

Madison raised her hand as if they were in a schoolroom, not the king's official office. "May I say something, Rafiq?"

He waved her forward. "Please. Everyone should have the opportunity to take a verbal shot at the king."

"That's not my intent," she said. "I simply wanted to let you know that when I've taken the twins for a stroll in the village, I've managed to talk with several of your subjects. They all seem to feel you are doing an excellent job."

"I am pleased to hear that." The first good news he had heard in quite some time, aside from Maysa's declaration of love. "All the more reason not to introduce a scandal."

Madison's gaze momentarily faltered. "I also took the liberty of digging into Boutros Kassab's history.

According to a few contacts I have in Europe, it seems he has a history of violence against women, specifically two of his three ex-wives and one mistress. Of course, he used his influence to get the charges dismissed."

"He is a known tyrant, so I am not surprised." He *was* surprised that Madison knew about Maysa's marriage to Boutros. Perhaps too much to be the product of a natural curiosity.

His suspicions were confirmed when she glanced at her husband before bringing her attention back to Rafiq. "Since Maysa suffered abuse at the hands of Kassab, we could leak that information. Then when you decide to publicly announce your relationship, people would know the reason behind Maysa's divorce."

He had been wrong to confide in Zain. "You told her about what Maysa endured when I emphatically asked that you not share that information?"

Zain seemed unmoved by Rafiq's ire. "Madison and I have no secrets. She is only attempting to aid in your happiness, and you will never be happy until you are reunited with Maysa."

When Zain stood and wrapped a protective arm around her shoulder, Madison said, "Thank you, sweetheart. And by the way, Maysa confirmed we're not pregnant."

Zain kissed her on the mouth, as if no one else mattered. The same way Rafiq had kissed Maysa only two short weeks ago.

"Then we shall have more time to practice in the next year or two," Zain said after they parted.

"Good lord," Adan said. "If you two do not stop this nonsense, I will send you both to your room and sell your children to the highest bidder."

Zain shot an acrid glance at Adan. "You are jealous because you have not kept company with a female in quite some time. Perhaps you should take care of that and leave the adults to solve Rafiq's problems."

As the brotherly bickering continued, Rafiq's temper arrived in the form of a solid slam on the desk. "Enough! I am capable of solving my own problems, and I am tired of the intrusion." He regarded Zain's wife. "Madison, I appreciate your assistance, but I will not be in need of the information. Revealing Kassab's tainted history will only force Maysa to relive a past she desires to forget and open old wounds that have finally begun to heal." Until he had inflicted the emotional wounds upon her.

"I understand your decision," Madison said. "And you can trust me to keep the information confidential."

Rafiq came to his feet and willed his anger to calm. "I am finished answering questions and entertaining suggestions, so if you will excuse me—"

"Not until you answer my questions, *cara mia.*"

As always, his former governess had an uncanny knack of appearing before Rafiq could escape the inquest. "I will allow one more question from you, Elena. But only one."

She wedged between a surprised Madison and Zain. "You will answer as many questions as I ask. First, do you love Maysa?"

He tracked his gaze from one expectant face to the other. "With all due respect, that is a private matter I will not address."

"Bloody hell, Rafiq," Adan said. "Just admit it."

"I assure you the sky will not fall on your head if

you say the words," Zain added. "Otherwise, I would have suffered several concussions."

"Do you love her?" Elena repeated.

"Yes, I love her." With all his once-hardened heart. "Are you satisfied now?"

The woman looked extremely satisfied, and somewhat smug. "Do you love her enough to spit in the face of convention and claim her as your partner for all time?"

When he failed to answer, Elena marched forward and stood immediately before the desk. "Rafiq, you have two choices, the first being you can disregard public opinion and ask Maysa to marry you because I know *she* is strong enough to handle any repercussions. Are you?"

He did not view that as a viable option. "And my second choice?"

"You can end up like me. Alone."

"You have never seemed to have an issue with being alone before."

"I was never truly physically alone, Rafiq, but I was lonely. I spent a lifetime loving a man who refused to acknowledge our affair for fear of upsetting the royal applecart."

His mind was fraught with more confusion. "What man is this, Elena?"

"Our father, you fool," Adan said. "I have suspected as much for years."

Elena looked completely baffled. "How could you have known?"

"I arrived late from the academy one night and I saw you enter his suite," Adan stated matter-of-factly.

"I assumed everyone knew and just never mentioned it out of respect for your privacy."

"Then you were the one sleeping with the king?" Zain asked, his tone heralding the shock Rafiq now experienced.

Elena lifted her chin, her eyes slightly misted with tears. "Yes, I was sleeping with the king. Right up until the day before he died. And no, I was not responsible for his death. I *was* responsible for giving him many memorable moments during his final hours on earth."

Adan kissed her cheek. "Good show, old girl. And while we're confessing…" He turned to address Rafiq. "I wish to apologize for sleeping with your wife."

The shock returned with the force of a grenade. "You did what?"

Adan held up his hands, palms forward. "Before you come across the desk to slug me, I wish to add I was only seventeen at the time. Rima apparently had a tussle with Shamil and she looked to me for comfort. I did not plan it, and neither did she."

If he heard one more revelation, he would not be responsible for what he would do to his youngest sibling. "You also knew Rima and Shamil were lovers?"

He shrugged. "I assumed everyone knew—"

"You assume too much, Adan," Zain said.

Adan presented a wry smile. "Obviously."

Rafiq turned a glare and a question on Zain. "Do you wish to confess anything?"

Zain held up his hands in surrender. "I solemnly swear I did not bed your former wife."

"I am so glad to know that, honey," Madison said.

So was Rafiq, if he could actually believe Zain. He no longer knew what to believe.

"It is now time to put the past to rest." Elena braced her palms on the desk, leaned forward and directed her gaze at Rafiq. "*Cara,* you have shown signs of being a great leader, yet most likely not greater than your father. But you can be a better man than your father. You can have the life you were meant to lead with Maysa, or you can enter into another loveless marriage and be miserable until your time on earth is over."

Or he could spend the rest of his life alone. He had no need to produce an heir, now that Zain had fulfilled that requirement. His father had completed his reign as a widower, and no one had condemned him for the decision. Of course, no one had known about his relationship with Elena. Yet he had dishonored the cherished surrogate mother to Rafiq and his brothers by not standing up to the elders and making a commoner his queen.

"I will consider all that you have said," he told Elena, the only answer he could presently give.

Elena straightened and smoothed a hand over her graying hair. "That is all anyone can ask. And I know you will make the right decision for all concerned, as I have taught you to do. Never forget what makes a man a true king and a hero. Honor."

And he had clearly forgotten that honor over the past few weeks. "If it is all the same to you, I wish to be alone now."

"Let us leave your brother to his thoughts," Elena said as she started toward the door, gesturing for everyone to follow her.

And everyone did, except for Zain. "I do have to know one more thing, Rafiq."

He released a weary sigh. "I am in no mood to answer more questions about Maysa."

"This doesn't involve Maysa," he said. "It does involve her brother. Why have you not yet dismissed him from the council?"

If he did, he risked Shamil revealing damning information to the press about his relationship with Maysa. Yet if he decided to make it known to the world that he was in love with the beautiful doctor, and he planned to make her the next queen, that would no longer be a concern. But the possible uproar over taking that course could be very concerning.

Since he had not quite reached that decision, Rafiq provided only a partial truth. "I had thought to ask him to step down first. If he does not, then I will demand his resignation."

"I personally would opt to humiliate him tomorrow at the meeting by relieving him of his duties," Zain said. "Perhaps he will then think twice before he tangles with another Mehdi and receives another broken nose."

After Zain exited the room, Rafiq weighed his brother's suggestion. He agreed that dismissing Shamil publicly would be effective, and worth considering. First, he had to determine whether he would attempt to reestablish a relationship with Maysa. A permanent, public relationship.

With that consideration rolling around in his mind, Rafiq would be forced to face another sleepless night—without Maysa. Would he be wise to ask her to make it his last?

You have shown signs of being a great leader, yet

most likely not greater than your father.... You can have the life you were meant to lead with Maysa....

Elena's words of wisdom suddenly struck a chord in Rafiq. He could be a better man. Maysa could assist him with that. In some ways, she already had. She was stronger than most men he had known, at times even him. Determined and intelligent. Worthy of respect. She had much to offer this country. She had much more to offer him. Much more than he probably deserved.

Rafiq could not bear the thought of spending another long day—and night—without Maysa Barad. Now that he had made the supreme decision to alter tradition, as well as his life, he had to formulate a plan. As the kernel of an idea filtered into his brain, a scheme that would cover two pressing issues at once, he smiled for the first time in weeks. He prayed that what he had planned would bring about Maysa's smile, too.

She wasn't particularly thrilled to be summoned to the palace by Rafiq's assistant, Mr. Deeb. Yet when Maysa had learned she was expected to speak on current health care issues before the royal council, her attitude immediately changed. She could not wait to enlighten each and every one of them.

And now here she was, waiting in the anteroom for her turn to finally have the chance to give the members a good dose of her reality. Unfortunately, the opportunity meant she would have to face Rafiq, as well as her brother, who amazingly still held his position on the governing board. Despite his verbal threats, and his physical assault on the king, Shamil had somehow come out of the situation smelling like a rose, while she still carried the thorns of Rafiq's rejection.

Maysa refused to worry over that now. She would walk into the room as the only woman among all men and let them know she was a force to be reckoned with. Her bravado began to diminish when Deeb appeared at the main door. "They are ready for you now, Dr. Barad."

And she was ready for them—for the most part.

After silently demanding her nerves be still, Maysa entered displaying a confidence she didn't exactly feel. To make matters worse, Rafiq happened to be the first person to invade her field of vision. And what a vision he was, dressed in his finest black silk suit, the official sash of the king draped around his neck, his face free of facial hair, his dark eyes without obvious emotion. She had no idea what he was feeling, only what she was feeling for him—undeniable longing.

"Gentlemen," he began in Arabic. "You all know Dr. Barad."

Maysa took inventory of their reactions and wasn't pleased with the results. No one spoke a greeting aside from Zain and Adan, although a few nodded in acknowledgment.

Rafiq pulled out the chair next to his and gestured her forward. After she settled in, she realized she was now face-to-frown with her brother. Lovely.

She turned her attention to the king as he outlined future plans for hospital expansion and patiently waited for her turn to present her thoughts on rural health care.

But before that turn arrived, Rafiq centered a bitter gaze on Shamil. "Sheikh Barad, as presiding Minister of Health, it is my opinion you have failed in successfully overseeing Bajul's faltering health care system."

Shamil's face turned so red, Maysa feared his head

might explode. "I take exception to your criticism, Your Excellency. I have served our people well."

"I disagree," Rafiq said, switching to English. "And I take exception to you sleeping with the queen, you traitorous son of a bitch."

Maysa had no way of knowing how many members understood the English curse, but she understood it very well. However, she had never heard Rafiq speak the words before, and she found it somewhat amusing, and appropriate for the situation.

Her brother stood so abruptly, he knocked his chair back in the process. "You are out of line, Rafiq."

Rafiq remained surprisingly calm. "And you are hereby facing charges of high treason if you do not vacate your position, and the premises, immediately."

Shamil sent a pointed look at Maysa before returning his ugly sneer to the king. "You are willing to make my sister your sacrificial lamb?"

A slightly mocking smile curled the corners of Rafiq's mouth. "No, but I am willing to appoint her as the new health minister, if she agrees."

Maysa looked around at all the confused men lining the table. But she didn't know if their confusion resulted from Rafiq offering a woman a position on the council for the first time in Bajul's history, or because Rafiq still spoke in English. "I would be honored, Your Majesty." Honored and thrilled and amazed.

"This is a travesty!" Shamil shouted. "A monumental mistake for this nation!"

"And men like you are a scourge on our nation," Rafiq said as he signaled a nearby guard, then returned to speaking in their native tongue. "Escort the sheikh to the airport and inform them that by my order, he is permanently barred from crossing Bajul's borders."

Shamil shook off the guard's grasp and pointed a shaky finger at Maysa. "You will regret this decision, and you will suffer the wrath of the people once they learn you are the king's secret whore. They will shun you."

"Not if she is the queen."

Shamil looked stunned, while Maysa turned wide eyes on Rafiq. "What did you say?"

"I am unofficially asking you to be my wife." And he did so where everyone could understand his proposal. "I will do the official honors after the meeting. You may give me your answer at that time."

As security escorted a cursing Shamil out of the room, Maysa sat in shocked silence. Yet several members of the council broke theirs by issuing protests over both Rafiq's decisions.

He commanded their attention by rapping the table with his palm. "Silence! I ask who among you has the right to judge Dr. Barad when she has done nothing but divorce a tormentor and care for the poorest of our people. Who among you has given more than your wealth to do the same?"

"She is a harlot who has taken the king as her lover," one man said. "She is a divorced woman who has no respect for the sanctity of marriage."

Rafiq glared at him. "And you do, Sheikh Saab? Do you not dishonor your wife nightly by bedding the innkeeper's wife?" He then turned to another protester. "And you, Sheikh Najem. Did you not divorce your first wife to marry a woman much younger than yourself?"

Najem looked as if he would like to disappear beneath the conference table. "It is different. I am a man."

"And that is where we differ," Rafiq said. "Both my brothers and myself believe we are overdue implementing changes in attitude when it comes to the backbone of this country, women such as Dr. Barad."

Zain and Adan verbally added their support before Rafiq spoke again. "Now that the business at hand is settled, including going forward with the water project, this meeting is officially adjourned."

Before Maysa could mentally digest the chaotic events, Rafiq took her by the hand, led her through the lengthy first-floor corridor, and up the stairs at a fast clip. He slowed a bit as they climbed to the third floor, but not enough for Maysa to catch her breath or gather her thoughts.

She suddenly realized they had arrived at the royal living quarters when she peered through the open bedroom door to her right. "What just happened in that meeting?"

"You agreed to become Bajul's newly appointed health minister to replace your brother, whom I have permanently exiled."

"And?"

He hinted at a smile. "I unofficially asked you to be my wife, and now I wish to make it official." Like a storybook hero, the king of Bajul went to one knee and clasped both her hands in his. "Maysa Barad, will you do me the honor of being my wife and my queen?"

She'd imagined this moment many times in her youth, and "youth" was the key. Now she was an adult, with adult concerns.

"Well?" Rafiq asked with a touch of impatience in his tone.

She wanted to say yes, but she wasn't quite ready to do that. "I'm still thinking."

He stood, his expression showing his disappointment. "I have asked too much of you, and I have waited until it is too late."

"I didn't say no, Rafiq. But before I say yes, I have to know what changed your mind."

"Not what, but whom," he said. "Elena forced me to see the error of my ways, immediately after she revealed she carried on a long-time affair with my father, who refused to make her his wife due to outdated mores."

Maysa was quickly reaching revelation overload. "How did they pull that off without anyone finding out?"

"Adan claims he knew, but Zain and I only heard rumors that our father had a mistress. We never suspected it would be the woman who raised us."

She, too, had heard the rumors, yet never in a million years would she have guessed Elena as the mystery woman. "It's sad to know that she was never able to show her love for your father out in the open."

"And that is what I am trying to avoid with us. I understand that I am asking you to endure continued bias, and I would not blame you if you refused me—"

"Let me stop you right there. As I've said before, I have survived much worse than a few insults. I survived the members' caustic remarks in the meeting only a few minutes ago. But if I agree to marry you, I will continue to be who I am, not who everyone feels

I should be. I will still be a doctor, and I will insist on treating the patients who need me."

Rafiq streak a hand over his jaw. "You realize that will require a security contingency at the clinic at all times."

That was something Maysa had yet to consider. "I accept that necessity, as long as the men do not frighten away my patients."

"They will also be required to accompany us when we travel to the outlying areas."

"We?"

His smile arrived, fully formed and completely gorgeous. "Yes, we. I believe I still have much to learn about our country's medical needs. Who better to guide me than you? However, I will make certain we have better accommodations, or at the very least, a comfortable cot for the tent where I will make love to you the next time."

"I will definitely agree to that, Your Majesty."

His features turned suddenly serious. "Then you will agree to marry me?"

She saw no harm in keeping him in suspense for a while longer. "I am leaning in that direction."

He slipped his arms around her waist and tugged her closer. "Maysa, if you refuse me, and I pray you do not, you must know I will never marry another. I refuse to settle for less than what we have together, an abiding love that has spanned years of separation. I will never feel for another woman the depth of what I feel for you. I simply cannot."

That alone convinced Maysa to deliver a resounding "Yes, I will marry you."

They sealed this unlikely betrothal, not with a contract, but with a kiss, as it should be. That kiss ended when a household staff member cleared her throat before she rushed by.

"Let us retire to my bedroom now," Rafiq said as soon as the woman disappeared around the corner.

Maysa glanced at the open door, specifically the bed, and questioned the wisdom in his plan. "I'm not sure I would be comfortable doing that, Rafiq."

"She never slept in my bed, Maysa," he said, as if he had channeled her concern. "I suppose I have been saving the bed for you, though it took me a while to realize I have been waiting for you all my life."

"And I am honored you reserved the permanent space beside you." As well as deeply touched.

"If you are also worried that I am only interested in making love to you," he added, "and I used a marriage proposal to achieve that goal, I assure you that is not the case. I have simply not been able to sleep without you in my arms."

Such a sweet thing to admit, but Maysa was still a bit suspicious. "It's a little past four o'clock, Rafiq. Isn't it too early to retire for the night?"

He presented an endearing grin, with a side of sexy devil tossed in for good measure. "Perhaps we could consider it a long nap?"

Now that her adrenaline level had plummeted, Maysa could probably nap standing up. She released Rafiq and stretched her arms above her heads. "I am very tired, so I suppose we could manage that."

Rafiq then swept Maysa into his arms, carried her into his bedroom as if she were already his bride and laid her on the bed for their "nap." After they undressed down to only skin, they did actually sleep for a while before they officially made love as an engaged couple. A soft, sensuous lovemaking session that almost brought Maysa to tears. Joyful tears.

And in the peaceful moments that followed, they were content to hold each other as if they had no other plans for the foreseeable future—until Maysa remembered they did have one monumental plan to make.

"When do you suggest we have the wedding, King Mehdi?"

He nuzzled her neck. "Tomorrow would be preferable, unless we can find someone to officiate tonight."

She elbowed Rafiq's side, causing him to release an exaggerated wince. "I am serious."

"And I am now injured, as well as serious about wanting to marry you quickly, before you change your mind. But I suppose we need sufficient time to make the arrangements."

"We only need a month at best," she said. "Just enough time to organize a small, intimate ceremony. Perhaps we should consider traveling south to the beach, or perhaps here at the lake. I have always thought it would be nice to marry without shoes."

Rafiq lifted his head from the pillow and frowned. "You do not wish to wear shoes or have an elaborate undertaking?"

"I wish anything but a large wedding. We have both been through the pomp and circumstance before. I see no need to repeat that now. And yes, I want to marry without my shoes and feel warm sand beneath my feet."

"I will leave the decision to discard footwear to you. But when a Mehdi king takes a new queen, he is expected to hold a large celebration in honor of the event, complete with a feast and thousands of people, most of whom he has never met, nor does he care to meet."

That was not Maysa's idea of a good time. "I will agree to the feast and the hordes of strangers, as long as we exchange our vows in private with only close friends and family in attendance."

He scowled. "I hope family does not include your brother."

"Bite your tongue, future husband. I would rather consume a plateful of salt than have Shamil at our wedding."

He kissed her gently. "I agree, my future queen. Your brother is not welcome in our world."

She smiled. "And for future reference, I prefer to be addressed as Dr. Queen. I believe I have earned the title."

Rafiq laughed then—a rich, deep laugh that provided masculine music to Maysa's ears. "As you wish, Dr. Queen," he said, followed by a lingering kiss. "And I believe I have thought of the perfect setting for our wedding ceremony."

"That cove by the lake?"

"No. The place where we began our journey together. Our past."

Epilogue

Exactly one month later, the reigning king and the physician queen exchanged vows, surrounded by olive trees and fifty or so of their closest friends and family. The bride had exchanged her preferred gauze dresses for a gown made of champagne-colored silk. The groom sported an open-collared, white tailored shirt with a beige jacket and slacks. Neither wore shoes, a sincere scandal in the making.

Maysa's attendants, Madison and Demetria, wore aqua dresses, while Zain and Adan reluctantly donned matching navy suits to meet their responsibility as groomsmen. None of the bridal party appreciated the no-shoe policy, a true uprising in the making.

Perhaps the ceremony wasn't quite as intimate as Maysa would have liked, but everything was going as planned...until two international news helicopters began buzzing overhead, forcing them to hurry their vows and the official kiss.

The disruption sent everyone to their awaiting cars for the brief trip to the palace. A trip too brief for the bride to agree to the groom's suggestion they begin the honeymoon on the journey. Just as well, Maysa decided. Had she agreed, the wedding guests would probably see guilt written all over her face.

Moments later, the newlyweds entered the massive banquet hall to a round of rousing applause. Maysa was extremely thankful for the show of approval and somewhat surprised. Fortunately, the press coverage had been favorable, and she hadn't been exposed to overt hostility, aside from the palace chef, who had not been pleased when she'd changed her mind about the menu twice.

Maysa could not recall being so blissfully happy, or so ready to begin her life with Rafiq. First, she had to assume her first duty as the queen—mingling with some of the most influential people in the world.

She spent well over an hour exchanging polite greetings with guests who'd waited a long while in the lengthy reception line to meet the monarchs. During a brief break in the line's flow, she surveyed the decorations made from bouquets of fragrant jasmine and the candles set out on the tables. And when one esteemed, unfamiliar guest held Rafiq captive with endless chatter, she turned her attention to the bounty of food spread out on the nearby tables. Enough food to feed half of Bajul, and she would swear more than half had come. By the time the last well-wisher left, she was ready to consume her fair share. Unfortunately, Rafiq had been detained again, this time by a woman at least twenty years his senior. That didn't stop her from fawning all over him, and Maysa didn't mind a bit. After this free-for-all food fest ended, the king would be taking her to Cyprus for two weeks filled with sea, sand and on-demand sex.

Thinking about the honeymoon led her to seek out her husband. When he caught her gaze and winked, she considered dragging him away now, a very unqueenly thing to do.

"Have you been enjoying your first hours as the queen?"

Maysa turned to Madison and frowned. "I am not enjoying having to wear these high heels. I'm definitely not enjoying the limited time with my new husband."

"They both take some getting used to," Madison said as she acknowledged a guest with a wave. "Both the heels on your feet, and the human kind who think it's their right to have the king's ear, even when that king is the groom."

Madison waved yet again, this time at a handsome, middle-aged gentleman. "I have no idea who that was," she said through a fake grin. "Some dignitary I invited I think. I believe he's from Albania, or maybe it's Australia. First rule of thumb, smile and pretend you know them, even if you don't."

"That's what I've been doing since we arrived, and I didn't understand what some of them said to me. It's a true disadvantage."

"I'll be glad to teach you some basic foreign greetings if you'd like," Madison said. "I know at least fifty."

"You and Zain will return to California before I master even five."

Madison brought her attention from the crowd and

gave it to Maysa. "Actually, we've decided to stay in Bajul indefinitely."

Maysa decided her sister-in-law deserved a hug for delivering such glad tidings. "I'm thrilled to know you're staying. I'm going to need all the support I can get. Rafiq will be pleased, too. But exactly why did you decide to relocate from Los Angeles and leave the beach behind?"

"We want the children to be raised here so they can learn about their heritage. And I want Cala to lead the future generation of Bajul's kick-ass women, just like her aunt Maysa, who defied all odds and received the ultimate prize."

"Rafiq?"

Madison frowned. "No. Premium tickets to the local sheepherder's ball."

Maysa grinned. "I was not aware of that perk."

"Of course I meant Rafiq, silly queen. He's always been considered quite a catch, just like Zain before he came to his senses and married me." Something, or someone, behind Maysa drew Madison's attention. "Speaking of our catches, here they come, plus the lone bachelor prince who mysteriously went missing after the wedding."

Maysa turned to see the approaching trio of gorgeous Mehdi brothers. Rafiq and Zain's resemblance to each other had always been remarkable, but even more so now that her husband decided not to regrow his goatee. Yet Adan, with his lighter-colored hair and skin tone, as well as his deep, deep dimples, did not favor his siblings aside from his tall stature and distinctive gait. Clearly he had inherited his looks from some unknown relative.

After Rafiq came to Maysa's side and kissed her soundly, Adan inserted himself between them. "Congratulations to the bride," he said, then leaned to kiss Maysa's cheek. "And my apologies for my tardiness in arriving here tonight."

Rafiq demonstrated his disapproval with a scowl and showed his possessive side by wrapping one arm around Maysa's waist and pulling her close to his side. "May I ask where you went after we left the grove?"

Adan adjusted his collar that seemed perfectly fine. "Since I am a gentleman, I will only say that I was preoccupied with a lovely little lady right here in the palace, and she is quite charming."

"Only you could manage to pick up a woman in less than an hour's time," Zain said.

Adan grinned. "Yes, I definitely picked her up."

Zain pointed at him. "Enjoy your freedom now, because mark my words, I predict you will soon meet that special someone and she'll drag you onto the marriage merry-go-round." When Madison glared at him, he added, "I meant she will introduce you to the state of marital bliss."

"You are wrong, brother," Adan said. "I intend to adhere to my plan of waiting until I am at least forty before I settle down. And as of this evening, I have decided to remain celibate for a while."

"That will most likely be the longest ten minutes of your life," Rafiq said, drawing laughter from everyone but Adan. "Now that the festivities seem to be dying down, have you notified the airport of our impending departure?"

"I have and the plane is ready and waiting." Adan began to back away as he spoke. "And I am prepared to deliver you to your destination safe and sound, after I say goodbye to the lady."

"Hurry," Rafiq called after his brother before Adan disappeared through the double doors.

Madison pushed up her sheer sleeve and checked her watch. "The celibacy thing didn't even last seven minutes."

The conversation continued until Adan suddenly returned with a beautiful baby girl wearing a pink satin dress, her thumb planted securely in her mouth. But not just any baby—Zain and Madison's baby girl, Cala.

He walked up to the group, a mischievous look splashed across his face. "Did I not say she was special?"

Zain kissed his daughter's cheek. "The most special lady in the world, and the niece of quite the deceiver."

Madison moved closer to examine Cala's dress. "Where did this come from?"

Adan's grin expanded. "I saw it in a boutique window the last time I visited Paris. I could not resist buying it for her. I bought Joseph a miniature tuxedo for the occasion. He's wearing it now, but unfortunately he passed out in Elena's lap and will be missing the party."

Who would have thought a reputed rogue like Adan would have such a soft spot for children? Not Maysa. She only wished Rafiq shared in his brother's enthusiasm. As far as she knew, he had never held his niece and nephew, and she wondered if he would ever recover from losing the child he'd believed to be his for months. Then as if by magic on this magical night, Cala reached for Rafiq.

Everyone went silent while Maysa held her breath as she awaited her husband's reaction. He hesitated a moment before he took the baby from Adan. Cala extracted her thumb, touched her uncle's face, then laid her head on his shoulder, as if she sensed he needed help with his healing. The scene was so very, very sweet, Maysa's already full heart filled with more joy.

"She apparently realizes who to go to when she needs her demands met," Adan said, shattering the silence. "I hate to disappoint you, Cala, but he will make you jump through hoops before he'll grant you your wish. But if you learn to curtsy—"

"She will not do any such thing," Madison chimed in. "Bow maybe, but never curtsy."

Rafiq tenderly kissed the now sleeping Cala's cheek before returning her to her father. "It is time for us to go now."

Maysa was more than excited to get on with the honeymoon and get out of her heels. "Good night, everyone, and thank you all so much for being there for us."

After doling out hugs and kisses, Maysa and Rafiq entered the armored limousine flanked by escorts on motorcycles. Adan took another car, leaving them alone at last.

Maysa rested her head on Rafiq's shoulder and sighed. "Today is perfect."

He lifted her chin and kissed her softly. "You are perfect."

He might not think so as soon as she asked the question she'd wanted to ask for some time. "Rafiq, do you want to have children?"

"At one time I was not certain I did, but now I am sure I do want children. Perhaps as many as five."

"You cannot be serious, Rafiq. We're both four years past thirty. We wouldn't have time to—"

He touched a fingertip to her lips to silence her. "I am not serious, but I would like to have two. I would also prefer to wait a year before we begin the process, but as Zain said, we may practice frequently until that time."

"I wholeheartedly agree with practicing often and waiting a year, but not any longer. We do need time together before we start a family."

"Fortunately, time is now on our side."

Thankfully, that was true. "There is something else we need to cover. Actually, a few rules."

"So we are back to rules again, are we?"

"A few minor rules. First, I believe it's all right to go to bed angry, as long as we make up in that bed before morning."

"You will receive no argument from me."

"Second, we both need autonomy and time away from each other now and then. We will appreciate each other more when we are together."

From the sour look on his face, evidently that rule did not set well with the king. "How much time?"

She tapped her chin and pretended to think. "I would say perhaps the occasional lunch hour, but never breakfast or dinner. We might want to shower separately—"

"I draw the line there."

She was not surprised by the command. "All right. I wasn't particularly fond of the idea anyway."

He gave her his smile and took her breath in exchange. "Anything else, my queen?"

"I prefer Dr. Queen, remember?"

He lifted her hand and laced their fingers together. "I prefer to call you the woman who saved me from a lonely life. The center of my existence. The love of my life."

The vows were less rushed and more poignant than those they'd exchanged earlier. Beautiful vows coming from an equally beautiful man. "And you, Rafiq Mehdi, have always been, and always will be, the king of my heart."

He touched her face with reverence, then said the words she would never tire of hearing. "*Ana bahebik.* Always."

She laid her hand on his palm, and entrusted him with the rest of her life. "*Ana bahebak.* Forever."

Dr. Maysa Barad-Mehdi had received several miracles at last—permanently reuniting with the man she had wanted most of her life, a career that continually fulfilled her and, most important, realizing that abiding love could be more than enough.

* * * * *

A sneaky peek at next month…

MODERN™

POWER, PASSION AND IRRESISTIBLE TEMPTATION

My wish list for next month's titles…

In stores from 20th June 2014:

❏ Christakis's Rebellious Wife – Lynne Graham

❏ Carrying the Sheikh's Heir – Lynn Raye Harris

❏ Dante's Unexpected Legacy – Catherine George

❏ The Ultimate Playboy – Maya Blake

In stores from 4th July 2014:

❏ At No Man's Command – Melanie Milburne

❏ Bound by the Italian's Contract – Janette Kenny

❏ A Deal with Demakis – Tara Pammi

❏ Wrong Man, Right Kiss – Red Garnier

Available at WHSmith, Tesco, Asda, Eason, Amazon and Apple

Just can't wait?

0614/01

Special Offers

Every month we put together collections and longer reads written by your favourite authors.

Here are some of next month's highlights—and don't miss our fabulous discount online!

On sale 20th June

On sale 4th July

On sale 4th July

 Save 20%
on all Special Releases

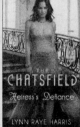

THE CHATSFIELD®

Enter the intriguing online world of
The Chatsfield and discover secret
stories behind closed doors…

www.thechatsfield.com

Check in online now for your exclusive
welcome pack!

Which series will you try next?

Wholesome, heartfelt relationships

4 new stories every month

Only available online

Awaken the romance of the past...

6 new stories every month

The ultimate in romantic medical drama

6 new stories every month

MODERN™

Power, passion and irresistible temptation

8 new stories every month

True love and temptation!

4 new stories every month

MILLS & BOON®
Book Club

Join the Mills & Boon Book Club

Want to read more **Modern**™ books?
We're offering you **2 more** absolutely **FREE!**

We'll also treat you to these fabulous extras:

- 🌹 **Exclusive offers and much more!**

- 🌹 **FREE home delivery**

- 🌹 **FREE books and gifts with our special rewards scheme**

Get your free books now!

visit www.millsandboon.co.uk/bookclub
or call Customer Relations on 020 8288 2888